MW01462754

MISTRAL

ROGUES OF THE ZATHARI
BOOK 2

STELLA FROST

Copyright © 2022 by Stella Frost

All rights reserved.

No part of this book may be reproduced in any form or by any electronic or mechanical means, including information storage and retrieval systems, without written permission from the author, except for the use of brief quotations in a book review.

Cover Design by Natasha Snow Designs

Editing by Hart to Heart Edits

Formatting by Stella Frost

ISBN: *978-1-944142-49-0*

READER NOTE

Dearest readers—I believe that reading should be enlightening, exciting, but above all else, fun. If you would like a detailed list of tropes and topics in this book, please visit my website at stellafrost.me and visit the Books menu.

Take care and enjoy!

PROLOGUE

Humanity once gazed up at the stars with wonder and curiosity. But in the year 2107, we looked to the stars in terror and anguish. When the great gleaming warships of the Aengra Dominion arrived in our galaxy, we assumed the worst. And when their first ships arrived on Earth's surface, their diplomats laid claim to the Earth as property of the mighty Aengra Dominion.

Humanity did not take kindly to being claimed, and they made a brief and ill-advised attempt at rousting the Dominion. Armed with superior weaponry and numbers, the Dominion fought back to protect their ships. A short, but brutal war left much of the Earth in ruins, with most of the damage wrought by humanity's inelegant and cataclysmic weapons. The planet was already in a downward spiral due to escalating temperatures and disease, and the arrival of the Aengra only hastened along its slow demise.

As an act of peace, the Dominion spent another ten years on

the Earth's surface, using their advanced technology to rebuild several large cities. They also established the colony of New Terra in the distant Imrathi Belt, the galaxy at the center of their mighty empire. Millions of settlers accepted the rule of the Dominion and left Earth for a better life, leaving their home planet to those who were deemed unfit to settle the new colony.

Now, in the year 2198, Earth is a backwater planet in a distant galaxy. The intergalactic corporation Ilmarinen Interstellar constructed an interstellar jump gate near Mars, making Earth an occasional stop for travelers in search of fuel or a visit to the quaint, decaying planet. The Dominion maintains a loose grip on Earth through their embassy that sends fewer and fewer colonists each year to New Terra. Much of Earth belongs to the lawless criminals and corrupt politicians scrambling for the scraps that remain. It is a place where dirty deals are made and the law is little more than words on paper.

Many unfortunate enough to be born on Earth since the great migration still look to the stars, dreaming of what lies beyond those great gleaming gates.

Some are fortunate enough to find out.

CHAPTER 1

Helena

Once upon a time, I dreamed of being a pretty princess, like the rouged and ruffled girls in the yellowed books of my youth. This was certainly not what eight-year-old Helena had in mind.

For one, my fairy godmother was a seven-foot-tall alien woman with muscles that would have made most human men cry. With one crimson-skinned hand, she gripped my jaw so tight I was worried she'd crush it to powder. She painted elaborate streaks of silver onto my eyelids and cheeks. Mumbling through my squished cheeks, I asked, "Arna, can you lighten up?"

Her vivid orange eyes narrowed. "I am barely touching you, little piglet."

Ouch.

She applied black powder to my lashes, then tilted my face

up firmly. I squeezed my eyes shut as she painted a chromed silver gloss onto my lips. Being pampered was one thing. Not that my life on Earth had been filled with luxury, but I could fantasize about it.

This wasn't it. I felt like a car being detailed, with Arna aggressively painting my face and her assistant Telah rubbing a glittery oil onto my chest and back so vigorously I was going to have a friction burn. I could imagine the janitors back at my old hospital scrubbing the windows clean until they squeaked.

The cramped dressing room on the Basilisk was filled with half a dozen women and three men receiving the same treatment. Across from me, the other Terran woman, Milla, was already being dressed like a mannequin. Her eyes were closed as she lifted one foot and then the other for her glittering green shoes.

I had never liked being naked in front of people but being snatched from Earth had forced me get used to a lot of things very quickly. I tried to look on the bright side; maybe I'd spent a very uncomfortable day with an alien woman wielding a laser in places only my gynecologist had seen, but I'd never have to shave again.

Without warning, Telah pulled the loose robe from my chest, baring me completely. "Up," she ordered.

Closing my eyes, I stood on a fluffy rug while the next team approached. I was no more than another piece on the assembly line. Hands grabbed my bottom like it was a piece of fruit in a market, while someone else strung an uncomfortable thong into place. I mentally drifted away as brisk hands rigged silvery straps all over me. Cold spray blasted against my skin, adding another layer of sparkle that stung. They were impersonal and efficient as they dressed and arranged me like a pretty little sex doll.

When they were done, Telah turned me around to a mirror. Painted in silver and wrapped in layers of silver straps and loops, the creature in the mirror was unrecognizable. Somehow, the brazen outfit made me look more naked than if I wasn't wearing clothes. Thin silver chains with dangling crystal drops draped over my hips and bare stomach. My long auburn hair was twisted up around a strange metal headpiece, set with dozens of shiny silver ornaments. I glittered like the old disco ball in Manny's back at home.

I missed my loose, shapeless scrubs, and the way I could hide in the drab fabric. I never thought I would miss anything about Earth, but I would have given anything to be back in my tiny apartment, where the air always smelled like stale fryer grease from the diner across the street, and I had to listen to my neighbors playing their creaky bedsprings at all hours of the day. I missed the people shouting and the bicycle bells and the late-night gunshots.

Maybe this was some sort of karmic punishment for all those times I dreamed of leaving Earth. Should have been more specific, I supposed.

Around the room, the others were dressed in similar outfits in different colors. Tonight, we were the Gems of the Galaxies, apparently. Boss Arandon had a real penchant for themes. His last sleazy soiree featured his stable of captives as a flock of flamingos. I was still finding shreds of pink feathers in my nether regions, so this was an improvement, even if I was going to have a wedgie for the next eight hours and glitter in my labia for the next eight days.

With a little shove from Telah, I joined Milla in the middle of the room. We'd both been snatched from Atlanta at the same time and became as close to friends as you could when you were captives on an alien ship hurtling through space a million miles from everything you'd ever known.

Milla's lithe frame was wrapped in a metallic green harness that accentuated her red hair. She squeezed my hand, spared a smile, and straightened up tall as Arandon's right hand and enforcer, Thenoch, walked into the room.

Wolfish yellow eyes gleamed against his cherry-red skin as he inspected us. Then he tipped his head, and we followed silently. My feet hurt already from the high heels, but I didn't dare complain. I'd learned the hard way that complaining got me nothing but more to complain about. "Piglet, drinks," he ordered. "Weasel, snacks."

"We have names," Milla said. Thenoch ignored us. "*Ashelo*," she muttered.

Thenoch glanced back at us, tilting his head. The tentacle-like growths hanging from his temples flickered a warning orange. If his dead eyes and furrowed brow didn't give it away, that little bioluminescent signal was a sure sign of danger.

I bit my lips to keep from laughing. Like the rest of the ship's staff and Arandon's guests, we had translator chips hooked over our ears. They fed us almost real-time translations for hundreds of languages, letting us communicate with each other and with Arandon's never-ending stream of wealthy guests.

But the chip couldn't translate anything that wasn't a real language. Once we figured that out, we'd started developing our own slang. It was petty and childish, but some days, it was all that kept me from breaking down and crying.

"*Otherem kufer,*" I murmured to her. Her eyes widened. *Mother fucker.*

"If you'd like to continue your games, I'll change your assignments to warm the lap of the Proxilar champion who just boarded." Thenoch snarled, the tips of his slender tendrils glowing red now.

I froze and shook my head. "No, sir."

"I didn't think so," he said. When he turned around, I tried to catch Milla's eye, but she was already drifting away, her face going pretty and blank. I desperately wished that I could mentally escape like she did.

Thenoch led us into the bustling kitchen, where four uniformed staff members prepared real food, not the reconstituted mush that we normally ate. My stomach growled at the sight of tiny crackers topped with curious blue spreads, thinly sliced cheeses, and something that looked like tiny octopuses sprinkled with chocolate shavings. One of the cooks shoved a silver tray loaded with shots of glowing blue liquor into my hands.

"Nice ass," one of the cooks crowed. There was a noisy guffaw.

I wanted to throw the tray of tiny octopi in his leering face, but instead I gave him a coquettish smile. "Thank you," I said sweetly, fanning my heavy eyelashes at him. As I walked out, I gave a swish of my hips.

Empty-headed and easy-going, that was me. That was the girl who survived.

The dining room of the Basilisk was dimmed to a hazy blue-purple glow. Floor-to-ceiling screens displayed the silhouettes of dancing figures, reminding me of the window dancers back in the Trench at home. Live musicians played on a trio of floating disks, high above the patrons. At a glance, I estimated three dozen guests gathered around the ornately decorated tables. There were a handful of humans, and a good number of Vaera, with new-penny copper skin and pointed ears. There were the odd, high-browed Il-Teatha with brilliant red skin like Thenoch and Arna, and a golden-skinned male with the peaks of bony wings rising from his back. I was fascinated with him, and the strangely cut garments he wore to accommodate those leathery wings.

With dread oozing into my belly, I noticed the huge Proxilar male in a corner with an Il-Teatha woman speaking quietly to him. I made a note to stay at arm's length from him. Just one of those big, bark-like hands could completely close around my neck and crush me like I was made of spun sugar. The Proxilar had a reputation for breaking their toys quickly.

And in the back of the room, sitting at his elevated table like a damned king, was Vehr Arandon. He was handsome, with impeccably styled bronze hair and razor-sharp cheekbones. Along the shaved sides of his head were ornate scars in spiraling patterns, clearly the work of an artist and not an accident. His ears were subtly pointed and adorned with tiny silver studs that complemented his tailored gray suit. He was coy about his origins, but Milla and I theorized he was part Vaera and part human. Whatever he was, he was one hundred percent shitbag, considering his swanky lifestyle was bankrolled by selling unwilling men and women.

Watching him from the corner of my eye, I began my rounds of the dining room, offering the little shot glasses to the guests. "Compliments of Master Arandon," I purred to each one. It was an elaborate dance, sliding between chairs without bumping anyone or putting my bare ass directly into someone's face. As I plotted a course for my next table, a human male crooked his finger at me.

Dammit. I widened my smile. He smirked in response.

Playing along was the way to go. I'd always thought I would be tougher, like the fierce women in the dog-eared books I devoured. It was easy to imagine myself as one of those fiery heroines who spat in their captors' faces and somehow got the better of the beefy mercenaries that crossed them. I was no quitter, after all.

But when I woke up, thousands of miles from home, surrounded by aliens examining my naked body like a tomato at the market, I'd had a rude and embarrassing awakening. I was not the fiery heroine. I was the quivering mess with runny mascara that needed rescuing.

Not that I didn't try. At the beginning, I mouthed off a few times, even fought back when Thenoch manhandled me. I now knew all too well what it felt like to have fifty thousand volts of electricity lighting up my central nervous system, and I didn't care to do it again.

My life plan had changed. Now, my plan was to behave, keep my head down, and pray that I'd figure it out eventually. The world had never been fair, but somehow, I magically arrived at the idiotic conclusion that things would turn around now. I'd develop some sort of brilliant instincts that would get me from this ship back to my home on Earth.

By my best estimation, that was at least six months ago, and I was still on this stupid ship with skintight leather between my ass cheeks and glitter in places it certainly did not belong.

But it was better than being dead.

Wasn't it?

I sashayed over to the human male. A gnarly scar twisted across his cheek, pulling up one corner of his mouth in a gruesome smile that matched his cold, dark eyes. "Pretty little diamond," he growled. He slapped his lap. "Come and sit."

"Oh, I'd love to, sir," I said sweetly. "But I have to make sure everyone has drinks."

"I've got something you can drink." He ran one hand up the back of my thigh, then palmed my bare ass. Revulsion twisted in my stomach. "Arandon's serving my favorite. Pretty Terrans."

"Oh, you're sweet," I cooed, sliding away from him to deliver glasses to his companions before making a hasty retreat. His touch still lingered, like a sticky stain on my skin.

My heart raced as I circled the room again. Milla was delivering little tarts filled with berries while the winged man gazed at her with raw lust in his glowing green eyes. What would it take to bribe him to fly us away from here?

As I returned to the kitchen to restock my tray with fresh drinks, Thenoch intercepted me. His warm hand closed on the back of my neck, uncomfortably hot. Someone really needed to tell him a simple *hey you* would suffice. "The human with the scar is looking at you."

"I noticed," I said mildly.

"Go entertain him a while," Thenoch said. He plunked a bottle of clear liquor onto my tray. "Boss wants him friendly."

"He's already gotten plenty friendly."

His grip on my neck tightened as one black-nailed finger dug painfully into a nerve. I buckled, trying not to whimper. "I misunderstood you, piglet."

"Yes, sir," I whimpered.

Tears pricked my eyes, but I hurried into the hall so he wouldn't see. Out in the short corridor, I leaned against the cool metal wall to catch my breath and compose myself.

Every time Boss Arandon held one of his parties, I hoped this would be the magical night when my luck would change. Whether it was a charming prince or a knight in shining armor with a boner for sleeping girls, I didn't care. I'd all but given up on my chances of escaping on my own.

After all, I only had to think about Sarah to remember the foolishness of hope. Sarah had been here a little while before I was taken, but she'd also been taken from Earth. And Sarah was not one to play along or keep her head down. She'd planned an escape for weeks, even getting Milla and me in on it, back before I realized it was a lost cause. Under Sarah's guidance, we'd learned the security rotations and the ship's floorplan well enough to find the armory and make the most efficient path to the shuttle.

After weeks of planning, Sarah went for it. After seeing Thenoch snap and beat one of the male captives, I'd lost my nerve and told her to wait. But Sarah was determined, so Milla and I covered for her so she could slip away during a party. She'd managed to lift Thenoch's key from his jacket without him noticing. But when she infiltrated the armory, the security system locked her in. In all our hours of furtive planning, we didn't even consider that there were cameras watching every inch of the ship. They'd left her there until the party was over, then dragged her into our sleeping quarters.

Thenoch beat her within an inch of her life. I'd never forget the way she screamed and cried, and then the way she just went silent and limp. Even worse, I'd never forget what a coward I'd been. When she cried *stop* for the first time, I was brave enough to step forward, directly into Thenoch's path.

"Enough. You're hurting her," I'd said, as if he didn't have her blood already on his knuckles.

That was all I got out before Thenoch's massive hand swung out and knocked my frontal lobe into orbit. I was still seeing double when he leveled his harsh gaze on me and said, "Anything else?"

I wanted to be brave, but I was a coward. *He'll kill me*, I thought. And I couldn't do it.

All I could do was stare in horror as he broke her to little pieces. When he left her bloodied and barely conscious, I did my best to put her back together. The medical equipment on board was far superior to anything I had back on Earth, but she'd still be scarred for life. Arandon had taken her to one of his auctions a few weeks later, and we never saw her again.

I tried not to think about it, but her face haunted me through too many sleepless nights. And as much as I wanted to deny it, I knew that I would share her fate sooner rather than later.

Thenoch crept up behind me. "Go, piglet."

"Otherem kufer," I murmured.

Fixing a smile on my face, I returned to the hall and headed straight for the scarred human. I tried to remind myself that he couldn't hurt me too badly if he wanted to stay in Boss Arandon's good graces. His people would grope and pluck and manhandle us all day long to make us presentable for his parties, but I hadn't been used for sex. It certainly wasn't out of any respect for us, but rather that Arandon fetched higher prices at auction if we hadn't been passed around to his entire crew. That went double for his customers, who didn't get free samples. Mystery and anticipation drove prices higher, he said.

As I approached, the scarred man grabbed the tangle of straps across my back and pulled me to him. I lost my balance and stumbled right into his lap. My tray went flying, but his friend shot one hand out to catch the liquor bottle before it broke.

His breath was hot and wet on the back of my neck, reeking of the blue liquor we'd been serving. As far as I could tell, it was infused with something that made people extra aggressive and horny.

Fantastic.

The man stroked my shoulder, making my skin crawl. His fingers came away sparkling with fine silver glitter. "What's your name, pretty little diamond?"

"Helena," I said sweetly. "What's yours?"

"Desmond," he said. "You from Earth?"

"Mmhmm," I said. "Are you?"

He grinned, drawing my eye to that oddly crooked smile. His features were handsome, but even without the scar, the cruelty in his eyes would have made him hideous. "I was. Now I'm from wherever the fuck I want to go."

"That sounds very exciting," I said. I started to rise, but he banded his arm around my waist. I stole a look across the room and caught Boss Arandon's gaze. His head dipped in a subtle nod. It was a sad state when your captor was the most comforting thing in the room. "Desmond, would you like a drink?"

I reached out to pour him a glass of liquor. Looping one arm around his thick neck, I slowly presented it to him. He skimmed his hand up my thigh, over my barely covered breast, where he lingered far too long, and finally took the glass in knife-scarred fingers. His bloodshot eyes leered at me over the edge of the glass.

"Pour us one, too," his quick-reflexed companion said.

I went to rise again, and Desmond yanked me back hard. "Pour your own, ya lazy fucks," he said. "She's got things to do."

My skin crawled as his rough hands gripped my thighs and spread them over his thick, muscular leg. *Keep your head down*, I reminded myself. *Just survive.*

He kept me there a while, as he and his buddies discussed stealing a shipment of medicines headed for a colony in a faraway galaxy. They laughed when they recounted the story of shooting some hapless Ilmarinen security officer in the belly, mocking the way he prayed to his gods as he bled out. I kept the liquor flowing and prayed that Thenoch would come and find something else for me to do.

"You're quiet," Desmond growled in my ear. His tongue slithered across my neck like a parasitic worm.

"Oh, it's just so interesting," I said. "I like listening to your stories."

His rough hand slipped up higher, cupping between my legs. I forced myself to remain still, like a possum playing dead. "I got something you'll find very interesting."

"And what's that?" I teased. Considering I was drier than the Sahara, I sincerely doubted he had anything I was going to enjoy. Unless he had a ticket back to Earth with my name on it wrapped around his dick.

"Unzip my pants and find out," he said.

"I'm sorry, I can't," I said.

His other hand wrapped around my throat. "You insulting me, little diamond?"

"No," I murmured. "My boss won't let me."

"I'll have a talk with your boss," he said. His thumb pressed slightly into my windpipe, just enough to hurt. "No one tells me no."

I entertained a delightful fantasy of breaking the liquor bottle over the table and ramming it into his leering face. I'd probably die an ugly death, but it might be worth it to be the first person to tell him *no*.

While I was still imagining which one of them would take me out, a warm red hand closed on my forearm. Thenoch glared down at me with those baleful yellow eyes.

No, not at me. At Desmond.

"Boss Arandon requests you not damage his merchandise," he growled. "Let go."

Desmond gave my throat another squeeze, then released me. Thenoch pulled me to my feet. As I stood there, frozen between two men who would gladly hurt me for blinking wrong, the man of the hour, Vehr Arandon, sauntered over. Gold lines were painted along his cheekbones and the bridge of his narrow nose. "Mr. Krix," he said warmly. "I see you've met my lovely Helena."

"A bit cold," Desmond griped. "Not much of an advertisement if you can't take it for a test drive."

Boss Arandon laughed. "I've heard such complaints before," he said. "I'll take it under advisement. I think having this little gem on your arm for the better part of an hour is quite a generous test drive. We'll be at the auction on Erebus in two weeks. You might bid on her then if you're interested."

My heart kicked against my ribs. Two weeks. Two weeks, and I would be off this ship and in the hands of someone who was willing to buy women.

Desmond's dark eyes skimmed over me. "Not sure your prices are worth it."

"My merchandise is well worth the price, I assure you," Arandon said. He offered me a hand, and I took it gratefully. From one monster to another. "Good evening, Mr. Krix." The crowd parted around him, and I followed. I could still feel Desmond's hands on me, his touch crawling like tiny insects.

When we returned to Boss Arandon's table, he glanced up at me, then tapped one shoulder lightly. I took my place behind him, gently rubbing his shoulders. He resumed his conversation as if he'd never left. A few of his guests spared me a fleeting glance, then carried on drinking their glowing cocktails and laughing at his jokes. I was furniture, and nothing more.

Even if I was slightly safer now, he hadn't intervened for my benefit. It was a power move to put people like Desmond in their place, and to remind them all that Boss Arandon was in charge.

A dark thought crossed my mind. I'd behaved myself until now, hoping against hope that someone would come along and save me. That Arandon would cross the wrong person, or get himself arrested. But it had been months. No one was coming. And I had no illusions that I could get out of here in one piece.

But maybe I could escape another way. I wasn't going into the hands of someone like Desmond, or the monstrous Proxilar in the corner. Back on Earth, I'd been a trauma nurse. And I'd developed an unfortunately grim niche; I had a gentle hand and a strong constitution when it came to women who'd been brutalized. Sometimes by strangers, but more often by men who supposedly cared about them. I knew very well what people were capable of.

I also knew that Vehr Arandon was always armed. There was a stun-gun in a holster under his arm, and at least one knife strapped to his leg. That gun was within a foot of my hand right this second. He'd still be laughing and sipping his expensive cordial while I blew his brains out through his ear.

There was no way I'd survive such a brazen escape attempt.

And while I hadn't quite committed to it, hadn't accepted the morbid reality of it, that was the point. I had two weeks to think of something better, but I knew for damn sure that they weren't going to hand me over to someone like Desmond. I would make sure of it, even if it was the last thing I did.

CHAPTER 2

Mistral

It was bad enough to be drugged to the gills and laid out like a slab of meat on the butcher's block. But if Evhina was going to gush lovingly about my brother and his new mate, she could have done me the courtesy of knocking me unconscious.

I closed my eyes while the pretty doctor wielded the whining saw to cut into my calf. "I'm just so pleased for him," she chattered. Thanks to the drugs, I didn't feel any pain, but I could feel the maddening vibration of the saw rattling up my leg, and the intense pressure as she opened a seam in my tough skin. "He brought me a delivery of antibiotics last week, and I got to meet her. She's charming, in a very down-to-Earth way."

"Literally," I muttered. He'd picked her up from Earth like a souvenir from the spaceport.

"And goodness, the way he looks at her," she said with a sigh.

The saw screamed against my skin again and sent a squirming sensation up into my groin.

I grunted. If she was one of my brothers, I'd have told her to shut the fuck up, but Evhina was both undeniably sweet, and wielding a bonesaw tough enough to slice through Zathari skin. Antagonizing her was in no one's best interest.

"Here we go," she said. She set the saw aside and put on a pair of magnifying glasses. Her pale blue eyes were comically huge, practically glowing against her copper-red skin. Her gloved hands brandished a pair of thin tweezers. She glanced up at me and scowled. "Hey. You know I don't like it when you watch."

"Some people like that, Evie," I teased.

Her wicked smile made me wonder what the hell the doctor got up to on her off hours. She chuckled and returned to her work as I stared up at the skylight. Soft blue leaves waved overhead, caught in the balmy breeze of a Phade summer day. "Were you working with Jalissa?" she asked.

"Not this time," I said. "Job on Kha'al."

"Care to elaborate?" With a blinding flash, she turned on a lamp and bent it to illuminate my leg.

"Not particularly."

"Shocking," she said. "Aha. There you are." There was an intense pressure as she dug into my muscle. The smell of blood and burnt flesh filled my nose and turned my stomach, but Evie had a gut of steel. "It must have been nasty if it got through you."

"It was a bomb," I said. "Superheated metal. Hot and sharp is a bad combination." I wasn't going to tell her that I'd been careless and distracted. Sometimes, we got a little too comfortable with our tough skin and forgot that we weren't actually invincible.

"Ugh," she said. "Why don't you do something safer? Go fly a ship like Havoc. I never have to pull shrapnel out of his hide."

"Maybe I like doing dangerous things," I said.

"Maybe I don't like worrying about you and your idiot twin," she snapped.

Rising on my elbow, I shot her a stern look. "That idiot..." I sighed. "That's fair. He's an idiot. But you should be glad we keep you in business." At the end of the cushioned table, there were silver clamps connected to my leg, which was filleted like a fish. The gauze underneath was stained a deep purple. Her gloved hands were soaked in blood, which didn't faze her one bit.

She scoffed. "Jalissa keeps me in business. You two just keep me drinking. Lay down, big boy." I flattened and let her finish her work. She found three more long shards of metal that had gotten under my hide and cooled. Each one hit her steel tray with a clatter. After she was done, she ran a scanner over my legs from hip to ankle to ensure she hadn't missed anything. "Anything else before I patch you up?"

"No. Well..." I patted my belly and averted my gaze. "I think I broke some ribs."

"Mistral," she complained. "Why are you like this? You stress me out."

I smirked as she pulled down the scanner on its ceiling-mounted arm. Pale blue light passed over me in a thin beam. She glanced at the screen mounted on the wall, where a pulsing red outline on a skeleton glared at us. "You would be bored if you didn't have to patch us up. And poor. Repeat customers are good for business, Evie," I said.

"Not when they're dead," she spat.

"I didn't die, obviously."

"Not for lack of trying," she snapped. She sighed. "I can't put a needle in your skin." She crossed the little exam room and took a vial from a freezer. After mixing it into a bottle of water, she shook it vigorously and handed it to me. "Drink."

I obediently chugged the sour-tasting mixture, which prickled down my throat like bad booze. "Are you drugging me to keep me out of trouble?"

"I don't have good enough drugs for that," she replied, lowering her glasses again. With deft, quick motions, she hand-stitched the torn muscle in my calf, then applied a layer of catalyst gel over the open wound. She pinched the seam, then used the white wand of a Caduceus emitter to accelerate healing. After a few minutes, she peered closely at it. "You're going to have a scar."

"Okay," I agreed. "I'll live."

She wrapped my calf in a tight bandage, then mounted the wand on a stand over my lower torso. The blue glow of it was harsh on my skin. A maddening itch began just under the skin, and I clenched my fists to keep from scratching. "Got the ants biting?"

"Oh yeah," I said.

"Good," she said.

"So do you grill Jalissa and her girls when they come to you?"

"They scare me too much for that," she said.

"And I don't scare you?"

"Not anymore," she said. "Wraith, yes. But you're a teddy bear."

I bared my teeth at her. "I am not a goddamn teddy bear."

Her full pink lips pursed. "Sure, Mistral. You're terrifying."

I could count on one hand how many people I'd allow to call me a fucking teddy bear. And the men we'd left dead in the jungles of Kha'al would certainly have taken issue with Evhina's assessment of me. There was a difference between being soft and being kind. Evhina was sweet and good at her job; she had no reason to see any other side of me.

A soft chime rang, and the Caduceus emitter went dark. She moved it and examined my skin. "You're probably not fully healed, but I'll fry your skin with too much more in one sitting," she said. She gently pressed her hand to my belly, producing a dull ache. "You want some painkillers?"

"I'm good, Evie," I said. "Thank you."

She moved the suspended medical equipment, letting me sit up finally. Blood rushed from my head. Though I intended to avoid a lecture by not telling her about my ribs, I felt better than I had in days.

I tugged my shirt back down to my waist and leaned over to roll my pants down. She was dabbing at my bare foot with a wet cloth, catching drips of blood.

Over the tips of my toes, Evhina glared at me. "Normally I'd say to stay off of your foot for a day or two, but I know you're going to ignore me," she said. "So instead, I'm going to charge you extra if you split it open and have to come back."

"Fair enough," I agreed.

She made me wait for another half hour while the numbing agent on my leg wore off. I couldn't sit still, so I limped around on one foot to check the security sensors on the windows and doors of her small clinic.

"You don't have to do that every time you're here," she said, sweeping the bloody gauze from the table and wiping her equipment down.

"Yes, I do," I replied. "If you get to lecture me about doing my job, I get to lecture you about safety."

"Except—" she protested.

"Evie, show me your gun," I ordered.

Her eyes rolled, but she complied. As she turned away from me, I caught a glimpse of the wicked burn scarring up the back of her neck, disappearing into her wavy red-gold hair. It turned my stomach; not because it made her any less beautiful but knowing that she had suffered. Neither Evhina nor our shared colleague, the infamous Jalissa Cain, had deigned to share the tragic path that led to a skilled and highly educated surgeon from the Dominion ending up on a backwater like Phade with forged identification papers and heavy locks on all her doors. We all had our sob stories, and hers wasn't my business. However, ensuring that she was as safe as she could be here on Phade was my business, even if she took issue.

She slid her hand under her desk and came up with a dual-function gun. I took it from her and checked the charge on it. I was ready to scold her for not keeping it charged, but the indicator on the underside of the barrel indicated a nearly full charge. With a faint smile, I turned it over and found the switch. "Stun?"

"I'm not a killer," she said. "It's easy enough to switch."

"Evhina."

"Mistral," she said, echoing my tone. She took the gun back. "Happy? I keep it charged."

"I'd be happier if you kept it on lethal settings," I said. "If someone like me comes through that door, stun is just going to piss him off. You may not get another shot."

"If you want, I'll switch it while you watch, but I'm going to switch it again as soon as you leave," she said sweetly. Gods, her mouth. She stowed it under the desk again. Then she smiled at me. "Your concern is appreciated. I'm fine."

I sighed. "Fine. I'm on the ground for a few more days. Call me if you need anything."

"You want to bring me lunch tomorrow?" she teased. "Or should I only call if I need manly Zathari rescue services? Perhaps a bit of growling to start my day?"

"Goodbye, Evhina," I said drily.

My leg was still tingling, but I could limp along well enough to walk out of her clinic in the Verdant Field, one of the quieter districts in the city of Ir-Nassa. The brutal summer heat beat down on me as I strolled down the winding side street and toward the main thoroughfare. At the street corner, an older Il-Teatha woman sold flaky brown pastries and bags of bright citrus fruit from a cart. I shook my head when she approached, stepping onto a sensor to hail the auto-shuttle.

A minute after I stepped onto the silver pad, an open-air shuttle drifted by and eased to a halt. A pair of Il-Teatha women with shopping baskets sat in the front, talking animatedly. White straw visors shielded their crimson skin from the sun. With the midday sun beating down on my skin, I envied that self-made shade. When I climbed onto the shuttle, one of them forced a smile, but the bioluminescence at the ends of her tentacles gave away her fear.

I kept to the back and watched the glittering city of Ir-Nassa blur by around me. Though the city was full of bright colors and flourishing neighborhoods, utterly unlike the dirty slums where we were raised, it never quite felt like home. Nowhere really had, since Viper and I were taken from Sonides. Whenever I arrived here after a job, I sought out a big meal, slept for two days straight, and then I was ready to go again. There was a restlessness in me that I could never calm, and I felt it like a shard of glass under my skin.

And between Evhina's endless chatter about Havoc and Vani, and teasing me about taking her to lunch, something else was awake in me. I felt a hunger in my core that wouldn't be sated with my imagination and my hand.

Maybe it was time for a foray into the night life of Ir-Nassa. It would be easy enough to find a nice woman who wasn't repulsed by my face and get this itch out of my system. Hell, I suspected if I went back to the clinic and invited Evhina back to our place to fuck her brains out, she'd accept. But that didn't feel quite right, and my brothers would never let me live it down.

A month ago, my brother Havoc had arrived here on Phade with an unusual cargo. I'd been expecting crates of antibiotics to deliver to our distant kin on Irasyne. Reliable as ever, Havoc had delivered the drugs, but he'd also brought four bedraggled human women with him, one of whom he swore was his starbound mate.

Bullshit.

Or so I thought, until I saw them together.

I'd always believed starbonding was superstitious nonsense that our ancestors believed before the universe saw fit to ruin them. But Havoc had fucked his way across the galaxies for nearly a decade and never once taken an interest in something serious. He once proclaimed that there was no woman alive who could handle him for life.

And now, he was absolutely lovesick for a pretty human from Earth. Just like that, he was tamed, and perfectly happy to be so. Not only was it unsettling to see that strange stillness in him, but it made me wonder if I'd been wrong all along. Maybe I was missing out on something. Maybe I was already searching, and that was why nowhere had ever felt right, why I couldn't sit still.

My watch buzzed, and I glanced down to see a notification of a new video message from Storm. I swiped to dismiss it for later. Whatever Storm had to say, it wasn't for public consumption. With any luck, it would be a job that took me off this rock again.

I didn't need the work, or the money. Years of mercenary work had padded my bank account nicely. Even with more than two decades between me and the slums of Sonides, I'd never quite shaken the idea that I was desperately poor, always one bad day away from going hungry. Unless it was something for a job, like a weapon upgrade or a decent suit, I barely spent any of what I earned.

But I needed to get moving again. Even Phade, which had long been a place of comfort and rest, was uncomfortable. For nearly a month, there had been a trio of human women in and out of our shared apartment. They were Vani's sisters. Not by birth, but I understood that. My twin brother Viper had been with me since one cell split into two. But the others—Havoc, Bishop, Storm, and Wraith...they were my brothers, too. We had crawled out of hell together, and in the process, had spilled enough blood to make us family.

So I couldn't blame Vani for caring for the women she'd brought from Terra, nor for Havoc's concern for them on her behalf. But gods, was I glad to be getting them out from underfoot. I hadn't been able to walk around naked in my own house in weeks. One of them was a decent cook, and she'd earned my begrudging affection with a plate of fluffy confections she called muffins. But that wasn't enough to make up for having to watch my step to keep from scaring them, nor going into the shower to find it ice cold and smelling of flowers.

Thankfully, Havoc had negotiated a deal with the landlord and bought an apartment just under ours. I'd been eager to get them out, so I carried ninety percent of their few belongings downstairs before the ink was dry on the contract.

When the curved, high-rise building came into sight, I pressed a red button on the side of the auto-shuttle. It eased to a halt at the nearest stop, and I hopped off. My watch buzzed to confirm the payment, and I headed for the sliding glass doors. Sheer walls bloomed with overgrown ferns and flowers growing from window boxes.

I swiped my wrist across the security scanner to open the doors to the small lobby. A second security door awaited inside, where an armed guard nodded to me. "Welcome home, sir," Rotek said. "Your female companions stepped out earlier."

"They're not my—" I sighed. "Thank you. I may be leaving for business again soon. Will you keep an eye on them?"

"Of course, sir," he said. The Il-Teatha male was nearly as big as I was, and he'd retired from the Speaker's personal guards on Firyanin. He'd been vague, but I suspected he'd put more than a few bodies in the ground in his years of service. There was a reason we paid good money for this place, knowing we'd be gone more often than not.

I headed upstairs and let myself into the quiet apartment. I breathed in the stillness, then slumped onto a cushion next to the low table. Finally alone. Now that Evhina's drugs had worn off, I could feel my heartbeat in my calf. I ignored it and checked my message from Storm. My watch synced to the visual display on the wall, and I was greeted by a high-resolution video of another Zathari male seated in the dim office at Vuola Lire.

Storm was the head of security at the exclusive casino on Firyanin, and he made it his business to know everyone else's business. He grinned at the camera. "Hey, shithead. I might have a lead on the guy selling Zathari women," he said. "It's not a clean shot, but it's something. We've got a guest coming in, about three days from now. His private security team contacted us ahead of time, so I looked him up. Vehr Arandon. I did a little digging, and this guy is scum. The word is that if it's got a warm hole to fuck, Arandon can get it for you." His nose wrinkled. "The boss can turn a blind eye, but...you know, I have excellent eyesight. Anyway, if you want to get in on it, book a flight today. He'll only be here a couple of days."

The anger that settled into my belly felt good. It wasn't that itching, shapeless agitation that plagued me every time I was here on Phade. It was a comet, shooting across the sky like a message from the gods.

I recorded a quick message back to Storm.

"I'm on my way."

※

Thirty-six hours later, I strolled off an enclosed, air-conditioned shuttle that had picked me up from the massive spaceport at Aliaros, the sprawling megacity that gleamed across Firyanin's central continent like a forest of metal and glass. I'd worn my nicest clothes, but I still felt out of place amidst the wealthy patrons of Vuola Lire, who avoided eye contact on the swanky shuttle.

A pretty Vaera woman in a sleek gold suit greeted me at the landing pad. "Mr. Mistral," she greeted warmly. "Mr. Storm is waiting for you. Follow me."

I suppressed a snort of derision. *Mr. Storm.* It was always a shock to see Storm in a position of authority.

Walking into Vuola Lire, I was instantly bombarded by a cacophony of sound and light. The casino itself was massive, with an outdoor racetrack, several exclusive clubs, and even a fighting cage. Wraith and I had both fought there a few times as a favor to Storm and a boost to our bank accounts. Gambling tables of every sort filled five decadent floors, while beautiful servers of every species and gender entertained with drinks and company.

Viper and I, along with some of the other Hellspawn, had certainly enjoyed the benefits of Storm's position here. A drunken night at Vuola Lire was a night well spent, if not one well remembered.

The girl in the gold suit led me to a private elevator past one of the bars, swiping her wrist against a reader. She gestured for me to enter, then followed me inside. "Was your flight amenable?"

"Yes, thank you," I said gruffly. Her eyes swept over me.

"Very good, sir," she said, her politeness a well-honed skill. "At Mr. Storm's request, we've comped a suite for you. I think you'll find it most comfortable."

She took me to an office two floors up, where we found Storm looking down at a round array of screens. Each showed dozens of camera feeds and digital readouts I couldn't even begin to parse. He had an eye for patterns, and he'd apparently developed a reputation for spotting a cheater before even the computers picked it up. And like me, he also enjoyed the occasional skull-cracking; I suspected that he'd pulled more than a handful of would-be troublemakers into a secret room and applied that massive strength to make his point.

Storm glanced up as I entered and grinned. He slid around the displays and clapped me into a tight embrace. "Looking ugly as always," he said warmly.

"I do my best," I said, giving Storm a tight embrace. He was one of the only people in existence who made me feel small. "What have you got?"

"Drinks? Pretty girl to sit on your lap?" he said. "All well-paid and well-protected, I assure you."

I chuckled. "I'm good. Let's look at this Arandon guy."

"All business," Storm said. "You don't change. Let's get some privacy, shall we?" He held up a finger, then closed the door to his office. He beckoned for me to follow him through a side door, which led into another cozy office. After sliding one hand under his desk, a faint white noise filled the room. My translator let out a faint ringing from the signal jammer he'd just activated. We both switched off our translators.

After checking something on his computer, he swiped broadly and sent something to a massive wall display for me to see. What had been a subtly shifting image of a coral reef faded into a man's portrait. He was handsome, with a reddish tint to his skin and pointed ears that were reminiscent of the Vaera. The warm smile was a sharp contrast to his cold eyes.

"Meet Vehr Arandon. He arrives on property tomorrow night at nineteen hundred IUT," Storm said, speaking in our native Zathari. "Viper's digging around on him, but he doesn't have much. Just rumors."

"Did you contact Bishop? Maybe one of his girls knows something," I said. For years, he'd worked as a bodyguard on Niraj, home to the fabled City of a Thousand Pleasures.

Storm's dark blue eyes widened as he said, "Shit, you haven't heard. His cover got burned, and he had to leave Niraj in a hurry. Perri's building him a new ID, but he's laying low for a while to keep the heat off of us."

I shook my head. "Shit. Is he all right?"

"Far as I know," Storm said. "He seemed okay. Wouldn't say much else. I talked to Jalissa, too, but she didn't know anything other than the name."

I scowled. "And you think he's selling Zathari women?"

A few months ago, I'd heard a wisp of a rumor while on a refueling stop with a mercenary crew. As the conversation got bawdier, one of the other mercs talked about visiting a brothel on Vakarios, which was already a bad start to a story. Too drunk to realize the idiocy of what he was saying, the merc had told us at great length about how nasty he'd gotten with this 'horned slut' that looked like a prettier version of me. When he put his fists at his crotch and talked about how he'd steered her by the horns while tears ran down her cheeks, I'd already decided how I was going to kill him.

He'd fucked a Zathari woman. One of my people, someone who could have been my mother, my sister, my daughter, if my life had gone differently. Gods only knew how the woman had ended up there in the cesspit of Port Vakarios, but I was certain it wasn't by choice.

Out of respect for the job, I waited until we'd finished our contract to kill him. Before he met his end, the merc had told me which of the brothels he'd visited, thinking I might spare him. To be fair, I made it quick, but there wasn't a chance in hell I was letting him walk away after the way he'd treated that woman. I didn't lose a bit of sleep over one less shithead tainting the universe.

But upon my own visit to the filthy brothel, they'd told me they didn't have a Zathari woman. A bribe of a thousand credits still didn't yield a lead, and I suspected they weren't telling me because I wore my anger like a fucking beacon over my head. I'd searched Vakarios for as long as I could stomach and left before I caught the wrong kind of attention. Asking bluntly where one might buy a living being could make me either look like a trafficker or a narc. Being suspected of being with the law on Vakarios was a death sentence.

I'd been on the hunt ever since. This was a thin lead, but it was enough to get me moving. This restless anger had a direction again.

Storm swiped through the file. "We don't have a lot. We know Arandon is very connected. We don't know where he actually lives, but he seems to run his operation from a Chariot-class ship called the Basilisk. It's somehow marked as completely clean in the Ilmarinen databases."

"So he's got some friends in high places," I said. Storm nodded grimly. "Friends that will be upset if he disappears?"

"Who can get upset about an accident?" Storm said with a shrug. "But you better be absolutely fucking certain before you make a move. Rumor is one thing. If any of this splashes back on you, I can't help you without jeopardizing this place. And that will end badly for me, and possibly the rest of you." He swiped at his file again. "Arandon travels with tight security. We're expecting a team of three, but two of them are usually in the crowd. His bodyguard is a mean-looking Il-Teatha guy. He'll head in first to sweep Arandon's suite before the boss comes in."

"Paranoid?"

"All these rich criminal fucks are," Storm said. "That's why I make so much money." He raked a hand through his short hair. "You can't do it on the property, unless you can make it look accidental. No investigations on my watch."

I'd already thought of that, and I had a few ideas. "I'm on it," I said. "Can you set up a meeting?"

Storm grinned. "I thought you'd never ask. I hinted that we had a few high rollers who might be interested in hearing about his business. He jumped at the chance, and I got you on the guest list." He dug in his desk and took out a sleek leather wallet. "Mr. Delthe, up and coming fuel baron."

Opening the wallet revealed a paper copy of an ID, along with two chips that could be inserted into my watch so that any scanner I passed would pick up the new ID. I raised an eyebrow. "Fuel baron?"

"Figured you wouldn't have to lie as much about your work on Kha'al," he said with a shrug. "From what I can tell, he likes to talk and show off his girls. Don't offer too much and make him feel important."

Oh, I was going to make him feel important. He was going to get my VIP treatment.

CHAPTER 3

Helena

One of my coworkers back at St. Anthony's used to always chirp about looking on the bright side. I thought she was annoying, but it was a helpful exercise, especially on long days when two more traumas landed in our lap for every one we stitched up. At least we had jobs. At least we weren't overrun by swarms of blood-sucking beetles like the western cities.

At least, at least, at least.

Before leaving the Basilisk, Arna and Telah dressed us in crimson and black, complete with sharp little metal spikes all over. His thorned roses, Arandon said. Too bad whatever genius fashion designer made these getups hadn't considered the realities of doing anything but standing very still. Every time I tried to get comfortable, another damn spike poked into me. I'd found if I sat carefully on my right butt cheek, I could go unscathed. At least the sharp points would keep roaming hands off us.

We were landing on Firyanin, they said. Despite my fear, I watched in wonder as we took Boss Arandon's shuttle from the Basilisk and headed down to the surface. The gleaming city below had to be ten times the size of Atlanta. Shuttles and hovercars swarmed over the ground like bees at a hive. There was so much light that it was nearly blinding. Massive spires rose here and there, and right in the middle of it was a huge green space and a glittering blue lake speckled with rainbow-colored sails. My heart ached at the sight of it. I'd never seen so much green anywhere but a book.

But instead of heading toward that sprawling green, we'd flown to the edge of the city, where spotlights arced back and forth over the gaudy golden casino. We landed, but we didn't leave right away. Instead, Thenoch and two of Arandon's security team left to inspect the security.

While he waited, Arandon painted thin golden lines on his face. I was impressed at his ability to do his own makeup, though I wouldn't have dreamed of making a comment about it. Thenoch returned a few hours later with a report on the security. Arandon listened intently, then clapped the big man on the shoulder.

"Girls," he commanded, snapping his fingers as he finally rose from his seat. His red eyes skimmed over me, and he nodded in approval. After inspecting Milla, he took two coiled straps from his pocket. My heart sank as he unrolled one of them. After he clipped a clasp to the ornate bustier with the conveniently placed ring between my breasts, I clenched my teeth.

Staring up at the ostentatious golden edifice of Vuola Lire, I tried to remember Kitty's advice. Sure, I was wrapped up in red leather and boots with heels so high I could barely balance, but at least I was on solid ground for the first time in months. After the non-stop, steady hum of the Basilisk, I almost felt uneasy on the solid stillness of the planet with its unsimulated gravity.

Yes. Perhaps I was on a leash like an animal, but at least I wasn't dead. How was that for looking on the bright side?

I glanced at Milla, who smiled at me before taking a deep breath. She inflated, her shoulders rising, her head lifted. Her expression was bland and vacuous, and I knew she was somewhere where nothing could hurt her. Not being treated like a doll, not being groped or insulted. She was somewhere else entirely.

I didn't know how to do it so well, but I tried. *I am perfectly happy being his little plaything,* I thought as we sauntered into the casino, trailing behind him like puppies. As we walked in, patrons in elegant clothes turned to watch. I wasn't sure if they were staring at Thenoch, Arandon, or the two leashed human women with half their bodies on display, but I told myself it was because I was so beautiful.

If I hadn't been on a literal leash, I might have enjoyed the spectacle of Vuola Lire. The interior was decorated in dark marble columns and glittering gold. It was so over the top that it surpassed tacky and cycled back to being beautiful in a chaotic way. There was so much to see that it was almost overwhelming, especially after months of being in a confined space. The gambling floors rose all around us in a jungle of neon light, but the central area was open. Lights swirled around as slender acrobats on silks swung and flipped through the air overhead.

Below them, several tables of patrons enjoyed colorful drinks and stared up at the show.

Something tugged at my chest, and I stumbled forward to see Vehr glaring at me. "Keep up," he said. "Don't stare like a tourist."

"*Ashelo*," I muttered.

Suddenly, the leash tugged hard, and I found myself right at his side. He cupped the side of my head like he was going in for an affectionate kiss, but his fingers dug hard into the joint behind my jaw. I bit back tears as he whispered in my ear. "Whatever nonsense you flout in front of Thenoch, you will not do it here. If you are anything but silent decoration, you will reap severe consequences. Do you understand?"

I nodded, keeping my eyes forward.

"Now, play sweet," he growled in my ear. As he broke away, a charming smile broke across his face, and I swallowed my tears as I fell behind him again.

A pretty woman in a gold suit greeted him, guiding him to an escalator and winding through one of the gambling floors. As we went, I scanned my surroundings for escape routes out of habit. Now that we were on the ground, it was more realistic. That city would swallow me up like a single teardrop in the sea, never to be seen again.

We passed a table where a man and woman were sharing a bottle of wine as they rolled strangely large dice with a pair of Proxilar in suits.

Hard wooden table, good for breaking glass.

Grab the bottle. Break it on his head. Get the leashes and run.

We passed by.

"Right this way, Master Arandon," the woman said.

There was a bar that surrounded a column with a golden cage. Inside the cage, a pretty woman in a feathered turquoise costume danced. Sexy bird was a strange choice, but she had a host of eager spectators buying drinks and staring up at her. Past the bar was a pair of golden doors blocked off by velvet ropes and two massive bodyguards.

As we approached, the men stepped aside and opened the doors onto a beautifully furnished room. Inside, the ostentatious gold décor was draped in red and purple silks that made me think of something from a fairytale. A slender Vaera male poured drinks at a corner bar while a waitress in a skimpy gold outfit delivered them to the patrons at the table.

Half a dozen men and a single woman sat around the polished circular table in the center of the room. "Mr. Arandon," a Vaera man greeted, rising from his seat. His golden eyes slid over me, then flicked to Milla. His lips parted at the sight of her. "Please, join us."

As they made their fawning introductions, I surveyed the gathered patrons. The woman spared us a quick glance with her eerie pale green eyes. A small, jeweled disc was rigged to her purple dress and covered only her left nipple, leaving the rest of her breast bare beneath thin golden chains. It was quite a look. After a passing glance, she returned to stacking her gambling chips in precise, neat piles. There were a few Vaera, humans, and a big, gray-skinned male with curling black horns.

Who looked the most promising for an escape? The golden-skinned woman with the fierce cheekbones would have been my first pick, with the whole gender solidarity thing, but she looked like she'd rather rescue a piece of pocket lint. One of the human men was older, with salt-and-pepper hair that made me think he could have been my father's age if he'd lived longer.

What about the gray one? I'd only seen a few of them before, but I knew he was Zathari. The Devils of Sonides, as Arandon called them. Maybe he'd use some of that devilish strength to get us out of here.

As if he heard my thoughts, he glanced up at me, and I was drawn in like he had his own gravitational field. His pale blue eyes practically glowed against his dark, stone-gray skin. Onyx horns curved away from his brow, then rose, reminding me of monstrous fangs atop his head. The left side of his face had raised, twisted scar tissue that ringed his eye and trickled over his jaw and down into his crisp gray shirt. I knew a burn scar when I saw one, and he was lucky not to have lost the eye.

His eyes narrowed, and I realized that I'd been staring for far longer than was acceptable for a pet. With my stomach tying itself in a knot, I averted my eyes and hoped he wouldn't call for my head for being so rude.

Arandon paused at the empty seat, and I hurried to take his jacket. "A drink," he said. He reached up to unhook the leash and settled into the seat, while Milla rubbed his shoulders.

I lurched forward, then remembered my act. Calm, easy-going, utterly brainless. I let my hips swing as I sauntered to the bar and leaned over it to survey the tools of the trade. Knife. Bottle opener. Good for opening big juicy veins.

If I wanted one of them to take me out, I'd go after the Zathari. No Proxilar here, so he was the best choice to snap my neck in a hurry. Better than the alternative.

My morbid little fantasies probably warranted a bit of introspection and some therapy, but giving myself an escape plan kept me sane. I didn't want to die. Even though I'd wanted to leave Earth for years, I didn't hate life. But the thought of being at the mercy of someone like Desmond Krix, or any one of the hundreds of assholes who'd attended one of Boss Arandon's parties...that was a nightmare. And if those were my options, then I was going to take the escape route that lay before me.

"A Thegaran twister," I said quietly. "Easy on the berry juice."

The bartender nodded, apparently unfazed by a grown woman dressed in a ridiculous outfit being walked about on a leash. While he mixed the drink, I stole another look behind me. The one with the horns was looking right at me, those big blue eyes cold and soulless.

My cheeks heated, and I turned around, only to realize that I had a choice between him seeing my nearly-bare butt cheeks or my embarrassed face cheeks. I wasn't sure which was worse.

When the bartender pushed the drink toward me, I squeaked, "Thank you," and hurried back to Arandon. I set the drink in front of him, then took my place behind him. As he took his first sip, I wished that I had poison for that sweet little drink.

I hadn't been a violent person before my abduction, but I'd never been forced to think about my own survival like this. And if anyone deserved such a splash of poison in his cocktail, it was Vehr Arandon.

The distinguished older man glanced up at Milla. "How much for the tall one?" he asked. So much for being our savior. The resemblance to my sweet late father ended at the gray hair.

"It's funny you should ask," Arandon said. "They'll both be

up for auction at Erebus. Very obedient and well-trained." He leaned in. "And fresh. I might consider a deal for the pair."

The man's eyes dragged over us, and I felt like he'd peeled off my clothes. "Very nice." Then he tilted his head. "Let me get a closer look."

Arandon unclipped the hook on Milla's bustier and patted her ass. Milla's smile never faltered as she sauntered over the older man. He glanced at Arandon. "May I touch?"

"Gently, please," he said.

The man ran his hand over Milla's body, cupping her breasts, sliding between her legs like she was just an object on display. His touch was light, but it made me want to cry. She didn't even flinch. "Milla, show Mr. Damiran what you can do with your hands."

Milla settled in behind the man and started rubbing his shoulders. Damiran sighed. "Oh, she is lovely."

"If you men are done playing with your toys, I'd like to play some cards," the woman snapped. She tossed several hexagonal chips into the center of the table. "Let's deal."

The one with the horns added his chips, then stole another glance at me. I could have sworn he flinched, but maybe I was paranoid. Then he nodded to Arandon. "Boss Arandon, if I could be so bold," he said.

"Mr. Delthe?"

"Your pets are from Terra, yes?"

"That's right," he said. "Carefully selected."

Carefully selected, my happy ass. I averted my gaze so he wouldn't see my thoughts on my face.

"I'm in the market for something from Terra," Mr. Delthe said. "Might I have a sample?"

My stomach took up residence somewhere in the center of the earth. *Say no,* I thought.

Arandon chuckled and handed me the end of the leash. "Go entertain Mr. Delthe, would you?"

CHAPTER 4

Mistral

I WAS ALREADY OFF-PLAN.

No. I was collecting information. Assimilating. Earning his trust. It certainly wasn't that my heart nearly stopped when I saw the doll-like woman look up at me with sheer terror in her eyes. The other one hid it well, but this one didn't. Her smile didn't reach her eyes, and it slipped when she stared at me.

I was used to that. Even without the nasty burn, I would have been intimidating, especially to a human woman from Earth who'd likely never seen someone like me.

She was absolutely beautiful, with a perfect body. Curvy hips, a round ass exposed by the skimpy outfit, glistening with some kind of sparkling treatment. As perfect as she was, I wanted to cover her up. I didn't want these men staring at her like she was a piece of meat they were about to tear into. And I knew she'd think I was the same sort of monster, but if she was with me, that kept her away from them just for an hour or two.

"Go entertain Mr. Delthe, would you?" Boss Arandon said.

Her expression faltered as she looked at me, but she fixed that bland smile on her face and walked over to me. My chest tightened when she handed me the thin leather loop connected to her chest. It was all I could do not to leap over the table, loop it around Arandon's neck, and choke him out in front of them. It was only my promise to Storm not to shit in his house that kept me calm.

I took the thin leash and raised my eyebrows. "Come and sit," I said, pushing back a bit from the table. She hesitated and perched on my leg, like a pretty little bird. She kept her distance, careful of the sharp black spikes on her blood-red outfit. Shitty design, unless you wanted to make sure no one got too close to the merchandise. Not a stupid move on Arandon's part.

After putting my cards in her right hand, I looped my arm around her waist and let my hand rest on her stomach. She jumped in surprise, then gave me a little smile. Her breathing was quick, her body tense under my touch. I wished I could whisper to her.

I won't hurt you.

As the dealer tossed more cards to us, I pointed to the ones I wanted her to discard. We lost the first round, but I won a pile of cash on the second.

"You're good luck, little rose," I said, giving her a light squeeze. "Get the money."

As we played, I was whirling through scenarios. I'd worked out my plan to poison him with a slow-acting agent. It took a few days, but he'd die of an apparent heart attack when he was a few days from here. Not the most satisfying kill, but it kept Storm and the casino clean.

But my stomach nearly dropped through the floor when he said *auction on Erebus*. The space station was cloaked in mystery, open by invitation only to a clientele with a fuckton of money and no morals. And if Arandon was going to be there, he was my ticket to finding who was selling women from Sonides.

Killing one little bug was satisfying, but incinerating the hive would be even better.

"Mr. Delthe?" the dealer asked politely.

I glanced up and realized the woman was staring down at me instead of playing my cards. I hastily chose two, but she raised her eyebrows at me. Her slender fingers drifted to two different cards and tapped lightly. I nodded my approval. She tossed them out and retrieved two more from the dealer to give me a hell of a hand.

Another big win.

"I may have to retrieve my good luck charm from you," Arandon said archly, tossing down his cards in a fit of pique.

I cleared my throat. "What do you want for her?"

The trafficker laughed. "Mr. Delthe, I hate to disappoint, but she'll be up for auction."

"Two hundred thousand credits right now, and I'll come and buy another on Erebus," I said. The table went quiet, and Arandon raised an eyebrow. I had no idea what a shitbag like him was selling human women for, but he clearly wasn't offended by me drastically undershooting it.

"Two hundred and fifty," he said.

"Make it three hundred and I'll buy both," I said.

He barked a laugh. "Two hundred and fifty, and I'll get you a ticket to bid on the other one." His teeth flashed a shark's grin. "Final offer."

"Done," I said. Even better.

He smirked, and I knew that I had overpaid. That only made me madder. *Erebus,* I told myself. Even Jalissa hadn't been able to get on the list.

I gently touched the woman's leg, and I realized she was trembling. There was still a faint smile on her face, but her eyes were filled with fear, a line forming between her penciled brows.

Arandon laughed. "You can do what you like with her now," he said. "She's yours."

"Let's see what she can do with her mouth," the silver-haired man said, his eyes shining with greedy lust.

"Fucking pigs," the Raephon woman snarled. For a second, the pale green of her eyes brightened, and I could see the reptilian slits lengthening. Perhaps she'd shift into her dragon form and bite Arandon's head off, saving us all some trouble. "Can you all do nothing without thinking of your cocks? It's a wonder you manage to make it through a day."

I agreed, though I hated being lumped in with Arandon and the others. The older man shot the Raephon woman an irritated look, then shrugged and tossed back the rest of his drink. The card game went on as if I hadn't just bought a woman like livestock.

Eventually, Arandon's bodyguard brought me a tablet to sign, validating a credit transfer. Using Mr. Delthe's chip, I paid the sum, signed it, and looked back at Arandon. "I trust you won't mind me taking her with me tonight."

"She's all yours," he said. His brow raised. "And if you'd like one of your own kind, I can arrange that for you."

Fury rolled through me, and I involuntarily gripped the woman's waist tighter. She didn't complain, but her hand closed on mine, pulling away slightly. I eased up, tilting my head at Arandon. "You can get Zathari women?"

"Not directly, but I have connections," he said. "Give me a few weeks, and I'll find you a pretty little horned bitch to warm your bed. It'll be just like home, Mr. Delthe."

I had to wonder if someone like Arandon had stolen my mother, leaving Viper and me alone and afraid. One day she was there, and the next, a man hiding behind a shielded helmet and tactical gear was stealing her away. I'd told myself that she went to prison, probably for stealing or some other petty crime, but I never found any records. When I got older and understood that the world was much bigger and nastier than I'd ever grasped before, I realized that something far worse had likely happened.

Some days, Viper and I reminisced about her, wishing that we would find her. But in truth, I prayed that she was long dead. I prayed that she'd fought back enough to force someone's hand, so that she wouldn't suffer at the hands of men like these.

"I'd like that very much, Mr. Arandon," I said calmly, imagining how satisfying it would be to crush his skull in my bare hands. "I do like to have options."

Arandon laughed. "Very good, Mr. Delthe. Very good."

We played for another hour, and the petite woman was still shaking when we finished. I sent her to retrieve a drink for me, just to give her a moment of space, and I quickly sent a message to Storm on my watch under the table. *Meet me in suite. Scan for bugs.* She returned soon after and handed me the drink.

After another few rounds that saw me twenty thousand credits richer, I feigned a yawn. "Mr. Arandon, friends, it's been a pleasure. I think I'll retire with my new toy, if it doesn't offend."

"Of course not," he said. "I'm pleased to do business with you. We'll deliver an invitation to the auction to your suite."

"Lovely," I said. I tugged on the woman's leash. "Shall we?"

CHAPTER 5

Helena

A YEAR AGO, I'D BEEN WEARING LOOSE, SHAPELESS SCRUBS WHILE I worked my ass off in a charity hospital in Atlanta. Every day, I was up to my elbows in blood and stitching idiots back together, because even after our world was fucked inside out, humans were still killing each other.

One week ago, I was holding my tongue while a tailor measured me and Milla for matching red outfits. I didn't even bat an eye when he palmed my breasts like he was checking for the best produce at the supermarket and measured absolutely every inch of me.

And one hour ago, Vehr Arandon had sold me to a Zathari male like I was a used car. Now, the huge man led me along on a leash like an animal, but I fought tears and kept my eyes up.

I had hoped the big Zathari might save me. There was something endearing about the way he'd handed me his cards, keeping one hand firmly at my waist instead of rooting around in my nether regions like he was digging for loose change. It was a low bar, but that simple measure of respect put him at the top of a long list. Clearly, I was stupid.

The twisted scar on his left cheek gave his eye a sinister turn. And the fact that he'd barely finished making a deal for me when he asked about buying more women...it made me terrified of what awaited. Did he want a harem, or was he anticipating being rid of me that quickly?

I struggled to keep up with his long strides, but he had barely spared a look back at me. His eyes were fixed ahead, so I stole a look over my shoulder. Long, marble-floored hallway. No security.

This was my only chance. Once I went into a closed room with the horned brute, it was all over for me.

I had to risk it.

Quietly, I grasped the clasp that connected the leash to the metal loop on my chest. Then I took a few big steps closer to him to let it go slack. Keeping it silenced against my palm, I unhooked the leash, then turned and ran. The high boots threatened to trip me, so I ran on my toes, every step a precarious fight with gravity. I didn't know where I was going to go, but anywhere away from him was a good start.

Heavy steps clomped after me. I didn't look, just ran like I'd never run before. Doors blurred past. The noise of the casino crescendoed, calling to me. I could disappear into that chaos.

Almost there.

I was nearly back to the elevator when a heavy hand closed on my arm. The force of it yanked me off my feet, and he swiftly threw me over his shoulder. "Please don't hurt me," I pleaded. "I'm sorry."

He growled and said, "Be quiet. You scream, and I'm going to let him know I'm very unhappy with my purchase."

Tears stung at my eyes. *Good move, Helena.* One chance, and I'd fucked it up. Now he was going to take out his anger on me. God, it was going to hurt. Maybe he'd kill me and put me out of my misery faster.

He paused and swiped his palm against the double doors at the end of the hallway. Golden doors swung open on a black tiled floor. He bypassed the big sitting room and headed straight for the luxurious bedroom. The bed was gigantic, covered in a plush black comforter and a mountain of red and black satin pillows. Another big Zathari sat on the edge of the bed. Two of them? With those big bony horns and eerie eyes, they looked monstrous. Beautiful in a harsh, cold way, but still monstrous.

My head spun as he flipped me over his shoulder again, but he was strangely gentle as he set me on my feet. Before I could bolt again, his big arm encircled my waist. I whimpered, and he growled. "Don't fight me."

I fought to stay still as the other man approached us. Holy shit. He was one of the biggest men I'd ever seen, easily six inches taller than the one who'd bought me. His horns were oddly short, almost like little twisted spikes at his hairline. They might have been cute, if he wasn't utterly terrifying.

"Look how pretty she is," the big one said. His warm fingers brushed up my neck, and he unhooked my earrings. He took something thin and black from his pocket, and I instinctively clenched, hoping it wasn't about to go into me somewhere. Instead, he flicked it open, emitting a faint blue light that reminded me of a medical instrument. When the light passed over the earrings, it turned red. His smile turned to a grim expression as he nodded. "Let's strip her down and see if she's clean."

"I'm clean, I swear," I whimpered.

Mr. Delthe clapped a hand over my mouth. "Keep your mouth shut or I'll find something to occupy it. This can be as easy or hard as you want it to be. Understand?"

Desperation ripped through me, but I nodded my head. Even as I nodded like a compliant little thing, I was scanning the room. Several big glass vases would give me something sharp to fend them off. And through a set of parted gray curtains, I could see the doors to the balcony. Maybe it was high enough to jump.

Mr. Delthe hauled me into the bathroom. There was a huge tub inside, easily big enough for two Zathari and one little human pet. The bigger Zathari started the bath, filling the room with a dull roar and a rising cloud of steam. Then he put his finger to his lips. Silently, he leaned over me and plucked the ornaments from my hair. One by one, the expensive baubles made a glittering pile on a towel.

By the time he was done, my hair was loose, and the mirror was entirely fogged over. The bigger man leaned over and wrote on the glass with one finger. To my surprise, he wrote in Aengran Common.

Won't hurt you. Play along. OK?

My brow furrowed as I nodded against the other man's palm. He slowly released me, and my legs nearly buckled from the adrenaline overload. "Take off your clothes," Mr. Delthe said gruffly.

My heart thrummed. What the hell was going on?

"Don't make him ask again," the big one growled. He pointed again to the mirror. "Take off your clothes."

Was this some sort of fucked-up Zathari game? And what the hell did it mean that I was a little swimmy in the head and feeling all warm and melty between my legs at the thought of it? Fear and anticipation had turned my brain into mush. I fumbled at the laces on the back of the bustier, but Mr. Delthe pried my hands out of the way and yanked it apart.

I let out a heavy sigh as the tight garment finally released me. With my cheeks flushing, I held the loose fabric to my chest. "Let it go," Mr. Delthe said.

Slowly, shamefully, I released the bustier and let it fall. But to my surprise, a warm, fluffy bathrobe settled over my shoulders from behind. I hastily closed it over my body and tied the sash in a tight knot.

"I'm tired of waiting for what I've bought," Mr. Delthe said. Kneeling behind me, he unzipped the high boots. Even though I'd sat on his lap for hours with his hands on me, this felt more intimate. The edge of one of those horns brushed against my bottom as he leaned closer to remove the uncomfortable boots. The feeling of his hands on me sent a shiver rolling through me, and I prayed to all the gods in all the universes that he wouldn't notice.

The bigger man gathered my discarded clothing and jewelry and threw it into the bathtub. He smirked. "Anything in your ass?"

Mr. Delthe started to lift the robe, and I whirled and slapped his hand. "Absolutely not," I snapped. His light blue eyes went wide, and I realized I had made a terrible mistake. "I'm sorry." But despite my reaction, he was smiling. He touched my jaw, holding it open. His head tilted as he peered inside.

What in the hell was going on? I was so baffled I didn't resist.

"She looks good to me," Mr. Delthe said. "Let's get her in bed."

A chill ran down my spine. There was a splash as my boots joined the clothing in the water. The bigger one rolled up his sleeve, baring a huge, muscular forearm. Then he plunged all my clothes and jewelry deep under the water and swirled it around.

The scarred one turned me around by the shoulders, lowering his face so he was at eye level. All the armor that made me look like a pretty little ornament instead of a scared little human was gone, and it was just me in a fuzzy robe. No more spikes to keep his hands off. But despite the harsh scarring and the slight twist to his eye, he looked concerned. The cold distance in his eyes was gone. "Mistral."

"Miss what?" I squeaked.

"Mistral," he repeated. He put out his hand. "My name."

"H...Helena." I glanced nervously at the other man. "I'm sorry, I don't know what you want me to do."

"Come in here and play with us," the bigger man said. As he brushed past me, he said, "Artemis, activate mating music."

"Yes, Mr. Storm," a polite female AI voice said from in the bedroom.

"For fuck's sake," Mistral complained. "Tell me you didn't—"

A low, primal drumbeat filled the room, and the other

Zathari flashed me a devious grin as he made a little thrusting motion with his hips. "Mating time."

I froze, but Mistral took my hand, guided me over the cold tile floor, then patted a big plush chair across from the bed. I sank into it, staring at him in confusion.

"Helena, I'm not going to hurt you," he said, his voice deep and gruff. My eyes drifted up. "And this fool surely isn't."

"Remember which fool got you here," the other one said, though he seemed unbothered by the insult. He waved, then opened a refrigerator and took out several bottles of fresh fruit juice. "Storm."

"What the hell is going on?" I whispered.

"Well, technically, you belong to us now," Mistral said. His nose wrinkled. "And I hope it was worth the money."

Storm sighed and offered me one of the bottles of juice. "It's fresh, and it's good. No booze, though we can make that happen. You look like you could use a drink."

I shook my head. "I think I might throw up." With my hands trembling, I took the juice and sipped it tentatively.

He just smiled and opened another bottle for himself. Then he plopped onto the edge of the bed next to Mistral. His voice was quiet, and his expression went serious as he spoke again. "When you leave here, you can go wherever you want. But we need information first."

My jaw dropped. "What information?"

"On Arandon," Mistral said. "Everything you can tell me, especially about this auction he mentioned."

"I don't know if I can help you," I whispered.

"Where's his base of operations? What kind of security does he have on his ship? Who else will be at the auction? Is he the only seller? Where's he getting the Zathari women?" Mistral said, rapidfire.

"I don't know," I pleaded.

"Come on," Mistral said sharply. "Surely you know something."

Tears stung my eyes, and I lost control for a split second. Then I bit the inside of my cheek so hard I tasted blood, focusing on the pain to drive back my emotions. "Let me think. Okay?"

A sharp knock rang at the door, and Mistral lurched to his feet. "Play along," he said. He shed his jacket and tossed it onto the bed. Heading for the door, he stripped his shirt off to reveal a body like carved granite. Blame it on shock, but I helped myself to an eyeful as he strode past me. The burn scar on his face stretched down the side of his throat and over one side of his chest, almost like something had dripped down his face. There was a lovely, sinuous shift of muscle over his back as he strutted past.

Did I have a thing for horned men all of a sudden? According to the throbbing pulse between my legs, I certainly did. Life had a way of shaking things up, after all.

On his way to the door, Mistral unzipped his pants. When he opened the door, someone cleared their throat. "Sir, we were just ensuring that you were pleased with your purchase." I recognized Thenoch's gravelly voice. Did he know what happened?

Suddenly, Storm let out a long, erotic groan that showed a drastic overestimation of my skills in bed. His eyes widened, and he gave me a vigorous nod.

"Oh! Oh!" I squealed. "You're so big! Yes, right there! Yes, sir!"

His lips broadened into a delightful smile as he mouthed, *Yes, sir?*

"Very pleased," Mistral said to the visitor. "My associate is getting her warmed up, but I'd like to get in there and show her what a Zathari man can do. Do you mind? I paid good money, and I don't need any further interruptions."

A noisy cough. "Of course, sir. Please enjoy. We'll have some of Ms. Helena's belongings delivered in the morning. We think you'll find some very appealing garments and accessories to your liking."

Not to be outdone by my squealing, Storm slapped his hands together rhythmically, and I let out another long, high-pitched moan. Even though he hadn't touched me, a lurid image of him fucking me from behind filled my head, and that sound wasn't entirely faked. My eyes drifted to Mistral, and I realized that it was him I imagined, gripping my hips tight as he drove into me.

Surely, under these circumstances, I could not be held personally responsible for the erotic fantasies rampaging through my adrenaline-soaked funhouse of a brain, nor for the situation between my thighs.

"Sure," Mistral said. "You mind if I get back to fucking now?"

"Of course, sir," Thenoch said. "Please enjoy."

The door slammed behind him, and he hurried back to us. "Goddamn," Mistral murmured as he returned. "You're a hell of an actress."

Storm snorted a laugh. "I hate to break it to you, but he's not that good in bed."

I glanced at Mistral. He was already putting his shirt back on, but the view of his muscular chest was enough to fill my head with beautiful streaks of gray. The thought of that big, powerful body looming over me was a delightful fantasy. Whatever Storm said, I was suddenly curious about exactly what Mistral *was* like in bed.

I had officially lost my mind. Space dementia, or something.

"Asshole," Mistral muttered. He settled back on the bed and took the bottle of juice from Storm. He took a drink, and the look on his face said he wished it was stronger. "Arandon had you bugged." He tapped his ears. "Earrings, maybe some of the hardware in your hair, too. Sorry to frighten you, but we didn't want to risk him hearing anything."

"Let me get this straight," I said. "You just paid him a lot of money for me."

"Not *that* much," Storm said. Mistral glared at him. " I mean, he has the money. Not that you were underpriced." He laughed. "Are you insulted?"

"I don't know what I am right now," I said. I took a deep breath. "And you don't expect me to sleep with you?"

"I mean, if you wanted to snuggle up and keep me warm, I wouldn't say no," Storm said. Mistral elbowed him. "But no. Neither of us expect you to fuck us."

"No fucking," Mistral agreed. His eyes shifted away from mine.

Too bad.

Not only was I discovering an unknown appreciation for Zathari men, I definitely had a thing for men who saved me from certain doom and expected nothing in return.

"And what happens if I can't give you the information you want? Are you going to give me back to Arandon?"

"Of course not," Mistral said sharply. "What do you think we are?"

"I think you're a guy who's connected enough that Vehr Arandon wants to play cards with him," I said. "And you're up to something. People don't just drop that kind of money out of the goodness of their hearts."

He chuckled. "You're cynical."

"I got kidnapped off my planet by a man who sells women into slavery," I said drily. "Wouldn't you be?"

Mistral nodded appreciatively. "I would at that. I want information, nothing more. You help me as much as you can, and then you do whatever you want. We'll get you somewhere safe. Back to Earth, if that's what you want." He held out his hand.

Surely it couldn't be that easy. But I'd been praying for someone to come along and save me, hadn't I? At least for now, I was out of Arandon's grasp. "What about Milla? The girl who was with me?"

"You were there. He wouldn't sell her to me," he said. "But if we can get into that auction, we can get her out."

"Can't you go steal her or something?"

"If Arandon knows I'm onto him, I don't get to that auction," Mistral said. He sighed. "I hate the idea of letting him leave with her, but this is one for many. I'll get her out of there." He offered his hand again. "Do we have a deal?"

I held my hand back. "All of them," I said. "There's at least a dozen more on his ship right now. You focus on rescuing everyone, not just killing Arandon. I'll do whatever I can to help you, but that's my deal."

He raised one eyebrow. "To be fair, Helena, I just bought two hundred and fifty thousand credits worth of information. You're not in a position to make more demands."

"To be fair, Mistral, I don't give a damn," I said. "I came in here ready to attack you so that you'd kill me. I don't have much to lose."

His expression melted into one of horror. He glanced at Storm, then back at me. Then he put out his hand again. "Give me your hand," he said. I reluctantly put my hand in his, watching as it disappeared into his grasp. His pale eyes, that icy blue somehow welcoming, met mine. "I will get everyone out of that auction that I can. My goal is to bring this motherfucker down, along with everyone he works with."

"And you can do it?"

His smile was utterly terrifying, and I was very glad to have him on my side. "Oh, I can do it. It's a matter of how big the *boom* is going to be. Is that a problem?"

I shook my head. "Get the others safe. I don't care what happens to Arandon afterward."

"Deal," he said. He shook my hand, then leaned in. "Let's figure out what you know."

CHAPTER 6

Mistral

After two hours of intense questioning, I could see the fatigue around Helena's brown eyes, though she gamely pressed on. When she stifled a yawn for the third time, it occurred to me that she'd been on a breakneck adrenaline ride for gods knew how long. I cleared my throat. "We've got enough for now," I lied. "You should get some sleep."

Her warm eyes widened a little. "I can stay up. Maybe some coffee?"

"When was the last time you slept in a real bed?" I asked.

Her eyes drifted to the luxurious pile of pillows. Hope flickered across her expression. "When I was home. I don't even know what day it is back on Earth. It's been a while."

My chest tightened. "Then you sleep in here," I said. "Storm and I have some calls to make."

"Are you sure?" Her brow furrowed. "I don't want to inconvenience you."

Sweet, gentle creature. I didn't know who this soft thing wearing my skin was, but I was struck with affection for her. It had to be some sort of peculiarity of human evolution, triggering an instinct for a more powerful animal to take care of her. Whatever it was, I would have turned myself inside out to make sure she didn't suffer an ounce of discomfort. "It's no problem." Then I gently touched her shoulder. To my unexpected delight, she didn't flinch. "You'll be safe here. We won't let anyone hurt you."

She nodded, then gently put her hand over mine. "I don't know how I can possibly thank you enough."

"Just rest. We'll reconvene in the morning," I said gruffly. I grabbed my coat and headed out of the massive bedroom, back into the sitting room where Storm was working at his portable computer. Silver contacts gleamed on his fingers as he worked on the complex holographic projection. At my approach, Storm looked up and smirked. "Don't say a fucking word," I said as I joined him.

"Did I miss the memo? Are we all picking up human strays now?" he asked. "Should I get my hands on one before I come home for the winter holidays?"

"She's useful," I said. And extraordinarily beautiful. I'd hurried to cover her up for her own sake, but not before I got an eyeful of her body, sculpted to perfection, every inch of her smooth and gleaming. It was all I could do not to touch her, to follow the lovely curve from the nape of her neck down to the soft little dimples just above her ass.

"Sure," Storm said. "Useful."

We'd gotten plenty of information from Helena about Arandon's ship, the Basilisk. She'd also talked us through a surprisingly detailed description of the internal layout. With her information, we'd be able to narrow down the build and hopefully get our hands on manufacturer blueprints if it was a standard model and not a custom build. We had descriptions and names for some of his security crew, including the hulking Il-Teatha male that had come to the door to check on my satisfaction with my purchase. I'd considered putting his head through a wall, but it might have blown my cover too soon. She didn't know the exact date of the auction, but securing my invitation would take care of that.

"Are you coming with me to this auction?" I asked.

Storm shook his head. "I can't leave on such short notice. And if they link me to whatever bullshit you're about to pull, it'll bring me down here. I'll help you however I can from here."

I nodded. His position at Vuola Lire kept us all connected and well informed, and it wasn't worth jeopardizing unless it was a dire situation. "I'll call Viper," I said. My twin would surely help us, especially once he heard that Arandon had a source for Zathari women.

"No go," Storm said. "He's escorting Vinau Vess to Niraj. They passed through the spaceport here a few days ago and launched from Borealis yesterday."

"Shit," I said. My brother had been unusually focused and well-behaved lately, having kept his position as the filthy rich CEO's bodyguard for over six months. "Where's Havoc?"

"Running a couple of traders to Kheralore," Storm said. "Could be a few days before he's back in touch, and then you could miss your window. I can get you a charter to Borealis, but I don't have a civilian ship for you. Any ideas?"

I sighed. "Yeah, I've got one, but we're going to have to get in bed with her and her snakes."

His expression went grim. "Careful of the monsters you play with. Owing her a favor is less than ideal."

I swiped through my encrypted data files, looking for my file for the Diamondbacks' incoming code. It was labeled only *JC*. There was no telling where the mercenary woman was, but she was famously reliable for getting in touch. I composed a vague message, using the code words she'd expect to convey my message.

Ms. Coral-

I'm in need of travel advice. Leaving soon from Borealis. Please give your recommendations.

Mistral

After logging into Arachne, an expensive but secure message transmission system, I confirmed payment to have the message transmitted at the quickest possible speeds. The message was directed to an address based in our current system, the Ormari Cluster. The Diamondbacks would have an agent assigned to collect messages and transmit them to Jalissa immediately.

When I was done, I paced. "What's the play here? Blow the whole station?"

Storm raised an eyebrow. "That's bold, not to mention stupid," he said. "No way you get enough access as a guest. Besides, if there are multiple sellers, that's a lot of collateral damage if you can't clear the victims out. You want that?"

I sighed and shook my head. "I don't want these fucks getting away with it, either," I said. "I've got money, but I still can't buy them all. Even if we could afford it, they'll just steal more. They need to be shut down permanently."

Storm snorted. "I'm sure the Dominion would be pleased to deal with a bunch of slavers. Especially when the slaves are pretty little things like your new pet, and not Zathari savages like us."

I scowled. "How are you more concerned about getting in bed with Jalissa than snitching to the Dominion?"

It was the Dominion that had come to our home planet decades before we were born, driving our proud people to war. It was the Dominion that had tightened their greedy hold on what remained, squeezing it dry. And it was the Dominion that had condemned my brother and me to a life sentence on Kilaak. They had given me plenty.

"Well, you've got a week to figure out how to shut down an indeterminate number of slave runners, free all of their captives, return them to their home planets, and trace their networks of contacts to eradicate the bigger problem," Storm said drily. "Unless your little pet in there is an expert hacker, I doubt that's going to happen. So if you can find it in your heart to remove your horns from your ass, I'd say that dropping a tip to the Dominion is your best option for putting an end to this ugly business. And if you call Jalissa, you owe her a favor, not me."

"I'll take it under advisement," I said. I scowled. "And she's not my pet."

"Right," Storm said. "That's the important part, Mistral." Despite his words, there was a faint smile on his face. He yawned. "I've booked a charter to Borealis for the day after tomorrow. Two silver class tickets for Mr. Delthe and his companion. I've already got Perri whipping up some papers for Helena just in case. After that, you're on your own."

"Thanks," I said. I sighed. "Really, thanks."

"If you find the guy taking our women, I'll back you up however I can," he said, wincing at his watch. "You want me to keep making calls?"

"I'll take over," I said. "I'm waiting up to see if I hear back from Jalissa. Get some sleep."

With that, Storm left me in the big sitting room alone. When he was gone, I crept to the door of the bedroom, which was still slightly cracked. I pressed it open silently, then lingered at the doorway to watch Helena sleep. Still wrapped in the bathrobe, she was nestled deep under the covers, nearly disappearing into the mountain of pillows. Her breathing was soft and even, and there was a faint smile on her face.

I had done a great many terrible things in my life, fighting for my survival and to protect my brothers. I'd done a few more because I wanted to, not for any noble reason. And arguably, I had done a few things that one might consider good, if not entirely unselfish. But I had never felt the way I did right now, staring at this lovely little woman sleeping in safety, knowing I had saved her from a far worse fate.

The satisfaction of a job well done soured quickly, when I remembered her matter-of-fact tone as she told me her original plan to attack Storm and me, hoping to provoke us into killing her. Death was preferable over us touching her. Perhaps she'd heard rumors of what men like us would do, and given what Arandon's other customers probably did, it wasn't unreasonable. But it still stung, and I vowed that I wouldn't give her any reason to fear.

Even if the sight of her, the feel of her skin, was almost irresistible. When she'd been moaning and squealing for our little charade, I'd almost gotten hard for real. It was hard to focus on Arandon's toady when I was thinking about Helena, wide-eyed and breathless while I fucked her silly.

No. I couldn't.

Instead, I spoke quietly in Zathari. "I will protect you," I vowed. "You will be safe with me."

CHAPTER 7

Helena

When I woke, I was curled up in a pile of clean-smelling pillows and silky sheets, like some sort of laundry-loving dragon. I sat bolt upright and looked around the gilded and marbled room.

No tiny cabin packed with three other women. No Arna yelling at us to get up and make ourselves useful. It had been a long time since I'd woken up without a backache and anxiety twisting in my gut.

I was free.

Well, technically, I was now the property of one big, strangely beautiful Zathari man with motivations I couldn't begin to understand. But it was a marked improvement. I rolled out of bed and listened at the door, where I heard Mistral talking quietly. After checking that my bathrobe covered me, I slid the door open.

Mistral paced in the sitting room, arguing with a holographic image. I was stunned at the sight of him. Instead of his tailored black dress shirt, he wore a snug gray sleeveless shirt that clung to every muscle of his chest and made me wish I could be reincarnated as a piece of clothing. One hand rested at the back of his right horn, twisting idly at the point like a worry stone.

"Last offer, Mistral," a woman's voice said. From my angle, I couldn't make out her distorted features on the projection. "She goes, or no ship."

"Fine," he growled. "If she gets in my way—"

"You'll what?" the woman teased. "Please, continue. If you don't need my ship, I'd love to hear you finish that sentence."

"Nothing," he bit out. "Thank you, Jalissa."

"You're very welcome, Mistral," she said. "I look forward to you owing me a favor."

The projected display went dark. My translator chip couldn't keep up with his furious diatribe, but I laughed when a helpful voice said *three-legged donkey fucker*. His head snapped around. "Did I wake you?"

"No," I said, padding toward him. "Is it late?"

His pale blue eyes were bloodshot. "It's...fuck me, it's nearly noon."

"I'm so sorry," I said. "I didn't mean—"

His brow furrowed. "Why are you sorry? You can go back to sleep if you want. You probably need it."

I smiled at him. "I think I'm good for now," I said. "Can I help you with something?"

"Not unless you've got access to a jump-capable ship that can meet us at Borealis Station in thirty-six hours," he said.

I shook my head sadly. "Sorry."

He yawned and pointed to a big, black suitcase next to the rounded couch. "Arandon's man brought that for you. He said I might find something I like inside." His nostrils flared, but he gave me a smirk. "I told him I was very pleased with the goods."

My cheeks flushed. "Thanks, I think," I said. He spared a smile as I approached the bag warily and opened it. Inside was a stack of lace and leather. Even if he'd adamantly declared there would be no fucking, I didn't entirely mind the idea of him seeing me in one of these ridiculous outfits. I held up one of the webbed garments. "What do you like?"

His jaw dropped. "You—I don't—you can wear real clothes," he stammered. Then his lips pursed into a sly little smirk. "Is that a standard accessory?"

Underneath the folded garment was a neat little tray with an arrangement of silver phalluses and butt plugs with gems, including one with a pink feathered tail that brought back flashbacks of the flamingo party. His wicked expression emboldened me. "I think they're for you."

He laughed, a genuine, rich sound that filled the room. "Pink's not my color. Do you have any real clothes?"

"I don't," I said grimly.

He spared a smile, which was all the more appealing for how rare it was. "You want some?"

Fifteen minutes later, I was dressed in a skimpy nightgown and an oversized bathrobe. I knew I looked ridiculous shuffling around the luxury hotel in a bathrobe, but the fact that there was fabric hanging to my knees made up for it. I hadn't been this covered in months.

The casino had no windows, instead featuring high-definition vidscreens that displayed a twinkling twilight sky. People were drinking expensive liquor for breakfast amid a constant jangling noise of machines, raucous laughter, and conversation. Now that I wasn't on Arandon's arm, I enjoyed the atmosphere, even if it was a bit overwhelming.

We stopped by a bistro, where Mistral loaded a bag with fruit and pastries. I picked at a flaky knot of bread as we descended a long escalator to the ground floor. There, past a restaurant and a crowded bar, was a promenade of boutiques selling jewelry, shoes, and outlandish fashion like I'd never seen. He gently touched my shoulder and murmured, "Pick out whatever you like."

I veered into the first boutique, where a tall, thin person with mottled gray skin intercepted me. Their elongated head and wide, expressive eyes were strangely welcoming. When they spoke, the voice was soft and gentle, with a lovely vibration almost like a cat's purr. "Would Miss care for personal tailoring?"

"Oh, I'm not sure," I said.

Mistral gave me a little push on the back. "Miss would care for personal tailoring. Anything she wants."

I froze, staring up at those big blue eyes. "You don't have to do this," I said quietly. "Just something simple would do."

He ducked his head, then glanced over my shoulder at the salesperson. "A moment, please." The salesperson nodded and stepped back. My stomach knotted around my spine. "I have the money."

"But it feels weird to let you spend it on me," I said.

"Who said you let me do anything?" he replied. His mouth

curved up slightly. "There's no strings here, if that's what you're worried about. You don't owe me anything."

I started to speak, then closed my mouth as butterflies swirled in my gut. It was so tempting to accept this kindness, but no one made this much effort for no reward. "You're sure?"

"I'm sure," he said. "Put it this way. I won twenty thousand credits off your former captor last night. Every bit of that should go to you, especially since you picked my cards."

He'd noticed. I'd have let him win more if I wasn't worried about Arandon catching on. "He's obvious when he doesn't have a good hand," I said shyly. "But you spent two hundred and fifty, which means you're still way in the red."

"That's not how math works."

I laughed. "That's exactly how math works."

"Not mine," he said sternly. "Go pick out clothes, or I'll pick them for you. And I have terrible taste." He nudged me gently, and I finally turned to join the salesperson, who was lingering at a respectful distance.

They ushered me past mannequins wearing dresses made of metallic cages and feathered capes. Through a heavy red curtain was a small platform surrounded by eight-foot-high screens. "Would Miss mind being measured?"

I laughed lightly. "You don't have to call me Miss. I'm Helena."

"Helena," they said, pressing their long-fingered hands together in a praying gesture. "Lovely. I am Ordohres."

"That's a beautiful name," I said.

Their blue eyes crinkled, and they smiled broadly. "Miss Helena is very kind." They gently tugged at my bathrobe, then gestured to the straps on my nightgown. "If you would not mind. Miss Helena may have her privacy." They took a remote and activated it, bringing up a partition that sealed me inside the screened area. My heart pounded. It was a little too cage-like for me, and I suddenly had a vision of the lovely alien tearing off their face to reveal Thenoch, laughing maniacally at me for thinking I'd escaped so easily.

"It will take only a moment," Ordohres said from outside. "All clothing off, then stand in the footprints."

After I shrugged out of the nightgown, I stepped onto the illuminated footprints. From several angles, pale blue light skimmed over me, and I watched as one of the screens began to display a three-dimensional image of a woman's body, with markings and numbers all over it. Then a flashbulb ignited in my face, and I reeled, squeezing my eyes shut.

The partition rumbled away, and I fumbled to cover myself again. Ordohres brought me a silky purple robe with an embroidered logo and said, "Compliments of the tailor, Miss Helena," they said gently. Then they beckoned to Mistral. "Would Sir care to help choose?"

He raised an eyebrow, then smirked at me as I finished tying the loose robe. "Why not?"

We sat on a big, curved couch, and Mistral put one hand on my thigh. To sell the act, of course. And my warm, fuzzy feeling, like I was full of carbonated joy, was entirely an act, too. I definitely wasn't enjoying having a big bad alien with deep pockets who vowed to avenge injustice on my behalf take me on a shopping spree.

All an act.

Ordohres set out a little half-dome display on a table in front of us, then gave me a tablet with a gallery of clothing designs. I selected an asymmetrical blue dress, which appeared on a model of my body. I gasped. "That's amazing," I said. The long blue gown was similar to the one the golden-skinned woman at the card game was wearing, with a large, jeweled plate over the breast. I had to admit, it looked good on me, or at least on the virtual me.

"Miss Helena may also choose a different color," Ordohres explained. I swiped until I found a rich red. I glanced at Mistral, who nodded his agreement. "If you do not object, we will select a flattering shoe and jewelry collection to match. For an extra fee," they added, glancing up at Mistral. He nodded, and Ordohres tapped a slider on my tablet. A jeweled bracer appeared on one arm, along with a tiara-like headband in the model's hair.

I officially loved alien shopping.

Mistral leaned over me and swiped rapidly through the tablet. An assortment of colorful strips that barely qualified as a pair of underwear, let alone a dress, appeared on the model. "Sir likes this one very much," he said. He pointedly swiped at the tablet to make the model turn around, showing the criss-crossed straps over her ass.

I smirked. "In black?"

"Yes, of course," Ordohres said. "A very alluring choice, Miss Helena. Very good."

Mistral was hard to read, so I couldn't tell if he was having a little fun at my expense, trying to lean into his wealthy playboy act, or some other inscrutable purpose. And worse, I couldn't tell why I felt all warm and bubbly over it, nor why I was picturing the glazed look of lust on that handsome face if he saw me in that skimpy black web. The roller coaster of the last twenty-four hours had clearly turned my brain inside out.

There was absolutely no reason I should trust him. Normal, law-abiding citizens didn't get invited to high-stakes card games with people like Boss Arandon, and they certainly didn't have the money to drop a massive chunk of change to free a hapless human that got sucked into an intergalactic trafficking trade.

But I was millions of miles from home. The only friend I had was Milla, who was still in Arandon's grasp. And that made Mistral the closest thing to an ally that I had. Even so, I would be wise to keep him at a distance. It would be too easy to let all of this sweep me away, to be so dazzled that I never saw the red flags. Once I saw what I wanted, the blinders were on. That was how I'd ended up in this mess to begin with.

As we picked out more clothing, I started to feel overwhelmed and guilty, knowing that it had to be incredibly expensive. But Mistral just nodded his approval. After the first time Ordohres approached the notion of an extra fee, they didn't ask again. Perhaps walking in here was enough to let them know that Mistral had the money.

I ended up with half a dozen outfits that would cover most of me, and another few that weren't much better than Arandon's choices. While I was picking out night clothes and underwear, Mistral glanced at his watch. His pale eyes widened. "I'll be back."

Ordohres helped me finish picking out my things, then

leaned in. "Sir will be very pleased with Miss Helena's new clothes," they said. "Lovely choices. Anything else?"

"I think that will be plenty," I said. I glanced back at him, pacing in the doorway of the boutique. He had one hand to his ear, brow furrowed. Then a look of relief crossed his face, and he smiled faintly. When he returned, he seemed more relaxed.

"If Sir is satisfied, then he may sign," Ordohres said. "Miss Helena's choices will be prepared by the morning."

"I'll give you an extra five percent if you can get it done by tonight," Mistral said. He raised an eyebrow. "Direct to you."

Ordohres smiled faintly. "It will be done. Thank you, sir."

When we left the boutique, I tugged lightly on his hand. "Good news?"

"I'll tell you upstairs," he said.

I wanted to trust him, but I had to listen to the cold, quiet part of my brain that told me to trust no one. After all, Vehr Arandon had bought me plenty of expensive clothes, too. Maybe Mistral would surprise me, but until then, I was going to be cautious.

As we strolled around the full loop of the bustling shopping promenade, I instinctively looked for exits and hiding places, little pockets of safety. With each cozy alcove and narrow hallway, I felt a little safer.

On the way to the elevator, I glanced up at him. "Thank you for buying me clothes."

"You're welcome," he said. He didn't quite smile, but there was a nice warmth to his eyes that made me feel guilty for doubting him. "I imagine it's hard to feel safe when you're that exposed."

"Most men wouldn't insist on covering me up," I teased.

"I don't insist on covering you up," he replied. One brow arched. "You're quite lovely uncovered, but you should have the choice of what you show and who sees it."

No, sir. I was absolutely not going to let that convince me that he was trustworthy. *Down, girl*, I told myself, even as my cheeks heated with the compliment. The bar was at his knees, at best. Best not to give him too much credit yet.

We hurried back to the room, where I watched his big hand sweep over the security lock. I mentally reversed it, thinking about the path I could take out of here if I had to.

Down the hall, fire stairs, onto the third floor of card tables where I'd disappear into the massive crowd. I could see it now.

Mistral tapped his watch. "We've got backup meeting us at Borealis. One of my brothers." He glanced at his watch. "I need to run a few errands and visit with Storm. He's getting a set of papers made for you."

"Do you need my help?" I asked.

He shook his head. "Why don't you use that gigantic bathtub?" he said. "And order something expensive to eat. Have you had a decent meal since leaving Earth?"

My stomach rumbled. "Not really."

He crooked a finger at me and gestured to the massive wall screen. "Artemis, display restaurant menus." A full-color display of a dozen delicious-looking dishes appeared. "Order whatever you want, but have them leave it at the door. Don't let anyone in here." He rooted in his bag and took out a gun. My heart thumped at the sight of the sleek weapon. "You know how to use one of these?"

"Not exactly," I said.

He pressed it into my hand, his bigger hands nearly engulfing mine. The dark gray metal was nearly the same color as his tough, warm skin. With one finger, he flicked a switch on the side. A tiny pinpoint of blue light illuminated beneath the switch. "Right now, it'll stun," he said. "Nice jolt to the nervous system, and your target will be immobilized for a few minutes." He flicked the switch, and the light turned red. "Now it's lethal. One hit will incapacitate. For most species, it'll be enough to cause cardiac arrest."

"Most?"

"Not me, or something big and nasty like a Proxilar," he said. "But the second shot will finish just about anything off."

I swallowed. "It wouldn't kill you?"

"You'd need sniper aim," he said calmly. "But after three shots on red, I'm not getting up without help." His even stare made my mouth go dry. "Does it help to know that?"

My hand trembled. "Why do you ask?"

"I know you're afraid, Helena," he said. "You can trust me, but you have every reason not to."

"I just…" I sighed. "I'm sorry. This is a lot."

His head tilted, and his gaze took on a sharp, incisive gleam. "You're not my prisoner, Helena. If you would rather go home to Earth right now, I'll get you a ticket and have you on a shuttle by tonight."

"Really?"

"Yes," he said. "Is that what you want?"

I stared at the gun, then set it down on the table between us. Was that what I wanted? For months, all I could think about was going home. But it wasn't quite *home* that I wanted, so much as *away*. I needed an escape, not a return. And I couldn't cower again, not like I did when Sarah needed me. "I want to help you get Milla and stop Arandon. I can go back after that," I said.

"I can arrange that." With that, he nodded to me and said, "Lock up behind me. Enjoy your bath."

CHAPTER 8

Mistral

As promised, Vehr Arandon delivered an invitation that night. It was printed on heavy paper, an unusual extravagance, and it featured a date in Ilmarinen Universal Time, along with a jump gate designation and a hailing code. After making the jump, we would hail the code for coordinates. The process was standard for people who wanted to keep their illicit activities quiet. It was hard to rat out a moving target.

And while I'd have preferred my twin brother for backup, I'd heard back from another of the Hellspawn, the men who had escaped Kilaak with me. Ember had just arrived on Phade for an unplanned vacation, with nothing on his schedule but soaking himself in expensive booze and frisky women. Faced with the prospect of some sanctioned violence that would soothe his conscience, he'd agreed to meet us at Borealis. He was easy to please; as long as I bought his ticket and kept him fed, he would be happy.

The plan was underway, and we were launching for Borealis in just a few hours. "Helena!" I called. "Let's go!"

There was a noisy clicking of heels as Helena scurried across the suite and burst out of the bedroom with a suitcase rolling behind her. My jaw nearly hit the floor. The first time I'd seen her, she'd been barely covered, and I'd thought she was one of the most beautiful things I'd ever seen. Now she was covered in a long, flowing dress, with her hair braided in an ornate style down her back. Somehow, she was even more alluring than before.

I was dumbstruck. I had been with plenty of beautiful women, but none had ever inspired such a fiery, possessive hunger like the sensation gnawing at my belly. She was a creature out of a myth, an ethereal being descending to the mortal realm.

And she was not for me. She was my responsibility for the moment, but she wasn't mine. What she needed was for someone to treat her like a person and care for her safety. I didn't take her away from Arandon just so she could be at the mercy of my raging lust.

Get it together, I scolded myself.

"Is this all right?" she asked, making a sweeping gesture over her body.

Is this all right?

Wrapped in gauzy pink and lavender, she looked like a blooming flower from the jungles of Irasyne. *All right* was an offensive understatement.

"It'll do," I said, hoping she hadn't noticed me gaping like an idiot. I handed her a small silver wallet.

She opened it and frowned. "Zaera Lavin. Personal assistant to Mr. Adalon Delthe. Assistant?"

"Fairly accurate. We couldn't exactly put property on it," I said. Her lips curved into a smile. I tucked that soft smile away like a precious jewel. "Regardless, you stay close to me. Understand?"

She nodded and tucked the folio into the small shoulder bag I'd bought her yesterday. I held up a slender silver bangle and beckoned to her. Her clean floral scent washed over me, prickling into my nose. I was desperate to touch her. "This has your ID chip in it."

"And it's legitimate?"

"Someone will have to look very closely to discover that it's not," I said. I took my time fastening the bauble, letting my fingers trace the underside of her wrist.

When I was done, she examined it and gave me another of those sweet smiles. "Thank you, Mr. Delthe."

"You're welcome, Ms. Lavin," I said, prompting a little laugh. "Shall we?"

✦

Three hours later, we were boarding a charter cruise from the massive Aliaros spaceport. The charter was luxurious compared to my usual accommodations. Far fewer rough-looking males, and much more genteel language. No one was bellowing *oi, the fuck are you looking at?* and there was a notable lack of firearms, which made for a generally more pleasant environment.

In the entryway of the Starcruiser Aedelia, a slender Vaera male in a tailored blue uniform welcomed us with a shallow bow. "Mr. Delthe, Miss Lavin," he said smoothly. "Allow me to show you to your cabin."

Storm had his fingers in an impossible number of pies, one of which was ticketing with Nafh Zaridi Transit. His connections had gotten us a private cabin, complete with a bed, a little sitting area with an external-facing window, and jump seats. The porter took our bags and secured them in a concealed compartment, then demonstrated how to unfold the jump seats so we could stay in the cabin for launch. "Of course, your silver status provides for complimentary drinks and meals. You may also visit the dining room if you prefer."

"Thank you," Helena said brightly. "This is very nice." He bowed slightly to her, then left us alone. Her eyes swept around the room, then landed on the bed. "Only one bed?"

"I don't need to sleep," I said, even as the blood rushed right out of my head and into the dumbest part of my body. There was no way in hell I would be able to sleep if we both laid there.

Her lips pursed, and I caught that wicked little smirk that said she was trying not to laugh. "All of this must be so expensive."

"We have plenty of money," I said. My tongue felt thick and clumsy. "Go ahead and pick a seat for launch." I had barely finished speaking when she obediently sat in one of the jump seats, graceful hands folded neatly in her lap. I didn't like the quick way she obeyed. I wasn't sure if it was fear of me, or that Arandon had terrified her into compliance, and she hadn't yet broken the habit. I did not, however, mind that she let me lean in to buckle her into her seat for launch. She smelled clean and floral, like sunlight and fresh flowers.

Her eyes followed the flurry of movement outside as the land crew prepared the ship for launch. After a series of recorded announcements, the ship rumbled to life, setting our entire cabin vibrating. I expected her to be more fearful, but she was calm and serene even as we surged upward to break through the atmosphere.

Beyond the window, the bright blue of Firyanin's sky turned to a hazy blue-gray, then darkened to the lovely midnight blue of the upper atmosphere, and finally into the endless black of the void. The shift between Firyanin's gravitational pull and the artificial gravity generator was nearly seamless.

After a few minutes of acceleration through the black and diamond sea, a computerized female voice spoke over the speakers. "The Starcruiser Aedelia has reached traveling velocity. At this time, it is safe for passengers to move about the vessel. Estimated arrival at Borealis Station is in twelve hours. Thank you for choosing Nafh Zaridi Transit for your luxury travel needs."

"What are we going to do for twelve hours?" she asked, carefully unbuckling her harness.

My head swam. What in the hell was I going to do for twelve hours in cramped quarters with her? If we stayed here, I was going to make a serious mistake. For someone so petite, she somehow filled the entire room with her presence. There was nowhere for me to look where she wasn't glittering like a sunbeam on the sea. "A drink?" I finally managed.

Good job, idiot.

"It's a date," she said, rising on shaky legs.

The Aedelia was relatively small, carrying no more than three hundred passengers. Judging by their dress, I guessed that a good number of them were destined for the luxury spas and high-end restaurants on Borealis, while another significant portion were using it as a waypoint to carry out business.

The ship was sleek and more ornamented than I was used to. Despite the tailored fashion I'd brought to sell my image as Mr. Delthe, wealthy fuel baron, I was out of place. No matter how much I groomed and polished, a Zathari male with a scarred face was going to attract attention. Nothing I could do about that. Hopefully having Helena's elegance on my arm softened the edges and made me look a bit more respectable.

I paused at a spiraling staircase and gestured to a scrolling holographic sign. "Cocktail bar?" I asked. She nodded eagerly, and I led her up the stairs to a cozy bar furnished in white leather and silver chrome. We claimed a corner booth, where a convex window at the front of the ship gave us an impressive view of the Ormari cluster. Firyanin was already far behind us, but the green gas giant of Torsyne was visible in the distance.

Helena was enrapt, and I dared to lean in a little closer. "Have you been to the Ormari cluster?" I asked.

She turned rapidly, and I found myself inches from her face. She blinked rapidly. "I'm not sure," she said. Her brow furrowed. "Boss Arandon moved around a lot, but the help doesn't always know where it is. All the stars look the same after a while." There was a bitter twist to her smile.

I nudged her shoulder and pointed. "That's Torsyne," I said.

"The pretty green one?" she asked.

"Is it pretty?"

"I think so," she said, holding her fingers as if there was a bauble between them. "It looks like a bead made from polished jade."

"It's a ball of gas."

"Use your imagination," she teased. "And where do you live, Mr. Delthe?"

I shrugged. "I move around a lot."

Her brow furrowed, but a petite Sahemnar waiter arrived to take our order. After I requested a Phade-specialty whiskey, Helena ordered a fresh-squeezed fruit juice, and I glanced at her. "No alcohol?"

"Not on a ship going a zillion miles an hour," she said with a laugh. She leaned in. "Can I ask something potentially offensive?"

"I'm intrigued," I said. "Go on."

The waiter returned with our drinks, and Helena sealed her lips. She smiled sweetly as they placed the deep purple juice in front of her. When they left again, she leaned in. "One, what are they? And two, is that a man or a woman?"

It was oddly charming that she was worried about offending with such a question. "They're Sahemnar. They're native to Firyanin," I said. "And they're neither man nor woman. They can all reproduce."

"Wow," she murmured. "That must be handy." Her cheeks colored. "I've met a lot of different people through Boss Arandon, but none of them before Ordohres in the boutique."

I chuckled. "I'm sure there's a few bad eggs, but I can't see many of the Sahemnar dealing with the likes of him. Their religion is very peaceful and altruistic, and they mostly stay on Firyanin." They were a little zealous for my tastes, but I'd choose aggressive politeness and slightly sanctimonious pacifism over the bloodthirst of some of our neighbors any day.

"It's a beautiful planet. I'd stay there too if I could," she mused. She plucked the sugared berry garnish from the edge of her glass and nibbled at it. Then her gentle expression sharpened as she stared at me. "Spill it, Mistral. I want to know who you are and why you just happened to be in a room with Vehr Arandon."

"Maybe I want to know the same about you," I teased. Her eyes widened, but she smiled. What the fuck was I doing?

I definitely should have gotten laid before leaving Phade. This was going to be a problem. I felt like I had when we first escaped Kilaak, when I was a wide-eyed virgin who'd been surrounded by filthy, sweaty criminals for nearly fifteen years.

"You first," she said.

"I'm a bad man, but not as bad as Arandon," I said.

"That is not an answer, and it's also a lie," she said irritably. "Bad men don't do what you did for me."

I leaned in and gave her a sly smile. "There are different kinds of bad, Helena."

She didn't recoil. If I wasn't mistaken, she looked even more interested. "And what kind of bad are you?"

"The kind that will pay good money to get you out of a situation like that," I said. "And not lose a bit of sleep over killing the people who put you in it. Does that bother you?"

"No," she said. "A few more people like you might be what the universe needs."

"My turn. How did you end up with Arandon?"

She sighed. "You still didn't answer me. You're good at evasion but I'm not stupid."

"Yes, I am, and you certainly aren't," I replied. "It's still my turn. How did he get you?"

"He had a really good carrot," she mused, stirring her drink idly. I frowned, unsure what Terran root vegetables had to do with the matter. "I lived my whole life on Earth. But I always wanted to leave." Her brow creased. "I guess I should have been specific. The Dominion still takes applications to resettle on New Terra, but it's expensive, and there's a long waiting list. A friend of mine told me about this humanitarian group that was taking applications for settlers to New Terra, so I went to a meeting and filled out some paperwork. They said they wanted the most promising candidates who could contribute to the betterment of the colony. They called me back for an interview. God, I was thrilled. I dressed in my best clothes, practiced a whole spiel about how I could contribute with medical experience. The last thing I remember is walking back into the lobby and seeing one of Arandon's guys. Then I woke up on the Basilisk and realized something was very wrong." She laughed bitterly. "For a split second, I thought maybe I'd passed the interview. Then I realized that being stripped down and having every bit of hair lasered off my body probably wasn't standard procedure for resettling colonists."

I shook my head. "I'm sorry that they lied to you." It was a particularly cruel trick, somehow worse than just snatching her off the street.

"I probably should have been more suspicious, but I wanted it so badly. Still, it could have been much worse." She chuckled. "I've been plucked like a chicken and had strangers touch me everywhere. And I mean everywhere," she said with a little shudder. "But Arandon was adamant about not sampling the merchandise. Short of a few foreign objects being inserted into places I don't care to mention in public, they left us alone."

"And do you really want to go back to Earth?" I asked. "After we shut down the auction, I mean."

Her brown eyes lifted to mine. Instead of answering, she was quiet for a while. "I don't know what I want anymore. Is that ridiculous?"

I shrugged. "It is what it is. Do you have any family there?"

"My last living family left for New Terra a few months before I was taken," she said. Her fingers drummed on the glass. "I had a job, but I imagine there's medical work everywhere. A few friends, but no one close. Like I said, I was ready to leave it behind when this happened."

"Medical work? What did you do before?"

She smiled. "I was a nurse. It's amazing that as shitty as life on Earth is, people still find a way to make it worse for each other."

A healer. Maybe that explained her calm. She reminded me of Evie with her even temper, even in the face of something frightening. I could easily picture her up to her elbows in blood with that same, even demeanor. "After we leave Erebus, you could go somewhere new."

She glanced at me. "I don't have anything. How would I even begin?"

"If I have money to get you out of a slaver's hands, I certainly have the money to get you started on a decent planet where no one is going to bother you," I said. Hell, I knew three humans who had just left Terra and probably wouldn't complain about another roommate, and they didn't really have an option, considering who was paying their rent.

And then she'd be close. Right at my fingertips, so I could see her again whenever I liked. Not that I was letting that influence my offer.

Her eyes shone. "You don't have to do that."

"I know I don't have to," I said. I nudged her foot under the table. "Look at me, little human. You think you could make me do anything I didn't want to do?"

When Helena looked, she *looked*. Her warm eyes raked over me, almost to the point of making me uncomfortable. Finally, she spared a little smile. "I think there are ways to convince bad men to do good things."

"Oh, really?" I said.

All the tactical experience and hard lessons of my life did not prepare me for Helena to rise from her seat and kiss me. It was light and soft, barely brushing the corner of my mouth. I nearly groaned at the touch of her fingers, grazing my chin. I turned ever so slightly, giving her permission. She kissed me again, and I could taste the sweet, fresh berry on her lips.

I wanted to tell her *no, I'm not good for you. You don't know what you're doing.*

I should keep it professional. I should have kept her at arm's length.

I didn't.

I didn't give a flying fuck what I should have done. Once her lips found mine, I was done for. The heat of her mouth was intoxicating. I drew her lower lip into my mouth, nipping slightly at her and basking in the soft gasp.

As she sank back into her seat, her cheeks were flushed. "I don't know what came over me."

It was sheer animal lust that came over me. Fuck my resolve. I was going to drag her out of here and peel that dress off. Just as I started to rise, the waiter returned. "May I interest you in an evening meal?"

CHAPTER 9

Helena

My heart raced as I pondered the menu. I didn't know what had come over me. There wasn't a person on Earth who would have described me as bold, but here I was, kissing Mistral in front of the whole damned bar.

Why? Because I wanted to. Because there was something burning in my core so intensely that I could barely sit still, and the only solution seemed to be on those soft, full lips that had been demanding to be kissed for the last hour. Every word out of his mouth drew my attention, until I realized I had to kiss him or I was going to scream. I had to know what they felt like, and now that I knew, I just needed to do it again and again until he peeled me off.

Though the menu was printed in Modern Aengran, kissing Mistral had rendered me temporarily illiterate. I finally glanced up at Mistral. "You order, please," I whispered.

His pale eyes skimmed over me. Then he shoved the menu back at the waiter, who looked terribly confused. "We'll order directly to our cabin. Thank you." He glanced at me and raised his eyebrows. I nodded.

My heart thumped as I followed him. I was already ahead of myself, imagining the delight of sliding that jacket off of him and exploring those big muscles and warm gray skin. And those horns. God, I wanted to touch them so badly it was going to drive me wild. An insistent pulse throbbed between my legs as we returned to our cabin.

I didn't do this kind of thing, but I was so far from who I was at this point, it didn't matter. I wasn't sure Helena Cage existed anymore. She left Earth on Vehr Arandon's ship, but I wasn't sure she ever made it off.

And whoever I was in this moment did things like this. She demanded what she wanted. As soon as the door slid shut, I reached for him, but he grabbed my wrists and held me away. "Helena, you are very lovely, but I can't," he said.

My cheeks flushed as the sting of rejection sunk deep. "God, I'm sorry. This is business. I shouldn't—"

"It's not you," he said sharply. "You're not here because you wanted to be. If not for Arandon, you would be millions of miles from here. I will not be like the man who stole you."

I laughed, and he gave me a stern look. "I'm not laughing at you." His head tilted. "Okay, yeah, I am. You couldn't be like Arandon if you tried."

"No?"

"You may have done bad things, but you aren't a piece of shit," I said.

"You don't know me," he said. "I could be worse than he is."

"I know what you did for me," I said. Despite his protests, he was inching closer. I hesitated, then gently gripped his shoulders. "You're probably right, though. That we shouldn't."

"Right," he murmured. "We shouldn't. I should go somewhere else and let you rest." His gaze never broke from mine. "That would be the wise thing."

"Yeah," I whispered. "Wise."

It was unclear who broke the standoff. All I knew was that I had a handful of his shirt while his fingers tangled into my braid, and then his lips were blazing against mine. His tongue met mine, teasing at first, then claiming. One arm wrapped around me, then the other, and I was pressed tight to him as he took over my senses. He had his own gravity, and I was helpless. Somehow, I ended up in his lap on the bed, and my hands found their way under his jacket.

Not sure how that happened. Really.

With a chuckle, he tossed his jacket aside and let me that much closer to that beautiful body. Then, much to my dismay, he lightly held my hands together in front of me, depriving me of the decadent warmth of his dark gray skin. "Helena, you don't have to do this to thank me."

I was breathless as I stared at him. "Is that what you think this is?"

"You told me you'd planned to provoke me into killing you so you wouldn't have to fuck me," he said. "This is a bit of a shift."

My stomach plunged through the floor. "It wasn't about you. I thought Mr. Delthe would hurt me. And it wasn't only you." I averted my gaze. "I can't tell you how many times I thought about how I would do it. But it wasn't about *you*. Whether you think you're good or bad or somewhere in between, I'm not afraid of you."

His pale eyes lifted to mine.

I risked a little smile. "And I seem to recall you and Storm promising there would be no fucking."

"That was to keep you from having a heart attack in front of us," he said. "Certainly not because I don't want to." There was a curious vulnerability in his eyes that made him even more magnetic. "Do you really want this?"

"If by *this*, you mean to touch you and get that shirt off of you, then yes," I said. I went for his waist band, but he caught my wrists again.

"You first," he said, kissing my lips before he let me go. His big hands deftly unzipped the long, flowing pink dress, letting it slide away from my skin. I rose and danced my way out of it, prompting a delightful smile. He reached for me, then stopped just short. "Are you sure?"

I laughed, grabbed his hands, and placed them firmly on my hips. "I'm sure. Your touch is the nicest thing I've felt in a long time. Even when I was on Earth."

His smile was incandescent. "Your ass is the nicest thing I've felt in a long time."

"You're so poetic," I teased. Then I kissed the tip of his nose. "I want you."

He growled and flipped me onto my back. That casual display of strength sent an instinctive twist of fear rippling through me, but I held it back. His gaze lingered on me as he slowly unbuttoned his tailored shirt, then peeled off the snug underlayer to reveal his broad, muscular chest. The scar on his face matched a longer patch of lighter scar tissue over the left side of his chest, trickling to a point at his bottom ribs. I wondered how he'd gotten such an oddly precise burn.

I was still staring and wondering when he lowered himself to me, sliding that wonderfully warm body against mine as he kissed my chest, then my throat, then returned to my lips. The sweetest friction ignited me like a match.

It was easy to lose myself in that warm, sweet touch. Something fiery was awakening in me, and I wanted to demand more, closer, higher, faster. I wanted everything all at once. But I was content. For the first time in a long time, I was safe.

Or was I?

A cynical part of me was still hesitant. I really didn't know this man. Maybe this was some twisted, long game. Maybe I was so dazzled by the pretty eyes and those irresistible horns that I was ignoring the massive red flag flapping in the breeze behind him.

And maybe, just this once, I didn't care. After all I'd been through, I decided that I had earned a chance at feeling something good. No one could judge me for making a little mistake. Just this once, I'd do what I wanted without a care for the consequences.

I lifted my hips and smiled when the steel warmth of his cock pressed to my cleft. "I wouldn't normally do this, two days after meeting someone," I said.

He chuckled. "I certainly would. Especially with someone like you." I went to unzip him, but he gripped my wrist lightly. "Not yet."

"I told you, I want you," I said.

His lips curled into a delightful smile as he dragged his cock against me, sending a shiver rippling through me. "I know you do, but I'll hurt you if we rush. We have time. At least ten hours, by my estimation." Then he lifted me easily, sliding his hands under the delicate lace of my panties. "Yes?"

I nodded eagerly. "Most definitely, yes."

He laughed and left a fiery trail of kisses down my chest, detouring to my hip before taking a meandering path down my inner thigh, to my calf, and finally to a curiously sensitive spot on my ankle. In a blur of pink, my panties went flying over his shoulder and landed on the door handle like a little flag. Then he sank to his knees in front of me.

Was this really happening?

Hell yeah, it is.

He lowered his head, kissing the soft skin of my mound, then licked me right up the center, parting my lips with that blazing hot tongue.

I gasped, then let out a giggle. "Oh, maybe you are a bad man after all."

"Very bad," he said.

"You should—"

He lifted his head. "Helena?"

"Yes?"

"You can keep talking but I'm about to have my mouth full," he said. One big hand splayed over my thigh, squeezing gently. "So it's going to be a one-sided conversation. I'll get back to you when you regain consciousness."

Good God. Somehow I knew he wasn't spewing the same stupid bravado I'd heard from men back on Earth.

Then he sealed his lips to me, lapping hungrily at my pussy. Warmth flooded me. I squirmed beneath him, and he hooked both powerful arms over my thighs to hold me in place. The security of it only made it better as I was locked in place, completely held by this ferocious, devoted creature. His tongue was as powerful as the rest of him, tickling across my lips and plunging into me in a relentless, torturous rhythm.

He paused and examined me closely, sliding one big finger through my lips. "I've only been with a human woman once before," he said. Then his eyes gleamed. "There it is." His tongue circled my clit, and lightning shot through me.

I squeaked, twisting against his firm hold.

He laughed, lightly teasing it with the tip of his tongue. "Love that little magic button." As he continued to work at me, he slid one finger into me, caressing me slowly. With that slow thrust, my body clenched around him, a prelude to what I hoped was coming next.

I was floating and flying under his control as he wound me tighter. A nonsense song of whimpers and giggles flowed from my lips as I rose on that pulsing wave of pleasure. Everything was a blissful haze, and he was gravity, pulling me closer and closer to a place where nothing else mattered.

He paused. "Helena, they're going to hear you if you scream." His tongue flicked across my clit. "Are you going to scream?"

"Probably," I bit out.

He chuckled and set about making sure I did. There was nothing tentative or graceful about it. Mistral was a glorious beast, consuming and devouring me with an intensity that was almost frightening. Two fingers slid into me, spreading me open, and the thought of him fucking me was enough to bring me to the edge.

My hips jerked, and he put one strong hand on my stomach to hold me down.

So close.

I clapped both hands over my mouth and felt my eyes rolling back as the pleasure overwhelmed me and I fell into the sweet darkness of the void.

I lost myself for a few seconds, and when I lay flat again, I opened my eyes to see him licking his lips clean. He slid over me and kissed my cheek. I rose to kiss him, then slumped. "I think you broke me."

"In a good way?"

"Oh yeah," I panted.

He lay flat next to me and grinned. "Was that your first time?"

"No, why do you ask?" Nerves fluttered through me. "Did I do something wrong?" Not that I'd done much at all, besides lie back and enjoy his attention.

"Gods, no," he said. "Arandon said his merchandise was fresh. I just assumed..."

"No, definitely not." I rolled over and traced his chest. "Are we going to have sex?"

"That *was* sex," he said. "Unless I misunderstood what your thighs locked around my neck meant."

"No, I mean are you going to..." I sighed. Considering he'd just been licking me like an ice cream cone, it shouldn't have been so embarrassing, but I couldn't squeeze the words out.

He raised up on his elbow and gently stroked my cheek. "I'm teasing you, Helena. Do you want me to fuck you?"

"I really do," I said. "When my muscles start working again. Right now, it's taking all of my effort to not melt into a puddle of Helena-flavored slime."

He laughed. "I adore your candor," he said. His big hand slid down to cup my breast. "Now, where were we?"

A chime sounded at the door. The mischievous smile evaporated as Mistral shifted into alertness. His eyes narrowed, and he placed one finger on my lips before rising. A voice emerged from the cabin's speaker. "Attention, valued guests. Please open chamber for an identification verification."

With a grim look, he said, "Let me handle this."

CHAPTER 10

Mistral

As much as I hated to see her covered up, I tossed my jacket to Helena, who hastily wrapped it around herself. My mind was spinning as I approached the cabin door. My papers were impeccable. Our forger, Perri, was well-paid to do impenetrable work. But sometimes that didn't matter, particularly when they saw someone who looked like me.

I quickly checked the disc on my watch, then grabbed the small wallet with Mr. Delthe's papers. With a deep breath, I released the smile Helena had left on my face and put on my stony mask. I hit the button to open the door and found a tall woman on the other side, with the golden skin and bright eyes of the Raephon. A headband with a blue-tinted lens covered one eye.

At the sight of me, her vivid golden eyes narrowed slightly. But she smiled evenly and greeted, "Good evening, Mr. Delthe.

I am conducting a routine identification check to ensure that all passengers are prepared to disembark at Borealis."

Sure you are.

I'd bet my horns that she clocked me the instant I boarded and had just been waiting for an opportunity to ruin my day. The destruction of Sonides, over a century ago, was at the hands of the Dominion, but they only accomplished it because our once-close allies, the Raephon, backstabbed my ancestors. Janderon, their lovely jungle planet, was untouched, its ancient cities still intact, while my people were plunged into poverty in the ruins of our ancestral home.

I handed her my documents, hoping that my silent *fuck you* made it to her. Blue light emitted from the lens to scan my papers. Text scattered across the curved lens. My heart pounded. *Come on, Perri.*

Our escape from Kilaak had left my face scarred, thanks to a well-placed acid round shot by a merc who knew exactly how to bring down a Zathari. After years of mercenary work, I had the money to have an expert surgeon repair my face, but my scars gave me an extra layer of protection that not even an expert forger could. The burn had altered several landmarks on my face that made facial recognition difficult. While someone might find me if they looked hard enough, no automated search would match me to the files for Tiro, the idiot teenager who'd gotten thrown into prison with his smooth, unmarked face.

Her eyebrows raised, but she handed back my ID. "And your companion?" she asked mildly. "Miss Lavin?"

"My companion is resting," I said. "I'll get her ID."

Wrapped up in my jacket, Helena was pressed as far against the wall as she could get, but she was calm as she pointed to her small handbag. When I returned, the Raephon woman repeated the process of scanning her ID.

While she was checking, I examined the woman closely. Her gray uniform matched the ones the stewards wore, and as far as I could tell, she was just an employee of the airline. Finally, she nodded and handed the papers back to me. "Mr. Delthe, where are you headed?"

"I'm headed to Borealis," I said. "Like everyone else on this boat."

"And after that?"

"Wherever I feel drawn," I said.

"Do you ever travel to Sonides?"

"Do you?" I asked, fixing a sharp expression on my face.

Her eyes narrowed, but her bland smile never faltered. Finally, she nodded to me. "Thank you for your time. Please enjoy the rest of your flight and your stay at Borealis."

I let out a shaky breath after the door slid shut behind her. Suddenly, I felt caged in, like the walls had ears. It took a considerable effort not to yank the door open and check the hall for incoming soldiers.

"What was that about?" Helena asked.

I shook my head and set her ID aside. "Later."

Her brow furrowed, but she smiled and made a beckoning gesture. I perched at the edge of the bed, but the easy contentment of being in bed with her was gone. Worry and seething anger twisted my mind into barbed knots. Helena kissed my shoulder, but I gently took her hands before she could start something I wasn't ready to finish. "If something happens when we get off this ship, you tell them you don't know anything about me. Then you get someone to call Storm."

"Mistral, I—"

"Helena, listen to me," I said sharply. She recoiled, but this was important. "You can get to him in his office with the universal frequency OC-MXH-8714. Say it back to me."

"OC-MXH..."

"OC-MXH-8714," I repeated.

"8714," she echoed.

"Say it again," I ordered. Frowning through it, she repeated it three more times for me, and I finally nodded. "If they ask, we met on Firyanin, hooked up, and you don't know anything about my business."

"I got it," she said mildly. "What the hell is going on?"

"Nothing, I hope."

"Do you want to be a little more vague?" she said, a note of irritation creeping into her tone.

I gestured to the door. "I don't know who's listening."

Her expression was curious, but she finally nodded. "Okay. Will you tell me later?"

"Maybe."

"Did you do something bad? Or does she just think you did?" There was a flicker of fear in her eyes. "Please tell me."

I wanted to shut down her questions, but I'd pulled her into my world. That made me responsible for making this tiny little sphere safe for her. "I got in some trouble a long time ago." Her eyes widened. "For stealing. Sort of. And because I'm Zathari, they threw the book at me and my brother and sentenced us to prison."

"So you don't hurt people," she said.

"Well...that's not true," I admitted. "I can't say anymore right now, but I'll tell you everything when we're somewhere more secure." I raked my hand through my hair. "I understand if you don't want anything else to do with me."

She grabbed my arm firmly as I started to rise. "Did I say that?" Her brow furrowed, and I could tell she wanted to press the issue. "Look into my eyes and tell me I'm safe with you."

I cupped her face in my hands. There was the tiniest flinch when I did, but she kept her gaze on mine. "I promise that you're safe with me," I said. "If it's up to me, nothing in this universe will ever hurt you again. I would rather throw myself into space than cause you an ounce of pain."

Her lips broadened into a smile. "That's a little much."

"I mean it."

"Please don't throw yourself into space. I would miss you," she said with a faint smile. She rose on her knees, holding her hands awkwardly. "Can I touch you?"

"You don't have to ask. Of course you can," I said.

"I do have to ask," she murmured. "I've had enough people touching me without permission for a lifetime. I know you're upset, and I don't want to make it worse."

My heart ached with the show of concern. "I'm fine now," I said. Her hands kneaded into my shoulders, and I let out a long groan of pleasure. "Now I'm even better."

She chuckled and dug surprisingly strong fingers into my neck, working out the tension and bathing me in hazy pleasure. I couldn't remember the last time someone had taken care of me like this. The realization that I was enjoying her attention instantly made me feel guilty.

I gripped her wrist and said, "You don't have to—"

With a light slap to my hand, she said, "Keep your hands to

yourself, buddy. If you really want me to stop, then say so. But I like touching you. And I really like when you do this."

"Do what?"

Her nails grazed over my scalp, fanning out and sending a ripple of goosebumps from head to toe. I groaned and leaned back into her, soaking up her touch like the sun.

"When you do that," she said, her voice wonderfully smug as she continued to massage my head.

Her hands cast a spell on me, slowly smoothing out the knots of anxiety and fear. Slowly, I became more and more aware of her, of the warmth of her bare chest against my back, the scent of her hair, the brush of her lips against my skin. We were safe here, at least for the time being. And I would be a fool to miss out on an opportunity to be with her.

The rhythmic motion of her hands stopped suddenly. "Is it all right to touch your horns?"

"Please do," I said. There was a dull pressure as she gently touched the bony curves. I gently grasped her wrist and pulled one hand down, placing her fingers on the sensitive skin at the base of my right horn. "Right there."

When she rubbed in a gentle circle, it felt like lightning straight to my groin. "How's that?" Her other hand matched the motion.

"Great," I managed, squirming as the throbbing sensation intensified. "It's very sensitive."

Her hands stopped. "Painful?"

"Pleasurable," I said, leaning my head back into her touch. Reluctantly, I plucked her hands away and kissed her fingertips. "Do you still want to do this?"

"Hell yes," she said with a giggle.

I rose and went for my belt, but she beat me to it. Her eyes were alight with excitement as she unzipped me. Her eyes were wide as she stared down at my cock. "You weren't kidding about taking it slow."

I hesitated. "If you're not ready—"

"Excuse me," she interrupted. She tickled her fingers down my belly before grasping my cock. "I said nothing of the sort." The mere touch of her delicate hand on that sensitive skin ignited a pulsing ache in my groin. Her eyes were full of mischief when she looked up at me. "Are you on protection?"

"Five-year implant," I said. "You want to see my card?"

She smirked. "I'll trust you."

"Are you?"

"On year seven of a ten-year coil," she replied.

"In that case, we're done talking," I growled. I pounced on her, covering the velvet-soft skin of her breasts in kisses. I grabbed one of the pillows and slid it under her hips, then rose to undress. Her eyes were hungry as I dropped my pants and kicked them aside.

"I appreciate you for your integrity and your wits," she said. I cocked my head in confusion. "But you are so damned hot."

A strange warmth washed over me. "Really?"

She made a beckoning gesture with both hands as she said, "Yes. Come over here."

Pressing my body to hers, finding my place between her legs was like finding home after a lifetime away. I rose onto my knees, lightly teasing at the flushed pink of her pussy as I gazed at her. The way those soft pink petals spread around me was intoxicating. "Are you ready?"

She nodded rapidly. "It's been a while since I had sex, so take it slow, please."

I stroked the inside of her knee, savoring the way she shivered. "Of course," I said. If fate was kind, there would be time to fuck fast and hard, time to bring her to desperate hunger and hold her on that edge of ecstasy until she begged. This was something soft and warm and wonderful, and I was going to savor every second.

Taking my time, I eased myself into her. Her body tensed, and I heard the catch in her breath as I stretched her open. "I'm fine," she murmured. One foot curled around me, trying to pull me in, but I could see the strain on her face.

"Helena," I said calmly. "Don't hurry me. I will be much happier if you're honest. We have time."

Her expression was oddly vulnerable. "Thank you," she said, exhaling in a long sigh. I ran my hands over her thighs, relishing that smooth, warm skin. Eventually, she lifted her hips and offered her hands to me. Slowly, I sank deeper into her, fighting the urge to plunge into that sweet, decadent warmth. I could see the flicker of fear on her face when I slid past the ridge on my cock, then a tiny gasp of delight.

Still holding myself back, I brushed soft kisses along her throat, slowly rising to claim her lips. "Are you all right?" I asked. "Tell the truth."

She nodded eagerly. Her pupils were already dilated. "You feel amazing," she breathed, holding my face tightly. I took it slow and gentle, taking my time to enjoy the subtle shift of her expression from trepidation to curiosity to pleasure. Her hands ran all over my body, and I imagined glittering trails marking my skin, like sweet little scars. As I rocked into her, the warm softness of her sex fluttered around me, squeezing me so hard I thought I would come any second. Her eyes drifted down. "You can come in," she said shyly. "All of you."

I raised my eyebrows. "Are you sure?" She nodded, and I lifted her hips, slowly introducing my *dzirian* into her. It was torture to go so slowly, when I could already feel the divine heat of her body kissing the sensitive skin. The round orb of the *dzirian* was pliable, with enough give that we could get inside a partner without causing terrible pain. Her body clenched tight around me, pulling me in, and we both gasped at the same time.

"Oh, my God," she whispered, staring down in wonder. I clenched my fists tight as her body squeezed me. I wasn't going to make it. "I can feel your heartbeat."

"I know." And so could I; each firm pulse pressed against the tightness of her body, producing a rhythmic rush of sensation that washed over me.

I hadn't felt this good in ages. Maybe ever.

I would have been content to lie there with her for days, but the pulse of the *dzirian* was intensifying. I held myself back, pressing one hand between us to bring her along with me. At the first brush of my finger over that perfect little pink bud, her whole body jolted and clenched around me. I groaned, and she let out a delightful squeal and laughed.

"Oh, shit," she giggled. I teased her again, and she drove one foot into the bed, driving her hips up into me. Her sheer delight and simple joy was breathtaking. Her body arched, and I could see the tension rippling through her as she fought it. There was a strange fear of losing control in some women that I'd never understood. There was nothing more beautiful than that moment of utter abandon. "I'm close," she whimpered.

"I know," I said. "I can feel you." Her eyes locked on me, and she suddenly drove her hips up to meet me again. Her breathing quickened, until every exhalation was a little whimper, a tiny affirmation of the way I made her feel. It was fucking intoxicating.

Her body clenched tight around me, and I kept teasing at her clit as I quickened my pace, thrusting in short, hard strokes to chase my own climax. She gasped and babbled sweet nonsense *Mistral there I can't oh yes Mistral Mistral* until it was a song made of nothing but my name, which had never sounded so beautiful. When she shuddered and gasped, I knew she was with me.

White heat rolled through me as I came, losing myself to blind, pure sensation. I was only vaguely aware of her legs wrapped around me. I opened my eyes to see her smiling up at me. Her cheeks were flushed, her lips full and red. With that lush auburn hair streaming around her face like a halo, she looked ethereal, like some mythological siren in the outer reaches of space.

Now I understood.

I understood why Havoc had a standing order with a juice bar on Phade to keep the Nomad stocked with Vani's favorite drink. I understood why he had that stupid look on his face when she walked into the room. Because he would have done anything to feel that glow of her affection. If she looked at him the way Helena was looking at me right now, I understood.

Helena wasn't mine. This was blind, stupid coincidence, not some mystical force of fate that had brought us together. I tried to tell myself that, but it might have been a lesson learned easier prior to fucking her, rather than in the glorious afterglow, when I was still buried to the hilt in that unbelievable heat that felt like the purest, sweetest thing I'd ever experienced. Every pulse of my *dzirian* was met with a lovely little fluttering echo of her body around it.

She lightly cupped my face. "Where are you?" she murmured.

"Inside you," I replied. She laughed, and I lowered my head to kiss her, slow and sweet, until she was breathless. "How do you feel?"

Her eyes gleamed. "I feel like you rebooted my brain. All I can think about right now is how good I feel, how hot you are, and...and how I could go for a snack." She kissed my nose, then smacked my ass lightly. "Want to get us a snack?"

"Is that code for sex?"

"That's code for get me something to eat," she teased. "Then maybe dessert. *That's* code for sex."

I chuckled. "Your wish is my command."

CHAPTER 11

Helena

When Mistral left me alone to find dinner, like a good little hunter providing for his woman, I hastily visited the tiny washroom, cleaned myself up, and put on fresh underwear. I expected to feel a sort of sinking shame as I realized what I'd done in a moment of sheer lust. But as I splashed water on my face, I was pleased with the woman in the mirror.

And I hadn't been kidding when I said he rebooted my brain. It was hard to think about the place I'd been before, every day overshadowed by constant dread. Mistral was like a calming drug that sanded all the edges off my anxiety.

Still, his dramatic reaction to the ID check worried me. Maybe his claims about being a bad man weren't overstated. And maybe I really had changed, because I was starting to care less.

The door slid open, and I startled. Mistral returned with a

heavy-laden tray in one hand and a bottle of fruit juice in the other. I laughed and took the juice from him, setting it on the table as he set the tray on the bed. Then he frowned at me. "You're dressed."

I glanced down. "Barely."

He smirked. "The whole time I was gone, I was looking forward to coming back and seeing you naked."

God, he could make a girl feel gorgeous. "Mr. Delthe, what would you like?"

His pale eyes gleamed. "I'd like you to take everything off so I can appreciate you."

I crossed my arms. "Then I want to see you, too."

"Really?"

"Really," I said, slowly releasing the clasp on my lacy bra. I released it, but kept my arms folded over my chest. "Now, you."

He let out a charming little laugh. "If you're waiting for me to be coy, you're misunderstanding me," he said. He peeled off his shirt in a single movement, then dropped his pants in a pile on the floor. I drank him in, letting my eyes sweep over him from those massive, carved calves up to the rounded curve of his ass, across the glorious topography of those sculpted shoulders. All of it gleamed deep gray like the clouds of a summer storm, so stark and beautiful. And of course, there was no ignoring the thick cock between his legs, which had been all mine only minutes ago.

I sighed. "So hot."

He responded by lunging at me, burying his lips in my neck as he grabbed my panties and pulled them down over my hips. I laughed in his grasp as I kicked my legs to let him pull them off.

"Happy now?" I teased.

"Very," he growled. Then he plopped onto the bed, legs spread, and opened a container to reveal a spread of crackers, meats, cheeses, and fancy little hors d'oeuvres like I'd served on the Basilisk. "You know, I don't know that anyone's ever called me hot before."

"Then people are stupid," I said flatly as I joined him in bed. "Have you seen yourself?"

"My scars don't bother you?"

"Should they?" I asked.

He chuckled. "I guess not." He grabbed a little tart in each hand, handing me one before taking a bite of his own. "Usually, people don't say anything. They just ask for a good hard fuck."

I shivered and tasted the little savory morsel. It was sweet and spicy, and tasted all the better considering this horned hottie had just delivered it right to me. "And would you prefer that?"

"You can tell me I'm hot *and* ask for a good hard fuck," he said, kissing my ear. "Who says you have to choose?"

"I'll keep that in mind." I glanced down, then gave him a mischievous look. Slowly, I teased my fingers over the curved bulge at the base of his cock. It was intimidating, but there was something wonderfully elegant about it, like it had been sculpted. I giggled at the thought of someone lovingly chiseling his cock out of stone.

"What are you laughing at?"

"I'm sorry, I was just thinking about how your cock is weirdly pretty—"

"Helena," he said, jaw dropping. "Don't call it pretty."

"Beautiful?"

He frowned.

"Ferociously handsome and unquestionably manly?"

He flashed a dazzling grin.

"I was thinking about how your cock is ferociously handsome and unquestionably manly. Like an artist carved it," I said, tracing my fingers over that soft curve. Even now, I could feel an insistent pulse beneath that soft, warm skin. "What is this?"

"*Dzirian*," he said, gently plucking my hand away. I frowned at him, but he smirked in response. "And if you keep touching it right now, this entire tray of food is going on the floor and you're still going to be hungry when I'm done with you."

"Oh no," I drawled, though I pulled my hand away and stole another tart with my other hand. "I was just wondering how that feels to you."

"It feels good," he said.

"Good?"

"What? I'm not a poet," he said. I gave him an arch look. He sighed, then popped the rest of the small tart in his mouth. After chewing thoughtfully, he placed one of my hands over his fist, then sandwiched his big hand over it. Then he opened his fist, following it with a squeeze from above. "It feels like that. When we lie together afterward, our heartbeats line up for a while." He did it again, and I was lost in the lovely memory of how it felt to lie there with him buried deep, my body dancing and shivering with each insistent pulse.

"Does it have a purpose?"

He tilted his head. "Makes you want to fuck me again. Pretty good evolutionary development if you ask me."

I laughed, and he just gave me a knowing smile. "I'm not arguing that point."

"When we're fucking, the *dzirian* produces a sort of..." he shrugged. "An oil, maybe? It helps our partners relax and feel more pleasure. I'm no scientist."

"Fascinating," I murmured. It made sense. Half an hour ago I'd have said there was no way that was going inside me, but it hadn't hurt me at all, beyond a bit of pressure. There was still a pleasant, warm tingle radiating from my core, as if I was drunk off of him.

As I was staring, his big hand slipped over my thigh and tickled across my clit. I squirmed away from him with a noisy giggle. "And what's that for?" he said innocently.

"You know damn well what it's for," I said. "That's the magic button that makes me scream."

He laughed and pulled me back against his chest, big legs surrounding me. One leg was casually splayed out, and I caught a glimpse of a dark seam, a fresh wound on his calf. I leaned forward and tapped it lightly. "What happened to your leg?"

"Shrapnel," he said calmly.

"As in an explosion?"

"Yes," he said, flexing his toes. "It's almost healed."

"How exactly did you end up with shrapnel in your leg?" I asked in wonder, turning to face him.

His icy blue eyes raked over me. "Things explode. Metal flies everywhere." He gestured down to his calf. "Shrapnel."

"That's not an explanation," I said. "Are you always so vague?"

He looked taken aback. "Am I vague? People don't usually ask me things."

"I'm asking," I said.

"Before I went to Phade, I was doing some mercenary work on Kha'al," he said. "Things got messy."

Suddenly, I was much more interested in something else. "Why were you really at Vuola Lire? You dodged me earlier, and then I got distracted with your mouth."

He puckered his lips. "Are you still distracted?"

I pushed my finger against his lips. "Yes, but I want answers."

"I want more kisses," he replied, lightly grasping my wrist and coming in for another one.

It took all my willpower to use my other hand to cover his mouth, because all I wanted was to drape myself over him and kiss every inch of his body. He let out a little groan of disappointment. "After you answer me."

He plucked my hand away. "Promise?" I raised my eyebrows, and he sighed. "A few months ago, I heard rumors that someone was selling Zathari women through Vakarios," he said, narrowing his eyes. "I hunted down a few leads but couldn't get anything concrete. A couple days ago, Storm called me, told me this Arandon guy was coming to the casino, and he had a reputation for trafficking. I got him to arrange a meeting, and the rest you know."

"And why again have you been telling me you're a bad man?"

He leaned in and gave me a shark-like grin. "Because I went there to…" He glanced over his shoulder, as if he was still afraid that the woman was at the door. "I went there to shut his business down."

I drew a finger across my throat and raised my eyebrows.

He nodded.

"Ah, yes, then you're a very bad man," I said in a deadpan voice. "Do you think he's the one selling Zathari women?"

"I don't know," he said. "But this auction is the best lead I've got to find out who is."

I nodded. "Why do you care so much? I mean, why is it your job to fix it?"

"Some things are just wrong," he said. "If I don't, who will?"

The way his eyes slid away from me told me he was hiding something, but I was enjoying the lazy calm with him. I decided to let him have his secrets for now. Even if he'd just fucked forty-two percent of my brains out, I wasn't entitled to everything going on inside his pretty head. I tipped his chin up. "Hey, serious man," I said. His lips pursed in a smile. "Can I ask you another question?"

"Kiss first," he said.

I obliged, and he took his sweet time, one hand sliding up my thigh as his tongue gave me something better to do than talk. By the time he was done with me, I had nearly forgotten what I wanted to ask. "Give me a minute," I said breathlessly. He chuckled to himself.

I pointed up. "This might be offensive, so I apologize. Why are your horns different than Storm's?"

He let out a sigh of relief. "I thought that would be much worse. It's a genetic thing. Why is your hair that color?" He shrugged. "Just a word of advice. If you ever meet Storm again, don't point it out. He's very self-conscious, especially after one of his girlfriends called them cute."

I burst out laughing. "They are cute."

His expression melted into one of utter horror. "That's just as bad as you telling me that my cock is pretty."

"It is!" I exclaimed. "Look at it!"

"Helena, we have to work on your interspecies sensitivity."

He shook his head. "Anyway, the shape and size is an inherited thing. My twin brother's are identical. His horns, not his cock." His head tilted. "Well, I guess that's identical, too. I've never looked that closely."

"You have a twin? As in another man who looks exactly like you?"

"Helena, I'm not sharing you with him," he said flatly. "We've shared way too much, and I draw the line here."

The consternation on his face made me laugh so hard that I snorted. "I'm sorry. That wasn't an invitation. I was just picturing two of you and wondering if that would be less scary or more scary."

"Maybe you'll meet him one day, and you can tell me," he said.

"What's his name?"

"Viper," he said.

"Is that his real name?"

He hesitated. "No. And Mistral isn't mine."

It didn't take a genius to figure that out. "What is your real name?"

"I can't tell you." His expression was odd; the subtle twitch of his lips and brows said he was fighting with himself. It seemed as if he wanted to say something and to hold it back at the same time. "It's superstitious, I'm sure. But—"

"Mistral is fine," I said gently.

With a little chuckle, he shook his head. "Zathari take several names over our lives. When I went to prison, my name was Tiro ehsan Adiya im Niza ara Khidresh," he said.

"That's a long name," I marveled.

The tension on his face eased. "Tiro was my birth name," he

said. "It means 'leader.' At birth, our mothers name us with their hopes for what we will be. The rest is about my parents and my home. Tiro, son of Adiya and Niza, who was born in the city of Khidresh."

"Say it again, please," I said, gently taking his hand.

He complied. There was a melodic flow to his native language, which took on a lovely timbre with his deep voice.

"But you don't use that name anymore? And you have another one?"

"That's right. As far as anyone knows, Tiro is dead. And my true name…" That tension crept across his face again.

"Is yours to share or not," I said. After brushing a kiss over his brow, I patted the bed next to me. "Lay down."

He glanced at me, gave me a mischievous grin, then obeyed, lying flat on his belly. Carefully, I straddled his hips. "Am I hurting you?"

"No," he said. "I am thinking very dirty thoughts, though."

"About what?"

"Hmm," he said. "I have a beautiful naked woman on my back. What do you think I'm thinking about?"

Countless men and women had called me beautiful in the last year. It wasn't a compliment anymore. It had almost become unpleasant to hear; an expression of covetous desire to do things to me that only Vehr Arandon was preventing.

But hearing it from Mistral made me feel warm and bubbly. It felt good again. It felt like something given rather than something scraped out of me.

I leaned in and gently ran my nails down his back. A shiver rippled down his spine, and his whole body shook a little beneath me. "Sweet gods of the void," he groaned. His fingers curled into the sheets, and I could see the veins rising on his forearms.

"No?"

"Yes," he blurted. "Please."

I took my time, soaking in the warmth of his big body as I scratched his back. The tension flowed out of him, and he eventually turned his head to lay on his crossed arms, a faint smile on his face. I was fascinated by the contrast of my pale pink nails against that rich, dark gray. Up close, his skin was faintly variegated with slightly darker specks, as if he really had been carved from stone. It was warm, but there was a toughness to it that was so different than mine.

This was such a silly, tiny thing, considering all that Mistral had already done for me. But I liked doing this small thing for him, wrapping him in a warm fuzzy blanket of good sensation. I did it for Arandon when I was his prisoner, though it had been to stay on his good side. This felt different, like I was wielding something powerful rather than clinging to whatever goodwill I could scrape together.

A light snore soon revealed that he had fallen asleep. After watching him for a while, I carefully extricated myself to sit at the window and watch the stars outside. Without the warmth of him pressed against me, I started to feel cold and anxious. We were headed into dangerous territory.

And while I was here having my fun with Mistral, Milla was still out there. The others from the Basilisk were still in danger. I couldn't do anything for them yet, but it felt wrong to be enjoying myself while they were suffering. And I was suddenly awash in the memory of Sarah, sobbing in pain, then screaming for help when they sold her off.

Tears pricked my eyes, and I covered my mouth to keep quiet. Mistral shifted, and I bit down on my own hand, holding my breath until the sting of tears passed.

I couldn't be a coward again. And I prayed that whatever came, he would put an end to Arandon and his depraved business. Maybe we could even find Sarah and save her.

It struck me as odd to think of the two of us as *we*. I hadn't been part of a *we* in a very long time. It was a nice thought, but I hoped that my trust in him wasn't going to come back to bite me, because there was no one coming to save me from Mistral if I was wrong.

CHAPTER 12

Mistral

I woke slowly and caught an eyeful of Helena wearing nothing but a pair of lacy red panties as she pawed through her suitcase. The rumbling of the ship told me we were nearing Borealis, its electromagnetic field stabilizing us for a docking. A fresh, flowery scent filled the room, though it didn't quite mask the smell of sex.

It was enchanting to watch her touching the clothes, head tilting as she thought carefully. With a warm twist of pride, I realized she was looking through the things I'd bought her. I had more money than I knew what to do with, and I would have happily spent more if she hadn't been so obviously uncomfortable with the luxury.

As silently as I could, I slid one half-numb arm from under me and grabbed her ass. She let out a sharp squeal of surprise, gasped, and tumbled into the jump seat. When she met my eyes, she burst out laughing. "You scared the shit out of me!"

"I could tell," I said. I felt hungover. "Did you put me to sleep?"

"Yep," she said. "Like a big lazy cat. You must have needed it." She raised an eyebrow and jerked her head toward the window. "Too bad you slept so long. We could have banged it out one more time before we arrived. But we're almost there." I let out a little growl and lunged out of bed, pinning her to the waist-high table near the window. Beyond the window, the gleaming silver construction of Borealis Station awaited. Its silvery glass domes reflected blinding light back at us. It might have been impressive, but I had absolutely zero interest in the technological marvels of Borealis when I had Helena in my hands.

I grasped her small breasts, holding her close as I kissed her neck. "Don't tease me, Helena," I murmured, rolling those sweet little peaks between my fingers. She laughed, low and quiet. "You know, there's all sorts of procedures before we can actually debark." Slowly, I slid one hand down, savoring the way her muscles fluttered under my hand, until my fingers brushed her wet folds. Something primal in me growled with satisfaction, that just my touch could conjure that sweet nectar from her. "Customs. Depressurization. Gravity recalibration."

She squirmed in my grasp. "Those are the least sexy words I've ever heard."

I held her tight to my chest with one arm, giving her nowhere to go as I curled my fingers into her. Her legs buckled, but I held her up. Her heart was pounding, each beat reverberating into my chest. "Are they? Seems like you like the science talk." Her hands clutched at my arm, nails digging in slightly as I continued to stroke and caress her. "The gravity on Borealis is slightly heavier than on Firyanin."

"Mistral, if you keep spouting science facts, I am going to lose it," she said.

"Oh, you're going to lose it, all right," I growled. I placed her on the table, her bare back pressed to the window. I briefly wondered if the windows were tinted, or if some lucky mechanic on Borealis was about to get a show.

Let them all see what they were missing.

Her chest was already flushed pink, her nipples tight rosy buds from my attention. Still holding her gaze, I slid my fingers into her pussy, curling into that soft, beautiful place that would drive her wild. Her body pulsed rhythmically around me, and she grabbed my shoulders firmly. With my thumb, I stroked her clit, watching as the shock of it rippled all the way up her body and into her widening eyes.

A chime sounded inside the cabin, followed by a chipper male voice on the speaker. "Mr. Delthe, can I interest you in a cocktail or a small plate before your departure? The chef recommends an assortment of pickled fruits from Irasyne, paired with a light red wine."

Her eyes went comically wide, but I never stopped fucking her with my fingers. "I'm satisfied," I said loudly. "Thank you."

"Thank you for your patronage," the chipper voice said. "Thank you for flying Nafh Zaridi Transit."

"Thank you for flying with Mistral Air," I growled into Helena's ear.

A wonderful little moan rippled out of her, and she threw her head back, that long wavy hair streaming behind her like a waterfall. It was a delightful display, her body arched toward me, her rosy pink pussy gripping my fingers. Her breathing quickened, until it was tiny, ragged sounds that scraped over her full lips.

"Helena," I said calmly. "Helena!"

Her dark eyes fluttered open. She couldn't speak, just let out a tiny, breathy sound as she clenched tight around me. Her fingers were curled so tight around the edge of the table that they were turning white, the veins standing out on her arms.

"Look at me when you come," I said. "I want to see it in your eyes."

Something ripped savagely through her from spine to shoulders. I was drunk on her, on the smell of her, on the way her beautiful body rolled and rippled like water. Then her eyes locked on mine, and I felt it all the way to the base of my cock, like a lit match. Her lips parted in a look of sheer shock, and she lurched forward, grabbing my shoulders as her whole body tensed around me. A long sigh escaped her as she slumped against me, aftershocks still fluttering through her and tickling at my fingers.

When she finally looked up at me again, I smiled, kissed her forehead, and withdrew my fingers. "Careful how you wake me up, sweet rose. I can always make time for that."

✦✦✦

An hour later, she was dressed, and we were filing into the crowd leaving the Starship Aedelia. Helena's face was still wonderfully flushed, though she had, unfortunately, put on clothes. I supposed it would attract the wrong kind of attention to parade her naked through Borealis.

I kept one hand on her back as we shuffled down an enclosed hallway and into the station itself. Around the massive outer ring, large ships were mixed in with smaller shuttles and jump ships. My skin prickled with dread when I saw the signature purple and gold marking of a Deeprun Dynamics ship, probably refilling the station's fuel stores.

Deeprun Dynamics was a massive mining corporation with dig sites in a dozen galaxies. In addition to providing fuel to quite a few planets and outposts, they ran the mining operation on Kilaak. Their shareholders got rich off prison labor, under the oversight of men who were just as violent as the prisoners they ruled over. And when we escaped, it was on a stolen Deeprun ship, with the bodies of their mercenaries turning the dried ground red with blood.

Since then, we did our best to avoid contact with Deeprun, especially since they still had bounties out on the Zathari savages who killed their men. I'd have to keep my head on a swivel here to make sure no one got too curious.

Like the spaceport back at Aliaros, the main concourse of Borealis Station was packed with bars, restaurants, and small shops. Animated signs pointed the way to the Night Horizon, an expensive resort that boasted a luxury spa and capsule rooms with a nearly three-hundred-and-sixty-degree view of space. A gaggle of Vaera women were headed that way, while a human male scurried behind them with a handtruck loaded with baggage.

I glanced at my watch, which was already syncing for messages. I had a message from Ember, confirming that he had arrived and was at the Sea's Edge bar. Another came from Jalissa Cain's mercenary, instructing me to notify her when I arrived.

The Sea's Edge featured massive screens depicting colorful underwater scenes. A polished wooden bar took up the center of the place, tended by a pretty Raephon woman in a white sailor suit. Her eyes lifted to me, then flinched as she glanced over her shoulder. A thousand credits said that Ember was in the corner.

I took Helena's hand and led her through the bar. Seated at a corner table, back pressed into the wall, was a man I hadn't seen in nearly a year. He had three massive plates of food in front of him; rice and raw fish by the look of it. He was methodically piling a sliver of pink fish onto a lump of sticky rice, then maneuvering it to his mouth when he looked up and saw me. His dark gray eyes lit up, and he dropped the chopsticks to come in for a hug.

For a small Zathari, he could give one rib-crushing hug. Finally, I clapped him on the back and pulled away to catch my breath. "Good to see you," I said. "I see you were hungry."

"I'm fuckin' always hungry, man," he complained. Then his eyes slid over Helena. "And you are absolutely stunning. Are you lost?"

She laughed. "I'm Helena," she said, putting out her hand.

"Ember," he said, squeezing it gently. His eyes flicked to me, and his nostrils flared slightly, like he was smelling the air. His sly smile said that he knew exactly what we'd been up to. "Helena, do you like fish? Come eat. I've got these little meat rolls coming." He pulled out a seat for Helena, then shoved the dome display at her. With his mouth full of rice, he mumbled, "Hit that button. Specials on the second page."

I envied the easy way Ember had with people. It helped that he was on the smaller side, even compared to Viper and me. His slender, curved horns almost disappeared into his tousled black hair. We used to give him shit about the obvious correlation between small horns and his equipment, but he definitely had it easier blending into a crowd. "You're going to spend your whole paycheck on this place."

"Good thing you're paying," he replied. "I've eaten nothing but protein mush for three months. And I was looking forward to going to Sarahi's for dinner when someone called and demanded that I get my ass up here."

"You missed Sarahi's?"

"And it's a damn tragedy," he said with a sigh. We had a standing invitation at the Sahemnar restaurant around the corner from our place in Ir-Nassa. Even Wraith cracked a smile when the elderly owners brought him a house special spiced to kill and called him *little grandson* like he wasn't twice their size and the scariest fucking thing on the planet.

Ember shoved one of the plates at Helena. "Eat. You look hungry."

With a chuckle, she took a lightly fried hunk from one of the plates. Her nose wrinkled as she examined it. "And this is..."

"Some kind of vegetable," he said. "I don't know. It's good." She bit into it delicately and smiled. Before she could give her thoughts, Ember blurted, "So, are you two fucking or what?"

Helena choked on the vegetable and covered her mouth while she coughed.

I raised an eyebrow at him. "Not at the moment. But in the

general sense, yes. Quite enthusiastically." I glanced at Helena, and her cheeks were scarlet red.

"Good for you," he said to Helena. "Because if you weren't, I was going to hit on you, but you've got that flush up here..." He gestured to his cheeks. "So I figured you were probably—"

"Ember, remember that talk we had about knowing when to shut the fuck up?" I asked. "And how you always miss the cues?"

He grinned at me. "Vaguely." He took the hint and stuffed his mouth with another pile of rice and fish.

I swiped at my watch, quickly composing a message to Jalissa's contact. "JC's girl will be here soon," I said. "Did Storm fill you in on what we're doing?"

His jovial expression faltered, and there was a hint of the fiery anger that lent him its name. "He mentioned."

"We'll talk more later," I said.

Helena cleared her throat. "Ember, what do you do for work?"

"I kill bugs," he said frankly. "Out on Tahukal mostly. Right now, the company is determined to set up a new site in the middle of the nastiest pit on Tahukal."

"You mean bugs?" she said, holding her fingers a few inches apart. "Like roaches?"

"No, I mean *bugs*," he said. His gray eyes drifted up, as if to sketch a picture of the height. "Bite you in half and fuck your corpse kind of bugs."

"Ember," I said sharply. "We're eating."

"That's disgusting," she said, though she sounded more impressed than afraid.

"Oh, it's nasty as hell," he said. "And honestly, I'd feel a little bad about it under different circumstances. I'm a big believer in leaving the natives alone, you know? But they're invasive. Some dipshit brought eggs from some other planet, and they got bigger, nastier, and smarter because of the atmosphere and the soil on Tahukal. Poor locals have been fending them off for years, and it's a losing battle."

"So are you on vacation?" she asked.

"Sort of," he said. "We were trying to secure a new dig site and stuck our dicks in a hive. Metaphorically, I mean. I'm not that—"

"Ember," I said.

"So, we got a bunch of soldier bugs who didn't like us getting near their queen. We had a nice little firefight, cleared the whole thing out, but the boss got his arm chewed off, and his second got a chest full of eggs. They're getting medical, and the rest of us are on a break while a load of medication runs through us and makes sure we're not going to shit out a monster." He shrugged. "So here I am, enjoying an expensive dinner on Mistral's dime in case I'm about to become a father to a bunch of carnivorous insects that eat my asshole on their way out."

Helena just stared at me, mouth wide open, and I shrugged. "This is Ember. He'll make you appreciate my lack of detail."

While Ember regaled Helena with tales of burning out a hive of carnivorous blood crawlers on Tahukal, the bartender brought out two more plates of food and a round of drinks. Ember was polishing off an impressive pile of thin, fileted fish when a light hand tapped my shoulder.

Adrenaline spiked through my veins. I slid my hand under my jacket and turned to see a slender woman with intense purple skin and faintly glowing markings on her cheeks. She was Helena's size, but her long, pointed ears and glowing violet eyes marked her as Aes-Jarra. Interesting. They didn't leave their system often. Jalissa was one of the few I'd ever met. "Mr. Delthe?" she asked politely.

"Ms. Vartai?" I replied.

Her mouth tugged up in a crooked smile. "Call me Kharadine," she said, brushing her fingers over her chin as she bowed slightly. I mimicked the gesture.

"Join us," Ember said. "You must be Ja—" His voice tapered off, and he patted at his throat in shock, then fear.

Kharadine was holding her fist tight in the open air over the table, and her eyes glowed brighter. "We have a friend in common. No need to air her business." She opened her fist, and Ember let out a long wheeze. Then she took the empty seat next to Helena and helped herself to one of the meat rolls. "I've brought the ship. I'll be flying for you."

I frowned at her. "I can fly it."

"Perhaps you can, but you won't," she replied calmly. "I will fly the ship. Those are the conditions of using it, which were agreed upon prior to my arrival."

Ember stared at her with sheer lust in his eyes. I'd stake my entire net worth on Ember trying to seduce her before this job was done. I would not, however, bet on his surviving the attempt. "I've got no issue with that."

"I'm pleased for you," Kharadine said. She glanced at me. "Will this be an issue, Mr. Delthe?"

"No. I agreed to her terms," I said. Against my better judgment, of course. I preferred to handle Jalissa like a loaded gun; useful, even necessary, but dangerous. And when I dealt with

Jalissa, I wanted an even exchange. She paid money, I did a job. This nebulous *favor* business was not how I did things.

Kharadine nodded. "Very good. I'm sure this will be a mutually beneficial expedition for both of us." As she took another of the meat rolls, her glowing eyes pulsed and lifted to look over my shoulder. I followed her gaze to see two officials in familiar dark gray uniforms approaching.

"Excuse me," one of them said. He was a Vaera male, with an imperious air that grated my nerves. "Your identification, please."

"Is that necessary?" I asked.

"Standard procedure," he said evenly.

"And that's why you headed straight for the Zathari, yes?" Kharadine asked mildly. "Do you have a protocol that dictates you start with the biggest men in the room? Or is there another reason you came straight here?"

The Vaera winced at her question. "Your identification, please," he repeated.

Ember sighed and handed his wallet over. I followed suit, keenly aware of the gun under my coat.

My heart pounded. Ember and I in the same place was compounding our chances of detection. I was already plotting our way out. I would kill every Ilmarinen officer on this floating hunk of metal before I went back to Kilaak.

Helena cleared her throat. "Excuse me. Don't you want to look at mine?" she said primly.

His eyes skimmed over her. "Yes, of course," he said, giving her offered identification a half-hearted glance.

Finally, the officer handed me back my ID. "Mr. Delthe, thank you for your cooperation," he said. He handed Ember his wallet back. "Mr. Ageros," he said. "Ms. Lavin. Ms. Vartai. Please enjoy your visit to Borealis."

"Thank you," Helena said sweetly.

Go fuck yourself, I thought, watching him wind back through the crowded bar. I jerked my chin toward them. "Get your shit. I want to get off this place as soon as we can."

CHAPTER 13

Helena

THIS MADE TWICE IN TWENTY-FOUR HOURS THAT I'D WATCHED Mistral go from utterly confident and calm to a tense, ticking time bomb. The tension in his jaw made the tendons on his neck stand out, and I was sure he was going to break the officer's neck.

Ember looked utterly chagrined to leave behind what remained of his feast. Kharadine patted his hand and said, "Life is difficult, dear. You'll survive. I've got some lovely proteins on the ship."

"Can't wait," Ember muttered.

As we hurried through Borealis, Kharadine walked ahead of us. Ember and Mistral walked on either side of me with their big travel bags slung over their shoulders. With two huge men on either side of me, I felt important and well-protected. But they both looked tense, and I caught Mistral checking over his shoulder a few times.

We passed through a section of the station packed with bustling shops and restaurants. A sign with blood-red lips advertised *Virtual Romance*. I watched a couple giving each other sneaky looks before dashing into the shop. At the end of the shops was an artificial garden with a suspended vidscreen playing advertisements for the station's offerings.

Past that, we went through a security checkpoint manned by two uniformed officers. Kharadine scanned her ID, then flipped it over to scan another pass. She typed on the display, which showed the message:

Vartai, Kimra. 4 passengers confirmed.

So she was like Mistral, with all kinds of fake names and forged papers.

Then she beckoned to us. My heart thumped as I swiped my ID to follow. A green light illuminated at the turnstile, letting me pass.

Past the massive doors was an austere terminal patrolled by a dozen uniformed officers. The outer wall was sectioned into wedges. Outside the thick glass windows, I could see smaller ships parked along a walkway. I felt small and insignificant, watching this whole world open up before me. Where were all these people from? Where were they going? My situation felt all-consuming, but the reality was that I was a tiny speck in a massive universe.

I felt a little lost, even overwhelmed as we followed Kharadine to a doorway marked *07*. She entered a long passcode, and the door opened to a narrow hallway. Inside, the air was frigid and dry. "Watch your step. She's a little shaky."

When I placed my foot on the gangplank, it trembled a little. I closed my eyes and hurried after Mistral. Soon, my feet found solid ground again, now on a smaller ship. It was sleek and stylish inside, with a big central area decorated beautifully, like our cabin on the Aedelia. "Welcome aboard the Impulse," Kharadine said. She lifted her eyes. "Rossi, please bring up the desk."

"My pleasure, Captain Kharadine," a male AI voice boomed. I jumped in surprise.

In the middle of the cabin, a circular portion of the floor rotated slightly and rose until it formed a table. The flat surface flickered, then illuminated with a loading screen.

"I'll be a moment," Kharadine called from the cockpit. "Stow your things in the cabin. Mine is locked, and there's one extra."

Ember glanced at me, then Mistral, clearly doing the mental math. His shoulders slumped, then he got a mischievous gleam in his eye. "I'll sleep with Kharadine."

"You certainly will not," she shouted.

Mistral smirked at him and gestured to one of the couches. "Surely you've slept in far worse places."

"And I could have been sleeping in a big bed with a nice girl in Ir-Nassa," he griped. "Maybe two."

"Poor baby," Mistral said, taking my bag. I followed him down a hallway and into the open cabin. It was similar to the one I'd shared with Milla and some of the other girls on the Basilisk, though much less crowded. Two stacked bunks with a narrow ladder took up one wall. He gave me a playful smile. "You want to share with me?"

"Hell, no," I teased. "You can sleep out there with Ember."

He growled and grabbed my hips, pulling me close as he

kissed my lips. "It wasn't actually an option, Helena," he whispered.

I reached behind him and pinched his ass. He jumped and gave me a look of mock horror. "I know that, Mistral. The question is if you want to be on top or bottom."

He pinned me to the wall, hands lightly securing my wrists. "We're going to share," he murmured in my ear. "But you can still be on top."

I laughed. "I like how you think."

There was a faint rumble, and the ship began to vibrate slightly. When we emerged, Kharadine was sitting on the couch waiting. "We'll pull away from Borealis soon. For now, we've got cover. No ears listening."

I sighed with relief. "Can I ask a question?"

"Yes, I'll join a threesome with you," Ember said. "As long as—"

Mistral shot him a look that would have melted steel.

"As long as you know I'm completely kidding. Because I respect boundaries," Ember finished.

"Why did you two get so tense when the Ilmarinen officer checked your ID?" I glared at Mistral. "And don't be vague. You did it on the Aedelia too."

"Because they're wanted criminals," Kharadine said.

Ember shrugged. "She's not wrong."

Mistral settled on the couch across from me. "We escaped from Kilaak."

I raised my eyebrows. "Mistral, I know you're a man of few words, but let's just assume you need to always use more than you think you do," I said. "Please. Explain everything like I just woke up from a coma."

"Kilaak is a prison planet," he said. "Me, my twin, Ember, Storm," he said. "And a handful of others. Normally, they wouldn't keep particularly good records, but we hijacked a Deeprun ship on our way out. Might have killed a few of their guys."

"They had it coming," Ember said.

"Don't they always?" Kharadine said.

"But what did you do?" I asked. "Why were you in prison?"

He sighed and pinched his nose. Ember just smirked at him. "My idiot twin and I thought it would be a good idea to steal a Dominion ship. We were sixteen and far stupider than anyone should be at that age," he said. "Couple of their officers got hurt, and neither of us was smart enough to realize that they had remote access to take over the ship in case of exactly what we did."

I stared at him in disbelief. "I've been over here worried that you were a serial killer, and you went to prison for a joyride?"

He scowled. "I told you that I wasn't going to hurt you. I didn't kill anyone until they put me in prison."

I turned to Ember. "And what about you?"

He just laughed. "Sorry, sweetheart," he said. "He's only telling you his story because you're fucking. If you want mine—"

"Ember," Mistral said sharply. He met my eyes. "There's still a bounty on us, but Deeprun shot themselves in the foot. The administrators on Kilaak don't keep good records. A lot of prisoners die on the surface, and more in the mines, so they don't always know who they've got. None of us use the names in the High Court's records. But we still stand out, especially in places like Borealis. Some people see Zathari in decent clothing outside the slums of Sonides and assume we're criminals."

"That's racist," I said.

"That's what I'm saying," Ember said. "I mean, technically we are criminals, but so is Kharadine."

"Guilty," she said.

"And that's why you told me to pretend I didn't know you," I said quietly.

Mistral nodded. "We spend a lot of money to have good ID. I've got half a dozen clean ones, but you still can't be too careful."

"The good news is that where we're going, everyone is a criminal, and they sure as hell won't be running you through the Ilmarinen databases for outstanding bounties," Kharadine said. She gave me a stern look, then turned to Mistral. "How do you feel about leaving the human behind?"

"She wants to help," Mistral said. His pale eyes drifted to me. "Don't you?"

I nodded, but I had to wonder. My insistence on helping him was one thing when I was answering a string of questions while I was safe in a luxurious hotel. Now we had mercenaries, an ally who apparently had psychokinesis, and an invitation to an auction that would be attended by people as bad as Vehr Arandon, if not worse.

What the hell was I thinking? Maybe it would be smarter to back out, to take up Mistral on his offer to send me back to Earth. But things had changed. I'd never thought that being with a man would make me dumber, but I wanted to stay at his side. And until I laid eyes on Milla and Sarah again, I wouldn't be able to rest.

"I do want to help," I said, my voice shaky.

"Can you snap someone's neck? Hack into a Chariot ship navigation system?" Kharadine asked. Her glowing eyes narrowed. "No offense, pretty girl, but you serve no purpose here but using up precious oxygen and giving the men erections."

Even though I was questioning myself, I was shocked at how angry her blunt assessment made me. Compared to what I'd heard on the Basilisk, it was mild, but it was like I'd completely lost my ability to hold back now that I was free. "How about you go fuck yourself?"

Kharadine was unruffled, which made me even madder. "Why are you taking her? You clearly have affection for her," she said to Mistral. "That will get in our way."

I spread my hands flat on the table. "I'm not an assassin, though if you give me an empty syringe, I can kill a man and make it look like an accident," I said. "But more importantly, I know every one of Vehr Arandon's men. I know that his body man, Thenoch, wears a gun on his right hip, and that he always has extra security dressed as guests, bystanders, whatever. They're average-looking, not people you'd notice, but I can pick them out of a crowd. You can't."

"I was just—" Kharadine started.

I raised my voice to cut her off. "I know that Vehr Arandon's drink of choice is a Thegaran twister, light on the berry juice, and that he's got an allergy to *ghiliash* honey so severe that just smelling it will make him sick enough to excuse himself to the nearest bathroom. One drop in his food and he'll be incapacitated until he gets medical attention. At least two of his bodyguards and one of his female companions will carry an emergency adrenaline spray, just in case," I continued. "I know that when he's bluffing at cards, he always plays with the earrings on his left ear. Never the right. You may have blueprints and know how to kill people, but I spent months with the very people you're trying to take down. And they have big mouths around anyone they see as beneath them."

Mistral was staring at me like he wanted to kiss me, but I was still mad as hell.

Kharadine nodded, but her imperious expression never faltered. "This is all good information," she said. "Write it all down, and stay here. "

"Vehr Arandon sold me to Mistral," I said. "And if he shows up at the auction without me, it's going to raise some questions. Most importantly, I know the people he's selling. They'll trust me."

"She goes," Mistral said quietly. "I'd rather not have any extra risks, but she's right. Besides, Arandon may be more amenable to conversation and dropping information when he sees a happy customer with one of his products."

Kharadine shrugged. "It's your call. But I hope I don't have to say I told you so later." She swiped across the table, which shifted to a display of a virtual armory. "This is what I've got on board. Courtesy of Jalissa."

Ember's eyes widened as he took in the display of guns. He tapped one to zoom in. "Sweet Wayfarers," he murmured. "I would marry this if I could."

"Look at the inventory and decide if you want anything else," she said. "We can have a shipment brought in by tomorrow if needed, but it's all on your dime, plus Jalissa's markup."

Mistral nodded grimly. "I'll give it a look."

Kharadine nodded. "I've also got a fairly standard toolkit." She glanced at me. "And a few empty syringes if you'd like," she said in a mocking tone. I scowled at her.

Mistral leaned back. "So what does Jalissa get out of this? Besides me owing her a favor. This is a lot for a favor."

Kharadine waggled her fingers through the air, like an insect crawling. "We're dropping crawlers on Erebus. She wants blueprints, security, to know everything about the system, and a list of everyone who comes on and off the ship. Information only."

"We both know she doesn't just want information," Mistral said.

"Do we both know that?" Kharadine asked innocently. "You don't need to worry about it. We all have our moral lines, and Jalissa doesn't like traffickers any more than you do. And if the Dominion gets word of a bunch of rich assholes selling and buying women on Erebus…"

He pinched the bridge of his nose. "I don't want to get in bed with the Dominion."

"Then don't," Kharadine said sharply. "This kind of bust is a kingmaker. And she would very much like to have another friend owing her a big favor, especially one well-placed in the Dominion Intelligence Force. You don't have anything to do with it." She chuckled. "Jalissa isn't interested in sharing credit with you."

"So shouldn't she owe me a favor instead?" Mistral asked. "I brought her this opportunity, after all."

"That's not how this works. You got your ship, now you pay up," she said. "You take down your scumbags, Jalissa passes on the information, I get paid, and we all go home happy, yes?"

As they continued to talk strategy, I felt increasingly out of my element. But when there was an opening, I leaned forward. "Kharadine?" Her brows lifted, her eerie, pupilless eyes wide. "I have an idea."

"Go ahead," she said evenly.

"I assume I'll go...in costume," I said, glancing at Mistral. "When Arandon sold me, they had put bugs in my earrings so they could listen in. Could you do that? Maybe even a little camera?" I positioned my hands over my head to imitate the elaborate headdresses I'd worn. "I would probably wear my hair up, so you could hide it there. If you're planning to turn information over to the Dominion, video evidence could be helpful."

Her brow furrowed, and I braced myself for her to outright reject the idea. But she nodded appreciatively and started typing. "That's not a bad idea. Let me see what I can find. Something small..."

They continued to talk for another hour before Kharadine rose and excused herself to the cockpit to compose a message to Jalissa. As the outsider, I could only piece together fragments, but I was guessing Jalissa was a crime boss or arms dealer. I didn't particularly care what she did if she was willing to make sure Arandon and his buddies weren't selling people anymore.

With their planning session finally ended, Mistral caught my eye and headed for the cabin. I followed and closed the door behind us. Inside, he let out a long sigh, like he'd been holding his breath for hours. "Are you sure you want to do this?"

"What, sleep with you?" I teased.

He smirked. "Go to Erebus," he said. "I'm sure this will be much worse than Arandon's parties. Say the word, and I'll send you back to Vuola Lire. Storm will put you up for as long as you need and make sure you've got personal security. It'll be the safest place in the universe."

My heart pounded. "I thought about it, but we need to help them."

"While I very much enjoy your company, I can do this without you," he said.

"I have to," I said. I twisted my hands as a squirming wave of guilt rose in my chest. "Can I tell you something?"

"Sure," he said, leaning against the bunk.

After pacing for a minute, I sat on the lower bunk and stared at the ground. I didn't want to see his eyes when they filled with disappointment. I told him about Sarah, and how I'd kept my mouth shut. Tears pricked at my eyes. "I just stood there," I said quietly. "She probably hated me. With good reason. If she'd gotten us out of there, I'd have gone, but I didn't stand up for her."

"You said you told him to stop," he said quietly.

"I did," I said. "And then he hit me, and I was too scared to say anything else. I was afraid he would hurt me like he was hurting her."

His firm hand gripped my chin and tilted it up. Tears spilled over my cheeks, and he gently wiped them away. "Helena, what do you think you would have accomplished by continuing to fight?"

"She wouldn't have been alone," I said. I tried to pull away, but he held my face firmly. "I wouldn't have been a coward."

"Would it have saved your friend from her fate?" he asked. "Do you think that all of his security and allies would have backed down because you let that man beat you bloody on principle? Or do you somehow think that your foolish boldness would have changed Vehr Arandon into a decent man who let all of you go?" My eyes drifted away from his, and his voice took on a firmer edge. "Look at me, Helena."

I reluctantly met his eyes. "It probably wouldn't have changed anything, but it was still cowardly."

His expression softened, and he sat on the bunk next to me. "Come here," he said. One strong arm looped around my shoulders. "I understand why this upsets you. The fact that you still fret about it speaks volumes of your character. But what happened to your friend wasn't your fault. We all do hard things to survive."

I sniffled once, then let out a noisy sob. "I'm sorry," I said, trying to push away from him.

But he didn't let go, and instead pulled me closer, where I was secure against his broad chest. "Let it go," he said. "All of it. Don't hold onto anything that weighs you down. These things that happened were not your fault, and you are not a coward."

Caged in those big arms, I quit trying to keep the lid on everything and let it flow out of me in ugly, ripping sobs. His hand cupped my head gently to his chest as I cried. It was all so fucking unfair. I'd tried to live a good life on Earth, and when I dared to look elsewhere, this happened. One mistake, and my life was taken away from me. Arandon snatched me, violated me, and treated me like an object, like a piece of furniture. And for what?

Two hundred and fifty thousand Dominion crescents. My life, my body, my freedom, all for an appallingly low number.

And I'd convinced myself *at least at least at least* like this was somehow all acceptable because it could have been worse. I'd lived in fear for...I still didn't even know how long I'd been gone. Men had touched me, whispered the filthy things they wished they could do to me, and I could still hear their voices echoing in my head. None of it should have happened to me, nor to anyone else.

And it hurt all the more because I was helpless. I didn't get out of it because I was clever or brave. The only reason I was safe now was sheer, dumb luck, because this beautiful man stumbled into my path with a good soul and the inclination to stop a bad thing happening in front of him.

Poison burst out of me, foul and putrid and stinging, until there was nothing left. I didn't know how long I cried, but eventually the tears dried up. Then I was afraid to look up, knowing how terrible I would look.

I realized dimly that he was still gently stroking my hair. When I was quiet, he spoke softly, though his deep voice was still a comforting rumble against me. "I'm not good at this," he said. "I don't know how to find the silver lining in everything, nor to make you feel better. But I give you my word that you will be safe with me. As long as you want it from me, I will make sure you don't have to be afraid or alone."

I sniffled and dared to look up at him. He gazed down at me, those big blue eyes so full of tenderness I could barely wrap my mind around it. "Thank you," I said. "And you're wrong."

"About?"

"You're very good at this," I said. As his lips curved, I brushed my lips to his for a soft kiss. "I'm glad you showed up in my life when you did."

"As am I," he murmured. "As am I."

CHAPTER 14

Mistral

THREE DAYS LATER, WE EMERGED FROM AN ILMARINEN GATE INTO the Fields of Thados, a galaxy of unclaimed planets. Several blocky mining vessels followed us through, presumably headed for one of the fuel-rich planets here. Far from here, the Theritanian Empire spread its influence, and everyone with half a brain cell knew that it would be here that they finally clashed with the Aengra Dominion. It was only a matter of time before the two greedy empires clashed over who got to defile the untouched planets first, and who would be stuck with the hollowed-out leftovers.

I rode in the cockpit with Kharadine, who was calm as ever as she navigated us away from the Ilmarinen gate and into empty space. She put her hand out. "Let's get directions to the party," she said grimly.

Using the projected screen, Kharadine typed in the hailing

frequency Arandon had given me. My heart thumped as we waited for a response. We sailed slowly through the open space past the gate, an eerie silence hanging in the cabin. I nearly jumped out of my skin when I heard something bang against the lounge table, and then a raucous laugh from Ember.

In the days of travel, I'd begrudgingly shared my time with Helena. She and Kharadine didn't get along yet, but she and Ember were thick as thieves. He tried to offend her with his goriest tales of bug hunting on Tahukal, but she matched him blow for blow with stories of medical woe from her days in the emergency room. I finally had to beg them to stop so we could eat dinner in peace. But it was good to see her smiling and laughing, especially after her anguished admission. I knew Ember wouldn't make a move, and I was happy to see her at ease. When I wasn't planning our incursion with Kharadine, I spent hours talking to Helena, who was as ferociously intelligent as she was beautiful.

I wished that I could wipe away all that had happened to her. And yet, I knew that if she'd never been taken from Earth, if her life had not transpired just as it had, we would have never met. Perhaps it made me selfish, but I wasn't sure I could have given that up if I had the choice.

The screen chirped with a response. "Transmission received," Rossi, the AI boomed. "Incoming message. Manual navigation vectors provided. Shall I plot course?"

"Yes, please," Kharadine said. "Play message."

The engines rumbled to life, and we surged forward as the message began to play. A pale-skinned Vaera man appeared on our screen. "Greetings, Mr. Delthe," he said. "My name is Odensrah Iban, and I represent the owners of the Erebus Resort. I will be your personal concierge for your visit."

"Excellent," I said, wishing I'd put on my fancy coat. "I look forward to visiting your establishment."

He smiled evenly. "Upon reaching the given coordinates, please hail this frequency again. At that point, we will provide a locator frequency to guide your navigation systems. Would you care for a companion to be provided with your accommodations? If you like, I can send a catalog."

My stomach twisted in a knot of anger. "That won't be necessary. I will have my own companion present."

"Very good, Mr. Delthe," he said smoothly. "Should you wish for additional company, you need only ask. We look forward to welcoming you to Erebus."

When the screen flickered off, I was overcome with the need to scrub myself clean. Kharadine gave me a glance. "You might sell the act better if you partake of their offerings."

"I'll take the risk," I said.

With the course set for Erebus, Kharadine and I returned to the central cabin, where we had begun preparations. "Ember," I called as we walked in. He and Helena came out of the galley, and to my delight, she passed me a cup of coffee before sidling up to me. I casually slung my arm around her waist and savored the way she molded to me, like our bodies were meant to fit together.

Sharing a tiny bunk meant for a human-sized body with two other keen-sensed people on board hadn't been ideal for making love to her, but I'd improvised. The other day, I'd stripped her bare, warned her that I'd stop if she made a peep, and proceeded to go down on her until she went limp. Her face was tomato red by the time I was done, and lipstick smeared both of her hands from the effort of muffling her sweet cries of joy. She'd gotten the sweetest revenge the next morning. I woke up hard as a rock, nuzzled into her, and ended up with her left hand over my mouth and her right stroking me until I was spent.

And just an hour before we approached the Ilmarinen gate, I'd bent her over the bed, covered her mouth, and fucked her sweet and slow until her whole body bent like a bow and her legs shook. Her muffled scream had vibrated up my body, and I swore I could still feel the blazing brand of her lips on my palm. When she smiled at me, I could feel the pulse of my *dzirian* still.

"We'll reach the coordinates at our designated space in approximately ten hours," Kharadine said. "At that point, we'll get another ping that will let us navigate automatically. They're keeping the location as quiet as they can."

"Can you scan for it?" Ember asked.

She shook her head. "There's an asteroid belt not far from us, and it's disrupting the sensors. I can start a scan, but we'll be on top of Erebus by the time it finishes."

Ember nodded. He raked a hand through his hair, then tested his breath and wrinkled his nose. "I should get cleaned up so I don't drag you down, Mr. Delthe," he said in a mocking voice. He excused himself to the shower.

Kharadine's eyes raked over Helena. "When you're dressed and ready to go, I'll get you wired," she said. She swiped across the table to reveal an intricate web of names and brief descriptions. When she wasn't entertaining Ember, Helena had given Kharadine detailed descriptions of both Arandon's victims and his staff. "I'll have your little bag of tricks ready by the time you're done."

Helena nodded, her expression somber. "I'll get started." She rose on her toes, kissed my cheek, and left us in the central cabin.

Kharadine's glowing eyes followed her, then landed on me. "You should leave her onboard," she said quietly.

"She wants to go," I said.

"Right," she said. "I thought I was talking to a Zathari mercenary with bulletproof skin and a hundred pounds on her. I see why you're intimidated by the tiny human who wants her way."

"Are you more worried about blowing the job or her safety?" I asked. Like I hadn't considered all the worst-case scenarios of someone there putting their hands on her. I was still considering leaving her onboard, but she was right about her ability to help us.

"Both, since you seem to care about neither so much as pleasing her whims," she said sharply. "Let's review."

We spent another few hours reviewing our plans. This job made me uneasy; on top of snitching to the Dominion, we were going into an unknown location with unknown patrons and unknown security. Our success and survival hinged on adapting quickly to what we found on Erebus. There was no question that Ember and I could adapt. Our escape from Kilaak had been meticulously planned for over a year, and it was still a shitshow of epic proportions.

But we'd done it. Regardless of what Kharadine thought I was risking with Helena, I already knew that I'd kill anyone who put their hands on her. That wasn't even a question.

Unfortunately, we weren't here to rain down blood and

death, as satisfying as that would be. Blowing Erebus into dust would have been easy. We were here to shut these assholes down and free their victims. And that was a much harder and more delicate prospect. Living, breathing people were much harder to work around than expendable crates of cargo.

My plan was to ingratiate myself with the other patrons on Erebus, while Helena's recorders fed information back to Kharadine. I intended to find out who was selling Zathari women, and if he didn't survive to be taken by Dominion officials, then that was an *oops* I could accept.

I had originally planned to keep my promise to Helena by bidding on Milla, but after days of debate, we'd decided it was safer to call in the authorities before the auction. We would send a call to Kharadine's contact approximately thirteen hours before the auction to confirm that it was on.

Though Ilmarinen Interstellar claimed to be politically neutral, they conveniently had Dominion officials on site at all of their gates. Their technology was the foundation of the Dominion's power and reach. And as far as the Aengra Dominion was concerned, their laws extended into any territory where they happened to be breathing. More often than not, that was a pain in my ass, but for this, I would welcome their overreach.

The plan was to have the Dominion ships arrive just before the auction, which would have all the patrons in place with their victims centralized. Kharadine theorized that would reduce the collateral damage to innocents while giving them the greatest chance of arresting the buyers and sellers. The footage we captured would confirm their involvement, in case any of them tried to deny it.

For our part, we were getting out of there before the auction. Helena didn't like that part; she wanted to have her hands on Milla and the others before we left. But there was a damned good chance this would all turn ugly. And if buyers started leaving with their new purchases as soon as it was over, some of them could slip through our hands. Letting the Dominion crash the party before it even began was the best chance for all the innocent people involved.

Ember returned from the shower with a pair of loose pants on. Several twisted scars stretched over his flat belly. Whatever he'd tangled with on Tahukal was deadly enough to slice into a Zathari hide, which was enough to make me shudder. As he rubbed a clean-smelling oil onto his brow and onto his horns, he looked me over. "You ready to be an asshole?"

I frowned at him. "What?"

"What's your name? What's your business?" he asked.

"Adalon Delthe. Phytridarium mining," I said.

"Oh yeah? Where?" My tongue was tied for a split second. Bullshitting was my twin brother's specialty. Ember whacked me in the arm. "Spit it out. This is an easy question."

"Fuck off," I retorted. "I keep my sites secret. I don't need a young upstart like you poaching my business."

He flashed a devious smile. "Good save."

"And you?" I snapped. "What's your deal?"

"I'm your bodyguard. I'm not here to talk," he said. He tilted his head. "Any interest in expanding your operation out here?"

Kharadine watched in amusement as we sparred verbally. Ember tripped me up a few times. Years of working for the Meritan-Corvus corporation on Tahukal had left him with more than just interesting stories about killer bugs; he knew his shit about mining technology.

"What about your pet?" Kharadine asked mildly. "Would you loan her to me for a night?"

"Touch her and I'll—" I blurted. Kharadine's broad smile made me angry. I took a breath and tried to think of those men at the card game. "I don't share my toys, Miss Vartai."

She just raised her eyebrows and headed back into her cabin. Ember glanced at me. "Be careful," he said quietly. "I don't know these guys, but I don't think they look at their sex slaves like you look at Helena."

"I can handle it," I replied.

He nodded. "You better. Because if we fuck up, she gets hurt."

I left him still polishing his horns and headed into my cabin. Helena sat on the floor with a small mirror propped up on the lower bunk. She was calm as she twisted locks of her long auburn hair up into an elaborate style, pinning each one into place with surgical precision. She wore the light purple robe she'd gotten from the boutique in Vuola Lire, making her look like a pretty little jewel.

I glanced at the bed, where two configurations of leather and lace lay. Calling them outfits was a bit of a stretch. "Can't decide?"

She sighed. "You tell me. I can wear real clothes, but I'll also wear one of those if it'll help you blend in with the other perverts."

I chuckled. "You will certainly not blend in wearing this," I said, picking up the lacy little black thing.

She glanced back at me. Her face was already partially painted, the dark liner making her eyes intense and somber. "If you want to look like one of these men, then it's better that I look like your toy than your equal. If not for Arandon, I'd say I could pretend to be your wife, but he knows what I am to you. Theoretically, at least."

If she continued speaking, I missed it. When she said *wife*, I lost my senses. The Zathari didn't marry in a traditional sense, and I was so far removed from my people that I wouldn't have known where to begin with any sort of bonding rituals. But I knew the word, knew the implication, and the thought of her at my side in some distant future was enough to make my head swim.

It was even more stunning because it felt right. Like she'd pulled back a curtain to simply reveal what had always been true, as real as gravity. If the Wayfarers had seen fit to find a mate for me, Helena would have fit the mold. And I didn't dare want it, because I feared that she would look closer and realize I couldn't possibly be good enough for her.

She tugged my hand. "What do you think?"

"I think you should pick the one that's more comfortable to sit on my lap in," I said, trying to mask my sudden introspection with a flirtatious look. Her lips pursed.

I watched with quiet fascination as she finished her hair, then clipped on some of the jewelry we'd bought. She went from being a beautiful wildflower, perfect just as nature made her, to a polished gem, cut and crafted to rigid perfection. Then she rose and let the robe fall away. Her naked body was dusted with a glittery substance, like she'd been wearing when I first met her.

"Helena, will you be extremely angry if I mess up your makeup?" I asked.

Her smile reached into my soul and ignited it. "I will be furious," she said. "But you can mess it up later if you like. You can leave handprints all over me."

"I will take that offer," I said.

She reached over, took one of the lacy black garments and handed it to me. "Help me," she said sweetly. Gods, she even smelled good, like flowers and vanilla. I was overcome with desire to bury my face between her thighs and drink her down.

I handed it back. "I can't."

"Why?"

"Because if I put my hands on you, you're going to have to start all over," I said frankly. "You make me a weak man."

She laughed. "Is this going to be a problem on Erebus?"

"I hope not," I said.

When she was finally done dressing, her gleaming body was covered in a configuration of straps and cutouts that boggled the mind. Only a thin filament of black fabric covered her sex, though sheer black sleeves covered her arms from wrist to shoulder. Black stockings hugged her legs nearly to her hip, hooked to her garments with thin silver chains. I was surprised at how she could look so naked while being covered nearly from head to toe. The thin slivers of glittering skin were all the more alluring.

My eyes raked over her.

She raised one dark brow. "What do you think?"

"I think you're the most gorgeous woman in the universe," I said frankly.

"You're just saying that to get me in bed," she teased.

"I'm saying it because I've already seen you in bed," I replied. I took her hand lightly. "Will you be offended if I say I like you better in the pink dress I bought for you?"

Her smile was so soft and sweet I felt like I was melting. "I like it better, too," she said. I crooked my finger, and she leaned in for a kiss. "Don't mess up my makeup. Hands off."

I groaned in disappointment, but complied and kissed her, savoring the taste of mint on her tongue. When I broke away, I whispered in her ear. "I like you best when you're naked."

She laughed and kissed my temple. "Of course you do."

Someone pounded on the door. "Kharadine's ready," Ember shouted through the door. "You better not be fucking."

"I'm going to kill him before this is over," I muttered.

Helena laughed and put her robe on to follow me into the cabin, where Kharadine was waiting with a tray of small cameras and bugs. The other woman carefully mounted two finger-nail sized chips onto the backs of Helena's earrings, then explained, "You can take these off and put them on your other jewelry, or just wear these the whole time. These will be audio only."

Helena gave me a longing look. "Mr. Delthe bought me these, so I'll wear them whenever he wants." Her voice was syrupy sweet, almost cloying. "Whatever he likes, I like."

"Ugh," Kharadine groaned. "I mean, that's great, but I hate the subservient act. I preferred you telling me to go fuck myself."

Helena snorted. "Me too. Give me the fucking earrings," she teased.

"That's much better," Kharadine said. She leaned over Helena to attach a camera to the glittering headdress nestled in her auburn hair. The lens was well-hidden by the gemstones and would capture whatever Helena looked at. She hooked another to a large button on my jacket.

Ember finished dressing in a surprisingly well-tailored suit. A holster peeked from beneath his jacket. I was surprised at how well he cleaned up, considering he spent most of his time covered in bug guts and blood. He brushed off his lapels. "Helena, how do I look?"

"You look very handsome," she said sweetly.

He beamed. "You look very…" He glanced at me. "You look very attractive in the most respectful way I can manage to say it."

"Thank you, Ember," she said.

Kharadine approached Ember to secure another lens to his jacket. He gave her a mischievous grin. "Kharadine, how do I look?"

She ran her finger from his chin to his bare throat. "Like you've left me a nice, exposed target," she said sweetly. Then she hurried to the cockpit and said, "Rossi, open hailing frequency."

An hour later, we glimpsed Erebus emerging from the shadowy sea of stars. Shaped like a top-heavy diamond, it was constructed of dark metal. It was easily as big as Borealis, but without the glittering bustle of ships coming and going. Ahead of us, another small passenger ship was coming in for landing.

Helena and Ember were crammed into the cockpit to watch, and even Kharadine didn't complain. The stark gray walls of the station were marked with runes and letters I didn't recognize. A crane was mounted to one side. It looked like it could have been a mining station, if not for the fact that it was orbiting in open space instead of digging minerals from the earth.

A robotic voice issued from the speaker. "Greetings, vessel IMS-H7-4217," it said. "Requesting permission for automated navigation."

"Permission granted," Kharadine said. When the screen popped up on her side, she hastily typed in her code. There was a little jolt, and she released the controls as the station brought us in for a landing. Inside the massive landing area, half a dozen passenger ships were parked and loaded into large bays. We were all on high alert, pointing out details and adjusting our plan. Ember noticed the armed guards patrolling in two concentric circles, while Kharadine noticed a set of concealed turrets at either side of the open doorway.

Soon, we landed with a light *thump*, and the concierge appeared on our screen with a video message. "Greetings, Mr. Delthe," Iban said. "We welcome you to the delights of Erebus Resort. When you are ready to disembark, please respond to this message, and we will escort you to our private lounge."

I glanced back at Helena and Ember. "Are you ready for this?"

"Whatever you say, boss," Ember said wryly.

Helena nodded. "Let's go."

CHAPTER 15

Helena

The moment we debarked the Impulse, a disconcertingly pale Vaera male approached us with a tray of glasses filled with amber liquor. "Greetings, Mr. Delthe," he said brightly. "I am Odensrah Iban, and I will be your personal concierge during your stay." He offered the tray, and Mistral lightly nudged my back. Right. Time to be eager little servant Helena. I brought him a glass, which he took quietly. The concierge glanced at Ember. "And this is your personal bodyguard?"

"That's right," Mistral said. He sipped the liquor. "He goes where I go. Is that a problem?"

"Not at all, sir," Odensrah said. He didn't even glance at me, which was probably for the best. I'd never seen a Vaera so pale; his skin was a disconcerting shade of pink that made him look sunburned. Behind him, a pair of brawny human men approached. "May we take your belongings to your suite?"

"My other assistant will accompany you," he said, glancing over his shoulder as Kharadine hopped from the boarding ramp. Her purple-black hair was tied up under a cap, and she wore a sharp black suit that covered her from neck to ankles. We should have switched roles. "Ms. Vartai will accompany my pet, should I need to be separated from her during my stay."

"Of course," Odensrah said. While the crew followed Kharadine, Odensrah led us to a black carpeted ramp. At the top of the ramp was an expanse of tinted black glass ringed in glowing red light. "Mr. Delthe, I trust you will find Erebus most interesting. We have exquisite dining, live shows, and spa services, tonight. May I schedule you for a visit with one of our fine masseurs?"

"I'll consider it," Mistral said. "We've traveled a while, and I look forward to a drink with better conversationalists than my bodyguard." He glanced at Ember, who spared a faint smile.

Odensrah laughed. "Yes, of course, sir," he said. I had a feeling that if Mistral said he wanted to eat a live human child with his bare hands, the concierge would have said *yes, right away, sir,* and brought him a menu of assorted babies fresh from the nearest maternity ward.

Anticipation prickled over me in a nervous rush as we reached the dark doors. It felt like we were stepping into another world entirely, where the rules of decency no longer applied.

Crimson silks draped over the looming stone archways like streaks of blood, making it look like an ancient temple from the books I used to read. Holographic flames surged from golden braziers. At four points around the lobby were stone pedestals, each one crowned with a nude woman painted with silver. It was only the subtle shift of their breathing that revealed they weren't carved from stone.

Across the lobby, I saw a golden-skinned man in a sharp white suit with two petite Vaera women trailing after him. Their skintight red outfits covered their arms and legs while leaving their bottoms bare, and I could see something twinkling between their cheeks.

At least I wasn't overdressed.

Odensrah led us down a long hallway, similarly decorated in fake stone. It struck me as odd that they had built this technological marvel in the depths of space only to recreate an ancient structure with the most rudimentary materials. Quiet, rhythmic music played from speakers, and there were plush red settees here and there. At one of them, an elegantly dressed woman sat with one leg kicked up on the opposite arm while an oiled male servant knelt with his face buried between her thighs. I noted, with dismay, that there were thin red welts across his back.

Past that, we walked into a large, round chamber that seemed to be the center of the station. At the center, another living statue posed on a high pedestal. A dozen silver cages surrounded her. They currently stood empty, but it didn't take a rocket scientist to know what they were for. A staircase spiraled around the outer perimeter, while several hallways branched off from the chamber.

I glanced back at Ember, expecting to find him drooling over the naked woman. But he was surveying the room intently, his gray eyes alert and moving rapidly. I tried to follow where he was looking to make sure we captured everything on video.

Odensrah led us down the left hallway, where a faint red light glowed from a doorway. The low hum of conversation and music rose as we approached. At the bottom of a short staircase was a crowded lounge. The darkened area was filled with plush couches and low tables. A hostess in a sheer white toga approached. Gold powder dusted her cheekbones and collarbones, gleaming in the low light.

Before handing us over, Odensrah gave me a brief look, then glanced at Mistral. "Would you like to store your pet for the moment?" He gestured to one side, and I could see through an archway to a line of silver cages. A scantily clad woman was inside the first one, her head bowed.

"Is it standard?" he asked.

I fought to maintain my bland expression. Being locked up wasn't a big change from the months I'd spent on the Basilisk, but I wanted to be close to Mistral. That was the safest place in the universe as far I was concerned.

"It is your choice, sir," Odensrah said. He gestured broadly into the bar. "Many patrons choose to keep their pets with them."

"Mine pleases me too much to be far from her," he said.

"Very good, sir," Odensrah said. "Argent will escort you to a table. While you enjoy a drink, I will transfer the information regarding your suite to your comms. When you're ready, simply activate the message, and you'll be guided to your suite. Enjoy your evening."

Without speaking, the woman in the toga beckoned and led us deeper into the lounge. The noisy clank of glasses and buzzing conversation was a stark contrast to the quiet of our travel for the last few days.

Mistral held my hand lightly while he sauntered through the area. Ember was close behind me, his hand at my back. Off to our right, several men surrounded a large table, where a half-empty bottle of liquor stood between their glasses. One of them was leaning on one elbow and listening to another, while a slender male vigorously sucked him off. His hand rested on the man's head, but he seemed utterly unfazed by having a conversation while someone serviced him.

At another table, a pair of women and three men spoke. One of the men had a pretty Vaera woman in his lap, wearing nothing but a tiny pair of panties. He toyed with her breasts like he was fiddling with a stray thread. Though she wore heavy makeup, I noticed the discoloration around her eyes and the sharp lines of her cheekbones, hinting at malnourishment more than great bone structure.

A large table at the middle of the bar seemed to be the heart of the party. At the center of the round table, a brass brazier held a holographic projector producing an illusory orange flame. There were several empty seats, but I froze, though Mistral continued to walk.

Sitting at the opposite side of the round table was Vehr Arandon. Milla stood behind him, her eyes fixed on something galaxies away. Arandon's eyes lit up at the sight of Mistral, and he beckoned. "Mr. Delthe, come and join us," he said warmly. I bowed my head, but not before I caught a glimpse of Thenoch, sitting at a table nearby with another rough-looking human. They must have been sent to the bodyguards' table.

At Arandon's invitation, Mistral approached, though he took a seat further around the table from him. Ember took one of the empty seats near Thenoch, giving me the faintest smile before turning away.

Before I could take my seat in Mistral's lap, Arandon said,

"And look at his lovely pet, recently purchased from my stable. He saw her and simply couldn't wait until the auction to purchase her. I'm sure you can see why." A dozen pairs of eyes turned to me, and I suddenly wished I had opted for normal clothes. "Helena, give us a turn, would you?"

I glanced at Mistral. He nodded slightly, and I turned around for them. Then Mistral placed his hand at my back. That tiny gesture was a comfort, a reminder that this was just an act. "She is very lovely," Mistral said. "And quite satisfying."

"Excellent," Arandon said. He tapped Milla's arm and flicked his hand toward Mistral. "Pour Mr. Delthe a drink."

"You're very generous," Mistral said, folding his big frame into the chair. I perched on his lap and leaned against him. Milla's eyes were wide as she approached us to pour him a drink. I didn't dare speak to her, but I wanted to reassure her.

Too bad we hadn't come up with nonsense language for *everything is okay and we're about to turn all of these jerks into the authorities so you can go home.*

There was a round of introductions, and I made sure to follow Mistral's gaze to each one as he repeated their names. I was shocked that there were two women. One had her own servant kneeling at her feet, while the other seemed to be accompanying her partner, a golden-skinned male with brilliant blue eyes.

"As I was just telling Mr. Takkarat here, there should be quite a selection tomorrow," Arandon said. "Only the finest merchandise from me." He leaned in. "I hope you're prepared to bid, Mr. Delthe. There's a brothel owner from Nocyria who has his eye on my other little Terran jewel here."

The implications of his words and what they meant for

Milla made me nauseous, but she didn't even flinch. Mistral's body tensed beneath me, but his voice was calm. "It will be no object, Mr. Arandon," he said politely. "As pleasing as I have found this one, I will be more than happy to pay very well for another. Her skin bruises easily, so I'm also in the market for something that can withstand a bit more intense activities. One of my own kind, perhaps. You told me you could arrange such a thing."

"Ah, of course," Arandon said. "If you'll give me just a moment." He pulled Milla down, whispered in her ear, and she flinched before scurrying away.

As they blustered, I found myself wondering at how civilization could spread across dozens of galaxies, maybe thousands, and there were still misogynist pigs no matter where you looked. Knowing there were people like Kharadine and her boss, Jalissa, who seemed to scare even Mistral and Ember, gave me some hope. But just once, I would have liked to show up fully clothed with a nearly-naked Mistral on my lap wearing nothing but a diamond-encrusted sock on his dick.

The thought of it made me laugh, and I pretended to sneeze to keep from attracting attention.

"I've been summoned," a booming voice announced. Mistral's hand dug into my thigh painfully, and I pressed my hand to it, lightly prying under his fingers.

Standing next to Arandon was a big Zathari male, with bright silver hair slicked back between tightly curled, ram-like horns with silver jewelry on the tips. He wore an asymmetrical jacket that crossed over in front, exposing a scarred chest and left arm. The raised scars on his arm were neat and precise, like they'd been carved. And behind him, on a thin silver chain, was a female Zathari. A sheer red dress barely covered her body, which was painted with intricate silver designs. Her face was partially covered with a mask of crimson leather, sealing her mouth. Her pale eyes were full of anger, though she was calm.

At the sight of Mistral, the big man gave a little bow. "Cousin," he greeted as he approached. "Daerathis Locke."

Mistral offered his hand. "Adalon Delthe," he said. There was something strange in his voice. "A pleasure."

Locke took a seat across the table, then tugged on the woman's leash. His jovial tone went harsh as he barked, "Kneel." Her lavender eyes drifted up to Mistral, then narrowed as she sank to her knees. In an eerie shift, Locke's voice went right back to that rich, pleasant timbre. "Arandon says you're in the market for a Zathari pet, yes?"

"I am," Mistral said. His voice was thin, and I realized his muscles were trembling beneath me with rage.

"I have to warn you, they're ferocious," Locke said, slowly twisting the woman's braid around his hand until she had to crane her neck. "It's a challenge to break them, but the triumph is so sweet."

"And how do you capture such ferocious creatures?" Arandon said. He gestured to me. "Humans are easy enough, but certainly the Zathari present a challenge."

Locke chuckled. "Ah, it's like any prey. Bait the trap properly and they'll come to you. The poor beasts are stuck on the shit heap of Sonides. When they're old enough to realize there's a world beyond their precious slums, they're desperate to leave." He shrugged. "So, I offer them a chance."

"They sell themselves to you?" Sparrek, one of the Vaera men, said incredulously. "Some sort of contract?"

The Zathari man let out a booming laugh. "Hardly. But they leap at the opportunity to leave for refuge on Irasyne. They pay a deposit, and we take them off Sonides on their own dime."

Listening to him be so glib about taunting these women, about dangling a better life in front of them only to sell them into slavery, made me furious. But my anger was nothing compared to the heat rolling off Mistral. I slid my hand into his jacket to rub his chest gently.

Locke glanced up at Mistral. "You know, cousin," he said. "There's nothing quite like grabbing them by the horns and steering them wherever you want them to go."

Mistral's pupils were dilated wide, his breathing accelerating. Beneath the table, veins protruded along his clenched fist. "And how long have you run this operation?"

"Ah, what's it been now? Fifteen years, I think," Locke said. "Never too many at a time. I deal in other merchandise as well. But I've refined my model. I can pick one of them up and have her ready to sell in six months."

"And their men don't stop you?" Mistral asked. "You and I both know how protective our kin are."

"Ah, well, you know how the Dominion is," Locke said. "As far as they're concerned, Zathari men are brutes and thugs. Easy enough to get them out of the way. There's always work to be done on Kilaak."

When Mistral's body shifted, I was sure he was going to lunge across the table and kill the other man on the spot. I was tempted to let it happen, but instead I whispered in his ear. "Don't blow this," I said, curling my hand around his jaw. I kissed his cheek and hoped that I was enough to calm him. "It's not worth it."

"Well," Mistral said calmly, plucking my hand away from his face. "I do look forward to seeing your merchandise tomorrow."

"Very good," Locke said. His dark blue eyes drifted to me. No matter how handsome he was, his eyes were cold and cruel. "It seems your pet could use a bit of discipline. Very rude to interrupt the men talking."

Mistral chuckled. "With all this talk of mouths and training, she wants to go back to our suite and suck my cock. Why would I punish such eagerness?" He patted my thigh. "But I'll certainly teach her not to interrupt."

But Locke was still glaring at me. His unwavering stare sent a chill down my spine. "Perhaps you are satisfied, but I am not. An unruly creature needs discipline." He crooked a finger at me. "I will show you how to control those outbursts." He grabbed the female Zathari's braid and yanked her to her feet. Her face creased with pain as he gestured to the contraption covering her mouth. "Easy enough to shut them up."

"You will do no such thing," Mistral said calmly. "Surely you don't intend to insult a potential customer by implying a lack of skill or competence. I will conduct my affairs as I see fit."

Locke stared at me, and I knew that if Mistral wasn't there, he'd have had me bent over and sobbing in front of the whole bar. I was tempted to stick my tongue out, just to drive home the fact that he couldn't touch me, but I wasn't sure he would stand down. Instead, I bowed my head and mumbled, "I'm sorry, Mr. Locke."

"What was that?" he asked.

"Go ahead," Mistral said, gently tipping up my chin. "Speak up."

"I'm sorry for interrupting your conversation, Mr. Locke," I said. "It won't happen again."

"Such sweetness," Arandon said, giving me a strange look, as if he was afraid I was going to blow his potential sales. Then his eyes alit as a well-dressed Vaera man sauntered by. "Ah, Lord Edymeri," he crowed. "Gentlemen, meet an old friend of mine."

The hours passed in a blur of introductions and smarmy conversation with despicable men. With each introduction, I turned to look, capturing their names and faces on camera before averting my eyes like a good little pet. I was chilled to the bone with each passing minute, with the casual way these people talked about buying and selling living beings like we were no more than animals. When it was just Arandon, I thought maybe it was just a human thing. Maybe the Vaera viewed us as inferior and saw no difference in keeping us than I would have with keeping a housecat. Though I certainly wasn't dressing up a housecat in skimpy leather and making it serve drinks.

But these people didn't stop at humanity. There was Daerathis Locke, bragging about how he scammed women who could have been his mother or sister. There was Arandon with his Vaera servants. There were even women here, apparently unconcerned with any vague notion of sisterhood. We met a man who was looking to stock his brothel with high-quality products, as he tried to rival the business at Niraj. If I heard one more man refer to us as inventory, products, or pets, I was going to scream.

The only thing that kept me sane was Mistral. There were some nasty comments, and suggestions of ways he might use or punish my body, but he always deflected it in a way that protected me. And he always had one hand on me, gently reminding me that he was still Mistral, not this foul façade.

Locke finally excused himself. "If you're interested in a show, there's a Zathari girl in the live show later," he said, raising his eyebrows. "Shall I save you a seat at my booth?"

"Perhaps I'll join you later," Mistral said. He cupped my chin. His blue eyes bored into mine. "But I made a promise to teach this one a lesson on how and when to use her mouth. It may take a while."

A wicked smile crossed Locke's face. "I'm sure there are patrons who would enjoy seeing it. A space could be arranged."

"I don't share," Mistral said. "I assure you, her behavior tomorrow will more than sufficient to show you that she's learned a lesson." He nudged me up and beckoned for me to follow him out of the bar.

Ember closed in behind us and whispered. "To your suite?"

Mistral nodded and swiped at his watch. A red arrow appeared on the display. We followed the directions through the station, up an elevator, and down a winding hallway to room 19. Mistral scanned his watch against it, and the door hissed open. He glanced at Ember. "Make sure no one followed us." Ember nodded and headed back into the hall.

The suite was massive, with more faux stone and crimson furnishings. Past the foyer was a sitting room with several lounges. One door led to a smaller bedroom off to our left, and another door at the back of the room was still closed. Several bags were set outside the closed door, while the hard-shelled suitcases carrying Kharadine's equipment were deposited in the middle of the sitting room.

As soon as Mistral closed the door behind him, he let out a

heavy sigh that turned into a growl of frustration. He wriggled out of his jacket and threw it on the nearest couch, pacing as he shook out his arms. The vigorous motion looked like he was trying to fling mud off his limbs. "I fucking hate these people," he said. "I hate that you had to sit there and listen to that."

I kicked off my high-heeled shoes and let out a sigh of relief. While he paced, I curled my toes into the fluffy rug and winced at the cramps in my feet. "It's worth it if this works."

"I guess. I need a shower after that. And the fucking Zathari. I'm going to break his horns off and shove them so far up his ass that he spits them out again." He pinched the bridge of his nose. "I should get back out there to see what I can learn. I just need a minute to breathe." He bumped the closed door with his hip, then froze. "Oh. Well."

I tucked myself under his arm and saw why he'd stopped in his tracks. "What the..."

Inside the bigger bedroom, it looked like a warehouse of sex toys and dungeon furniture. There was a big bed with loops and hooks all over its posts, and a wall rack crowded with all sorts of leather implements, from cuffs to whips to impossibly huge phalluses. A strange, hot pulse awakened between my legs. I wouldn't have imagined myself the kinky type, but I was definitely curious and up for experimenting with Mistral.

"Did you ask for the kinky upgrade?" I teased.

"I think it's standard," he drawled. Then he gave me a hungry look. "See something you like?"

I smirked. "I see a lot of things I like. Didn't you say you needed to punish me?"

His jaw dropped, and he gently cupped my face. "That was an act."

"I know, silly," I said. "I was kidding."

He kissed my lips gently. "I need you to know that. You are...I feel stupid just saying you're wonderful. It's offensive. Like calling the sun bright. And I never want to hurt you."

"Mistral, I know all of that was an act." The tension on his face eased. Then I jerked my head toward the door. "You and Ember probably have work to do. And I need you to help me contact Kharadine to make sure everything gets back to her."

"Mm," he said, coming in for a kiss. "You're right. So dutiful."

I put a finger to his lips. "Go get your work done, Mr. Delthe. And then we can play."

CHAPTER 16

Mistral

THE HARDWARE ON THE WALLS WAS DOWNRIGHT INTIMIDATING. Still, the thought of exploring with Helena sent a surge of heat to my groin. I wanted to make love to her, to feel something sweet and pure after the depravity of the men in the bar. I wanted to wrap her up and shield her so that her world was small and safe.

But there was work to be done, and I owed her my best work outside the bedroom before I could enjoy her inside. I reluctantly left her to undress while I joined Ember in the sitting room. Using Kharadine's loaned equipment, we set up the signal jammer to prevent people from listening into our room. Then we scanned the furniture, the light fixtures, power outlets, everything I could think of. We found nothing, but it only made me worry that the builders of Erebus were much cleverer than I had hoped.

"We should get back out there and sweep the place," Ember said. "Leave Helena here for now. The drunker they get, the worse they'll behave."

"I was planning on it," I said. "How did I do?"

"Pretty good," Ember said. "But you better get your temper locked down. If we see Locke again, Helena won't be there to distract you. And I'm sure not going to kiss you and calm you down."

I hated it, but he was right. "Send a message to Kharadine and have her come and sit with Helena."

He nodded. When Helena emerged, she wore the soft purple robe again. She looked more at ease now, with her hair down and pinned back from her face.

Heat bloomed in my chest at the sight of her. She was so good out there, I could hardly believe it. The way she'd swallowed her pride and apologized to Locke, the way she'd watched my body language closely enough to know when I was on the verge of screwing everything up...she was amazing.

She brought us her earrings and hairpiece. "Do you need to upload these to Kharadine?"

"She's going to come and wait with you when we leave," Ember said.

Helena frowned. "You're going back out?"

I nodded grimly. "I want to get my eyes on the entire station, maybe meet anyone that wasn't in the bar earlier."

With a nod, she padded over to a small kitchen in the corner of the suite. Then she moaned in delight as she pulled out a big tray of sliced cheese, fruits, and sweets. She plucked a folded note card from the center. "For Mr. Delthe and companions," she read. She chuckled and bit into a big hunk of cheese. "Correction. For Helena and herself. You two can go now. I'm happy."

"I'm offended," Ember said. She lobbed a berry at him, which he caught easily before devouring it whole. "Slightly less offended. You better leave some for me."

"You're not my boss," she teased.

Ember looked to me expectantly, like a little child looking for his mother to intervene.

"Eat it all," I told her with a little laugh.

"Dick," Ember muttered.

Helena crooked a finger at him as she sat on the couch with her tray, and he eagerly joined her. He was uncharacteristically patient, waiting for her to pick out a handful of treats before he dug in. She glanced up at me, then to the empty space next to her. "I was thinking…what if you could get a message to Milla? Or to Locke's Zathari girl? She looked miserable. Surely she'd help you."

Joining her on the couch, I took a plump berry from the tray. "I wish we could. I'd be concerned that they're bugged or that they'd accidentally let something slip. Every person we involve is a chance to blow the whole thing."

"I guess that means Vehr Arandon can't have an unfortunate accident tonight," she mused. My little mercenary.

"Kharadine is rubbing off on you," I said. I squeezed her thigh. "We've got to behave. We don't want anyone getting paranoid and pulling out of the auction."

A few minutes later, Kharadine arrived with a bag over her shoulder. She glanced around the room, then settled onto the couch and opened a portable computer. "I dropped the crawlers while you three were enjoying yourselves," she said drily. "They're on the move. Got one in their security office doing its thing."

"Enjoying ourselves is a stretch," Helena said. She held out her jewelry for Kharadine. "I got as much as I could."

Kharadine nodded appreciatively and took a little wired tray from her bag, then connected it to her computer. She set the jewelry in the tray, eyes glowing as she typed rapidly. Then she looked up. "You can go. We're fine here."

She might have been an underling, but Kharadine had Jalissa Cain's imperious attitude down pat. As far as they were concerned, the Diamondbacks reigned at the top of the food chain, followed by everyone else in the universe. "Keep the doors locked. Let us—" I started.

"Mr. Delthe, if someone that isn't you comes through that door, they'll have me to deal with," Kharadine said without looking up. "I've got this. You can go."

My hackles were raised as Ember and I left the room. I hated having Helena out of my sight, but I liked the idea of her locked in with one of Jalissa Cain's girls. If Kharadine had to choose between saving my life or Helena's, she wouldn't even think about it.

Ember stayed at my side while we made a circuit of the main floor. I estimated we'd gone about two-thirds of the way around the ring when we reached another stone archway blocked by heavy red curtains. Ember pressed one of them aside, then froze. A uniformed Vaera male stepped through with one hand resting on his gun. "May I help you, gentlemen?" he said brusquely.

"My apologies," Ember said. "I was looking for the bar for Mr. Delthe. We must have gotten turned around."

The guard glanced at me and smiled faintly. He gestured behind us, hand in a firm bladed gesture. "Continue back the way you came. We do have a proprietary app to aid in navigating the station," he said pointedly.

"Thank you," I said smoothly. "Come along."

We explored in the other direction, passing the dark glass doors that led to the landing bay, and further past that. Like at Vuola Lire, there were a few small boutiques with jewelry, clothing, and more sex toys. There had to be more dildos on this station than actual dicks.

In the center of the shopping area, a vidscreen displayed directions toward the spa, the observation deck, and the amphitheater, where the much-discussed live show would take place. The arrow gave way to a short video clip featuring writhing bodies, leaving no question what the show was. Ember nudged me. "The rest of them are probably there," he said grimly. "I'm not saying I want to, but…"

"I can't do it," I said. "Helena could have been in this place if circumstances were different. And I will lose my shit if I walk in and see a Zathari woman getting fucked for an audience. Seeing that woman on a chain with Locke was bad enough."

"Agreed. I wouldn't stop you, and all of this would be for nothing." He cleared his throat. "I want you to know that I'm not trying to steal her."

"What?" I asked.

He looked embarrassed. "Helena. She's beautiful, but I'd never make a move. I know she's yours, but I do like being around her."

My heart thrummed at that. Was she mine? "I appreciate that, but she's her own person. You don't need my permission to be around her," I said. "I think she likes you, too."

His pained expression smoothed into an easy smile as we continued walking. I wouldn't deny that a primal, possessive instinct awoke in me when I saw the way Helena laughed with Ember, but it wasn't the same way she looked at me. He wasn't taking anything that was mine any more than a tree was taking the sun from a blooming flower. His affection for her pleased me, because he would protect her if she was in danger.

At the opposite end of the ring, we found another curtained archway, where we were turned away by another firm but polite guard. In my mind I sketched a rough layout of the station. About one quarter of the circle was inaccessible, likely comprised of maintenance, security, or private rooms.

For such a secretive place, there were relatively few patrolling guards. I supposed that the security kept most of the undesired element from ever landing on the station. I was also certain there was security in plain clothes throughout the entire station.

We spent another hour circling the station, then stopped at a small bar tucked away near the observation deck so it wasn't quite so obvious that we were doing reconnaissance. This job might be the most important thing I'd done since we escaped from Kilaak. And back then, we had all the time in the world to plan, along with more than a dozen half-unhinged Zathari with violence to spare and no innocent bystanders. I had twelve hours, Ember, and a pretty little human who needed my protection.

Staring out at the endless sea of stars beyond Erebus, I

prayed to the Wayfarers that I was competent enough to pull this off. Everything I cherished depended on it.

CHAPTER 17

Helena

I FROZE, MY INSTINCTS TAKING OVER WITH THE KNIFE TO MY throat. *What now?*

"Go into the elbow," Kharadine barked, pushing against the back of my head. I lunged, nearly choking myself in the crook of her elbow. The dull cheese knife skimmed harmlessly off my skin, and I dropped my weight to flip her over my shoulder. She let out a *oh-woah!* sound as she sailed over me and landed on the plush carpet. Her violet eyes flashed as she smiled up at me. "Good girl."

Still breathing hard, I offered my hand. "Thanks. That was fun. When do I get a knife?"

"Let's not get ahead of ourselves," she said, gesturing to her gun on the table. "No need to get that close if you've got a gun. This is defensive. For someone like you, you're already in trouble if they get in close."

"Someone like me?" I said irritably.

Her head cocked. "Someone who isn't trained to kill. Quit taking it so personally and be realistic. Even if you were trained, someone like Mistral would break you in half if he got his hands on you. This is for an emergency only." Then she put the knife down and beckoned to me. "One more time on the choke, then we'll work on a simple groin shot. Dicks are easy targets."

There was an instant of instinctive panic as she grappled me again, but I shoved it down. As I was twisting in her grasp, the door slid open. Suddenly, I was tumbling to the floor amidst a chorus of shouts. My blood was practically boiling with adrenaline when I rose to find Ember pinning Kharadine to the ground. His big hand pinned her throat to the ground, but she had a knife—a nice sharp one, not the cheese knife—at his groin. His gray eyes were wide and panicked, and he was making little choking sounds.

"Hey!" I exclaimed. "I'm fine. She was teaching me self-defense."

Mistral trained a gun on Kharadine, his blue eyes narrowed with murderous intent. His eyes drifted to me.

"Look at me. I asked her to teach me something," I said calmly. "No one's hurting anyone."

Ember glanced at Mistral. Then Kharadine kneed him in the groin, shoved him off, and scrambled to her feet. In a blur, she grabbed the gun and leaped over the couch, putting half the room between her and the Zathari. Ember rolled onto his back and groaned, his eyes closed in pain.

"You're okay?" Mistral asked me. He was breathing hard, his eyes still fixed on Kharadine.

"I'm fine," I said.

"Overprotective, idiot males," Kharadine muttered. She raked her loose hair back. "She's fine. Thanks for babysitting, Kharadine. Thanks for flying across the fucking universe, Kharadine. Thanks for—"

"Thank you, Kharadine," Mistral said. He holstered the gun and offered his hand. "I'm sorry. I didn't expect to walk in and see that. This place has us on edge."

She scowled and waved her hand dismissively, not taking his offered handshake. "Anything new?"

"Not much," Mistral said. "Got the lay of the station, but it seems that most of the traders were at the live show. We didn't go in."

Her brows arched, but she just nodded silently and walked up to him and unfastened the camera from his lapel. Ember scowled at her and took off his jacket, tossing it over the couch for her. After she took off the bug, she gathered her belongings and left silently.

When she was gone, Ember retrieved a towel and filled it with ice, pressing it to his crotch. "That was fucking dirty," he complained.

"That was impressive," I said. "No offense to your dick."

He glared at me. "Full offense to my dick. We saw you in trouble and reacted."

"You left me with her," I said. They exchanged a look, but I waved it off and pointed to the kitchenette. "Ember, I ordered you dinner. House special, and it smells really good."

His angry expression melted away, and he limped over to peek under the silver tray. His gray eyes widened. "Helena, you're my favorite human," he announced.

"How many do you know?" I said.

"Enough that you should be flattered," he replied.

Mistral glanced at me. "We're going to retire. And yes, Ember, I mean fucking. You need anything else?"

He was already digging into the massive dish of stir fry, picking out a hunk of meat. Then he glanced at our bedroom door, shook his head, and took the tray into the other room. "I don't need to hear you in there," he said drily. Then he crowed, "Holy fucking shit, there's a hot tub. And bubbles! Fuck yeah." The door slammed, and we heard the rush of water.

"He's a simple man," Mistral said. "Good call on the food."

I just smiled up at him. "That's why I'm his favorite human."

"He has good taste," he said, leading me into our room by the hand. "Too bad for him that you're my human." He closed the door behind me, then held my wrists lightly. "Are you up for this? After being here, I understand if you're not. I just need to be near you."

I grasped his face and kissed him. "I was ready to drag Kharadine in here and tell her to pick a toy if you didn't come back soon."

"You might get more than you bargained for with Kharadine," he said.

"I was counting on it." He laughed and lifted me easily, then carried me back to the bed. His big hands stroked my thighs as I slowly unbuttoned his crisp gray shirt. "What did you see out there?"

His expression faltered. "Mostly security. Not many patrons. They were probably at the live show, and we couldn't do it."

I cocked my head. "Why not? It's for the job."

"Because I don't think the women here are doing it by

choice," he said, frowning. "Like that Zathari woman. I can't have that in my head, even for tactical reasons. Watching it feels like complicity."

My throat clenched, and I gently cupped his face, tracing his cheekbones with my fingers. "You are such a good man," I murmured.

His brow furrowed. "I don't know that I am."

"Is this your 'I'm a bad man, Helena' spiel again?" I asked. "We've been through this."

"No. I just…" He sighed and shook his head. "This isn't what you wanted tonight. We were supposed to be having fun."

I gently combed my fingers through his hair, prompting a soft smile. "We have time. What's going through that pretty head?"

"My pretty head?"

"Sooner or later, you'll accept that you're hot," I said. Despite his somber mood, a smile flickered across his face. "What's going on?"

"I've done some bad and some good in my life," he said. "But finding you and coming here feels like it's the most important thing I've ever done. For the first time, my choices are making an impact on someone else for the better. If we pull this off, it's going to do more than line some rich asshole's pockets. This matters."

"So why are you so gloomy?"

"I'm not gloomy. I just know that when this is over…" He stared at me for a long while. One big hand covered mine and pressed it to his cheek. "When we leave here, I'm not going to be the same. You've changed me, and I don't know how to handle things being different."

In the wake of his words was a strange resonance, like church bells echoing through a stone sanctuary. There were volumes he wasn't saying, and I was afraid to let myself dream of hearing it clearly. If he turned me away, I would certainly never heal.

And I did it anyway, because he was right. This mattered. I took a breath, bared my throat to him, and prayed he wasn't going to rip it out. "Are you going to take me with you after this?"

"Do you want to go with me after this?"

"Absolutely," I said, without an instant of hesitation. "I don't know what you'll do after this, either, but you don't have to do it alone."

"Really?" he asked. "You trust me?"

"I do. And if you're a bad man, then I like your kind of bad." He smiled, and I gently stroked his brow. As my fingers grazed that velvety soft skin around his horns, he sighed happily and closed his eyes. "Can I give you some advice?" He nodded. "Worry about tomorrow when it comes. What you're doing—"

"What we're doing. You're important, too."

My chest swelled with pride. "What we're doing is tough. And you need to have your head in the game tomorrow. You can't be worried about what happens afterward."

"And for now?" he said quietly.

"For now, just be here with me. Is there anything that we can do to help Milla or Locke's woman without endangering them tonight?"

"I've thought in circles around it, and I can't figure it out," he said.

I nodded. "Then we've done what we can for tonight. And

tomorrow will be a new day. Can you let Mr. Delthe wait outside, and just be Mistral with me right now?"

"I can handle that." He took my hand and kissed my fingers lightly. "After this…" he hesitated. "Things will be better. I promise."

I peeled off my loose shirt. Mistral's eyes ignited with desire. "I think they're pretty good right now," I said. "Especially with you under me."

His eyes drifted up, and I followed them to an elaborate system of rails above the bed. Several big metal rings hung from thick chains. "You like me under you, huh?"

"What are you thinking?"

"I'm thinking I want to tie you up and devote all of my attention to you," he said. "What do you think?"

"I think I'm ready to be the center of your attention," I said.

Ten minutes later, I was wondering what I'd gotten myself into as he laid out loops of deep red rope. I fingered one of the loops and found it soft and silky. He laid out a pair of scissors next to it, then took my hand lightly. "Do you trust me?"

"I do," I said without hesitation. "Will it hurt?"

"It shouldn't," he said. "Unless you want that, but I don't particularly like causing pain. But the thought of your body wrapped in red bows is quite appealing." He kissed my brow. "You tell me to stop if you get scared or anything hurts."

I nodded. "Tell me what to do."

"Let me take care of you," he said.

He slowly pulled my hair into a ponytail, his fingers grazing over my scalp. Then he gently pushed me onto my back and grasped one ankle to bend my leg. He kissed the insides of my thighs slowly, then started to loop the soft rope around one leg.

His deft fingers tied a knot along the outside, then formed a new loop. When he was done, my leg was tightly bound from knee to ankle, with a line of intricate knots and a pretty red bow at one end.

I was already on fire, wet and warm when his fingers brushed my sex before tying my other leg. He was in no hurry, and I found myself enjoying the constant skimming of his hands. It was like watching an artist at work, and I was his masterpiece of woven scarlet. When he was done, he gently grasped my arms and lifted me, so I was kneeling on the bed. "How do you feel?"

I wiggled my hips. "A little helpless."

"That's the idea," he said. Then he circled behind me and brought my hands behind my back. His warm lips blazed a line of kisses from the nape of my neck as he wrapped the rope around my wrists. There was a delightful comfort to the restraint.

"Okay?" he said quietly.

"Yes," I murmured.

"You are so beautiful," he said, wrapping the long tail of rope over my shoulder and around my chest. The warm rasp of his hands and the slide of the rope ignited a rolling blaze in me. Loops of rope went around my upper arms and my chest, and I was secured. He slid his fingers under the loops and tugged. "Feeling okay?"

"Yes," I said. "What are you going to do now?"

"Touch you," he said. His big arms looped around me and pulled me back to him. Then a blindfold covered my eyes, plunging me into darkness. He kissed my ear, then my throat, as those big hands explored me and brushed away the lingering fear. "Just breathe with me."

I felt the expansion of his broad chest, his heart pounding against my back. I let myself relax into him. He rubbed my shoulders, eventually sliding his hands around to tease at my nipples. The feel of his hands sent a lightning bolt straight to my core, and I instinctively pushed my chest into his grasp. He chuckled against my ear. "How do you feel?"

"So good," I said. The rope hugged me tight, the pressure of it strangely reassuring.

"Nothing hurts?"

I shook my head. The realization that I could go nowhere, do nothing to get away from this, was immense. I breathed deep, and when I exhaled again, I released a lifetime of struggle and grief and frustration. Thirty-two years on a desolate planet, and after the worst stretch of my life, I was flying through the stars with Mistral. I was weightless, floating through some strange place where all I had to do was feel.

And I felt so good. It had taken so long to find this that it nearly broke my heart to think of what I had lost along the way. How many days and months and years I had been without this, without him. There had been a yawning emptiness in me, a decades-long drought, and he was pure, clean rain.

Tears trickled from my eyes.

"Helena, what's wrong?"

"Nothing," I murmured.

"Then why..." His finger traced my cheek, so gently, and I let out a soft sob. "I'm cutting it. You have to tell me if it hurts."

"No!" I protested as he shifted away from me, breaking that sweet, warm contact. He slid the blindfold off, and then there were two beautiful blue eyes filling my vision, one ringed in that oddly pale scar tissue. Fear filled his eyes as he cupped my cheek. "You're not hurting me. I promise."

"Then what's wrong?"

"I've never felt like I could just let go. And I can't believe I'm here with you and that anything could feel like this."

He smiled. "What do you want me to do?"

"Can you just hold me for a while? You make me feel safe," I said. His entire demeanor shifted, as if something illuminated him from within.

"You can have anything you want, Helena," he said roughly. He held up the blindfold, and I nodded. He gently slid it over my eyes again, then kissed my cheek. "I'm right here."

"Thank you," I whispered. He continued to explore me, but one arm remained tight around my chest, anchoring me to his body. It went beyond sexual, although my body was on fire. My head was swimming, and I felt like my mind was going somewhere beyond my body, soaring out into space.

Back on Earth, no one rushed in to save me or dry my tears. Everyone had their own unbearable loads, and they couldn't pick up someone else's. I'd tried sometimes, and shamefully, there were times when I knew someone else needed a hand, and I simply couldn't do it. I'd looked the other way and hoped that someone—not me—could help.

So I didn't know what to make of Mistral, someone who would step in to save me, someone who would devote himself to my pleasure. And not just my pleasure; he had prioritized my security, my safety, my comfort. Just because of who he was, not because I had earned it. He had space for me. It seemed impossible, and yet it was right here in front of me, all around me where I couldn't ignore it.

My chest tightened again, and I wondered what the universe had in store. I didn't want to go back to Earth, and I didn't want to go anywhere without him. But we were so different; once we were out of this strange situation, surely he'd realize he didn't want me around to complicate his life. And the thought of standing on solid ground, looking up at the night sky and knowing he was out there somewhere without me…it was enough to break my heart.

"What are you thinking about?" he asked.

"How good you feel," I said. I tried to lighten my tone. "And how good you are with your hands."

He chuckled. "I think you're hiding something."

"Just worrying about silly things," I said.

Then he kissed my cheek. "Then I'll distract you."

The bed shifted. I was suddenly alone, and cold without his blazing hot skin at my back. Then he lifted me, and I squeaked in surprise. When he set me down, my ass landed on warm skin, and then I realized—

"Holy shit," I squealed as his tongue parted me from below. I tried in vain to rise on my knees, but I was right where he wanted me, with my pussy at his mouth. His tongue swirled against me, spearing into me as I clenched rhythmically. "Holy…"

"Mm," he agreed, his voice vibrating against my most sensitive places. As the flat of his tongue caressed me, I wriggled in vain, but he just hooked his arms over my thighs and held me there at his face and ate me like I was the sweetest dessert.

The sensation washed over me, rhythmically at first, then chaotic as climax started to tear its way through me. I rolled my hips against him, and he growled, vibrating up into my body.

White-hot pleasure twisted up through me then, pulling my whole body taut. My muscles strained against the rope, and they pushed back, as if to say *there's nowhere you can go. You're with him, just accept all of it.*

I didn't want to go anywhere else or be anywhere else. I just wanted to float here forever, caught in his gravity and drawn closer until there was no escape.

My whole body clenched in anticipation as he gently untied the loops on my legs, one at a time. "Are you okay? Tell me how your hands feel."

I wiggled my fingers. "I'm good. I'm so good," I whimpered.

He laughed and put one finger into my hand. "Squeeze and tell me."

I squeezed it and said, "It's fine."

"Good," he growled. Then he lifted me up easily, reminding me of that massive strength, and put me on the ground. "Feet." When I planted my feet, he wedged his foot between them and kicked my legs out wider. I shivered as he bent me over the bed, planting one hand between my shoulders. "Is this too much?"

"No," I whispered. "I want you so badly."

"Do you want me to fuck you, Helena? Bent over, bound, blindfolded?"

I wiggled my hips at him. "Please. Don't leave me like this."

His head nudged at my entrance. I shivered in anticipation, trying to wiggle myself back onto him, but his hand kept me pinned to the bed. He was gentle but unyielding as he stroked me and teased his cock against me. Then he slid in slowly, so big and warm and solid, and I whimpered with sheer desperation. Finally, we were anchored together. As I lay there at his mercy, my heartbeat matched the pulsing of the *dzirian*, as if we were sharing a pulse.

One hand curled around the ropes at my back and tugged them a little tighter. I groaned in pleasure. "Beautiful little rose," he said, withdrawing with agonizing slowness. "The way you squeeze me drives me fucking wild. Tell me what you want."

"I want you," I said. "I want you inside me. Please."

He took it slow and deep at first. With each stroke he thrust upward, finding the perfect spot inside me as he nearly lifted me off my toes.

As I murmured in soft, whimpering nonsense, he fucked me harder and faster. I felt his hand start to rise, like he was going to check on me again. Damn his concern. I blurted, "Don't you dare stop!"

He let out a growling laugh, and he gave me exactly what I asked for. It was magnificent, and I was flying through the abyss. He rocked into me, so hard and deep, and there was nothing to hold me except for him and his powerful hands. His bindings held me tight and made me weightless at once, and I surrendered to him.

You're not going anywhere. You won't fall apart.

Before I knew what was happening, something hard pressed to my clit and vibrated. The shock of it made me squeal, and he let out a rich laugh. "Surprise."

"Oh shit, oh shit," I whimpered, rising on my toes. Then I couldn't speak, just whining and begging in wordless moans. It was within reach, if I survived long enough.

"Helena, you don't have to be quiet," he said, breathless as he rocked into me. "Let this whole fucking place know you're mine. Let the whole universe know."

"I'm yours," I said breathlessly. "All yours."

"You first, rose," he said, slowing his pace as he increased the pressure of the vibrator. Something terrible and wonderful unfurled in me, reaching sharp claws down my legs, and I was suddenly glad he was there to hold me so I didn't explode into a thousand pieces. I pressed my face into the bed and screamed until my throat hurt, letting out all the frustration and anxiety and grief of the last year of my life. Pleasure ripped and burned through me, leaving something pure and clean in its wake. There was Mistral and only Mistral left. Then there wasn't even him, just a raw feeling of *good beautiful hot wet pure*.

His hands planted on either side of me as he thrust into me and stayed, letting out a deep groan as he finished. As I clenched tight around him, drawing it out of him, I had the strangest flash of an image in my head. I could see my own body, flushed pink against the red ropes, with stone-gray hands splayed over a bowed spine. Everything was fiery heat and hunger.

Then I snapped back to myself, where my breathing was ragged and quick, almost a sob as I came back to reality. He tugged lightly on the rope. "Do you want me to take it off?"

"Not yet," I murmured. He withdrew and joined me, lifting my head to lay on his thigh. I couldn't see him, but he loosened my hair and stroked it gently. "I meant it, you know."

"What?"

"That I'm yours," I said, glad I couldn't see his face. My whole body was still pulsing rhythmically, and I could feel his seed, warm on my thighs.

His hand paused. "Helena, you're your own."

"I know, silly," I said. "But I can be yours without losing me, can't I?"

He was quiet for a while. "I hope so." I drifted in and out as he gently stroked my hair, following the line of my shoulder. Eventually, he shifted and untied me slowly. With each loop undone, he kissed my skin gently. There was a burning ache as my shoulders were freed, but he immediately gathered me into his arms and held me tight. I lay there for a long stretch, just listening to his heartbeat, feeling the rise and fall of his chest. "I'm glad you said that."

"Why?"

"Because it makes me feel better about wanting to kill all those assholes who looked at you," he said matter-of-factly.

I chuckled. "Murder is so romantic."

He let out another rich laugh. Then I finally opened my eyes to gaze at him. Sweat trickled from his damp hair, and he looked half-drunk with those hazy blue eyes. I slowly traced the outline of the scar on his cheek. Pain flickered through his expression, so I lifted my hands instead to touch his horns. "Only downside of having my hands tied," I said. "I couldn't do this."

"You keep doing that, and I'm going to bend you over again."

"Oh no," I said. "I should definitely stop. I'll do that any second now."

He grabbed me and pinned me to the bed, sealing my lips with a ferocious, bruising kiss. "You are such a gift, Helena." He kissed my forehead. "Tomorrow might get ugly."

"I know," I said quietly. "Can we not talk about it for now?"

"Just for a moment," he said. He gently stroked my cheekbone. "I want you to know that no matter what happens, I will keep you safe."

"I know you will," I said. His eyes were still concerned, so I stroked his brow. Then I pushed on his chest. "Lay down. Let me take care of you."

"Naked back massage?"

"I'm a simple girl," I said as he rolled over, letting me climb onto his hips. His back was streaked with sweat, but I liked seeing him messy and unpolished. I dug my hands into his shoulders, and he groaned. "And just think. Once we've rested, we just have to get up and get out of here. And then things will be better."

"So much better," he said dreamily. "Meaning?"

"You know what that means, Mr. Delthe," I teased. I smacked his ass. God, he had an ass like a stone statue.

He wiggled underneath me. "Watch it."

"Oh, I'm watching it, and the view is great," I said. He laughed, and I continued working at his muscles. "I'm just thinking that it would be a shame not to try a few more of those things before we fly out of here with our asses on fire."

"Mm," he groaned. "We can try whatever you want. Always."

I liked the word *always* on his lips. I liked the promises he made, and I knew that he would do his best to keep them. But as the glow faded, and he drifted into a soft doze, I realized that it might not be up to him. We were drastically outnumbered, and there was a good chance that we'd fail. Once all these people went their separate ways, we might never find them.

I tried to reassure myself. He was going to do everything in his power, and so would I. And if the full force of the Dominion couldn't stop this, then it wouldn't be for lack of trying. Our efforts had to mean something. One of these days, the good guys had to win.

I was still lost in thought when a big hand closed on my wrist. "Are you back there thinking?" he asked.

"Maybe," I said. Suddenly the world spun, and I ended up on my back with a big, beautiful man staring down at me.

"We can't have that," he murmured.

I smiled. "I can think of a few ways you could distract me."

He gave me a wicked look. "Oh? Show me one," he said.

"You first."

CHAPTER 18

Helena

A SHRILL ALARM PIERCED THROUGH MY LOVELY, DREAMLESS SLEEP. I groaned, then smiled as I realized a big warm arm was anchored around me. At the sound of the ring, the arm tightened around me. "Just a few more minutes," Mistral grumbled into my neck.

He was breathing heavily within seconds, but a fist pounded on our door. "Hey, you sex fiends, wake up!" Ember chirped. Though I had come to really like Ember, I wouldn't have minded if Mistral shot him through the door.

Mistral growled. "Fuck off!"

"Time to get up," Ember said. "If you don't come answer the door, I'm coming in with a bucket of ice."

"I'm going to dump him in space," Mistral complained. He kissed the back of my neck, then rolled out of the huge bed.

"I'm coming." He yanked the door open, naked as a babe. "What?"

"You have an auction time yet?" Ember asked, apparently unfazed by his friend's nudity.

"Still waiting," Mistral said. "Give me twenty minutes to shower and work up the willpower not to kill you." He slammed the door, then glanced back at me. "I'm sorry."

I gave him a slow look up and down. "Oh, I don't mind the view," I teased. Unlike Ember, I was thoroughly fazed by the sight of a naked Mistral.

He headed for the bathroom, then stuck his head out. "Are you coming?"

"Not yet," I muttered. I slid out of bed and practically skipped across the cabin to meet him.

His mouth slanted to mine for a kiss, but he held me at a bit of a distance. "I don't have the time to take care of you properly," he said. "Because Ember is a fucking fiend for punctuality. I guarantee he's got a timer going."

"Mm," I said. "Then I'll just look forward to celebrating this being over." He smiled at me, a genuine, sincere smile that was different from his *I'm about to put my hands on you and remove your panties whether you like it or not* smile, and different still from his *I hate this, but I'll smile so I don't bite your eyeballs out* smile. My experience was limited, but I liked to think this warm, soft smile was only for me.

We showered quickly, and I enjoyed washing his broad, muscular back a little too much. Somehow, my hands kept drifting down to cup his stone-carved butt. It was just right there, begging to be touched. Turnabout was fair play, and I had to remove his hand from its mission between my legs, warning him that I would never forgive him if Ember burst in here while I was riding the Mistral train to Orgasm City.

I sat on the edge of the bed and watched him towel off. God, I could have looked at him all day and never gotten tired of it. "Mistral, can I ask you a personal question?"

He glanced over his shoulder. His fingers slowly massaged a gleaming oil around his horns. There was something so charming about watching him get ready. "That's alarmingly open-ended."

"I really appreciate that you're taking all of this so seriously," I said. His eyes narrowed. "And I know this is important work. But is there a specific reason it's so personal? I thought you were going to kill Locke last night."

"I wanted to," he said calmly. He pawed through his bag for a pair of sleek briefs that hugged his powerful thighs. "Locke is hurting Zathari women, which is personal."

"And that's all? Species solidarity?" I knew damn well that wasn't all, and I hoped that he was going to take my hand instead of pushing me away.

He was quiet as he tugged on a dark undershirt that clung to his muscular frame, then sat on the bed next to me. "No, that's not all." He traced the back of my hand idly, sending a shiver up my arm. "When my brother and I were young, we lived on Sonides. Do you know much about it?"

"Only that the Zathari are from there, and what Locke said last night," I said.

He scowled at that. "It's where the Zathari originated," he said. "They say it was beautiful once. But it all fell long before I was born, and old Sonides only exists in memories now. The Aengra Dominion did what they do best. They wanted our planet, and they fought long and hard to take it. In the end, my people were betrayed by the Raephon, and Sonides fell under the Dominion's rule. These days, it's a sovereign planet with a Dominion puppet in charge. You can either swear loyalty to the Dominion, or you can scrape by in the slums. Not hard to guess which we were."

"That sounds hard," I murmured. And all too familiar.

He shrugged. "Things were difficult, but we didn't know any different. Our father was arrested when we were still in our mother's belly. That's relatively common in the poor neighborhoods, so we grew up with half a dozen mothers and aunts who made sure none of us went hungry. But when we were thirteen, someone took our mother." His voice deepened. "We were helping her and a friend carry food back from the market, and someone jumped them. Big men with helmets concealing their faces came out of nowhere and dragged them off. They dropped smoke grenades that filled the whole market, and then they were gone in a blink. All I remember is half of the code on their vests. We thought maybe it was a Dominion raid, but the format of the code doesn't match any of their ID systems. But in the end, it doesn't matter. Someone took her away, and we never saw her again."

My heart ached for him. "I'm so sorry. That must have been devastating."

His gaze was somewhere far away. "She wasn't the only one, either. They took a dozen women just from our neighborhood, some barely more than girls. They never returned."

"Do you think it could have been Locke?" I asked quietly.

He shrugged. "If he's telling the truth about how long he's been in business, it couldn't have been. That was twenty-four years ago. But it could have been someone like him. As soon as I found out someone was stealing Zathari women, I was furious. But it never occurred to me that one of our own would do it, and the fact that he does it by offering them refuge..." He sighed. "My mother wanted to take us to the refuge on Irasyne. If someone had promised her a new place to go, she might not have looked too closely. Especially if it meant getting my brother and me somewhere better."

My eyes stung. "I know that feeling."

He nodded, then leaned over to kiss my temple. "I suppose that's why I felt so strongly about helping you. I doubt Locke took my mother. But he's taken someone else's mother. Someone's sister. Someone's daughter. And—"

A fist pounded on the door. "Time's up!" Ember shouted.

"Just a minute!" We both bellowed in unison. At that, Mistral chuckled and clutched my hand, bringing it to his lips for a kiss. "And now you've seen my soft underbelly."

I teased at his flat stomach, scratching it like I was petting a fluffy kitten. "Not too soft." I hesitated. "Is that how your face was scarred?"

"That's another entirely different mess," he said. "For another time." He sighed and rose, but I tugged on his hand. His eyes were solemn when he looked down at me.

"Thank you for telling me about her. I know it hurts," I said quietly. "You mentioned before that her name was Adiya. Is that right?"

He took a breath, then hesitated. "That was her nickname that she shared with others. Zathari don't share their true names with people outside of their intimate circle. To know someone's name is to own part of them, and we don't take that lightly." The sting of rejection threatened to overwhelm me, but he leaned in and kissed my forehead. "But you are my *sharhanass* now. You are in *my* circle."

"I am?" I asked.

His head tilted, and I was fascinated with the way the light gleamed over the onyx curve of his horns. "Aren't you?" There was more of a question there than he was saying aloud.

"I'd like to be," I said. "I think this is more than just playing dress-up and some really great sex, isn't it?" Wasn't it? I watched my hope hanging in the air, threatening to shatter into a million pieces.

His slight nod was overwhelming. "It has been some really great sex, but yes, it's more." We both laughed nervously, and he rested his forehead against mine. "My circle is very small, but I would like you bound in it. Her full name was Adiryet." There was such love in the way he said her name, even as pain flickered in his eyes.

"That's beautiful," I whispered. I wanted to know his name, to have the confirmation that he felt for me what I felt for him. But I held my tongue.

He cupped my face gently and kissed my brow. His lips blazed a path to my temple, to my cheek, and finally to my ear. "I trust you to keep this safe."

I nodded silently, trying not to burst out of my skin.

"Vethylas Khel," he said quietly.

Overcome with warm joy, I just wrapped my arms around his big frame, squeezing tight as I shaped the name within my mouth, holding it safe within the warm confines of my body. The whispering sounds of it fit my quiet, serious Mistral, somehow strong and reserved at the same time. I didn't know all of his traditions, but I knew this was a monumental expression of trust. "It's a beautiful name. And I'll keep it safe. I promise."

"I know you will. And I'm grateful for you," he said quietly. He kissed the top of my head. "When you're dressed, come join us."

I felt buoyant as I pondered my clothing. Since Mistral appeared in my life, I had been living in each moment, set on getting to the next step toward...what? Toward returning to my old life? Healing what had been broken inside of me?

I wasn't sure what my future held. I wanted all of this ugliness of slavers and Erebus to be over, but I liked my adventures with Mistral. And I suspected—and hoped—that he had just given me not only his name, but a promise.

Loose pants and a modest robe were a nice change after having my body on display yesterday. After braiding my damp hair, I emerged from the bedroom to find Ember and Mistral sitting on the couch with a domed display projecting a colorful screen. I was unsurprised to find a big breakfast spread already laid across the table. Ember was gesturing with one hand and clutching a pastry in the other. There was a platter of meats; some familiar, like sausages, and others I didn't recognize. Half of it was gone already, no doubt in Ember's gut. I had to marvel at how much the man ate while managing to remain whipcord lean. He glanced up and smiled at me.

"How's your dick?" I asked.

He choked on his pastry and coughed violently. "Helena!"

"What?" I teased. "I'm a medical professional, and you were injured."

"Do you want to look at it and give me your opinion?" he replied.

"Ember," Mistral said sharply.

"She started it," Ember protested.

"I did," I said with a laugh. Ember just shook his head at me as I took a flaky pastry and perched on the edge of the couch. "Any update on the auction?"

"Eight tonight. It's six now," Ember said. "I just told Kharadine to make the call."

My stomach twisted into a knot. "Then we've got to get moving. I'll pack my things."

He nodded. "As soon as she confirms that the message was received, we'll go."

Could it really be this easy? One night of discomfort and forced smiles, and we'd bring the whole thing toppling down after a leisurely breakfast?

Of course it wouldn't.

I knew it wouldn't be that easy, because the universe had never worked together quite so neatly. It had thrown me a bone with Mistral stumbling into my path, but that was the only freebie. My suspicion was confirmed when we received a message from Kharadine. The message was short; just a video that said, "We've got a huge fucking problem. I'm on my way to you."

Five minutes later, she stormed into the suite wearing her dapper black suit. Though she was dressed to kill, her braided hair was disheveled. "Jammers on?" she barked.

"Everything's on," Mistral confirmed. "We're secure."

Kharadine paced. "I sent the message and got a confirmation of receipt." She threw up her hands. "But when I started preparing the Impulse for launch, the hangar crew came and told me to shut it down."

Mistral frowned. "Why?"

"Because they don't allow any traffic in or out on the day of the auction, which extends for twelve hours after the auction ends." She shook her head. "I told them Mr. Delthe had a critical business emergency that needed his attention, and they told me there were no exceptions. They were already locking everything down. Everyone knows this, apparently. Excuse me for not being a regular at fucking slave auctions. I wasn't aware there was so much etiquette involved with being a walking piece of garbage."

"Probably to make sure people don't run off without paying," I said quietly.

"Who knows," Kharadine said irritably. "What I do know is that unless you want to shoot your way out right now, we're stuck until after the auction. We're not going anywhere."

My stomach tied in a knot. "Isn't there someone we can talk to? Would someone take a bribe?"

Kharadine chuckled, giving me the tiniest smile. "Trust me, I tried. I even told the security guys that Mr. Delthe would make it well worth their while to bend the rules and open the for just a few minutes," she said. "No luck." As she paced, the markings on her skin glowed bright. Loose strands of hair floated around her face, carried on that strange psychic current.

"Did you get into their system with the crawlers?" Mistral asked.

She shook her head. "I've got a 3D model of most of the station, but we didn't breach the computer system. I could have gotten in, but they'd know someone was hacking them, and they might have alerted the other scumbags to leave. I didn't want to risk it."

"So what do we do?" I asked. "Is the whole operation screwed?"

Kharadine shook her head. "The Dominion is already on their way. We're just not leaving before they arrive. I say we lock down in here."

Mistral shook his head. "We need to be out there."

"Stupid alpha assholes," Kharadine spat. "Why?"

His eyes flashed with his anger as he rose. "Because he and I are practically bulletproof. And if the assholes from the Dominion come and start shooting, we can keep the innocent safe."

"Just tell your people that we're on your side," Ember said. He tapped his fingers against his slender horns. "We're not hard to pick out in a crowd."

There was a long silence as Kharadine and Mistral glared at each other. He shook his head and said, "She won't, because Jalissa wants the credit. And if she tells them that two Zathari men are working for her, that means the Diamondbacks aren't doing it alone."

"Are you always so fucking cynical?" Kharadine snapped. She paced. "Jalissa hires mercenaries all the time. You're not special. I didn't say anything because I assumed you wouldn't want the Dominion on the lookout for two Zathari men with bounties on their heads."

Ember wrinkled his nose. "Yeah, well—" His head tilted. "Wait, really?"

"Bullshit," Mistral said.

"It's not bullshit," Kharadine said. "I know Deeprun

Dynamics would pay good money to have your heads." Both men bristled. "Believe it or not, I'm not trying to actively fuck you over. Jalissa likes you for some reason."

"She does?" Ember said eagerly. Kharadine and Mistral both glared at him. He threw up his hands. "What? It's a compliment."

Kharadine was about my size, but with the way she squared up to Mistral, you'd have thought she was unaware of the difference between them. Her presence was massive. I envied that about her. She pointed at the domed display. "Your call, boys. I'll send another message right now and tell them you're here, but if they happen to run your faces through a database, that's on you. I say you stay put and avoid it."

"That's not going to happen," Ember said. "Tell Jalissa to pull some strings."

Kharadine raised an eyebrow at him. "The deal is long done, and amnesty for a couple of Zathari outlaws isn't in it. What do you want me to do?"

Mistral was quiet. "Tell them we're with you. Just tell them two Zathari males."

"What about Locke?" I asked.

"Somehow, I think Locke isn't going to be protecting anyone when this goes down." He shook his head. "Don't give them our names. I'm easy enough to pick out," he said, tracing the scar on his face. "Locke has silver hair, which should be enough to distinguish him from us."

Kharadine sighed. "I'll make the call. I still think you should stay here."

"Noted," Mistral said.

"And ignored," Kharadine muttered. Her eyes drifted to me.

"If you're going to risk yourself, fine. But at least leave Helena here."

Without a glance for me, Mistral nodded his agreement. I put up my hands. "No. I'm going with him."

"No, you're not," he said. "There's no reason for you to be in the middle of things."

"But—"

"No," he said. "And if you think I won't tie you down to keep you safe, try me."

CHAPTER 19

Mistral

I didn't like having Helena's ire directed at me, but I far preferred it to seeing her hurt. The sting would pass. My head was reeling as we tried to regroup. Our previous plan had stopped with us getting the hell away from Erebus well before the Dominion arrived.

I wasn't stupid. Dominion soldiers would take one look at me and Ember and round us up with the others. After all, I'd been playing the part of a rich, amoral scumbag since yesterday. If we survived it, there was a decent chance they could figure out we weren't who we claimed. That would be enough for the Dominion to send us to trial for some made up offense.

But hiding away in the room was unthinkable. It was one thing to keep Helena safe, but both of us could protect the more fragile creatures onboard. Unless the Dominion came prepared with acid and rocket launchers—highly unlikely on an enclosed station—they'd have a hard time knocking us down.

Ember sighed. "Well, we can keep bitching at each other, or just accept that the plan's changed. It's like this one time when we were scouting out a new dig, and the boss was set on this nice little spot at the foot of Doryagu Mountain on Tahukal. But we get there, and there's a Reaper colony, and they're pissed."

"And what exactly do you do in that situation, bug boy?" Kharadine asked.

"Rocket fuel, flamethrower, fuck shit up," Ember said with a shrug. "Because the other option is letting those nasty bastards run up on the ship, and that's just bad because their young ride on them and crawl up inside your—"

"That's quite enough," Kharadine said sharply.

"I'm just saying," Ember said. "The situation has changed. You can cry about it, or you can light something on fire. Metaphorically." He pondered. "Or literally, I guess."

She sighed. "If you insist on going, then you need to be armed."

"You sure they're not going to be checking?" Ember said. "If I was hosting an auction for a bunch of rich assholes, I sure wouldn't let them come in carrying."

She shook her head. "You should find out."

Ember departed to dress in his bodyguard-appropriate suit, while I returned to the big bedroom to dress. Helena was glaring at her open suitcase with an expression that could have melted steel. As I passed, I said, "What did the suitcase do to you?"

"I'm not happy with you," she said flatly.

"I'm aware," I replied. "And I will survive it."

Her brown eyes were full of fury when she looked up at me. "I hate sitting in here like a helpless little doll."

"No one said you were a helpless little doll," I said. "Don't put words in my mouth."

Her lips were sealed, but I could hear her as clearly as if she had spoken. *I don't want you getting hurt. I need you.*

My head tilted. "You need me?"

Her cheeks colored. "What? I didn't say that." She grabbed a handful of fabric and perused it. Then she balled it up and tossed it back into the suitcase in favor of a white dress. I stared at her in wonder.

I know it sounds crazy, but we can communicate, Havoc had told me. I'd thought he was entirely full of shit, because Havoc was so often full of shit. But I'd had to eat my words when I watched him and Vani across the room from each other, both laughing as if they heard something the rest of the world didn't.

This couldn't be happening. Was it because I had told her my name? Or did I feel safe telling her my name because something in me knew that she was destined for me? Because when I was holding her, it was like two halves had finally become one, and it was the most natural, beautiful thing I'd ever felt.

No. Some idiot romantic had taken over my brain for a split second there, planting the idea of a starbound mate.

I sighed. "I understand that you're upset with me. But I need to protect you."

"Who's going to protect you?"

"Ember," I said. She frowned, and I gently cupped her chin. "Ember is steel and stone. You are light and music. Both valuable and important. And just as I have no intention of taking

Ember to bed, I have no intention of taking you into battle. Do you understand?"

"I do, but I still don't like it," she said quietly. "And you're saying nice things, but I'm not just light and music. I'm a nurse. I went to school to learn how to save lives, and I'm good at it. If people get hurt out there, I can help them."

"I understand that," I said. "And you can help after the smoke clears. You can't help anyone if you get hurt, too." I knew that this wasn't just about me. She was soothing the sting of her guilt and shame in whatever way she could. This was her friend all over again.

She sighed. "I'm still not happy."

"I know," I said. "You want to be distracted? We have time now."

Her lips parted, but she scowled at me. "I know what you're doing."

I took a big step to close the distance between us. Even with her at arm's length, I could feel the space yawning open. "What am I doing?"

"You think you can shut me down with your sex appeal," she said.

"I can," I said. And if she didn't seem genuinely upset, I'd have pinned her down, put my head under her dress, and proved that I could turn that brain off quite easily.

A smile played on her lips before she remembered to be mad. "No, you can't." Her brow furrowed. "I don't want to sit here worrying about you out there."

I sighed and sat on the bed, leaning back on my elbows to watch her pace. "Do you want to be selfish or do you really want to help?"

Her pretty face pinched in an angry expression. "What?"

"If you stay here and worry about me, the worst that happens is you have a few hours of uncertainty and a nervous stomach," I said. "No offense, Helena, but you can handle that." Her nostrils flared with irritation, but I continued, "I want there to be something for us after this. Don't you?"

She nodded silently.

"If you go out there with me, you will occupy all of my attention," I said. "I'm selfish, too, and if it came down to you or someone else, it wouldn't be a choice at all. So if you think that you're more important than the dozens of people we came here to save—"

"Enough," she said. Her heavy sigh turned into an adorable little growl. "Now you have to go and put logic into it."

"I'm so sorry," I teased.

She finally nodded. "I don't like it, but you're right. But you better make me a promise." I just raised my eyebrows. "Be careful. And don't do anything stupid."

"I'm a Zathari male," I said. "I can't promise not to do anything stupid. That's in our genes."

She huffed. "I'm serious."

"So am I," I said. I was suddenly buffeted with a strange, twisting sensation in my belly. My throat tightened. Helena's eyes were glistening, and she scrubbed furiously at her face. With a start, I realized that she wasn't just upset about being left out. She really was worried about me, a feeling I hadn't experienced in a long time. "I promise I'll be careful."

I reluctantly left her to join Ember in the sitting room. He looked at me nervously, his gray eyes flitting to the door and back to me. I shook my head a little and gestured to the door. "Let's go."

As we emerged from the suite, I triggered my watch to call Odensrah, our unctuous concierge. Erebus might have been a den of depravity, but they had impressive customer service. The pink-skinned Vaera was waiting in the lobby when we arrived and greeted me with a shallow bow. "Good morning, Mr. Delthe," he said. "What can I help you with? Shall I get you a table for breakfast?"

"No," I said. "I want to know what it takes to get my ship out of here."

His expression fell. "Sir, are you displeased with your accommodations?"

"They're quite enjoyable," I said. "But I received a call early this morning that I am needed as soon as possible to deal with an emergency at one of my dig sites. This requires my immediate attention."

He shook his head sadly. "I'm afraid it's auction protocol. Beginning at midnight on auction day, there is no traffic. No departures until twelve hours after the final bid and all lots are paid."

"So you're telling me I'm a prisoner here?"

He shook his head again. "I'm terribly sorry, Mr. Delthe."

"Then get me someone who can make it happen," I said. "Who's in charge of this place?"

His brows arched. "Sir, I do apologize, but I cannot provide you with a meeting with our proprietors. We offer a great many options for entertainment, and I will ensure that you are given priority to launch when we are cleared after the auction. Will that be acceptable?"

"What do you think, Mr. Iban?" I asked coolly. "Given what I've just asked, do you think that leaving a full day from now sounds acceptable?"

His pink cheeks went sickly pale. "If I can be of further service—"

"I have a question," Ember interrupted. "I watch Mr. Delthe's back. Are they going to be checking weapons at the door?"

Odensrah nodded. "There will be a security presence to ensure that all buyers and sellers are protected. You are welcome to remain with Mr. Delthe, but no weapons will be permitted."

Ember scoffed. "I don't trust your security."

"I assure you that they are well-trained," Odensrah said.

"Yeah? How many?" Ember asked. Clever man. "I saw one skinny Vaera guy that I could have broken in half yesterday. I'm not impressed."

Odensrah's chest puffed. "Sir, I assure you that our security force is quite capable of protecting Mr. Delthe. There will be at least a dozen officers assigned to the auction venue. Most of our standard security is redirected to the venue during auctions in case of heated tempers."

"You bringing in extras? I saw this real mean-looking Il-Teatha guy at the bar last night," Ember said. "He puts his hands on Mr. Delthe, and I remove his hands."

"Our standing security force is quite capable," Odensrah said. He forced a smile. "Mr. Delthe, allow me to book you a table for lunch at our chef's table. On the house, of course."

"I suppose that will do," I said imperiously. "One more thing. My companion was poorly behaved last night, and I've chosen to let her meditate on her behavior after a punishment in our chamber. How can I be certain no one will bother her? Several of your guests made quite lewd comments about her, and I will not tolerate any man touching what belongs to me."

Sarah nodded. "Yes, of course, sir. Your room has its standard security, and there will still be guards posted at the entrance to the lodging zone." He glanced at his watch. "I will make your lunch reservations, sir. Please inform me if I can do anything else to improve your day."

I turned and left him reeling, already calculating as I walked down the wide hallway. Ember walked at my side. "You want me to try to get in with the security guys? See what kind of arrangement they'll have inside?"

"I don't want you getting too close," I said. "I don't want anyone suspicious of us."

We took a leisurely stroll of Erebus, our prison for the next day. Here in the depth of space, there was no sense of time. Night and day meant nothing, but everyone silently agreed to follow Ilmarinen Universal time, so we were still in the early hours of morning. Considering how late the party had gone last night, I suspected many of the buyers would be sleeping until at least lunchtime.

I froze when we emerged into the large open area where we'd seen the cages yesterday. Though the silver constructions had stood empty yesterday, each now held a living being. I saw two human females and one male. One of the females was Milla, the woman who'd been with Helena. There was another Zathari woman, this one gagged like Locke's captive, and a rare sight, an Arrikaini woman. Two Erebus guards were posted in the area.

At the foot of each cage was a digital display giving information about the inhabitant. Planet of origin, size, and some other details I cared not to think about. The readout on the Zathari woman's cage indicated that she was quite skilled at oral sex and had her ass trained. Dread prickled down my spine at the thought of Locke forcing proud Zathari women into his "training."

I wished I could tell them all this wasn't going to happen to them. But if one of them let something slip, it could blow the whole thing.

We spent another hour moving throughout the station to get a feel for their security. Ember identified most of the weapons he could see, murmuring quietly to record notes on his watch. My watch alerted me that Mr. Iban had made us a lunch reservation. Upon our arrival, a young Vaera woman led us through the lushly decorated restaurant to a private booth with a convex window overlooking a sea of stars.

There at our private table, Ember was uncharacteristically serious. "This could be a shitshow," he said quietly.

"Yeah," I agreed.

"You think we ought to just stay in, like Kharadine said?" he asked.

"Probably."

"Are you going to?"

"Of course not," I said.

He smirked. "I take it your girl isn't happy about that."

"She's not, but she'll be fine," I said. I picked at an exquisitely rare cut of meat. "Do you believe starbonding is real?"

He looked up from tearing into a piece of bread. "Why the hell would you ask?" Then he gaped. "You think Helena is your mate?"

"I don't know. Havoc met this girl, and they're..." I shrugged. "I wouldn't have believed it was real until I saw them together."

His brow furrowed, and he set down the remains of his bread, chewing thoughtfully. "I don't know what I believe. Does it matter?"

"What do you mean?"

"If you care about her, then who cares if it's some magical mate bullshit?" he asked. "That's your girl."

I chuckled. "You keep things simple, don't you?"

"Everyone says that, but they just mean stupid," he said wryly. "And I'm smart enough to pick up on it."

"You're not stupid," I said.

"I know I'm not. The rest of you are. You all make things more difficult than they should be and wonder why you're unhappy." He reached over, cut off a piece of my filet, and ate it. "You're sitting here worried about whether she's got some cosmic connection to you when you've got her staring at you like you're a god. Beautiful woman likes you. You like her. Don't overcomplicate it."

"You really are smart," I said.

"I know. Try to keep up," he replied with a shrug.

When we returned to the suite, I found Helena and Kharadine chatting on the couch. I half expected to walk in and find Helena dressed in one of her tantalizing outfits, ready to deliver an ultimatum about going with me. But she was dressed casually, listening intently to Kharadine talking about the Loom messaging system. They'd ordered food, judging by the silver trays strewn around the table.

I waited for them to finish and acknowledge me before I

jumped in. Between a mercenary and my mate, I preferred to remain in their good graces. "Any update?" I asked.

Kharadine glanced at her watch. "Last I heard from my contact, they're on schedule. We'll get you wired up in a couple hours."

We spent the next few hours reviewing the blueprints Kharadine's crawlers had recreated. Though we were stuck on the station now, we looked for strategic points to stash the innocent bystanders, as well as several access hallways for Ember and me to get the hell out if we had to. I knew that everything would change the instant the shots started flying, but this gave me the tiniest bit of reassurance that I might not be destined for prison.

Early in the afternoon, Ember and I took another stroll around the station, where we found increased security, just as Iban had promised. The silver cages in the foyer were all full now, with interested buyers inspecting the prisoners like they were sizing up a new piece of furniture.

Eventually, we returned to prepare for the auction. I stripped down to my undershirt and donned a protective vest from Kharadine's armory. When I was zipped up, I buttoned up one of my nice shirts and let Kharadine secure a camera on one of the buttons. She held out a piece of folded red silk. "Got something for you," she said.

I watched as she unfolded it to reveal several coin-sized devices with glass bubbles in the center. "Smoke bomb?"

Her glowing eyes were mischievous. "If you need to make yourself scarce, drop it and step on it," she said. She had another bundle for Ember, who eagerly tucked it into his breast pocket. "Don't eat it, bug boy." He just laughed and adjusted his cuffs.

Kharadine nudged Ember, who followed her into the kitchenette, where they became suspiciously focused on the contents of the refrigerator.

Helena rose from the couch and took my hands. She was calm, her anger from earlier having dissipated like a summer storm. "Be careful," she said.

"I will," I agreed.

"You're going to watch out for Milla, right?"

"For all of them. Just like I promised you," I said.

"Good." Her brows arched as she lightly grasped my chin. "Just so you know, Kharadine has been teaching me things. If you don't come back, I'll drag you back. And not in a fun way."

I laughed despite myself. "I'll keep it in mind." When I bent to kiss her brow, the delightful idea that she was my mate rolled through my mind again. If we got through this and I didn't end up in prison, I had her waiting.

That was quite a promise, and something worth fighting for.

★★★

My heart pounded as we strolled through the station to the auction. Dozens of men and women milled outside the double doors. Two guards were posted there, each wearing sleek body armor and large sidearms.

Two waitresses in sheer white togas circulated through the small crowd with cocktails. As I took a short glass filled with amber whiskey, I saw Daerathis Locke looking my way. I nodded in greeting, but he approached instead of giving me the same in return.

He offered a hand, and I shook it, entertaining a lovely

fantasy of tearing his arm clean out of the socket. "Mr. Delthe," he said warmly. "My girls will be lots five, six, and eight. I recommend that you bid early, as Boss Eld Fahren from Nocyria has an eye on them. But surely you would know much better how to handle a Zathari woman."

"I appreciate your recommendation, Mr. Locke," I said pointedly. If I ended up in front of a judge, I wanted a recording with Locke's name and face on it. "I'll watch for them."

While Ember and I waited for the auction, I made small talk with several of the men I'd met last night. Most had no companions with them, which was a relief. I was biting my tongue as a Vaera woman blathered about the joys of her personal pleasure slave when a somber chime rang out. At the sound, the gathered crowd fell quiet. The double doors behind the guards opened onto a dark theater.

A golden-skinned male emerged, dressed in an oddly sharp, asymmetrical white suit. I couldn't place his origins; his skin said Raephon, but his glowing red eyes and pointed ears were something entirely other. His voice was deep and powerful when he said, "Welcome to the evening's auction. Please enter. You will find a seat assignment on your personal comms momentarily."

I glanced at my watch and found a number *11* on the face. Plush settees were arranged in arcs around the stages, each with a small digital screen on a stand. The screens displayed numbers in glowing white, and I quickly found my assigned seat.

As soon as Ember and I sat, a waitress brought us drinks. I waved her off and glanced around the room. As I did, Ember tapped my toe with his foot. I glanced down and saw him flashing two fingers. Following his gaze, I saw two guards on stage, cloaked in shadow just behind the wings. He leaned in to whisper in my ear.

"Plainclothes guy serving drinks," he said quietly. "My right." I followed his description and saw the unusually bulky human man, whose tailored jacket didn't conceal the line of the gun at his back. "And the Vaera girl at the bar."

I glanced over my shoulder to see a small bar at the back, where a tall, slender Vaera woman was pouring more drinks. As she stirred, her sharp yellow eyes were scanning the room. "Good eye," I replied. He pointed out two more potential plainclothes security, though I was sure one of them was just a no-necked human in a poorly tailored overcoat. Time would tell.

Within a few minutes of entering, the white-clad man took the stage with a dramatic flourish. "Connoisseurs, I am Nova, and it is my pleasure to welcome you to Erebus," he greeted. "Where only the most elite may offer their wares, and discerning buyers can purchase with confidence. I am thrilled to present tonight's offerings. Before we begin the bidding, my assistant insists on reminding you of protocol."

A petite Vaera woman stepped up to the stage. Her sharp black suit and tight bun were conservative and severe, clearly an effort to distinguish herself from the women being sold to pay her salary. "Each of your seats is armed with a discreet button on the left arm," she said. I glanced down and saw the round outline set into the dark wood. "All bids will increase by ten thousand credits. Once placed, they are non-refundable. All items for auction will be held afterward until payment. You will be dismissed, one at a time, from the auction space to meet me and claim your items afterward. As the auction progresses, you will find more details about each lot on your individual screens."

I hoped Kharadine was paying attention. I carefully sent a message through my watch.

Tell them to wait until the auction ends.

The Vaera woman nodded to Nova, who retook the stage. He gestured broadly. "Without further ado, I present the first lot of the evening. Lot number one is a pure-blooded Vaera female, standing two meters tall," he said. A crimson-skinned female crossed the stage, stark naked. Her heavily-shadowed eyes were wide with terror. "We'll just place it right here for your viewing pleasure."

The woman followed his instructions to stand on the stage, and a small dais rose beneath her. It rotated slowly, giving a full view of her body. The screen that had directed me to my seat now displayed a picture of the woman's face. I noticed an arrow to swipe, and I did it out of curiosity. There was a picture of a woman's sex, spread open awkwardly like a cut of meat. I cringed and looked away.

Every one of these fuckers was going down.

"Bidding begins at seventy-five thousand credits," Nova said. "May I add that she is untouched, making her quite a purchase for any eager buyer." Behind him, part of the wall brightened with a digital display of the bidding price.

My skin crawled as it rose in a series of quiet chimes to a hundred and twenty-five thousand, then slowly until it paused at one hundred and fifty-five thousand credits. Nova stepped forward. "Ladies and gentlemen, surely someone wishes to take this beautiful Vaera piece home." The bid ticked up twice more, then quieted. Eventually, a lower chime rang, and he shouted, "Sold!"

With no applause or numbers, it was oddly anonymous. I glanced around, then realized the rest of them were staring resolutely ahead. *Now* they were ashamed of themselves? When I looked back, the Vaera woman was hurrying off stage, her head hung low.

"Lot number two is a statuesque human female from Terra," Nova introduced. My stomach sank when Milla walked across the stage. Her rich red-gold hair was tied up in a bun and secured with a gold circlet. Every inch of her skin shimmered with a metallic powder that made her look like she was carved from crystal. On the screen, Milla's picture appeared with her lot number. At first glance, her expression was neutral, but I could see the profound sadness in her eyes. If not for dumb luck and a tip from Storm, my Helena would have been up there. Someone here would have bought her, broken her, and discarded her like trash. The mere thought of it made me want to tear someone's head off. "Bidding will begin at ninety thousand credits."

There was a noisy series of chimes as bidders drove the price up quickly to one hundred and sixty thousand credits. I hit my own button. Even knowing that the outcomes didn't matter, I owed Helena this. I kept pressing the button until the bidding stalled at two hundred and fifty thousand credits.

"Sold!" Nova exclaimed. A gold star appeared on my screen, indicating I'd won the auction.

The auction continued, and I found myself feeling ill. When the first Zathari woman crossed the stage, all I could think of was my mother, naked and alone and terrified in front of evil, hungry men. Wondering about her sons, praying to uninterested gods for deliverance. The first of the Zathari was a slender woman with tiny curled horns who sold for two hundred and twenty thousand credits. I wondered if she had children in Khidresh who wondered where their mother had gone, if there was an auntie who made increasingly empty promises that she would be home soon.

Next across the stage was the woman who had accompanied Daerathis Locke the night before. Unlike the others, she was escorted by a guard, and her hands were cuffed to a slender chain belt around her waist. "Our next lot is a purebred Zathari female from Sonides," Nova said. "Quite a lovely rarity. Please be advised that this particular lot may take a powerful hand to tame, but the reward is surely worth the effort."

As soon as he started the bidding, the chimes were nearly deafening. They were lining up to discipline her and abuse her. I quit watching when it hit three hundred and sixty thousand credits. Instead, I watched her closely. Her head was down, but I could see the shift in her muscular legs. I caught her sidelong glance at Nova.

No, cousin, I thought desperately.

But she was Zathari, and if there was one thing we were good at, it was fighting losing battles against impossible odds. She dropped and swept Nova's legs from under him with a swift kick. Then she lowered her head and butted the guard with her horns. He lurched backward, one bloody hand clapped over his eye. In a surprising display of strength, she leaped into the crowd, clearing the first two rows easily. Shouts and a few laughs rose as she ran for the exit.

Hating myself for it, I jumped up and intercepted her. My

fingers dug into her wiry arms as I pulled her close. She snarled at me beneath that mask, and I grabbed her braid firmly. "We're getting you out of here," I hissed in Zathari. "Don't get yourself killed before then."

"Mr. Delthe," one of the guards said, gently tapping my shoulder. "Thank you for your assistance."

I released her to the guards, who grabbed her arms. Her bright lavender eyes found mine, and I gave her the slightest nod. Her brow furrowed, and I saw her gaze slide between me and Ember. "Don't bruise her," I said imperiously. "I intend to purchase her and take her home." When I said *take her home,* her eyes flitted to me. I raised one eyebrow to punctuate it and hoped that she understood my meaning.

Despite being knocked on his ass, Nova was up again and laughing. Thanks to her display of defiance, the bidding had shot up to nearly six hundred thousand credits. I could have bought a jump ship for that. Nova raked his slick silver hair back and said, "Perhaps I need say no more. You will certainly have your hands full, but what an adventure."

The bidding continued, and the woman stared directly at me. I ignored her, hoping she would get the hint and not give us away. Finally, the bidding ended at eight hundred thousand credits.

For the next hour, they brought out men and women from all over the galaxies. People chatted and drank as if they weren't trading in flesh, and I was increasingly on edge. Around the fourteenth sale, my watch buzzed with a message from Kharadine.

25 minutes.

A chill prickled down my spine, but I maintained my

composure, already watching and making a plan. After thirty-two living beings were sold right in front of me, Nova clapped his hands. "This concludes today's auction," he said. "As my assistant explained, we request that you pay for your lots, and you will then be guided to pick up your purchase."

I checked my watch.

Onboard.

My heart raced, and I rose from my seat as if to stretch. Nova's assistant hurried out to him, then whispered in his ear. "Ah, friends, we have been informed of a potential ventilation issue to this room. I do apologize for the interruption, but may I please request that you return to your cabins at this time. You will find emergency oxygen supplies in the washroom of each cabin. You will be notified shortly when we can resume operations safely."

There was a noisy buzz of conversation around the room. Across the chamber, I saw Daerathis Locke shaking his head angrily as he spoke to one of the waitresses.

Then I heard the most terrible and beautiful sound.

Boom.

Angry klaxons wailed over the speaker system, interrupted by a female voice. "Attention Erebus passengers," it said. "Emergency. Emergency. Please return to your cabins immediately." It repeated the message. The back doors of the chamber opened. Shouts rang out in the distance. Behind us, the crowd was rushing out. Sure enough, the Vaera bartender had her hand on her ear and a gun in her hand as she followed the crowd.

I glanced back at Ember, who nodded to me. Instead of fleeing, we rose and headed to the stage, where two uniformed guards immediately put their hands up. "Sir, you must return to your cabin," one of them said, pointing to the back of the theater.

For two days, I'd been on my best behavior, pretending to be one of these assholes who had enough money to buy myself an exemption from common decency. I'd swallowed my rage and doled out my approval of unthinkable immorality.

And finally, it was over.

I tackled the guard into the stage and took the sidearm from his hip. His fist swung around to my side, but it had all the impact of a toddler having a tantrum. I switched the gun to *stun*, jammed it under his chin, and fired. He went down hard, and I looked up to see Ember standing over another fallen guard. We both clambered up to the stage, where Nova's assistant was peering out from the wings. Her hand was sneaking under her coat.

Zig-zagging to throw off her aim, I swept her legs from under her and caught her neck before she hit the ground. She cried out as I hauled her up by the hair and put the gun to her chin. "This is set to kill," I lied. "Where do you take the slaves you sold?"

"I can't, I don't—"

Ember loomed in front of her and grabbed her face with one huge hand. He ignored her whimpers and said, "Listen, lady. You're kinda cute and I don't want to crush your skull with my bare hands, but I don't have time. Where are they?"

Straining against his grasp, she pointed offstage. I shoved her at Ember. "Bring her with us."

Ignoring her protests, Ember dragged her after us as we hurried into the wings. Flashing red lights illuminated the dark backstage area, where I made out the outlines of benches and tables. The eerily calm robotic voice still announced, "Emergency. Emergency. Please return to your cabins."

A hand swung out of the dark. I caught the wrist, clipped the owner's ankle, and bore him down to the ground. Before the guard could move, I fisted my hand into his collar and slammed his head against the ground. I didn't check to see if he was awake, just rose and kept moving.

The shouts and high-pitched sounds of stun weapons was close now. We emerged from the stage area into a narrow back hallway with the austere monochrome of a staff-only area. The Vaera woman pointed frantically down the hall. "They're in 5A," she blurted. "I swear. Please don't kill me, please—"

I barreled down the hall to 5A, which was unguarded but locked. Ember shoved up the woman's sleeve and planted her wrist comms against the security panel. A green light flashed, followed by the door sliding open.

Something slammed into my chest, and I went flying backward into the opposite wall. My head swam, and I focused my eyes to see a uniformed Vaera man in the doorway with a huge sidearm. Behind him, dozens of naked men and women cowered in fright. I glanced back at Ember. "Let her go," I said. Then I grinned at the guard. "You and me now, buddy."

Mr. Delthe was somewhere back in that gods-forsaken auction house. Vethylas Khel was with Helena, a figment of a dream of who I might be someday. This was Mistral, who emerged from the hellish, smoke-filled pits of Kilaak with a flexible conscience and a taste for blood.

Planting my foot against the wall, I launched myself toward the guard and tackled him. As I stumbled into the room, another shot hit me in the back, but it found no purchase between the protective vest and my tough hide.

I fought with the Vaera man, slapping the gun out of his hand as I went for my own. I stunned him, watching as his eyes rolled back. Then something thin and hard went around my neck, and I couldn't breathe. I clawed at the cable, following the hands up to lean, muscular forearms. I hurled the owner over my shoulder and wheezed for air.

A female Vaera guard lay unconscious at my feet, a strong steel cable wrapped around one outstretched arm. I shook off the daze, but then the world went white as something smashed into my face and clipped my horns, landing in the sensitive place where bone met skin. Exquisite, blinding pain rolled through me as I fell back. When I opened my eyes, I saw Milla standing over me with a metal stool.

"You're not going to take us," she said. She was no longer distant; she was absolutely present, with fury burning in her eyes. "Not like you took Helena."

From beyond the doorway, I heard heavy footsteps, and then Ember yelling, "We're trying to help!"

I lurched to my feet and wrenched the stool from her. "I'm here to help," I rasped. Her eyes narrowed, then widened as they drifted up over my shoulder.

Before I could turn around, something bit into my ear, and the world went white.

CHAPTER 20

Helena

THE WHOLE WORLD WAS NOISE AND CHAOS. SOME WOMAN HAD been yelling, "Emergency. Emergency!" for ten minutes, while voices echoed up and down the hall. When it started, Kharadine pointed to the couch and ordered me to sit. She paced. "It's fine," she said. "This is fine."

I wished Mistral had stayed here. What if they thought he was one of the bad ones and just killed him on the spot? And while I knew I would only distract him, it made me crazy to sit here in safety while he was beyond my reach.

After another ten minutes of emergency warnings, a fist pounded on our door. I jumped in surprise. Kharadine rose and looked pointedly at me. "You stay put. If they ask you anything, you let me handle it. Got it?"

I nodded. She rushed past me and hit the speaker system. "Who is it?"

"Dominion Intelligence Force," a brusque voice said. "Under Code 34-A27, you are ordered to comply."

They gave us half a second to gape at each other before the door slid open. Two armed officers swept in, guns sweeping in a wide arc. Six months ago, I would have been overjoyed to see armed Dominion officers barging into my room to rescue me. Now I was just annoyed. Where the hell had they been when I actually needed them?

When Kharadine put up her hands, I followed her lead. "Keep your hands up. Is there anyone else in the room?" one of the officers asked.

Kharadine shook her head. "Only us." The guard approached, patting Kharadine down from neck to ankles. When he turned to me, I gave him a cheeky smile and opened my robe, giving him an eyeful of my matching purple underwear.

He gaped at me, then quickly lifted his eyes. "She's not armed."

"Please come with us," the first guard said.

"I need to speak to Watchcaller Al-Shara," Kharadine said. The guard's brow furrowed. "Right now."

"I'm not authorized to do that," the guard said.

"I am," Kharadine replied. "Call her."

"Ma'am, I have orders to move you to another location."

"We're not going anywhere," Kharadine retorted.

The second guard raised a gun. "This doesn't have to be difficult."

"We're innocent in this," I said quietly.

"Then there won't be any issue with joining us for some questions," the first guard said. "Move."

Kharadine's eyes flared, and for a split second, I thought I was about to get the action I was missing without Mistral. But she put her hands up slowly and nodded. I followed close behind her, with one of the Dominion guards on either side of us.

Outside, the Erebus station was in chaos. There were distant shouts amidst the noisy, agitated buzz of conversation. Well-dressed patrons were handcuffed to chairs and shouting about lawyers while Dominion officials scanned their faces. I looked for gray skin and dark horns, but I saw no sign of our Zathari, nor the silver streak of Locke's hair. I wasn't sure if that was a great sign or a terrible one.

The guards led us to a set of double doors. All around us were shattered glasses and the faint smell of alcohol, as if people had dropped drinks in their hurry to escape the slave auction. Inside the doors was a dimly lit theater, with a rainbow display of lights streaking across the room. There were more officials with white and red caps administering medical attention to groaning guards, but I was more interested in the unusual audience.

Dozens of shell-shocked men and women in fluffy bathrobes perched on the leather seats while a harried-looking waitress served glasses of water. There was glitter and eyeliner everywhere. Judging by the tear-streaked faces, these were the people who were being auctioned. I saw several women doing the familiar dance of unwinding tight, uncomfortable hairstyles, their faces slack with relief.

At the front of the theater, I saw a familiar head of red hair at the front of the theater. My eyes stung as I hurried toward her. "Milla," I breathed.

Her dark makeup had run in streaks around her eyes, but she was as beautiful as ever. She hugged me, lifting me clear off the ground. "I thought I would never see you again." She pulled away and gently squeezed my shoulders. "How are you? Did that awful man hurt you?"

I shook my head. "I'm fine. He's the reason that this got shut down. Have you seen him?"

"He was helping?" she asked slowly. A look of horror washed over her face.

"Yes...why?"

"I hit him with a chair," she said. "And then the Dominion officers shocked him and took him away."

My belly twisted in a knot of fury. "What? Why the hell would you hit him?"

"Because he bought you and you disappeared and then he showed up to buy me, too, and I just thought I finally had a chance to escape," she said, through hitching sobs. "And I was so tired of them pawing at me and calling me *it* and—"

I threw my arms around her. "It's okay," I said. "I'm so sorry, Milla. It makes perfect sense. I would have hit him, too."

But that wasn't the end of it. She bawled into my shoulder. Her legs went out from under her as the weight of our situation finally crushed her. I guided her to the couch and held her tight, stroking her disheveled hair. Just the way Mistral had held me, I held Milla. People stared, but they looked sympathetic, not judgmental.

"It's all okay now," I murmured into her ear. "You're safe now."

Over Milla's shoulder, I watched half a dozen Dominion officials walking slowly around the room to speak to the gathered men and women. I recognized several more of Arandon's victims from the Basilisk. Kharadine sat quietly, but her eyes were alert as she scanned the room.

"What happened to you?" Milla asked finally.

"Well...it's been an adventure," I said with a faint laugh. "I can't tell you everything yet, but the man who bought me is a good man. Ever since we left Vuola Lire, we've been figuring out how to stop this auction."

Her eyes widened. "Really?" Then she gasped, her eyes drifting up.

I followed her gaze to see the tall, slender Zathari woman who had knelt at Daerathis Locke's feet. Like Milla, she wore a fluffy bathrobe with the Erebus logo on it. I barely recognized her with her face uncovered. Her long braid was undone, letting thick purple-black waves spill over her shoulders. She crouched in front of me and asked, "May I speak to you privately?" Her voice was gentle and musical, not at all what I expected.

I nodded, then glanced at Milla. "I'll be back. Stay with my friend here," I said, gesturing to Kharadine.

The Zathari woman led me to the doors, where two Dominion officials were posted. Both were Il-Teatha, with slender, bioluminescent tendrils laying neatly against the shoulders of their dark blue uniforms. The female shook her head apologetically. "We have to ask that you stay here for now," she said, her voice deep but gentle. The rich timbre of her voice was like getting a hug made entirely of sound. "Can I get you something? Food, drink, or maybe a blanket to keep warm?"

"I must use the facilities," the Zathari woman said quietly. "I was chained up all day and have been holding it quite a long time. It hurts."

The woman's face fell, and her tendrils glowed a soft, grassy green. "Oh, sweet sister, I'm so sorry," she said, her demeanor softening. After being manhandled by Arna on the Basilisk, this woman was a delightful surprise. She glanced over her shoulder. "There's one just around the corner. The halls have been cleared, but I can escort you if you would feel safer."

"I think we'll be okay together," I said brightly.

"Yes," the Zathari woman said. "We will be only a moment. Thank you for your kindness."

I followed the Zathari woman around the corner and through a heavy red curtain that cleverly concealed the entrance to an elegantly decorated restroom. She closed the door behind us and locked it. "Aura," she said.

"What?"

"My name is Aura," she repeated, offering me her hand. I gently shook it, marveling at her strong, warm grip. "You were with the Zathari male. Tell me about him."

I was suddenly struck with a wave of jealousy. It was stupid, but I sure didn't want this statuesque beauty asking about my Mistral. "Why?"

"Because I need to know which side he's on," she said.

"He's one of the good guys," I said. "We came here to shut down the auction."

With a wince, she pressed her long, elegant fingers to her temples. "I feared as much."

"Why do you say that?"

She sighed. "At the auction, I decided to make a break for it. I hoped that I could get to the launch bay and take over Locke's ship, but if not, I would force someone to kill me in the process. Cowardly, I know."

"Completely logical, actually. I thought about the same thing," I said.

"After what Locke did to me, the thought of another filthy pig violating me was too much," she said. "I jumped off the stage and made a run for it, but your Mr. Delthe stopped me. And then he whispered in my ear that 'we're here to help' and not to get myself killed. I don't know who he meant by *we*, but I believed him."

"He was telling the truth," I said. "We were recording Locke and all the others last night."

She nodded appreciatively. "I'm glad to hear it, but the truth will not do him much good. The Dominion arrested him."

My heart threatened to burst from my chest. "Did you tell them anything?"

"I didn't know what to tell them, so I kept my mouth shut," she said, shaking her head. her brow furrowed. "I saw them take Delthe and his bodyguard, but I lost track of Locke. I'll do what I can to help you get the others free if they'll help deal with Locke."

"You will?"

"Whatever I can," she said. "Locke has more women in captivity. This was a start, but they need our help, too."

A strange shiver rippled down my spine.

Helena? Can you hear me?

I whirled around. I had to be going crazy, because I had definitely just heard Mistral's voice in a tiny, locked bathroom. Like an idiot, I peeked under my robe, then touched my ears, as if I was wearing a hidden earpiece.

Helena? Try to talk to me.

The words were faint, as if he was shouting over a hurricane.

"What are you doing?" Aura asked.

"I hear him," I said. "Shh."

Her pale eyes widened. "You hear him?"

Closing my eyes, I tried to picture his face and think back at him.

Hi. I don't know how to do this but I hope it works. Can you hear me?

I got a sense of someone *shushing* me, a brush of a finger against my lips.

You don't have to shout. Are you all right?

Yes, I'm fine, but what the hell, Mistral? Where are you? What happened?

Strangely, I felt the sensation of him folding his arms around me and breathing a sigh of relief. As he did, I felt a strange pull, like there was a string tugging at my spine.

Long story. Tell Kharadine they arrested me. I'm in our suite. Don't know about Ember.

Someone rapped on the door. "Ladies? Are you all right?" The Il-Teatha woman with the soothing voice was outside.

Aura winced. "We should go back."

I nodded and followed her out. The Il-Teatha woman's uniform read *Nabeiros*. "Thank you…Officer Nabeiros," I said.

"Sentinel Nabeiros," she said warmly. "Do you need anything? We can have supplies brought in if you're hungry." Her red eyes were curiously warm as she turned to Aura. "Or if you need medical attention. Whatever we can do."

"I think I'm fine now. Thank you," Aura said politely. She

took my arm lightly as we followed Sentinel Nabeiros back into the theater.

I was beyond confused by what had just happened. Had I somehow become psychic? Maybe being in space and jumping through wormholes in the Ilmarinen system had given me superpowers.

Aura whispered in my ear. "You hear your mate?"

"My mate?" I whispered. Not a word I'd have used, but it seemed appropriate.

"Delthe," she said. "He is your mate, yes?"

I stopped and stared up at her in confusion. "Is he?"

"Did you just hear him speaking in your head?" I nodded. "Among our people, this is a sign that two mates are starbound. It is most auspicious, a sign that the Wayfarers themselves have brought you together as fate decreed."

"What the..." I murmured.

I had a million questions for Aura, but when I returned to the theater, a male Dominion officer was waiting for me. He straightened and gave me a curt nod. "Miss...Helena?"

"That's me," I said cautiously. "Why?"

"Can we talk to you?"

"Only with my friend," I said, beckoning to Kharadine. We followed the officer up to the stage and around a corner. Backstage, there was a whole assortment of padded black furniture like the things in the cabin I'd shared with Mistral.

The officer led us into a small, tidy dressing room. Except for a large bottle of shimmering oil on the counter, it was pristine. A polite Vaera woman in a sleek uniform perched on a stool, her spine ramrod straight. "Miss...I'm afraid I only have Helena," she said to me.

"That'll be fine for now," I said.

"I'm Sentinel Saronas," the woman said. "I have been assigned to talk to you and the other victims here. I'd like to help you arrange travel back to your home as quickly as possible. Milla Townsend tells us that you're also from Terra."

I glanced at Kharadine, and she nodded. "I am."

"Can you tell us how you ended up here on Erebus?"

Out of the corner of my eye, I saw Kharadine shaking her head. "It's all very confusing," I said, hoping I sounded empty-headed. "It's sort of a blur."

"I see," Saronas said slowly. Her eyes skimmed over me. "Can you confirm that Mr. Adalon Delthe purchased you against your will?"

Kharadine cleared her throat. "We need to speak to Watch-caller Al-Shara."

Sentinel Saronas's eyes widened. "She's very busy."

"She'll make time for me," Kharadine said. "Get her on the line and tell her Kimra Vartai is calling. "

CHAPTER 21

Mistral

Things could have gone worse, I supposed. I was alive, although my head was pounding like a bunch of mercs were systematically firebombing my brain cells. I was fairly sure Milla had snapped one of my horns in half with her damned chair. Furthermore, someone had known exactly how to drop a Zathari and stuck an electric prod into my ear and shut down my brain long enough to cuff me.

Now I was handcuffed in the sitting room of my suite, with three Dominion officers glaring at me. Worse, one of them had taken my wallet and scanned my face with a 3D camera. That meant they were about to run my ugly mug through every database they had.

"For the last fucking time, I'm not one of them," I said, straining against the cuffs behind the chair. "How many other Zathari men do you have cuffed?"

The Dominion soldier paced in front of me. The patch on his uniform read *Zan Elyon*. "The foul-mouthed one that says he works for you is down the hall. That's it."

I swore. "You let Locke go?"

Zan Elyon crouched, putting himself on eye level. His crimson eyes narrowed. "Mr. Delthe, I know who you are," he said. "Your colleague Vehr Arandon told us you were an eager customer of his. You like buying sex slaves? You like beating soft little human girls who can't fight back?"

Son of a bitch. I shook my head. "It's not what it looks like. Do you have Daerathis Locke in your custody or not? Big Zathari male, silver hair?"

He shook his head. "Not that I know of."

"Fuck," I swore. "You need to find him."

"Mr. Delthe, you should worry about yourself," he said. "The Dominion has very strict laws about trafficking. And we've got you traveling with a woman you purchased from an admitted dealer, as well as bidding on another tonight."

Fucking Arandon had sold me out to save his own hide. I'd bet that he gave up every one of his customers in a heartbeat. He was probably signing a deal before the smoke cleared.

"In case you were too stupid to notice, I was trying to help them," I said, realizing even as I said how stupid it would sound to them. I shook my head. "You have to listen to me. Check the passenger list. If you don't have Locke, then you're missing one."

Zan Elyon looked me over. As he was glaring, there was a terrible shudder that rolled through the station, and the lights flickered. Another series of alarms went off, and he darted for his partner. A voice issued over the speaker. "H-Class

Dominion personnel report to launch bay immediately. I repeat, H-Class Dominion personnel report to launch bay immediately."

Of course, it was my luck that my guy wasn't H-Class. When the lights stabilized, he continued pacing in front of me. I stared at him. "Get Helena. She'll tell you what happened."

"I'm sure your sex slave that you've terrorized into submission will vouch for you," he said.

"Go fuck yourself," I snarled. Then I closed my eyes. Unless I had suffered a mental break, Helena was my mate. A starbound mate, the thing I'd decreed impossible until just months ago. I'd heard her in my head, felt the joy and relief when she heard my voice.

Helena? I need you and Kharadine at the cabin. They let Locke go.

I was hammered with a powerful wave of emotions; I felt fear and anger and lust all at once. Wayfarers above, her emotions were huge. I liked that about her, but it sure was loud in my skull.

I'm coming right now.

"Mr. Delthe, we hear you're in the fuel business. What's your company called?"

I just smiled at him and braced for the inevitable backhand flying my way. His fist barely registered as pain. "Did that make you feel better?" I asked. "You can do the other side if it helps." It would take a lot more than a pissed-off Vaera to put a dent in my hide. Maybe he'd break his hand and give me something to smile about.

He bared his teeth. "I know you're dirty."

"You don't know anything," I said. Our friend Perri had carefully built us histories that held up to normal scrutiny, but a

Dominion officer with an axe to grind would probably see through it eventually.

My only saving grace was my face. The last pictures the Dominion had were taken from Deeprun Dynamics security cameras at the mining station on Kilaak. My scars had come after, when Deeprun mercs tracked us to Vakarios and came prepared with sulfuric acid. Perri had told me several times that whoever shot me and Viper had done us both a favor by altering half a dozen key identification points. Their AI would be hard-pressed to find me based on a current picture.

I hoped.

There was a sensation of a hand brushing my neck, then my horns. I squirmed as raw desire rolled through me. I could feel a pulsing heat, like a thread that tugged rhythmically at the base of my spine.

Helena?

Almost there, I heard.

Can you not think dirty thoughts about me?

An indignant flash of anger. *I'm not. I was just thinking about being happy to see you and how...oh. I was thinking about touching your horns.*

I smiled to myself.

"What are you smirking at?" Zan Elyon asked.

"Nothing," I said. "Gas."

The door slid open, and the three officers straightened suddenly, each saluting with a rigid, bladed hand placed at their sternum. I glanced back to see an elegant looking Raephon woman in a long, blue overcoat storm into the room. "You're dismissed," she said. "Go to the launch bay."

"Ma'am, we—" Zan Elyon protested.

"You are dismissed," she said sharply.

The tugging sensation at my neck intensified, and I didn't even have to look to know that Helena had just rushed into the room. Kharadine was hot on her heels, and to my surprise, the Zathari woman who'd been with Locke. Helena headed for me, but the uniformed woman held up a hand. "You sit."

The door rushed closed. Helena said, "Can you uncuff him, please?"

"No," the uniformed woman said calmly. Her bright amber gaze was calm and unwavering. "I am Watchcaller Al-Shara of the Dominion Intelligence Force. Do you understand what that means?"

"Not sure," I said. "But I'm guessing the rest of my life is in your hands right now."

Her lips pursed into a faint smile. "Indeed. We have a mutual friend." She gestured broadly to Kharadine. "I am aware that you have assisted in this raid."

"If we're going to be honest with one another, I did a bit more than assist," I said drily. "Our mutual friend only knows about this auction because of me." I tilted my head toward Helena, who beamed. "Mostly because of her, if I'm being honest."

"Regardless, we are now in an awkward position. My people have just arrested more than two dozen individuals with intent to buy or sell sentient creatures illegally. And you are one of them," Al-Shara said.

"But he—" Helena protested.

"If you interrupt me again, I will have you removed," Al-Shara said sharply.

Helena's face turned red, but she clamped her lips shut. *I'm going to kick her in the head,* she thought. Her anger was oddly charming, if terribly noisy.

"It was an act," I said calmly. "I bought Helena from Vehr Arandon to save her. Would you have preferred that I let him keep her? You clearly were doing so much, perhaps I shouldn't have interfered."

Al-Shara gave me a faint smile that evoked a snake about to strike. "I am not an idiot, Mr. Delthe," she said. "Ms. Cage has explained what you did. And surely you understand that regardless of your justified actions, you look as guilty as the rest of these men on paper." She rubbed her brow. "This raid is very good for my department."

"Are you getting a promotion? You're welcome."

"If all goes well," she said, clearly not caring about the jab. "But things have changed. There are three passengers from the Erebus manifest not accounted for. Daerathis Locke, Arryn Zelrek, and Ilanna Sil. We believe Sil was accompanying one of the buyers and may be in hiding somewhere on the station. We identified the other two as traffickers from the video surveillance Ms. Vartai sent to me."

"Locke got away?" I asked.

"It appears that he headed for the launch bay as soon as we breached the station. He set off explosives and forced the landing bay doors open," she said irritably.

"Can't you stop them at the jump gate?"

"We'll certainly try," Al-Shara said. "But it appears that they're using a signal jammer. We've lost track of them for the time being."

I glanced at Helena. She was smiling, despite the bad news. I gave her a questioning look.

"Mr. Delthe, you have some very resourceful companions," Al-Shara said. "One of whom claims to know where Daerathis Locke's center of operations is, but she has not deigned to share that information with me."

Realization dawned on me, and I looked up to see the Zathari woman smiling at me, a gleaming predator's smile.

"I want you to understand me, Mr. Delthe," Sentinel Al-Shara said. "We rounded up more than two dozen criminals today. Even if we don't catch Locke, I will most certainly be in a new office by this time next week. But I have no tolerance for abusive men who victimize women. I will not turn a blind eye to Locke and his business."

"Get to the point," I said.

Mistral! Helena's voice snapped in my head. *Be nice.*

She smiled faintly. "I have an offer for you, Mr. Delthe," she said. "I know you and your Zathari companion are using fake IDs. Very good ones, I should add. My compliments to your counterfeiter." My mouth went dry. She folded her hands neatly. "I'm not going to ask you who you really are, because I don't care. You bring me Locke, and I will ensure that you were never here on Erebus. You bring me his business and his records, and I'll make sure you don't exist as far as the Dominion is concerned."

My ears were practically ringing. "What's the catch?"

"No catch," she said. "Take out Locke and send us a location. We'll make sure anyone else he's holding is transported safely home."

"Why?"

"Because it's the right thing to do," Al-Shara said.

"I didn't know Dominion soldiers knew what that was," I said.

Her pupils elongated into slits, betraying the dragon beneath her elegant façade. "And I hear that Zathari criminals don't know an extraordinarily generous offer when they see one."

"And if I tell you no?"

"Mis—" Helena blurted. "Mister Delthe!" she snapped. "He'll do it."

Watchcaller Al-Shara smirked at me, her reptilian eyes glowing. "Does your human friend speak for you?"

I glanced at Helena. I would have dealt with Locke either way, but I hated shaking hands with the Dominion. They had shit on my life over and over, and it was happening again. But this woman held my freedom and my future with Helena. It wasn't even a choice.

"I'll do it."

CHAPTER 22

Mistral

The Dominion wasted no time in getting us back in action. An hour after I shook hands on a filthy deal with the gods-forsaken Dominion, the Impulse was refueled and launching from Erebus and into the unclaimed wilds of the Arippa Cluster.

I'd barely had a chance to catch my breath before Al-Shara's subordinates rushed us out of the cabin and down a side corridor to the launch bay. Ember was in a foul mood, his shirt spattered with deep purple blood. The five of us buckled in tight for launch, and we were soon on a course for the Ilmarinen gate with a ticket to jump the queue on Dominion business.

I wanted nothing more than to hold Helena close, but I knew she'd have to pry me off if I got my hands on her now. Instead, I took her hand and smiled. A surge of warmth rolled over me, and I had an odd flash of pink flower petals, like I was cocooned within a massive tropical bloom.

Her voice filled my head.

I'm glad you're okay.

You too.

The Zathari woman unbuckled herself and surveyed the lounge. Then she finally offered me a hand. "Thank you for your assistance," she said politely. Despite her bare feet and bathrobe, she had a regal bearing that reminded me of my mother, who had always looked elegant even in her faded, oft-mended clothing amidst our humble home. "You may call me Aura."

"Mistral," I said.

Ember was almost shy as he approached her, offering his hand. "Ember." She shook both of our hands and nodded politely. Not many Zathari lived outside of Sonides or Irasyne, and those that did were mostly male. In the years since I'd gone to prison, I could count on one hand how many Zathari women I'd met.

"We were glad to help," I said. "I'm very sorry for the way you were treated. And I apologize for putting my hands on you at the auction."

She chuckled. "It is kind of you to offer, but you owe me no apology. You saved me from self-destruction. In return, I want to help you take down Daerathis Locke."

"Can you fight?" I asked.

She smiled at me, another of those toothy, hungry-lion smiles. "Before Locke and his men took me, I was one of the Alleymen in Olatihr," she said.

"No shit," Ember murmured. His eyes drifted over her, though it was a look of appreciation and respect, not lust.

Helena tilted her head. "What's that?"

"The agents of the Dominion on Sonides do not always see fit to protect people who look like us," Aura said. "The Alleymen ensure that our neighborhoods are kept safe by whatever means necessary."

"It means she can kill you with her bare hands," Ember said. He looked almost shy. "My younger brother is an Alleyman in Afh Saida."

"Unfortunately, it wasn't enough to protect myself from Locke," she said darkly.

"He fooled you?" Helena asked.

Aura shook her head. "I had seen Locke and his people come to Olatihr several times. They even wore odd clothing, presenting themselves as emissaries from Irasyne. But I noticed that they rarely, if ever, took men or the elderly. We respect our elders, and it would have been proper to take some of them to a kinder place."

"They wouldn't fetch a high enough price," I said.

"That's right," Aura said. "I hadn't figured it out yet, but I was suspicious, so I asked if they could bring someone back to tell us how things were on Irasyne. But they said that was impossible, because no one would want to come back to the slums after the beauty of Irasyne." She shook her head and continued, "That was enough for me. I knew that if our people were happy, they would have been willing to come back and encourage us. I was prepared to report them to the Dominion and have them investigate, but I was ambushed in the market. I woke up chained on Locke's ship."

"Fucking asshole," Ember said. "He said he'd been doing it for fifteen years."

Aura shrugged. "He must have moved around Sonides. Perhaps others got suspicious too, and he simply moved to another city. He is careful, never taking too many or visiting too often. I mourn the lives he destroyed, and I will take great pleasure in razing that place to dust. Even better if I get to kill him."

"Where is his operation?" I asked.

"He keeps a place on Rubresan," she said bitterly.

"No one lives there," Kharadine said.

Ember swore. "Fuckin' Deeprun Dynamics does. Big-ass mining operation." He glanced at me and shook his head slightly.

Anywhere Deeprun was, we didn't want to be. "Is he working with them?" I asked.

"Not exactly," Aura said. "His factory is near one of their mining sites. His primary business is upgrading jump ships. I can assure you that the Dominion will not track his personal ship easily. He can rotate identification codes without alerting the Ilmarinen system. The Dominion will be looking for a ship that no longer exists."

"Can you navigate us to his factory?" Kharadine asked. "And is that where you were kept?"

She shook her head. "He has another facility built into the mountains nearby. I know that it faces west, and you can see the Deeprun station far in the distance."

"That's good," Kharadine said. "Rossi, get me a map of Rubresan." She swept her hand over the rounded table as it lit up with a loading screen.

"And are we certain that's where he'll go?" Helena asked. "What if he goes...literally anywhere else?"

"She has a point," Ember said.

Kharadine nodded to her. "It's possible. But if he's got more women locked up, then he's probably going home to move them in case the Dominion tracks him down."

"We go to his farm," I said. "I'm more concerned about freeing the people there before Locke decides to get rid of the evidence of his crimes. Maybe the Dominion stops him at the gate, and maybe they fuck it up. Either way, I want that place shut down." I glanced at Aura, who nodded in agreement.

"Then Rubresan it is," Kharadine said. She ducked into the cockpit to begin plotting a course.

The ship's AI boomed, "Course set for Ilmarinen Gate AC B-1. With current speed indicators, expected arrival in the jump queue is nine hours and forty-seven minutes, with a jump at approximately sixteen hundred hours IUT."

The map of Rubresan had appeared on the table by the time Kharadine returned. We surrounded it, staring down at the expanse of white. Rubresan was an icy wasteland of a planet, but Deeprun Dynamics had discovered valuable fuel deep under the ice.

Kharadine glanced up. "Once we make the jump, it'll only be about ninety minutes before we land on Rubresan. We need a plan, and then we need to eat and get geared up."

I nodded to her, then gestured to Aura. "Come help us find it."

It took an hour of searching the planet for the various Deeprun mining stations. Our first two had no mountains nearby, and the third was much too small. But when we zoomed in on a fourth location, even the blurry view of the Deeprun station was enough to make Aura gasp. "That's it," she said.

"You're sure?" I asked. The image resolved, showing the familiar silhouette of a processing facility. I'd stared at a similar building for years, wondering when I would snap and burn the place to the ground.

"I stared through bars at that place for months," she said. "I would know it anywhere."

We traced a sightline from the station to the nearest mountains. And hidden there in a valley was a curiously flat, level spot. Perfect for landing ships, one might say. The darkened mouth of a cave opened onto the landing pad, and I was willing to bet money that was where Locke was holed up with his captives.

"Talk to us about what's inside," I said.

"Do you want to know about the whips and chains or the security?" she said archly.

"I want to know who I need to kill to get the rest of them out."

She smirked at me. "I tease, cousin. My apologies. It has been a long time since I had a real conversation. I have lost the art of sarcasm." She glanced at Kharadine. "Can you give me a screen to draw?"

Kharadine swiped the map away and brought up a blank white page. Aura sketched three rectangular floors, giving a rough idea of where stairs would be. She was hazy on details, but she confirmed that there were at least half a dozen armed guards on site at any given point. "I do not know about other security measures, but I know that all of the guards are armed with electric weapons," she said. "It is unfortunate, but they are very well prepared to deal with the three of us."

"Four," Kharadine said.

"Will any of the others fight if they're freed?" Ember asked.

"Possibly," Aura said. "There's at least one other woman who was an Alleyman in Khidresh. Locke's had quite a hard time with her, too. But I don't know what condition she's in right now. Better not to count her in our numbers."

I shook my head, trying not to think about what she was really saying. "If they're caged, let them stay there until the shooting stops." I winced. "I don't mean to make light of your ordeal, but the last thing we need is a bunch of terrified naked women underfoot, especially if Locke's security is armed with acid rounds."

"Agreed. They'll be safer behind steel walls," Aura said. "As far as I know, the only way in or out is through the bottom. If we block it, he has no way out."

I nodded to her. "This is very helpful. Thank you."

We spent another hour sketching potential routes for our incursion, but this was just like Erebus. It would be messy and unpredictable, and it would all be over by the time we knew what was going on. Eventually, Kharadine swept her hand over the table to clear our notes, then headed into the galley. Then I heard a noise of surprise.

With my curiosity piqued, I followed her into the galley and found Helena leaning against the counter. On the small table was a pyramid formation of protein bars and a fresh pot of coffee. "If you guys need to eat, I'll get something going," she said. Like most small ships, the galley had a reconstitutor that would hydrate dried rations. I felt a bit guilty that I hadn't even noticed her leaving.

I smiled faintly at her. "Was it driving you crazy to sit still?"

"Yes, okay?" she blurted. Then she shoved a cup of coffee at me and Ember.

Ember was, as always, much smarter than I gave him credit for. "Helena, this is the best coffee I've ever tasted. Thank you."

"It's absolutely terrible, but thank you anyway," she said.

Kharadine gestured. "There's some Sahemnar curry in Bin 4A. Put that in."

"I am sure I know some Sahemnar that would take issue with you putting their name on anything from that machine," Ember said. "But I'll eat it."

Fifteen minutes later, we had individual plates of fragrant mush. Despite the off-putting texture with its mealy lumps purporting to be rice, the taste was halfway decent, and it was good to get something in my belly. Though Ember and I had dined at the exclusive restaurant on Erebus, this was more appealing because of Helena's thoughtful nature.

Before Aura had finished half of hers, Helena made her another portion and refilled her coffee.

Thank you, I thought at her.

She glanced up from her coffee and smiled. *Don't get too used to it.*

I laughed to myself, prompting a strange look from Ember. But I ignored it, then rose and stretched. "What's our ETA, Rossi?"

"Guest passenger, we have approximately five hours until we reach the queue," Rossi said.

"I'm getting a nap. If I'm not up in four hours, you have permission to kick me out of bed," I said to Ember.

Kharadine nodded to me, then glanced at Aura. "Let's get you some actual clothes, shall we?"

I beckoned to Helena, and she followed me into the small cabin we'd shared on the way to Erebus. Our bags were stowed neatly, another little flash of that need to keep order.

I stepped toward her for a kiss, but she pulled back. What had I done? "Are you all right?"

"Are we starbound?" she asked. Her eyes were fixed on the floor.

It felt like she'd punched me in the gut. "Where did you learn that word?"

"Aura told me about it," she said, her eyes still down. "She made it sound like some sort of magical thing. And it sounds crazy, except I can hear you in my head and have a conversation with you, so maybe it's not so crazy. Or we're both crazy."

"I didn't truly believe in it until now, but yes, I think we are," I said. I perched on the edge of the bunk and took her hand lightly. My heart pounded. Why wouldn't she look at me? "Is that bad news?"

Her warm brown eyes spilled over with tears when she finally met my gaze. "Of course not. God, I hate this. Ever since I met you, it's just waterworks all the damn time. I barely ever cried until you came along."

I chuckled and patted the bed next to me. She sat next to me, her legs touching mine. "There's nothing wrong with your emotions, Helena. They make you colorful." And they made me feel strong. Honored even, that she could let herself be vulnerable with me and give me the chance to help.

"Colorful. That's one way to put it," she said with a sigh. She hesitated before meeting my gaze. "Is it good news to you?"

"That you're bonded to me?" She nodded. Something reached into my chest and squeezed so hard I thought I would burst. "Helena, I gave you my name. I think something in me knew what we were already. I have never felt for anyone what I feel for you. It's the best news I've ever gotten," I said, trying to figure out how to show her what I felt. I thought of the way we'd laid together yesterday, half in a daze from making love, just breathing in each other, skin to skin, as if the world no longer existed.

Something pushed back at me. I felt like something scratched my back lightly, then grasped my face. But she still looked so sad. "Good. I'm glad," she said. Despite her words, her voice was full of anguish.

"Helena, what are you hiding? You're sad, and I don't understand it," I said. "Are you not happy to—"

"It's not that!" she said. "It's just that now I have so much to lose. And you have to go and be a hero, and I could lose you. This was supposed to be over." Her head fell as she tried to fight tears. "It's not fair."

"Oh, sweet rose," I murmured. I gathered her into my arms, holding her tight. It was so strange to be the center of her attention, to be wrapped up in such concern and affection. "They're not going to kill me."

"You don't know that."

"I do," I said calmly. "Because if anyone tries to stop me from getting back to you, I'm going to kill them."

"But what if—"

I pulled away, holding her face firmly so she had to look up at me. "I will kill them. There is nothing in this universe that will stop me from getting back to you. Certainly not a piece of shit like Daerathis Locke." I kissed her lips gently, lingering as she opened for me. "Do you believe me?"

"I believe you'll try," she said quietly. "But—"

"Trust me," I said firmly. "I have fought through far worse things than a handful of slavers on Rubresan, and there wasn't a beautiful, brave mate waiting for me like there is now." She drew another breath to protest, but I shushed her with a kiss, teasing my tongue against hers to give her something better to do than fill her own head with fear.

When I broke away, her cheeks were flushed, and she was smiling faintly. "You know you can't completely defuse me with a kiss."

"No? Should I try again?" I said.

She sighed. "You won't let me go with you, will you?"

"Absolutely not," I said. "I want you to stay here and prepare to help the women we bring out of there. Given what Aura has said, they'll need someone that doesn't look like me to comfort them and give them medical attention."

"I could help you inside. I can hang back until things are clear," she said hopefully.

"Is this about Sarah?" I asked.

Her eyes flew open, like I'd slapped her. Even as she shook her head, I could feel the unpleasant squirming sensation of guilt that coiled in her chest. "Yes and no," she finally said.

"You know my opinion on the matter. You weren't a coward then, and you aren't one now. What you did on Erebus proved how brave you are," I said gently. Her eyes lifted to me, filled with such vulnerability. Her entire heart rested in my hands, which was a terrifying responsibility. "You walked into a place filled with evil and you stared it in the eye, even after what you went through. You did it with no weapons, no bulletproof skin, nothing but your wits. You are one of the bravest people I've ever met."

Tears spilled from her eyes, and she shook her head. "I'm not."

"You are," I said firmly. "And whether you believe me or not, I need you to stay here. Get supplies ready to help anyone who needs it. I'm no expert, but wouldn't that be safer for everyone, including your patients?"

"I suppose," she said. Her brow furrowed, and then her expression melted into one of resolve. "Okay. I can do that for you."

"For both of us. We're a team now," I said.

"We're a good team," she said quietly. I nodded and kissed her forehead. Then she gave me a wicked smile. "Did you really want to take a nap, or was that code for sex?"

I laughed. "Can it be both?"

"I hope so," she whispered. She glanced back at the cabin door, then tugged off her shirt quickly. "You better be quiet or Ember's going to cockblock you."

I nipped at her ear and whispered. "I'm not the noisy one," I said, sliding my hand under her panties, finding her already warm and wet. She was hungry and fierce as she kissed me, gasping as I slid my fingers into her to warm her up. A wave of heat rolled through me, and I realized I was feeling her desire, an overwhelming wave of heat with a biting edge of sadness to it.

She fumbled at my pants and yanked them down, staring at

me intently as she shimmied out of her loose pants. I grabbed her hips, ready to devour her like a fine dessert, but she grabbed my horns and steered me away. "I can't be quiet if you do that," she said.

"I'm that good?"

"You know you're that good," she said wryly. She slid her panties down and let them fall, revealing that beautiful, curvy body. I was already hard and aching for her as she climbed into my lap.

"I don't want to hurt you," I said.

"You won't," she said, stroking me gently. Our hands met around my cock, guiding me to the sweet warmth between her thighs. She rolled her hips against me, resting in my lap with the *dzirian* pulsing against her. Her eyes fluttered, her fingers curling into my shoulders. Slowly, she rose and sank onto my cock.

Her tiny gasp betrayed pain, and I held her hips firm. "Go slow," I whispered. I knew she wanted me, and she wanted me to be pleased, but I couldn't stand the thought of her in pain. I captured her lips in a kiss as she slowly sank onto me, until I was buried deep in her.

Her arms folded around me, her lips sealed to my bare shoulder. There was the faintest vibration of a muffled moan against my skin as she began to move, keeping me tight within her. I was buffeted with her emotions, like a blistering desert wind. I couldn't pinpoint the feeling, but I felt as if she was trying to hold me not just there between her legs, but within her arms, within her entire being. She wanted to wrap every bit of herself around me so I would be safe.

She wanted to protect *me*.

Her concern was an axe splintering through ice, and something in me split wide open with that realization. I felt like a bundle of raw nerves, more vulnerable and exposed than I had ever been in my life. Her teeth grazed my skin, and I gently pulled at her braid, forcing her to look at me. "I'm coming back to you," I whispered. "I promise."

Her gaze was intense, almost unsettling, but she nodded and quickened her pace. I let out a soft groan, and she calmly put her small hand over my mouth, capturing my quiet declarations of pleasure and keeping them for herself. That blistering intensity overwhelmed me, a white-hot wave rolling through me as I came inside her.

I dimly realized she hadn't climaxed and tried to bring my fingers to her, but she grabbed my hand firmly and brought it around her waist. Her slender arms wrapped around me so tight I thought she might crack me in half, and I followed her lead. "You didn't—" I whispered.

"I don't need to," she replied. "I need you right here with me." The pulse of my *dzirian* within her was intense, almost painful. I was drowning in a sense of need and affection. It was sharp and hot, and I realized that I no longer knew what belonged to me and what belonged to Helena. The line between us was blurring.

I was overwhelmed and confused, an unusual experience for me. I'd been with women who desired me and didn't hesitate to scream it into the night. I knew that in their way, my brothers cared for me, even if it came dressed in profanity and pointed insults. My twin loved me as ferociously as I did him, even if it sometimes felt like our arms were linked with jagged wire long embedded in scar tissue, impossible to untangle. As a child, my mother had loved us with a quiet gentleness, tucking us into bed with tales of the Wayfarers. That sense of stability was ripped away when she disappeared.

Helena was something entirely different. On the surface, she was soft and beautiful, but there was a burning intensity I'd missed until now. She cared and loved with every cell in her body. This woman was marking me as sure as a red-hot brand on my skin, declaring to the entire universe that I belonged to her.

No hesitation.

No doubt in her mind.

She claimed me as her own.

I was almost afraid to look at her, for fear that she would realize I wasn't enough for her and I would be left cold and empty for her absence. Whatever happened, I would never be the same after being touched by her.

But when I dared to meet her eyes, she was wide-eyed and vulnerable, those soft hands tracing my cheeks. "If your gods sent you to me, then they better bring you back to me," she said softly.

"They won't have to," I said. "I'll come back to you no matter what."

CHAPTER 23

Helena

Emerging from the Ilmarinen gate, I felt like my entire body had been compressed into a tiny grain of sand, then blown up in a nuclear explosion. Space travel was long stretches of boredom—though well spent when it was just Mistral and me—punctuated by short bursts of absolute terror.

When we emerged from the whirling chaos to the sight of a massive purple-blue planet veiled in thick white clouds, I was filled only with dread, not wonder. As soon as the ship's AI confirmed that our engines were functional, Kharadine gave orders to begin prepping for their incursion. Once the route was set, the others were changing clothes, leaving behind the tailored suits and bathrobes, in Aura's case, to don body armor and holsters.

Even knowing my limitations, I hated being left out. I felt frail and useless, especially as I watched Aura pulling on a snug bodysuit from Kharadine's gear. It had felt good to be a part of the mission at Erebus, to do something to help. Even though Mistral had made it clear I could help after they left, I didn't like the feeling of sitting safely inside the ship while they were all in danger.

But I also knew pouting around the ship was the last thing anyone needed, so I took it upon myself to clean up the galley, then followed behind the others and gathered their discarded clothes to hang them neatly.

"Strap me in," Ember ordered as I passed the armory. I whirled on my heel, only to see Kharadine reach over the table to tighten the buckles on a holster over his back. Completely intent on the work at hand, Mistral was checking a gun that was half my size. I'd never seen him like this; he'd always been playing a part and using his words like weapons.

His head was down, fingers moving deftly over the sleek lines of the weapon. And maybe I was objectifying him just a little, because I was quite enjoying the snug black tactical gear that clung to his perfect, sculpted bottom.

He glanced up at me and nodded. No smile, but there was the tiniest flicker of warmth in his eyes.

I wanted to be selfish and demand that he stay here. Aura had been vague, but I could put together her hints and Locke's bluster to know that she had been treated far worse than I had at Arandon's hands. The Zathari women down there needed someone bold enough to save them.

But why did it have to be him? Maybe it was my old friends anxiety and crippling dread, and maybe it was prescience, but I couldn't shake the feeling that something was going to hurt him. I felt like I was about to watch him walk away from me forever.

"Hey," Kharadine said, jerking her chin toward me. She had traded her dapper black suit for sleek tactical gear, with matte black armored plates over her chest and back. "Come here."

I perked up and headed into the armory, where Kharadine laid out two weapons. One was a stun gun, a little bigger than the one Mistral had loaned me when he left me alone in the casino. The other was an arm-length black rod with three sharp prongs on the end. She pointed to the gun. "You know what to do with this one."

"Point and shoot," I said.

She nodded, then handed me the rod. "Locke's got some Zathari and Proxilar guards. If anyone gets to you, there's a good chance that they can close on you before you get a second shot. You see one of them, you put this somewhere soft." She turned to Ember and pressed it lightly under his chin.

"Hey, you need to ask for consent before you put that on me," Ember said. "I like a little—"

"You keep talking and I'm turning it on," Kharadine said.

"Is that a promise?" Ember teased. "You can squeeze it right now if you want. Go ahead."

Kharadine scowled at him. "I'll do it."

"Go ahead," Mistral said, smirking slightly.

There was a distinct, high-pitched whine when Kharadine hit the switch. Ember twitched slightly, squinting with one eye. The smaller woman's jaw dropped. She pulled the weapon away and activated it again. Blue sparks danced between the metal contacts. "What the fuck?"

"We're built tough," Ember said. He took it, then gave me a stern look. "Helena, if you ever do this to me, I will lose my significant affection for you." He pressed a finger to his ear. "You want to drop one of us, you've got a couple choices. Inside the ear. Anything that's wet and soft." He opened his mouth wide, then pressed just under his eyes. Then with a coy smile, he put one hand over his groin. "Right in the sack. But that'll be a challenge unless you're trying to spice up your life with Mistral, and I hear he—"

"I'm comfortable doing this mission with three. Keep talking," Mistral said calmly. He nudged me, then tapped the base of one horn. "Right here in the soft spot, too."

With an agile spin, Ember grabbed one of Mistral's horns and jerked his head to the side, then pressed the rod close to his ear. "The ear is the easiest one. No natural defense. You grab a horn and pull as hard as you fuckin' can. No matter how big they are, they'll go where you steer."

Mistral pushed him off and took the rod, then handed it to me. "Gun first. If they—"

"I know, don't let them get close," I said. "Kharadine told me."

"Helena, come with me," Kharadine said. She headed out of the armory, down the hall to the cockpit. I hurried behind her. As she went, she said, "Rossi, establish temporary leadership profile for Passenger Helena. Designation Acting Captain."

"Establishing profile," Rossi said. "Please read the text on screen to build vocal profile."

When we reached the cockpit, the large display showed several paragraphs of dry text about the Ilmarinen gate system. There was also a list of commands about opening various doors and arming security. At the orders of the AI, I read them slowly and loudly, until Rossi said, "Profile complete."

"What's this?" I asked.

"You're not sitting on this ship to do nothing," Kharadine said with a faint smile. "And I want you to know you're not staying here because you're a woman."

"I'm staying because I don't have the same skillset you do," I said. "If I go with you, then the rest of you have to worry about my safety, and that's a detriment to the mission. And I'm going to be ready for medical help here."

There was an unusual warmth in her eyes. "That's right. But an extra set of eyes is always helpful. And you're going to take over the ship temporarily."

Fear rolled through me. "I don't know how to fly a ship."

She chuckled. "You don't have to. Rossi knows how to do everything. Unless the ship is so damaged that he can't function, you'll be fine. And in that case, you have bigger problems, like plummeting to a fiery death."

"Very reassuring."

"I try," she said. She pointed to the captain's chair. "Sit."

Buoyed with excitement, I took her order to sit, running my hands over the wide arms of the captain's chair. There was a trio of large flat screens with dozens of readouts. The dashboard, for lack of a better word, had surprisingly few buttons and levers, though there were several illuminated panels on either side of me.

"Once we land, we'll launch a small drone that'll let you keep your eyes on us. After that, you're going to move the ship at least one kilometer away, so that if Locke has a turret defense system, he doesn't blow the Impulse to shreds. Meanwhile, you'll maintain visual and communication. If you see backup arriving, you tell us. Anything you think is important, let us know," she said.

"That's a big responsibility," I said.

"You were a doctor, right?"

"Nurse," I said.

"Did you ever save someone's life? Keep them from bleeding out?"

I had the uniquely awful experience of holding someone's internal organs in my hands while a doctor frantically patched them up. "More than a few times."

"This is probably way easier than that, and you have Rossi to help you," Kharadine said. Her brow lifted.

"I guess I've moved up from consuming oxygen and causing erections," I said archly.

"I was unkind before. I was not wrong, but I misjudged you. I'm sorry for that," she said, offering me one gloved hand.

I shook it and smiled. "How will I tell Rossi what to do? I'm not sure of the words to use."

"Try telling him to navigate to Rubresan," she said.

I cleared my throat, feeling silly. "Rossi, please plot a course to Rubresan."

"Acting Captain Helena, we are currently on course for Rubresan. Would you like me to modify our speed or landing point?"

"No, thank you," I said. I glanced at Kharadine, then tried again. "Rossi, how long until we land?"

"We will land in approximately forty-three minutes," he said.

"Rossi is an extremely advanced AI," Kharadine said. "If

you can tell him what you want, he'll ask you the right questions to clarify exactly what he should do. He also won't let you do anything that would harm the ship or yourself. So unless you figure out how to shut him down, you can't crash the ship."

"Okay," I said nervously. "Thank you for giving me something to do."

"Don't thank me. Just do a good job." Her hand squeezed my shoulder, then she turned to shout at the men. "Get your asses moving. Prepare for landing."

I hurried back to the cabin to change into some real clothes, then quickly braided my hair. As I emerged, Mistral was headed in. He pinned me to the wall, lowering his head to kiss me long and hard.

When he broke away, I stared up at him. The words rolling through my head were terrifying. I wanted to blurt it out, but it felt like the wrong time to hit him with those three magic words. Mate or not, that was huge. He looked surprised, and I wondered if it had somehow slipped through. But he just smiled faintly and patted my ass lightly. "Get back to your seat, Captain."

"It sounds good, right?"

"Looks even better," he said appreciatively as he followed me.

When I got to the cockpit, Kharadine sat in the second seat, gesturing to the captain's seat. "He's yours right now."

I glanced at her, but she just pointed to the screen. Trial by fire, then. "Rossi, update please."

"Acting Captain Helena, we will enter Rubresan's atmosphere in approximately three minutes. Prepare for entry."

The windows of the cockpit darkened, and there was a quiet mechanical whirring as the shielding plates covered them.

I shouted over my shoulder. "Sit down and strap in," I said as the ship began to vibrate violently. My teeth chattered as I held tight to the seat. I felt like my body was turning to stone.

"Adjusting gravity generator," Rossi announced. The crushing sensation faded. "Acting Captain, we have entered Rubresan's atmosphere. Oxygen levels are slightly lower than advised. Breathing support is advised for surface expeditions. External ground temperature is currently negative thirty-eight degrees Celsius."

"What's the ETA to our target?" I asked.

"Ten minutes," Rossi replied.

"Rossi, enable stealth protocols," Kharadine said, glancing at me. "Sorry, I forgot to tell you that one."

"Stealth protocols engaged," the AI announced.

"I'll talk him through the landing," Kharadine said. "What do you do after we leave?"

"Launch the drone. Move away one kilometer." I hesitated. "Rossi, show me a map of our destination, please."

The screen brightened, showing the marked peak. I pointed to the southeast. "I'll go this way. Further from the mining station."

"Smart girl," Kharadine said. "You've got this."

Tensions were high as they finished preparing. I joined them in the central cabin, where they were loading weapons into their holsters and testing small masks that hissed air. Mistral and Ember looked terrifying, dressed in black with matte black armor plates over their chests and legs.

"Landing in sixty seconds," Rossi announced.

There was a rumble and tilt as we neared the ground. Kharadine nodded to me. "The Impulse is yours now. Go."

I glanced at Mistral, then said, "Fuck it." I rose on my toes to kiss him firmly on the lips. "Go kick ass."

He grinned at me. "Anything for you."

"Fucking get a room," Ember said with a laugh. "Helena, you got one of those for me?"

I smirked at him, then kissed his cheek. "Go kick ass, Ember."

He brushed his fingers across his cheek, then grinned. There was a strange, almost feral tilt to his smile. It evoked sheer madness, and I was glad that I wasn't on the wrong end of his focus.

I hurried back to the cockpit and took my seat. Below us, the icy expanse of Rubresan was rising fast.

Kharadine called, "Rossi, open boarding ramp," she yelled. "Acting Captain Helena has the ship."

"Opening ramp," he said.

"Here we go," I said. There was a jolt as the ramp descended. "Launch drone, Rossi."

"Displaying drone view on Screen C," he said. At my right, there was a slightly distorted view of the yawning cave mouth.

"Comms check," Kharadine said. "Kharadine." All four of them announced their names, and I saw their voice profiles appear on the screen to my left. My fingers drifted over *Mistral*, who was listed as second in command to Kharadine. Of course.

"I've got you all," I said. Regardless of what Kharadine said, I was starting to panic. Seeing their names pop up on my screen made me feel like I was holding four lives in my hands but forced to watch from a distance. It was like trying to do surgery with my hands tied behind my back.

"We're on the ground," Kharadine said. "Move."

"Rossi, close boarding ramp and set a course from this point," I said. "Can I touch the screen?"

"Acting Captain Helena, please tap the screen to indicate your new location." The map was no longer the blurry map we'd been using, but a far more detailed one.

I sketched a circle to the southeast. "Find me a safe spot somewhere around here."

"I have calculated an ideal spot that is slightly further east. Is this acceptable?" A blue indicator flashed to the east.

"Yes," I said. As the ship lifted off, I realized I was separated from Mistral for the first time in days. I'd been lonely for much of my life, even on the rare occasions I'd been in a relationship. Having him so close through all of this had been a sweet, unexpected comfort. I liked being part of a pair with him.

Be careful, I thought, focusing my mind on Mistral.

There was a sensation of surprise that snapped back at me, then a soft, warm feeling. *I will. Let's keep it quiet for a while so I can concentrate.*

Watching the four of them disappear into the dark cave mouth, I started to fret, but I caught myself. I wasn't just his little bedwarmer, although I'd certainly enjoyed our time in bed.

I was his partner now. If what he believed was true, then we were bound together by some force beyond the natural world. And I was all but certain that I loved him, as insane and impossible as it seemed.

Because of that, I was going to be as razor sharp as I was

when I assisted in emergency surgeries back on Earth. I was going to be the teammate they needed and do what they couldn't.

I've got you all, I thought, scanning back and forth between the displays. So far, we had no movement outside the cave.

"Rossi, can you detect movement in the area?" I asked.

"Yes, Acting Captain Helena," he said. "I will alert you of any movement within a three-mile radius."

Over the comms, I heard quiet breathing, then a whispered, "Two on my right." There was a noisy shout, then I saw Ember's voice profile spike. "One down."

"Two down," Aura confirmed.

I wanted to ask Mistral how things were going, but I had to trust him to do what he was good at. They were in. Now all I could do was watch and pray that they all came back in one piece.

CHAPTER 24

Mistral

Gods, I loved to fight. The adrenaline and sheer bloodlust were a welcome respite after stuffing myself into a suit and pretending to be a smarmy rich asshole. As the armored Proxilar male charged me, I planted my feet and slammed my shoulder into his midsection. By the time he hit the ground, I was already spinning around to slam my foot into his face. When he bellowed in rage, I shoved my gun into his gaping mouth and pulled the trigger. Proxilar brains splattered everywhere.

Between Ember and Kharadine, the remaining security fell like dominoes around us. The sterile, steel-lined corridors were lit by low blue light. I felt like I was climbing through a glacier. "Second floor," Aura said.

In a two-by-two formation, we hurried up the stairs. I held up my fist and listened at the door. Low voices talked. "Motion detected outside. Get Mr. Locke to the safe room," one of them said.

The fucker was here.

I kicked the door open, knocking a body over on the other side. There were shouts beyond, but I didn't care. We were in the thick of it now, and the Hellspawn didn't do subtle.

We rampaged through the second floor. Lights flashed, and there was a terrible chorus of shouts as they scrambled. I heard one of them yell, "Fuckin' Dominion's here!"

"These are all cells," Aura said as we made our way down the hall. Small glass panes allowed only a tiny glimpse within the rooms. I kept my eyes forward. I didn't want to bear witness to their indignity, and they didn't need to see a Zathari man leering at them.

Halfway down the hall, a terrified-looking Zathari woman burst from a cell, with a Vaera male hiding behind her. Heavy metal cuffs were locked around her wrists and ankles, and there was only a ragged shift hanging from her too-thin frame. A blood-red Vaera hand was curled around one of her horns, yanking her head back. There was a silver knife gleaming just below her eye.

"Just step aside, or I'll blind this bitch," a rough male voice said.

Her dark green eyes were wide and bloodshot. I put out my hand and spoke calmly in Zathari. "Don't worry, cousin. He's not going to hurt you."

Kharadine tapped my back, and I lifted my arm to let her pass. "Why don't you let her go? I might be inclined to let you leave," she said, her voice eerily calm.

"Back up," the Vaera snarled. His fingers twitched around the knife.

Then there was a strange glint as the knife started to turn away, his wrist twisting unnaturally backward. Kharadine's eyes glowed blinding white as the man's hand moved away from the woman's face. "The fuck?" he protested, staring in horror at the blade.

"Duck," I barked.

The Zathari woman dropped to her knees, and the Vaera male stumbled after her, his hand still tangled in her chains. I fired a single shot that blew the back of his skull out. The woman screamed as blood splattered her back.

I gestured to Kharadine. "Get her up. Find her somewhere safe."

With her eyes fading back to normal, Kharadine nodded. She knelt and took the woman's arm. "It's okay now. We need somewhere to hide you for just a few more minutes."

Aura joined them and said, "Sister. This floor, and the one below us, are clear." She held up a blood-spattered security medallion. "Get everyone down to the spectator's room so they're ready to escape quickly. Check every single room. Can you do that?"

The other woman looked like she might faint, but she nodded. Her eyes drifted to me, then to Ember, and she frowned. "I will. Thank you." She immediately bolted for the end of the hall and planted the medallion against the silver pad next to the door. The door slid open, and she emerged with another Zathari woman.

"Guys?" Helena said in my ear. "Uh, Helena here. A ship just landed on the pad. Either he's bringing backup or that's his ride out of here."

"Shit," I said. I pointed to Kharadine and Ember. "You go back down, make sure he doesn't leave and no one else gets in." I glanced at Aura. "You with me?"

Blood splattered her angular features, but she looked exhilarated. "All the way to the end."

Behind us, the freed woman was opening cells amidst a rising chorus of frantic voices. I let Aura lead up to the next floor. She threw the door open, then dove to the side to avoid the incoming blast of gunfire. When it ceased, Aura let out a bloodcurdling battlecry and lunged at the phalanx of guards emerging from a large room. One yelled, "Get him out!"

There were two Zathari, a lanky Il-Teatha, and a single human among them. Before I could decide, Aura raised her gun and sniped the human from the end of the hall. I snarled and lunged at one of the Zathari men. He fired a round at me, and I whirled around to take the impact with my back. There was a *thump*, as if something had punched me, and then I smelled the foul scent of a burning chemical.

"You dirty fuckers," I said.

Before he could shoot again, I lunged at him and grabbed the gun. As we tussled, Aura dove over the Il-Teatha male and kicked my guy in the back of the head. He reeled, and I took advantage to grab his horns and wrench them apart. He let out a scream of agony, and blood dripped from the base of one horn. In his distraction, I swept his legs and jammed my gun into his open mouth. One lethal blast had him going limp, his limbs twitching. I finished him with a second shot, wishing I could have made him feel half the suffering he'd inflicted here.

Aura screamed, and I looked up to see her cowering with her arms smoking. The Il-Teatha man was down, but the other Zathari laughed cruelly, ejecting a spent shell. "You forgot your place, bitch," he said. His back was to me as he took another glass cartridge from his belt.

Through the frame of his broad legs, Aura's gaze drifted to me. Then she clasped her hands and begged, "Please, just don't hurt me. You can do what you want. Just like before."

"That's right," he said, his shoulders slumping. I crept closer, then reached through his legs from behind and grabbed his crotch. He squealed like a little girl, and his knees buckled.

"Who's a bitch now?" I growled. His horns were partially filed, but there was plenty to grab onto. I seized them and twisted his head around violently. His spine disintegrated in a ripple of cracking bone, and he went limp.

I offered her a hand, careful not to touch the acid. "Get that jacket off," I said. She nodded, fumbling to get the armored jacket off. There were a few coin-sized splotches that had already eaten through, bubbling on her dark skin. Her fingers twitched, and I could tell she was trying not to complain. "Find some water. Rinse it off fast."

"I'll stay with you," she said.

"Get that off first," I said. "If it gets too deep it'll destroy your nerves and you'll lose the hands." I tapped my face. "My brother lost an eye. I was lucky."

She nodded. "In a minute."

I sighed. Stubborn fucking Zathari. Apparently it wasn't limited to men.

At the end of the hall, a set of tinted glass doors had to be the entry to Locke's office. With Aura trailing behind me, I shot both doors out in a satisfying rain of glass. The office was quiet and empty. The suit coat tossed over the chair was the only sign that anyone had been here recently.

A pitcher of water stood on the table, and I used it to douse her burns. Only a tiny whimper escaped her gritted teeth.

"Elevator," Aura said, pointing to the back of the room. There was a folding screen, but just above it I glimpsed the silver seam of an elevator. We hurried through and hit the button. "His safe room must be below."

"Fuck, fuck, fuck," Ember swore over the comms. "We took out his backup, but Kharadine's hit. Hey, babe, you gotta just put some pressure on that."

"Don't fucking call me babe," she wheezed.

"What do I do?" Helena asked. "Should I bring the ship back?"

"Not yet," Ember said.

"I can help!" Helena protested. "Making sure people don't die is literally my job!"

There was a terrible cry of pain, and I said, "Get here. Ember, get Kharadine out to the ship. Come back and join me below if you can. Helena, bring the ship to the landing pad, but let him come to you."

"Got it," Ember said.

Helena was breathless. "Two minutes!"

It was heartless, but I pushed Kharadine out of my mind. There was no room in my mind for concern. Either Ember and Helena would save her, or they wouldn't. I trusted them to do their jobs while I did mine.

The elevator was agonizingly slow as it descended. When it dinged to a halt, I pressed myself into the front corner and gestured to Aura. She followed my lead, and when the doors opened, two more corrosive rounds exploded against the back wall. I popped my head around, then back. Three rounds followed. Aura ducked low, then launched herself out of the elevator.

I followed, aiming at the first thing that wasn't a Zathari female. A Proxilar male lunged for me and caught me by surprise. He caught my collar and a handful of my pants, then hurled me back to the elevator. I slammed into the wall with a bone-rattling impact, but I bounced back up, breathing hard.

"Gonna have to hit me harder than that," I growled. Behind him, a Vaera male slumped to the ground with Aura glaring down at him.

Carved directly into the cold gray stone, the basement level was cold and claustrophobic. Three silver doors stood along the cramped hallway, with one set much wider than the others. And at the far end of the small room, I saw Daerathis Locke peeking out from the open doorway.

I raised my fists like I was going to swing on the Proxilar. His broad lips spread in an idiot smile, and he mirrored my stance. When he swung one rocklike fist, I dodged and jammed my electric prod into his eye. He went down like a ton of bricks, convulsing violently. I glanced at Aura. "Want to finish him?"

She grinned, and I left her to kill him while I barreled toward Locke. The silver-haired Zathari stepped out from behind the door with a massive weapon on his shoulder. I kept charging as he pulled the trigger, and then the fist of an angry god planted in my gut and threw me clean off my feet.

I was still reeling when I heard the *clunk* of a spent shell hitting the ground. When I eased my way up, I felt the sharp pain that all but guaranteed my ribs were broken. Still, I lurched for him. As I went, I swept up the Vaera's discarded gun and fired a corrosive round at Locke.

He turned to run into his office, but the glass canister shattered against the back of his head. He swiped one arm over the back of his head and bellowed in pain as he wiped away burnt hair and melting flesh. "Well, Mr. Delthe," he snarled, eyes wild. "Guess you wanted a piece of my business bad enough to do something."

"I brought the Dominion down on you," I said. "And I came here to ruin your fucking life. How does that feel?"

The cool, calm demeanor of Erebus was gone. He was pure fury now. He lunged at me, and we exchanged a flurry of bruising blows. Despite his bluster about Zathari men being savages, as if he was a nobler sort, he was as brutal as any man I brawled with on Kilaak. As I whirled away from him, I saw a monitor on the wall. Ticking red numbers indicated a countdown.

Fuck me.

He was willing to blow the place to get rid of the evidence. I slammed an elbow into his ear and shoved his face into the desk. "Aura! He's going to blow the place. Get upstairs, and get all the women out." She nodded and bolted for the stairs without missing a beat. "Ember, where are you?"

"Getting Kharadine on the ship," he said, breathless. "Almost there. You gotta hold on so you can kiss me later."

"Put her on the ramp," Helena said. "I'll get her inside. You go back and help them."

Sweet, ferocious woman. My mate.

"Stop the timer," I said. "You're going to kill us both."

Locke struggled against me. "I've got my way out."

There was less than three minutes on the clock. Where the fuck was he going in three minutes from down here?

"Tell you what, Mr. Delthe," he said, breathless. "Step aside, and I'll get you clear before it blows. It'll be our little secret. No harm, no foul. Except the destruction of two decades of work, but what's a little betrayal between friends?"

Two minutes.

"Stop the timer," I said, looking around the room. It was sparse and minimal, clearly not where he usually conducted business. No conveniently placed big red switch.

"Step aside," he snarled. "The switch is somewhere else."

This was a ploy, but he was my only chance of survival.

I released him and let him pass me. He bolted for the wide doors in the hall and swiped his wrist over the security panel mounted on the wall. Cool air billowed out. In the low light, I saw the gleaming line of a metal rail set into the ground.

As soon as the door was open, he spun around and drew a gun from his back. He shot three rounds at me, each of them sizzling noisily through my body armor.

"Asshole," I said. I lunged at him and bore him to the ground.

Something tremendous rumbled inside the compound. It felt like a ship with no shielding trying to re-enter the atmosphere.

"Mistral?" Helena's voice echoed in my ear. "Where are you?"

"Get the ship away!" I shouted.

"Mistral?" Ember said. "Oh, f—"

The violent rumbling was drowned out by Helena screaming in my head. Her fear was so intense I felt like I was going to pass out. My vision blurred, splitting apart with glowing screens and bloody hands.

Mistral, answer me! Where are you?

With a growl of frustration, I tried to push her away, narrowing my focus on Locke. My vision cleared just in time to dodge a blow from Locke. I caught his arm and slammed it into the stone wall to make him drop the gun. Then we fought like I used to back on Kill, just brute force, fists smashing into faces for the satisfaction of it.

It would take just one opening. I fought like I'd never fought, guarding my flank, watching like a hawk for my moment. His anger got the best of him. Throwing a wild punch twisted his torso away from me.

I slammed my foot into Locke's knee and shattered it. His shrill scream was the most satisfying sound I'd ever heard. He collapsed, trying in vain to get up on one good leg.

Sweeping up his gun, I placed the barrel at his eye. "I'm glad you got away from Erebus," I said. "This way, I get to kill you myself."

"Enjoy it while it lasts," he wheezed. "You'll be following me into the void."

One shot, and Daerathis Locke was no more. He deserved a much worse death, but I was content to leave his worthless corpse here in the ground below his cesspit of an operation. If I got out of here, I could tell Aura and the rest of the women that he would never hurt anyone again.

As I rose, the compound was crumbling. Shattered rubble burst through the open doorways and slammed into me. My feet caught, and I went down on my knees, planting my hand on the ground.

As my hand closed on the cool metal, a massive electric shock rolled through me, and the world went white.

CHAPTER 25

Helena

IF ONE MORE PERSON TOLD ME I WAS DOING FINE, I WAS GOING to stab them in the eye. I had just dragged an unconscious and half-dead Kharadine up to the ship and held her throat closed with one hand while I screamed at Rossi to power up the Caduceus emitter. Then I burst into tears because I yelled *fuck* at the perfectly nice AI and he didn't seem to care, just said *yes, Acting Captain Helena* because he had no emotions while I had all of them at once.

And just when I got the bleeding to stop, a stream of half-naked Zathari women piled onto the ship in a fluttering chorus of voices that overwhelmed my translator. And then came Ember, absolutely drenched with blood, followed by Aura, with her arms half-melted.

And no Mistral.

I called for him over the comms. No answer.

Then through our bond. No answer.

"Where is he?" I shouted over the commotion.

Ember hung in the doorway of the cockpit. Blood splattered his face, and his eyes were wild with fury. "Get the ship in the air," Ember said. "The whole place is going to blow."

"He's in there!"

"If you let all these women die for him—" Ember growled. His gaze softened. "We'll get back to him. Zathari are tough."

Aura met my eyes and nodded. "He told me to get them all out. He knows what he's doing."

Of course he did. He was being a big fucking hero and sacrificing himself. Just like I knew he would.

"Helena, you have to get us clear," Ember said, grabbing my arm firmly.

There was a lump of ice in my throat as I surveyed the scene around me. A dozen women, all bewildered and desperate. A trail of blood marked the path to the cabin where I'd dragged Kharadine to patch her up. Tears spilled over my cheeks as I said, "Rossi, launch now. Get us back to our recon spot."

"Launching now, Captain Helena," he said.

I covered my eyes as the ship shuddered, engines firing to lift us off the ground. I shoved my way through the crowd of rescued women and plopped into the captain's chair, trying to find him.

Mistral, answer me. Where are you?

It was silent for the entire short flight. When we landed with a *thump*, Rossi helpfully informed me that we had reached our destination.

Seconds later, the feed from the drone went white, and I let out a clipped cry. There was only silence. A minute later, I felt him, but it wasn't the warm comfort of his touch.

There were no words or thoughts, just sheer pain and despair, a white-hot lightning bolt right between my temples. My whole body locked up with the pain, and I tasted blood in my mouth as I bit my tongue.

And then there was nothing at all. It was so empty, the silence was almost deafening.

A violent sob tore out of me. I'd just felt him die. I had just found him, and now he was gone. The only promise he'd ever broken to me.

Ember ducked into the cockpit. "Hey, I—" He hesitated. "What's wrong?"

I raised my head, and he shrank back at whatever he saw. "He's gone."

His jaw dropped. "You can't be sure of that."

"I felt it," I said. "We're starbound, and I felt it."

His jaw tensed. "I know this is worst time to tell you this, but we have to launch. We need to get to the Gate so the Dominion can pick up these women. I'll stay behind and look for him, but you need to get the rest of them out of here."

"No," I protested.

"The ship can't stay powered up forever," he said. "If we sit here, we burn fuel. And if we run out of fuel, we'll freeze to death." He shook his head. "I know you don't want to hear this, but Mistral wouldn't want that."

"Please don't say that to me," I said. Tears spilled down my cheeks. "How can you be so cold?"

"I'm not cold. But I'm not going to put the rest of us in danger for him," he said. "You may love him, but I've known him for almost twenty years. And this is exactly what he would do."

"You don't know that," I said.

"I know that given the choice between saving a bunch of women or saving me, it wouldn't be a choice at all," he said. "I know that like I know my own name, and I think you know it too."

My chest tightened, and I felt like I was going to throw up or punch Ember in the face. Maybe both. I furrowed my brow. "Rossi?"

"Yes, Acting Captain Helena?"

"Do you have an optimized fuel setting? So we can stay on the surface a little longer and still make it to a fueling station?"

"Calculating," Rossi said. A flurry of calculations and meters flicked across my central screen. "By reducing heating and ventilation to sleeper cabins and reducing water filtration temporarily, we can remain on the surface for approximately ninety minutes before we must launch to refuel at Ilmarinen Gate AC-B1. Shall I make the adjustments?"

Ember shook his head. "Helena, please. I don't want to make this worse, but I will override you if I have to. Kharadine needs medical care. We've got a ton of extra weight with all these passengers. And if anything goes wrong on launch, we don't reach the gate. Dead in the water."

"I hate you right now," I said, knowing it was unfair.

He didn't even flinch. "I know. I can live with that." His gray eyes flicked to the screens. "You launch it or I will."

For a moment, I wanted to force the issue. If he forcibly removed me from my seat and took over, then I wouldn't have to know that I'd left Mistral down here. Then I could hate him instead of myself.

"Rossi, prepare for launch to Ilmarinen Gate," I said through my tears.

"Preparing for launch," the AI said. "Acting Captain Helena, I have a reminder set from Captain Kharadine to contact a classified Dominion hailing code upon completion of the mission. Shall I open communication?"

I glanced at Ember, and he nodded. "Yes, please," I said.

The screen lit up with a human male in a blue Dominion uniform. "Yes, ah..." he said, tilting his head quizzically. "I was expecting someone else. Ms. Vartai?"

"Ms. Vartai got shot in the throat," I said bluntly, displaying my blood-stained arms. "Are you Watchcaller Al-Shara's guy?"

He blanched. "I am a contact for the Watchcaller, yes. Has the mission been completed?"

"He blew up his own place, but we got the girls out," I said. And not the one person I wanted. I wanted to scream it at the top of my lungs and make sure they all knew how much this had cost. And I felt so much shame for that awful thought, knowing that Mistral was incapable of being as selfish as I was right now.

Completely unaware of my turmoil, the officer smiled. "Excellent news. Do you need aid?"

Ember leaned over my shoulder. "We need help. How soon you can land a ship down here?"

The officer nodded eagerly. "Watchcaller Al-Shara ordered a medical ship into orbit as soon as you passed through the Ilmarinen gate into the Arippa Cluster," he said. "We can be on the ground in less than an hour."

Ember nudged me and whispered. "Refueling."

"Can you refuel us?" I asked.

"Of course," he said. "Please send me your exact coordinates to begin navigation."

"Thank you," I said. The screen went blank, and I managed to hold it together long enough to say, "Rossi, send our current coordinates to the address I just called."

"Done, Acting Captain Helena," he said.

"I'll leave you alone," Ember said quietly. He raked one bloody hand through his hair and hesitated. "Just so you know, I didn't want to leave him. He's my brother."

When he left me alone, I stared blankly at the screen. A readout confirmed that our coordinates had been received by the Dominion ship.

"OC-MXH-8714," I said to myself. I was going to have to call Storm and tell him that his brother was dead. That he'd sacrificed himself like a big damn hero. "Rossi?"

"Yes, Acting Captain Helena?"

"That big jerk made me a promise," I said, scrubbing tears from my eyes.

"I'm sorry, Acting Captain Helena. I do not understand the command," Rossi said. "Please rephrase."

"Never mind," I said, lurching out of the captain's chair. This was my ship for the moment, and I got to make the rules. I stormed out of the cockpit and down the hallway to find Ember. He was in the armory scrubbing blood from his bare arms.

His head snapped up as I walked in. "Are you all right?" he asked.

"I'm angry as hell," I replied. "Your stupid brother made me a promise. And until I see his body so I can yell at it for breaking that promise, I don't accept this. So I need something to do until we can go find his stupid corpse. And you're helping."

"That's our girl," Ember said warmly. I caught him wiping his eyes as I plunged into the chaos.

For the next hour, I made my way around the cabin trying to turn my despair into something positive. I found a local anesthetic and slathered Aura's arms, then gently flushed the wounds and wrapped them in gauze. Ember waved off my attempts to check him out, so I gathered all the clothes Mistral had bought me and took them to our new Zathari passengers. Ember even brought me some of his shirts, though he quickly retreated to the cockpit when one of the women started crying at the sight of him.

Most of our rescued passengers looked too thin, and Aura confirmed that they were both underfed and drugged to keep them weak. I went through the galley and prepared all the food we had. It was bland and mushy, but I was surrounded in a chorus of weeping *thank yous* from our new passengers. Some of them didn't have translator chips, so I relied on Aura to communicate what little I had to say.

The whole time, I felt like I was going to break down if someone looked at me wrong. Every breath was a struggle to hold back the tears. I knew he was gone, because the universe was a bitch. Every time I thought I had something beautiful, it was snatched away. It took my father. It took my chance at New Terra. And now Mistral was gone. I didn't believe what I'd said to Ember, but anger kept me moving when despair would trap me in a pit where I was useless.

I couldn't believe in Mistral's gods, because they had to be impossibly cruel to bring us together only to let him die. There was no fate or destiny. Just cruel, dumb chance.

The women were smiling and grateful, eager to speak to me as I brought them more food and drink, but I had to excuse myself. Their joy was so beautiful and gratifying, and it made me angry. They didn't deserve my spiteful mood, so I excused myself to check on Kharadine, who was still unconscious. Thick white bandages covered the barely closed wound on her throat.

The ship's onboard medical kit was better than anything we had at my hospital back on Earth, complete with a monitoring system that told me her heart rate and blood pressure were within safe ranges. It was a little odd, considering normal for Kharadine was far too low for humans, but the green star indicated all was well. She probably needed surgery and a blood transfusion, but that was beyond my abilities.

As I watched over her, Rossi's voice boomed through the ship. "Captain Helena, incoming Dominion vessel. We are receiving a request to come aboard."

"Give them permission," I said quietly.

"Yes, Captain," he said.

I left Kharadine and waited at the boarding ramp. Several uniformed officers—all female—stood at the bottom. One of them looked human; probably one of the settlers from New Terra. She waved. "I'm Medical Officer Braddix. May we come on board?"

"Come on," I said, my voice rough.

The woman headed into the cabin, then froze at the sight of our huddled rescues. "Good evening," she said brightly. "My name is Medical Officer—"

"Hold on," I said. I tapped my ear. "They've been prisoners a long time. They don't all have working translators." I lifted my eyes. "Rossi, please translate into Zathari."

"Yes, Captain," he said.

As the officer continued, Rossi echoed her in Zathari. "We are medical officers from the Aengra Dominion. We would like for you to all come onto our vessel and allow us to take care of you. You have nothing to fear."

Several of the women looked skeptical. After what they'd been through, I didn't blame them. Aura glanced at me, then nodded. She spoke in Zathari, then gestured broadly toward the boarding ramp. At that, half a dozen of the women rose and followed her, with a few more stragglers.

"We have someone seriously injured. She's unconscious and stable, but she needs more help than I can give," I said. "Can your people come and get her?"

"Of course," Officer Braddix said. She pressed a finger to her wrist. "Send medical team to transport an unconscious patient." Her eyes drifted over me. "And you? Are you injured?"

I shook my head. "I'm fine," I said blankly. My body felt empty and hollow, like I'd been viciously scraped out. But there wasn't a scratch on me, just like Mistral had wanted.

A few minutes later, a team was gently moving Kharadine through the ship on a hovering gurney. The Zathari women had left their dishes in a neat stack, even folding their discarded rags. I slumped onto the couch and buried my face in my hands. I couldn't even cry now that I was alone.

Pain suddenly twanged between my temples. It was like white noise, almost deafening. Then it faded again. Heat rolled through my body as adrenaline rushed through me.

Mistral?

There was another powerful throbbing in my head, then a sensation like the faintest tug at my hand. There were no words, but I felt the way he touched me, the way that thumb traced over my back, the tiniest touch to tell me he was there.

All at once, my emotions ran wild. Dangerous, fiery hope ignited in my gut. "Ember!" I yelled. "I need you!"

He burst from the cockpit. "What's wrong?"

"I hear him," I blurted. "I think. I don't know. We have to go look." I headed for the boarding ramp, but Ember grabbed my arm. "If you try to stop me, I'm going to punch you in the face. I know it won't hurt you, but it'll make me feel better."

He gave me a sad smile. "I was going to tell you to put on a coat. It's fuckin' cold out there." He jerked his chin toward the door. "I'll go with you."

Mistral? I thought. *I'm here. Please answer me.*

Nothing.

"We need to get closer to the compound again," I said, dashing back into the cockpit. "Rossi, get us ready to launch. Send a message to the Dominion vessel. We'll be back."

CHAPTER 26

Mistral

My mother once told me that when we died, we returned to the stars to gaze down upon our people and guide their paths. There, we would whisper knowledge to new souls ready to take form.

There was nothing to gaze at here but thick, choking darkness. My entire body ached, and it was so cold that every breath was like sandpaper on my throat. Surely if I was in this much pain, I hadn't made it to the peaceful void of stars. That, or the ancestors had left out some key information about the afterlife.

With aching arms, I twisted around and tapped my watch. The faint blue glow was enough to illuminate the squared-off tunnel around me. I shone the light back. The corpse of Daerathis Locke lay amidst the rubble of his former den of depravity. At least if I died in an icy tomb, he went first.

The faintest whisper tickled at my ear. It was my name on the wind, a whisper across a crowded room, just enough to snag my attention.

Mistral.

The familiar feeling of her was enough to bring me to the brink of tears. From half-dead to hearing my mate. My head pounded, but I tried to respond to her.

I'm here. I'm under the rocks.

There was only silence for a while, and I wondered if I had simply imagined it. This was the second nasty shock I'd gotten in two days, and my brain was probably deep-fried. I glanced at Locke again. "I'm not dying down here with you," I spat. "I made a promise."

Think, Vethylas.

The electrified rail that had attempted to remove my soul from my body had to be connected to another facility. Maybe to Locke's factory. An underground tunnel would conveniently avoid both the harsh weather and detection. And an underground tunnel had to go somewhere that wasn't here.

My joints ached as I struggled to my feet and limped to Locke. A quick check of his pockets yielded a gun and an extra magazine of those acid-loaded rounds. Cursing him with the filthiest Zathari curses I knew, I removed his watch and pocketed it.

I started walking, careful to stay to one side so I didn't get another shock. As I walked, I occasionally reached out to Helena.

Helena, are you there? Please answer me. I need to hear you.

Nothing. Had she given up? Left me behind? I couldn't blame her if she did. If Ember was half the man I thought he was, he'd have made sure that Helena left and got the women out.

As I walked, I started planning ahead. If I got out of this tunnel, Locke's guys were probably on the other end. I had a couple weapons on me, probably enough to take a few out. Assuming I survived, I could steal one of his ships. Then I'd return to Phade, get in touch with Jalissa, and hope that Kharadine was still with Helena.

It didn't even cross my mind that I wasn't going to make it back to her. The gods themselves had brought us together, and not even this motherfucking mountain falling down on me was going to keep me away from her.

Still feeling the ravages of electrocution, my muscles protested hiking in a subterranean tunnel in freezing temperatures. Even my tough hide couldn't protect me from the monster that was the wicked cold of Rubresan.

Helena, Helena, I thought in a singsong. *Where are you? I can't wait to be in the sun with you.*

Nothing.

I refused to entertain the nightmare scenarios worming through my thoughts like Ember's carnivorous larvae. Maybe I'd hallucinated that voice. She could be off the planet by now. Killed by Locke's backup crew. Succumbed to the cold. Imprisoned by the Dominion. Back on Terra where I'd never find her.

My racing thoughts were poor company on that long, cold walk beneath the frozen ground. I just kept thinking of her, holding that sweet smile in my mind. I imagined how it would feel to have her arms around me while I buried my face in her hair and breathed deep.

And then, like a miracle, there was that tiny little scratch at the back of my neck, then a light finger across my brow. I tilted my head, as if her hand was there to catch me.

Her voice was so soft I could barely hear it. *Mistral?*

I'm here, I thought. *I'm heading out of the tunnel. I think it connects to Locke's factory.*

I felt a burst of warmth that had to be joy and relief. *I'm coming. Just keep walking. Keep talking to me. What are we going to do when we get off this icy hellscape?*

Laughter bubbled up in me, and I coughed violently. *Anywhere you want to go. Somewhere warm.*

Beaches. And real food. No more protein mush.

Agreed.

Though I felt weaker with each step, I could feel her now. It wasn't just wishful thinking, but an insistent tug, as if she had jammed her hand right into my chest and grabbed my heart. There was no denying the bond that entwined us.

It was quiet for a while, and then I felt her, stronger now. *I'm on my way to you. It's clear up here.*

The thought of seeing her spiked my adrenaline, and I managed a quicker shuffle through the darkened tunnel.

Her voice rang out in my head. *Get off the track!*

A sleek, enclosed cart the size of our shared bunk passed me with a quiet humming sound. I heard the *thump* of hands pounding the glass as it came to a halt. The roof lifted with a quiet hiss.

Helena exploded out of it and ran for me. Her face was scratched, her clothes bloody. I didn't pause to ask questions, just grabbed her around the waist and held her so tight that she let out a little *oof*.

Her emotions rolled over me in a deafening, blinding wave

of relief and joy and terror and fury. It was heat and fire and utterly consuming, and I knew that all of those strange things boiled into a powerful, nuclear reaction to create love.

This was love. I was bathed in fire and so much beauty that I could never be the same.

Her tears felt like boiling water against my frigid skin. She pulled away briefly, running her hands over my face. "Oh, my God, you're freezing," she fretted. "I'm just so glad… you're cold…okay, we have to go." She grabbed my hand and dragged me toward the small vehicle. I climbed in first, and she settled between my legs as the roof sealed over us.

In the low light, I could still see her eyes gleaming. "Hello, Captain," I said, my voice barely more than a whisper. Breathing and talking hurt, but everything was better now that she was close.

"Hello, mate," she replied. "Two things."

"Hm?"

"I love you," she said. "I thought I lost you, and it was the worst moment of my life."

I love you.

I forgot everything but Helena. I only knew that she held my entire life in those three words, and that whatever else I was, I was hers.

"I love you," I murmured, pulling her closer so I could touch her, tracing the full curve of her cheek. "And the second thing?"

"Don't you ever do that to me again," she ordered. She actually smacked me in the chest, awakening the pain in my ribs. "No more being a hero."

"No promises," I said. I caught her hand. "Careful. I think I broke something. Or several somethings."

Her face went slack with horror. "Oh, I'm sorry," she said, cupping my face and kissing me gently.

"It's all right," I said. "You know what will make me feel better?" She just smiled and leaned in close, letting me wrap my arms around her. Her head rested on my shoulder, filling my lungs with her sweet scent. And there, beneath a crumbled stronghold in the icy depths of a frozen wasteland, I was warm and whole for the first time in my life.

When the vehicle came to a halt, she lifted her head and winced. "Ember had a little too much fun. Just a fair warning."

The roof of the small shuttle lifted, and I was bombarded with the smell of gunpowder, burnt ozone, and blood. Helena climbed out and offered me a hand. I rose into a harshly lit entryway. Beyond it was a huge open hangar. Acrid smoke filled the room, where the unmoving bodies of half a dozen unfortunates lay on the ground.

A beautiful, black-hulled jump ship was in the middle of the hangar, its boarding ramp down. A noisy clatter came from across the room, and I drew my weapon. Helena touched my arm lightly. "It's just Ember."

"Holy shit," Ember crowed. He emerged from behind the ship carrying a gun that could have blown a hole in a small planet. "Helena, cover your ears. I would fuck this thing if I could."

Helena shook her head. "You're supposed to wait for me to cover my ears before you say the disgusting thing."

"I can't help it," Ember said. He grinned at me. "What's up, shithead?"

"I'm fine, thanks for asking," I said. Fine was a bit of an overstatement. Every muscle fiber in my body hurt.

He shrugged. "She told me you were alive." His horned head tilted back toward the bloody aftermath of their arrival. "I ruined your welcome party and killed all the guests. Sorry."

I smirked. "And the boat?"

"Well, the Dominion's not going to pay us jack shit for all this trouble," Ember said, depositing the massive gun on top of a pile of cases. The asshole was going shopping. I admired that about him. "I like the things that go boom. You can take the ship."

Helena looked pained. "They're not going to let us keep it."

Ember looked at her incredulously. "Who's *they*? No one's letting me do anything," he said. "You two are taking the Impulse back to Kharadine. I was never here. I'll get this bird to Phade, and you can do what you want with it from there." He approached me and gave me a tight embrace. "Glad you're not dead, you ugly fucker."

"You too," I said. "Try not to stick your dick in anything explosive."

He smirked. "No promises."

We left Ember with the stolen ship and emerged into the bitter cold of Rubresan. The Impulse sat on a landing pad outside the hangar, partially off the concrete. Snow piled on the ship's dark nose. Several more bodies lay on the ground, hands stretched away from the ship. I gave Helena an incredulous look. "What the hell happened?"

She pinched the bridge of her nose. "Your brother is insane. He somehow triggered an emergency release on the cargo bay while the ship was landing, jumped out, and started shooting."

"That sounds about right," I said. We boarded the ship, and I made it only a few steps in before I had to touch her, had to wrap her in my arms. I was rougher than I meant to be as I pinned her to the wall of the cargo bay, curling my fingers into the nets. Her eyes were wide as she stared up at me. "I love you." I slanted my mouth to hers, devouring her in a kiss, wishing I could draw her all the way in, to cage her inside the safety of my body. Her hands curled into my belt and yanked me closer. "Let's get off this rock," I growled to her.

"Mmhmm," she said. "I'm taking you to the medical ship."

"You certainly are not," I said.

She shot me a glare. "I most certainly am. One, you nearly died. Two, this is Kharadine's ship."

"And if I refuse?"

Her head tilted. "Let's not make ultimatums," she said. Then a wicked gleam lit in those warm brown eyes. She slid her hands under my waistband, warm fingers almost painfully hot against my chilled skin. "Let's talk about what I'm going to do after they check you out."

Her hands were inching closer and closer. "I'm listening."

"Well, considering we were rudely awakened on Erebus before we got to play with anymore of those wonderful toys..." she mused. "And you *are* a hero." Her lashes fluttered. "I think I might get on my knees and worship this cock of yours."

My jaw dropped at the blunt, filthy words from my sweet rose. Then I grinned. "You could skip the medical part and do that now."

"Not until you've been cleared. I could injure you, and I couldn't have that on my conscience." Despite her words, one hand drifted closer, fingers just brushing the hair above my cock.

"You're a medical professional. I'll take the risk," I said.

"I won't," she said sweetly, withdrawing her hand abruptly. "Buckle up."

✦

Six excruciatingly long hours later, I strongarmed the Dominion doctor into letting us leave. A thorough examination revealed I was healthy—and therefore perfectly capable of enjoying Helena's mouth on my cock. I was still stiff and sore from touching the electrified rail, but I wasn't staying on a Dominion ship for that.

They offered to escort Kharadine to safety when she woke, but I didn't want to risk her ire. I could only imagine her fury upon waking alone without her ship. The Dominion doctors had clearly been given orders not to ask questions, and they simply marked Kharadine as "Patient A" and assured us she would likely wake tomorrow with little lasting trouble.

While the doctors gave me an infusion to loosen my muscles and restore my electrolytes after being shocked, Helena left me briefly. When she returned, she confirmed that the Zathari women were safe and being cared for by female officers.

Once I was cleared, I insisted on returning to the Impulse, which was docked in the hangar bay of the medical ship as it trundled toward the Ilmarinen gate. I'd managed a hot shower on the medical ship, and I felt like a new man as we climbed into the quiet emptiness of the Impulse. "That wasn't so bad, was it?" she teased.

"I had motivation," I replied, my cock already stiffening at the thought of what she was going to do. There was pure mischief in her eyes as she flounced past me, then jerked her chin toward the big, curved lounge in the central cabin. This where we'd played cards, plotted undercover missions, and now, where I could finally be alone with her again.

I watched her hungrily as she paced in front of me. She paused, and I gently grabbed her legs, running my hands up the back of her thighs. She was wearing some rough, oversized coverall that had to have come from the Dominion ship. I wrinkled my nose. "What is this terrible thing?"

She laughed. "They gave it to me because I didn't have anything warm," she said. Her eyes twinkled. "You don't like it?"

"I mean, you could wear anything and still be the hottest fucking woman in the universe, but honestly, I hate it," I said.

Never breaking her gaze, she raked her long hair back into a high ponytail. "Then do something about it," she teased, slowly winding an elastic around her hair. With a growl, I yanked the zipper down to reveal lacy black undergarments, one of the revealing pieces I'd picked out for her at the boutique in Vuola Lire. Back when I'd picked it out, it was mostly a joke. I hadn't ever imagined I'd see her in it. And here she was, a gift from the gods. "Find something nice?"

"Mm," I agreed, running my hands over her smooth, warm skin. Goosebumps rippled over her skin from my touch. I slid my hands up to remove the ugly garment from her shoulders, leaving her in only the skimpy lingerie. "Rossi?" I said.

"Voice not recognized," the male AI said.

She snickered. "Rossi?"

"Yes, Acting Captain Helena?"

"Heat," I said. I gave her a pitiful look. "I'm still cold."

"Turn up the temperature, please," she said sweetly. Then she plopped down on my lap, sealing her lips to mine as the temperature rose. Her kiss was divine, but I wanted more than this soft sweetness. Hunger overwhelmed me, and I drew her in, making up for the fear of losing her. She was breathless, almost fighting as we kissed.

With a soft little whimper, she broke away and shifted down to her knees. I spread my legs for her, watching in rapt fascination as she unzipped my pants. For all the fucking we'd done since we met, she'd never done this. It wasn't for lack of trying, but I'd always been so horny I couldn't keep my hands off her. Given the choice, I wanted to be inside of her.

But I was so tired, and the thought of her devoted to me was so appealing I was afraid I was going to come before she even touched me. Desire throbbed in my belly, turning to a dull ache in my balls. She lifted my cock and gazed at it like it was a delicacy. Without saying a word, she licked my *dzirian*, the warm flat of her tongue awakening a fire in my groin. Her lips pursed into a kiss, and she took her time, making her way up the curve of my shaft before she finally flicked her tongue over my head. Then she sucked at my head, slow and sweet, before she pulled off with a decadent noise.

"Mistral," she said, her voice taking on a rough, dark tinge I liked. "Is it all right if I use your real name? When it's just the two of us?"

"Always," I said gently. "It belongs to you now. I didn't know it then, but it was chosen for you."

She smiled, still stroking me slowly. "Vethylas," she murmured. The sound of it on her lips, along with that pale hand stroking my cock, reached something into my chest and squeezed. Then the tiniest flicker of fear crossed her face. "Help me if I don't do it right. Okay?"

"You'll be perfect," I said. "As always."

Her smile brightened, and then she took me in, her head bobbing slowly as she stroked me. As the warmth of her mouth blazed around me, I was already floating away. Suddenly, I felt a prickle of sensation at my neck, the sure sign that our mate bond was active. I felt her affection, and I hoped that she could feel the plain and simple *good wonderful* that was rolling through me.

She took me deeper, and I watched in wonder as my cock disappeared into those full pink lips, bumping against the back of her throat. With a little cough, she backed away, breathless as she stroked my slick shaft. Her eyebrows lifted.

"You're perfect," I murmured. "Just like that."

In I went again, and a low, sweet hum rumbled through my cock and into my balls like thunder. Her ponytail bounced as she worked me vigorously, noisy and wet. She made little sounds of satisfaction around me, and I let my hips rise slightly to meet her. Without breaking her rhythm, she reached up for my hand, guiding it to her head. I groaned and gently gripped her ponytail, simply letting the weight of my hand rest there. She let out a primal growl around me, and somehow came closer, body rising, pressed against my thighs as she worked my cock until I was on the edge.

She was perfect. My cock jerked, and I thrust into her mouth as I came. Her tongue swirled from below as she swallowed me down. My brain shut down, and I could only see brilliant rose red.

She was all mine. And I was hers, for the rest of time.

Even when I was finished, she lingered, slowly suckling at me, withdrawing one slow inch at a time until the head of my cock emerged from her lips. I watched her in wonder as she gently released me, then placed a single kiss on my slick shaft, like she was putting it to bed. I gently cupped her face, and she tilted into my touch. Her brow lifted in a silent question.

"Helena," I growled. "I think you melted my brain."

She grinned, her lips flushed and full. "Good."

"Mm," I agreed. "Can I ask a favor?"

"Anything," she said, rising to climb into my lap.

"Can I have that again without getting electrocuted and nearly freezing to death?"

She laughed and kissed my forehead. "I think that can be arranged."

CHAPTER 27

Helena

Twenty-four hours after I found Mistral, Kharadine was cleared to leave, which meant we could finally get out of the icy orbit of Rubresan. But when she banged on the cabin door and barged in, she had a message.

"Hey, you better have on clothes," she growled. "They want to see you before we go."

I frowned. "They?"

"I'm getting up in five seconds, so leave unless you want to see everything I've got," Mistral warned her. "One—"

She slammed the door before he went any further. We both dressed quickly, and since I'd given my clothes to the Zathari women, I had only my lacy undies and the coverall. Mistral grumbled when I put it on, and I reminded him that he could buy me clothes more to his liking later. I politely, but firmly rejected his suggestion to go naked at all times.

He was tense as we emerged from the boarding ramp and into the hangar bay of the medical ship. Then he froze. A dozen Zathari women formed a circle around the boarding ramp, all dressed in coveralls like mine. A few still looked frightened, but they were all calm. Standing just at the base of the ramp was Aura, looking as elegant and fierce as ever.

"They will not openly admit it, but I refuse to let the Dominion take all the credit for this," Aura said quietly. "Your cousins know that it was not the soldiers that fought to save them, but one of our own."

I looked back at him, and I could have sworn there were tears in those icy blue eyes. His hand rested at my back, fisting into the rough material.

"We thank you," one of them said, bowing her head to him. She held out her hands, beckoning to him. He glanced down at me, and I nodded.

He hesitated. "I only did the decent thing."

"Which is more than any other had done for us," one of the women said. She boldly stepped forward and took Mistral's hand. He tensed, but she pulled him closer and rose to kiss his cheeks gently. "Thank you."

Suddenly, half of them closed around my mate, some kissing his cheeks, others simply touching his arm. A few of them hung back, but they smiled and nodded. Watching him, I was filled with pride that threatened to split me open. That was my mate. His single-minded focus on justice for his people had led him to me, and then to all of them. How many shattered lives had he swept up just in the wild chaos of the last few days?

"Where will you go?" he asked. "Do you need us to escort you?"

Aura nodded and gestured broadly to Kharadine. "Only to Borealis. Captain Kharadine has arranged for a transport ship to meet us there, and we will make our way from there."

He nodded. "My brothers and I keep a place in Ir-Nassa. Should you ever need somewhere safe, reach out to us. Kharadine knows how."

Aura nodded to him. "Some hope to go to Irasyne," she said. Then her light eyes narrowed. "And some of us will continue what you started. There are still others that Locke already auctioned away. If they live, we will find them."

Mistral nodded. "You need only call. I'll be happy to rain down hell. And I've got backup with big guns and bigger grudges."

Her grin was a predator's hungry grin. "I will remember that." Then she strode forward and clasped his arm. "Thank you, cousin."

While they talked, I saw the medical officer who'd come onboard the Impulse to help move Kharadine. She caught my eye, then beckoned. "Excuse me," I whispered, stepping away from the ramp to join her. The woman immediately walked back to the ship. "What do you need?"

"Watchcaller Al-Shara has a call for you," she said.

My heart thumped as I followed her around the bend, and into a small, private conference room. A big screen illuminated with the elegant woman's familiar face. "Ms. Cage," she greeted. "I hear that congratulations are in order."

"And for you, too?"

"Mm," she nodded. "Shutting down a dozen high-level traffickers is quite a feather in my cap. I wish for you to inform your horned partner that the records have been swept. He was never here. And while I am certainly not giving him carte blanche to flaunt the laws of the Dominion, consider me a friend in the future."

I smiled. "Thank you," I said. "I'll tell him."

I rose, but she said, "That's not why I asked to speak to you. In our interrogations of Vehr Arandon, we've discovered that he conducted his operations by posing as a Dominion official offering settlement on New Terra. That's how you were abducted, yes?"

"Yes ma'am," I said.

"If that is what you wish, I have already secured a settlement for you," she said. My heart leaped into my throat. "A paid residence in the upper district of Alnova, along with a generous allowance to cover your living costs. We can have you there within three days."

My throat closed. It was all I'd ever wanted.

She smiled faintly. "If you need time to consider it, there is no rush. This offer stands, though I cannot extend it indefinitely."

I hesitated. "What about Milla? And the others you rescued?"

She nodded. "Considering your active involvement, the paid residence and allowance is a special offer for you. However, we are aiding all the survivors in returning home or in resettling in our colonies as they desire. Camilla Townsend accepted an offer to settle in Alnova."

"And she'll be safe?"

"As safe as any other resident," Al-Shara said. "Nowhere is perfect, but certainly safer than she was on Terra, and exponentially safer than she was in Arandon's possession."

"Thank you," I said. "And what about the others? There were others he sold before this. Will you be able to find them?"

She hesitated. "That may be a more difficult task, but one of my first initiatives in my new position is tracking down the other victims."

Her lack of confidence was evident, but I nodded. "I'd like to know what you find out. Especially a girl named Sarah," I said.

"I'll make a note of it," she said. "I've spoken to you as an officer of the Dominion, but let me offer you some advice from another woman. Your companion was certainly bold and succeeded in aiding many people. But men like him live dangerous lives. You should consider where you will end up if you remain with him."

I considered telling her where she could stuff her consideration. But instead, I dug into my reserve of control and calm, honed by months aboard Arandon's ship. I simply nodded. "Thank you for the advice."

When I returned to the hangar, I found Mistral pacing at the boarding ramp. He frowned at me. "Are you all right?"

"Fine," I said. I forced a smile. "Are we ready?"

"Let's get home," he said.

Home. What a thought.

An hour later, we were leaving the icy orbit of Rubresan behind. The Zathari women were packed into the ship, talking quietly, while Kharadine had retaken her seat in the captain's chair. As some of the women started to press toward Mistral again, he shot me a nervous look.

I can't deal with the compliments, he thought.

I suppressed a smile. *Poor baby. That's what you get for being a hero.*

He gave me a pained look, and I realized that his heroics had earned him at least a little bit of help. I frowned and put my hand to his forehead. "Mistral, you should lie down," I said loudly. "After all you went through, you need your rest."

"I'm fine," he protested, his voice a little too loud.

"I am a medical professional, and I insist," I said, shoving lightly at his back. He wedged between two of the women and back into our shared cabin.

He perched on the edge of the bed and mouthed, "Thank you."

Hey, guess what?

His brow lifted.

I unzipped my coveralls to show him the slivers of lace beneath. His jaw dropped, and he started to rise.

"You should really rest," I said loudly as I zipped up again. His jaw dropped as he gave me an incredulous look.

You monstrous little tease.

With a satisfied smile, I closed the door behind me, sliding through the crowd to join Kharadine in the cockpit. I let out a heavy sigh. "You feeling okay?"

"I'm great," she rasped. Her violet gaze raked over me. "You?"

"I'm good," I said, Al-Shara's offer still echoing in my head. "Al-Shara just made me an offer to go to New Terra."

Kharadine chuckled. "Isn't that what you wanted?"

"I did before," I said. "I don't know if I do anymore."

Kharadine shrugged. "Then don't go."

"His life is dangerous."

"Safe lives aren't for everyone." She glanced over at me. "You know, if you need a job, I've got a crew of girls you'd like. I think Jalissa would like you."

"As in your crime boss leader that scares Mistral and Ember?"

She grinned. "That's the one," she said.

"I don't think I'm cut out for action like you," I said.

"I was a librarian," Kharadine said, raising her eyebrows. "Can you believe that?"

"I absolutely cannot," I said.

She laughed. "It's a long story, but I'll never go back. I'd rather die pulling those women off Rubresan than of old age in a stack of books."

"Yeah," I murmured. "It does feel good. Maybe not enough, though."

"How so?"

"How many people were sold through Erebus, or elsewhere? They're scattered all over the galaxies," I said.

Kharadine raised an eyebrow. "Rossi, display my reports from the server crawlers."

The third screen switched from an external view of the stars to a dense text document. "What's this?"

"Guns are great, but information is real power," Kharadine said.

"Spoken like a true librarian. I thought you couldn't get into the Erebus servers."

She beamed. "Funny you mention that. Once the Dominion arrived, I had my crawlers go for the Erebus servers again. At that point, I didn't care if they knew. I also got them onto most of the passenger ships. I may have released another set on the medical ship just now."

"And what did you find, theoretically speaking?"

"A fuckton of information," Kharadine said. "But I can tell you that Vehr Arandon's cyber security is shit, and if he kept records of where he sold anyone, I've got it."

Hope welled up in my chest. "Can you send me what you find?"

"Sounds like someone is more cut out for action than she thought," Kharadine teased. "I'm not transporting Mistral all over the galaxy."

I glanced at her. "We may have stolen a high-tech ship from Locke."

"May have?"

"Possibly."

"Look at you," Kharadine said. "You're already cut out for the Diamondbacks."

I laughed. "I don't think so."

"We'll see."

The trip from Rubresan back to the Gate was quick, and another quick trip on the other side brought us back to Borealis. I accompanied Kharadine into the massive hangar of Borealis, where she greeted a Vaera woman in a killer black suit, complete with a cape. Okay, I had to admit that being in the intergalactic women's cartel had appeal if those were their sartorial choices.

We bade the Zathari women goodbye, watching as they followed the Vaera woman into a larger ship. Mistral finally emerged from the cabin as we took off again for Phade. Though I had already made my choice, Al-Shara's offer was a heavy weight on my chest. Even Kharadine's suggestion was thrilling.

Never before had my life been so full of possibilities.

When our course was set for Phade, Kharadine rose and stretched. "I'm getting a nap," she said. "You're in charge if something goes wrong." With that, she disappeared into her cabin, leaving me alone in the cockpit.

Mistral joined me in the cockpit, where I stared out at the stars. "Captain Helena," he teased. "It has a nice ring." I smiled at him, and he immediately frowned. "What's wrong? Something's bothering you."

"Is that a mate thing? Knowing I'm worried?"

"Must be," he said. "What is it?" I told him about Al-Shara's offer, watching his expression falter. He managed to regroup, his stony expression utterly neutral. "Isn't that what you wanted?"

"I did," I said. "That's what Helena Cage of Earth wanted." My head tilted. "But I don't think that's who I am anymore, is it?"

"Then who are you?" he asked.

"I'm your mate," I said. "Helena Cage of...wherever in the universe she wants to go. I want to be where you are. Is that what you want?"

He nodded. "That's what I want. More than anything I've ever wanted in my life." He offered me his hand, and I took it, savoring the weight of his grasp. "There are still things I have to do. This shit on Erebus was a reminder of how many assholes are out there."

"And it's your job to stop it all?"

"Sometimes," he said. He glanced at me. "Sometimes no one else will."

"Then I'm going with you." I took a deep breath. "I need you to do one more favor for me."

"No."

I stared at him in confusion.

"No favors. You ask me for what you want, and I'll do my best to give it to you. That's how this works now."

My cheeks heated, and I nodded. "I like that. Kharadine might be able to find the other people Arandon sold. If we can find Sarah, I want to help her."

"Consider it done," he said. "Anything else?"

"That easy, huh?"

"That easy," he said. Then he gave me a knowing look. "When it comes to you, I'm very easy."

"You sure are," I teased.

"Honestly, I'm surprised Kharadine didn't try to recruit you," he said.

I laughed. "Funny you should mention that. Helena Cage, Empress of Crime, has sort of a nice ring to it."

"Wayfarers save us all," he muttered.

CHAPTER 28

Mistral

Two Weeks Later

Daerathis Locke was a piece of shit that deserved a far worse death than I'd given him, but he'd built one hell of a ship. I'd wanted to name our new ride Helena, but my Helena insisted it was too confusing, especially when we started talking about packing things into her backside. Fair point. Instead, we'd called her the Night Rose, and while there was already a woman who owned my entire heart, I certainly loved this ship.

After a brief respite on Phade, I received a data package from Kharadine, courtesy of Evhina. It was a neatly organized file of Vehr Arandon's sales records going back for years, and she'd isolated a file with the name *Sarah Lundy*. There was a note informing me that the rest of the data was being sent to the Dominion, but that Helena might be particularly interested in Sarah. She hadn't even finished asking, "Can we—" before I told her to pack her things.

And now we were headed to meet with Nestus Maor, a wealthy Vaera trader who grew rare fruits on the rich soil of Zaalbara. He was eager to meet me, or at least, to meet the wealthy Mr. Adalon Delthe, who had expressed a sincere interest in investing into his farms. Generous soul that he was, he'd invited me and my companion to meet him at his estate, which overlooked his fields.

We weren't certain Sarah was there, but Storm had found Maor in the guest archives of Vuola Lire. He'd stayed there within the last three months and checked in with a female companion. It wasn't much, but it was something.

We followed the directions to land at the secure landing pad, and I rose from the captain's seat. Helena sashayed out of the cabin with my coat. I groaned and looked away. "For fuck's sake," I complained.

She looked down at her tiny outfit. There was *glitter* on her chest, making it impossible to not look at her perfect breasts, all pushed up like gravity didn't exist. "What? You don't like it?"

"How am I supposed to concentrate with you looking like that?" I said. She smacked my ass, then held out my coat for me to dress. The woman couldn't walk past me without grabbing a handful.

Not that I minded.

"That's the point, my love," she said, rounding me to straighten the asymmetrical garment. "Maor will be distracted, making your job easier."

"I think you just like to get me hot and bothered," I said.

"I do also like that," she agreed. "It usually works out well for me."

When we emerged from the boarding ramp of the Night Rose, a well-dressed Vaera gentleman awaited with a woman in a neat black uniform. "Mr. Delthe," Maor greeted. "I'm pleased you made it." His eyes raked over Helena, and I satisfied myself with the thought of punching him. "And your lovely companion. Would you like to leave her inside?"

"I'll take her with me," I said.

"Let's have a tour of the orchards, shall we?" Maor said.

As we followed him to a smaller vehicle, I glanced at Helena. *Is that Sarah?*

Not her.

We sat through his tour as his driver guided us around one of the orchards, packed with trees heavy-laden with plump blue fruit. The *macarloshi* were a delicacy, sold as-is and fermented into wine for wealthy palates. I kept my hand on Helena's leg, nodding along as Maor prattled about the expected harvest, his desired expansions, and complaints about some of the locals who apparently objected to him buying up their land. I read between the lines and gathered that he'd slaughtered some of the locals to quell their objections.

Asshole.

Eventually, we returned to his estate, where he invited me in for drinks. With Helena trailing after me, I followed him to a veranda that overlooked the lush expanse of orchards. And when his maid brought out a platter of sliced fruits, crackers, and other snacks, another woman was close behind. Dressed in a short red dress, her dark hair swept up in a sleek bun, her gaze was downturned, and I could see the fingerprint-shaped bruises on her forearms. They were a dozen shades from deep blue-black to faded yellow.

"My companion," he said. Without being told, she immediately started massaging his shoulders. She glanced up at me, her brow furrowed. Her eyes fixed on Helena.

That's her, Helena's voice rang out in my head, so loud I nearly shouted in surprise.

I made small talk about my imaginary business, of how the greedy bastards at Deeprun Dynamics had nearly shut down one of my drilling operations. After two rounds of drinks, I leaned forward. "Mr. Maor, I hope it's not too forward," I said. "Might I have a taste of your companion? I do appreciate a Terran woman."

He raised an eyebrow. "Shall we trade for a bit of dessert?"

Helena gasped, giving me a demure look. Then I nodded. With the bland smile masking her sharp attention, she rose as if to accept Maor's invitation, but didn't leave my side. "Of course." Sarah's shoulders slumped as she headed toward me, but I watched as she assumed a mask of calm. "Where did you purchase her?"

"Purchase?" he spluttered. "No such thing."

"It's our little secret," I said. "Clearly we share tastes. Perhaps we know some of the same procurers."

"An old friend, Vehr Arandon," Maor said. He shook his head. "But that's not a name I'd drop these days. Apparently he got greedy, and the Dominion grabbed him." He looked expectantly at Helena, but she remained at my side. "Don't be shy, pet. You're a pretty little thing, aren't you?"

With Sarah at my back, I glanced at Helena and nodded. "I'm

a human being, you asshole," she said calmly. "Not an animal. Not a pet."

His eyes went comically wide. "What is—you let her speak to you this way?"

"Sarah, do you want to be here with Mr. Maor?" I asked, glancing back at her. Her eyes widened. "You can speak freely. If he even thinks about touching you, I'm going to blow his head off."

"No," she blurted.

"Security," Maor squawked.

"Are you here willingly?" I asked.

"No," she said, her voice cracking. "He bought me."

There was a thundering of footsteps as two brawny Vaera emerged from the lush gardens, guns drawn. "Sir?" one of them barked. Helena was already in motion, grabbing Sarah's arms and pulling her down to safety beneath the table. I drew my gun and stunned both of the security guards, leaving Maor defenseless.

Maor scrambled back from his chair, looking around frantically.

"Sarah, does he have any other slaves?" I asked.

She shook her head. "Just me."

"She's not—" Maor protested.

I flicked the gun to the lethal setting and aimed. "Sit down," I said sharply. He slowly sank into his seat. "You're going to tell the rest of your men to stand down. I'm leaving with this woman. If you even think of sending someone after me, I'll report you to the Dominion. Considering they just busted Arandon and all of his cronies, they're extra hungry to arrest the buyers."

"You wouldn't," Maor said incredulously.

"Watch me," I said. I pushed back my chair, drained the rest of my drink, then nodded to Sarah. "Do you want to leave?"

She nodded eagerly, and I held out my hand. She took it, and Helena hurried after us. "Stay close to me," I said quietly. "He's probably going to start shooting."

As we hurried around the side of the house, Helena grabbed my wrist. "Athena, power up engines and arm external defensive systems," she said. There was a buzz, then a green indicator on my watch.

Sure enough, when we reached the Night Rose, a line of no-necked goons in black blocked our path. "Let go of the woman," one of them said. "We might let you walk out of here."

"I recommend you stand aside," I said. "One of my ladies is going to hurt you."

They glanced at Helena, and one of them laughed. He actually grabbed his crotch. "Come on baby, I got something you can hurt."

I extended my arms around Sarah and Helena. "Athena, activate radial wave." I whirled around, shielding the women as a shock wave burst from the ship. There was a deep thudding sound, and then a clatter as the men fell to the ground. One twitched violently.

Sarah screamed, but Helena shook her head. "They're not dead," she said. As we approached, the boarding ramp lowered, and I ushered them up it.

Maor ran across the landing pad, surveying his fallen men in horror. "I will ruin you. Watch your back."

"Good luck with that," I told him. I wanted to kill him outright, but Helena had discouraged me from cold-blooded murder. I'd actually hoped he might open fire, so I was justified, but I'd made her a promise to show mercy when possible.

Sarah burst into tears as the ramp rose behind us. "This is just a dream, isn't it?"

Helena hesitated, then said, "Do you remember me? From the Basilisk?"

Sarah nodded, still weeping. "You're the one who tried to protect me."

Helena froze. Her shock came through our bond loud and clear, hitting me like a hammer to the skull. "Protect you?"

"When Thenoch was beating me," she said. "You tried to intervene."

"I didn't try very hard," Helena said, her expression somber.

Sarah's head tilted. "It was more than anyone else did. And you took care of me afterward."

"But I—"

"Helena," I said quietly. "Leave it alone."

Before she could say anything else, Sarah threw her arms around my mate and sobbed. "It's okay now," Helena said gently. "We're going to take you somewhere safe, okay?" She gently extricated herself and took Sarah into the galley, murmuring something about coffee, and I headed to the cockpit. She hurried back a minute later, handing me the heavy earrings she'd worn for our rescue mission.

"You all right?" I asked.

Her eyes were red with tears, but she nodded. "Yeah, I am. I love you."

"Love you," I replied. My fierce, protective girl. Gods, she was perfect.

As I took off, I sent an encrypted message to the

Dominion enforcement outpost on Zaalbara. I had no intention of leaving Maor alone. I quickly uploaded the audio file from Helena's earrings, attached it to my message, and sent it. They'd be crawling all over Maor's estate soon enough. He could sing all he wanted about Adalon Delthe and his imaginary mining operation. If we kept this up, I'd have to come up with another slimy alter-ego, but it was a worthy casualty to rescue Sarah and give Helena some peace of mind.

I'd been alone in the cockpit for an hour when Helena returned. She wore a loose robe over her skimpy outfit, and her hair was down, just the way I liked it. "Is she okay?"

She nodded. "I think she's in shock. I told her she could stay with us. Well, with the Earth girls," she amended. "I don't think she's in a place to figure out anything past today. But for now, she's sleeping."

"Willingly?"

Helena smirked at me. "Not entirely. Poor thing probably hadn't gotten a decent sleep in months." Then she sighed. "Thank you for doing this."

"I told you before, and I meant it. You just have to ask for what you want," I said. "Do you feel better?"

She nodded. "I do. All this time, I've thought she must have hated me. And she thought I helped her."

"Imagine that," I said. "It seems like some very wise and generous Zathari told you the same thing."

She playfully smacked my arm. "Of course you'd say that. You like me."

"Excuse me, but I do not like you," I said. "I absolutely adore you."

With a happy sigh, she sank into the other chair. "After this, where will we go?"

"Home," I said. "Well, to Phade. As much as that's home. Viper's coming to meet you."

"Really?"

"Technically, he's coming home to have someone do maintenance on his eye," I admitted. "But I want you to meet him."

"And after that?"

"I'm going to take you somewhere nice and warm," I said.

"I like where this is going."

"And we're going to sleep," I said. She frowned at me. "Or, we could have a nice bottle of wine, a big bed, and you tell me what you want me to do to you."

"Thank God," she said. "I thought you must have had an aneurysm for a second."

Thirty-six hours later, we landed at a hangar in Ir-Nassa. It was strange to have my own ship now, but I liked the sound of Captain Mistral. And I certainly enjoyed my first mate, who held my hand lightly as we strolled down the street to the high-rise apartments with Sarah in tow.

As I suspected, the Earth girls were thrilled at a new arrival. The pretty blonde one, Amira, shoved a plate at me. "Take this upstairs. We thought you were home, but the man up there said he's your brother," she said. "I was afraid to go back up."

I shook my head. "He's much nicer than I am." Gods help them if Wraith came home to visit any time soon.

Helena kissed my cheek. "I'll be up shortly. I'm going to make sure she's settled in," she said. There was a peal of laughter, and I realized that there was probably no better place for Sarah than amidst a gaggle of women from Earth who'd been through something like she had. Vani's "sisters" had worked for a crime boss and had been subjected to mistreatment by him and his goons. I left them in a chorus of chatter, one of them crowing about how pretty Sarah's hair was.

I banged on the door before I walked in. "Viper?"

The apartment was cool and quiet, but I heard water running. A minute after I walked in, Viper emerged from the hall with a towel around his waist. His short-cropped dark hair was slicked back between his horns. Releasing the towel, he threw up his hands and headed for me. "I thought I missed you!"

I embraced him, then pulled away with a pointed look downward. "Cover your dick. My girl's coming up."

"Uh, your girl? What in the entire fuck?" I noticed his artificial eye was dim, and realized the glass lens inside had been removed, covered instead with a solid metal cap. The sculpted gray prosthetic that normally covered the internal mechanisms was gone, too, giving a close view of the metal plates grafted into his skull. The asymmetry of his face was slightly disconcerting.

When we were making our escape from Kilaak, we'd almost lost Wraith when half his leg got blown off. Stubborn beast that he was, he'd kept fighting, but by the time we made it to Vakarios, Wraith was half-dead from blood loss and completely delirious from travel. Deeprun crossed our paths again, and we shielded Wraith from an acid round that would have surely killed him. I'd been lucky that it only melted part of my face and chest; I'd been sure Viper was a dead man when it got in his eye. I'd never forget the horrific sounds he made when the others held him down to flush it out.

"Long story," I said.

"I've got time," he said drily as he gathered his towel.

"What's wrong with your eye?" I asked. While I'd chosen not to have my face repaired, Viper had no choice if he ever wanted to blend in again.

He winced. "Got in a scuffle. I took a hit from this ugly fuckin' Proxilar enforcer, and I think he knocked something loose. It's been off ever since. I swear it's shocking my brain sometimes."

"Those are called thoughts, little brother," I teased.

"I know. They're confusing," he replied. He put one hand up to cover the exposed mechanism. "Is it going to scare your girl? I've got a patch, but it makes me look like I've got panties on my face."

I shook my head. "She's tough. Don't cover it up."

He nodded. "The Clockmaker is working on the lens for me right now," he said. "Swears he's got some upgrade that will let me see heat signatures. That man is off his nut."

"But he's good," I said.

"He is good," Viper agreed as he settled onto one of the big cushions around the low table. This was one of the few traditions the Hellspawn held onto; for months, this little place had no furniture except this table and a couple of ragged blankets folded into squares. This was the way we'd eaten every day of our lives until the day we were taken from Sonides. Family meals mattered.

I set Amira's plate on the low table. "The Earth girls sent this up for you. They're afraid of you. What the hell did you do?"

"Nothing!" he protested. "I was minding my own damned business and one of them barged in here. I didn't know what was going on. I raised my voice, and she ran off so fast I didn't know what the hell happened." Then he lifted the cover on the plate and sniffed. "Oh, shit, that smells good."

"Yeah, you ought to apologize," I said. "The little blonde one can cook."

He tore off a piece of bread and chewed it, his one good eye rolling back. "Fuck. I'll get on my knees and grovel if I have to. Speaking of, sit down and explain yourself. No more stalling asking about my eye."

Helena took longer than I expected, so I gave Viper the quick version of what happened. From hearing about the Zathari women being stolen, to working with the Dominion, right up to grabbing Sarah from Maor's hands. He just shook his head.

"I got your call about helping, but Storm said you were already gone," he said. He sighed. "You should have waited. I would have loved to have helped you kill that asshole."

"I know," I said. "On the bright side, there's plenty more assholes out there for killing."

"That there are," he agreed. "You think he's the one that grabbed Mom?"

I shook my head. "I don't know. I doubt it. Jalissa's girl, Kharadine, has his records. If she finds something, great." He nodded, chewing thoughtfully. We'd both accepted years ago that we would likely never find her.

"And you think this girl is your mate? For real? Not just mating, as in…" He made a lewd penetration gesture with his hands.

"I know what mating is, Viper," I snarled. "Yes. I know. I thought it was bullshit, too. But I can't deny it."

I expected him to be more skeptical, but he just smiled. "That's beautiful." He tilted his head. "First Havoc, now you? Hell, maybe one of those girls is my mate."

"Then you really should apologize before they find someone much better looking," I said.

He laughed. There was a quiet knock at the door, and it swung open on my favorite sight. "Oh, shit," Viper murmured. His pale blue eye raked over her, drinking her in slowly.

She looked almost shy as she walked in. "You must be Viper." She stuck out her hand. "I'm Helena."

He rose, looked her over, then gently hugged her. "Yes, you are," he said.

When he let her go, she looked at him, then me, then back again. "Holy shit. You really are identical."

"Well, except..." As Viper pointed to his empty eye socket, I touched my scar. The tandem gesture made her laugh.

Viper smacked the table. "Helena, I think we need drinks. I want to hear about Erebus. My treat. Sarahi's?"

"Put on clothes first," I reminded him. "And then, yes. Sarahi's."

"Right," he agreed. He hurried back down the hall, and Helena sidled up to me. "Does he like me?"

"He likes you," I whispered. "He has good taste like I do."

She smiled and rose on her toes to kiss me. "Good." Then she glanced over her shoulder. "You need to get him drunk so I can bang your brains out after dinner."

"Consider it done."

CHAPTER 29

Helena

Two Months Later

Summer in Ir-Nassa was brutally hot and beautifully bright. After the dusty landscape of Earth and the dark hold of Vehr Arandon's ship, this place was like living inside a flower bouquet. From the window of the clinic, I could see the edges of the marketplace, where hundreds of colorful tents sprang up each day to sell everything from bolts of silk to fresh fruit to live crickets.

At the sound of a tinkling bell, I bustled out of one of the exam rooms to find a young Il-Teatha woman cradling her arm. Blood-soaked linens wrapped her forearm, and the tiny lights at the end of her tendrils flickered red, indicating her distress.

"Hi!" I greeted. "What's going on?"

"I had a bit of an accident," she said, clenching her teeth.

"Oh, no," I said. "Come on, let's get you taken care of. I'm Helena."

"Isalie," she greeted.

Though I'd turned down Kharadine's offer to join the Diamondbacks, she and Mistral had introduced me to Evhina, a doctor on Jalissa Cain's payroll. In the last month, I'd removed a few bullets, assisted Evhina with a skin graft, and reset a few broken bones, all for people with whom we shared a mutual friend.

When we weren't discreetly helping Jalissa's associates, we stayed busy with people from the neighborhood. Cuts and broken bones and minor illnesses found their way here, and we sent most people on their way quickly.

It was like being back in school, as I learned each day about different species and their medical peculiarities. Drugs that would have poisoned a human were common antibiotics for Il-Teatha, and Sahemnar ran such low blood pressure that I would have thought they were already in cardiac arrest if they were human. Luckily, we had a good computer system that made recommendations. Most of what I did was provide reassurance and advice, and occasionally wipe away tears.

Within half an hour, I had young Isalie patched up with a prescription for a scar-reducing ointment. I saw another few patients and administered antibiotics, patched a nasty road rash from a tumble in the street, and assisted Evhina with placing a contraceptive coil. At the end of the day, I bade Evhina goodbye, reminding her I'd be gone for a few extra days. She gave me a knowing look as she said, "Enjoy your vacation."

When I emerged from the clinic, I found Mistral waiting across the street, under the shelter of an auto-shuttle stop. He was distracted, glancing down at his watch, and I enjoyed the view for a few seconds. His asymmetrical tunic revealed one bare arm, his lean muscles cut to sculpted perfection. His hair had grown out just long enough that the warm breeze caught it, reflecting blue-black in the sunlight.

He still did the occasional run off the planet with his brother, Havoc, but he'd spent most of his time lately on Phade, working security here and there. I'd also learned that my handsome mate had an outrageous bank account because he'd spent the last ten years doing lucrative, if slightly shady work, and rarely spent any money on himself. I had quickly adapted to letting him spoil me rotten whenever he wanted, though I usually insisted on picking something for him. The argument *but you look so handsome, and that makes me happy* usually worked.

I hurried across the street and bumped him with my hip. "Hey, handsome. You want to take me somewhere?"

"Sorry, I'm waiting for my girl," he said. "Have you seen her? This tall, prettiest woman in the city? Cute little ass that swings when she walks?"

"Haven't seen her," I said. "I guess you're stuck with me. On the plus side, I'll put out if you buy me something pretty."

"Guess you'll have to do," he said. He leaned down for a kiss. "Ready?"

Our trip took us back to Vuola Lire, where Storm had hooked Mistral up with another suite. I laughed when we walked into the big room where we'd first crashed together in the most confusing night of my life. "This time we can actually have sex, instead of faking it," I said.

"You know, I think I was already falling in love with you

when you started squealing about how big that imaginary dick was," he said. "Even if you were talking about Storm, not me."

I laughed and poked him. "You know, even then I briefly thought about actually doing it with you."

"Did you really?"

"Sure did," I admitted. His smile could have lit the room, and it didn't evaporate for at least twenty minutes.

We met Storm for dinner, then strolled through an art installation on the second floor of the massive resort. Acrobatic dancers performed in the open air, and Mistral held my hand while we stared up at them, twisting and flying across the open space. Even gravity couldn't keep them down.

After sampling from a spread of desserts at the patisserie, he suggested a stroll through the botanical gardens outside, but I finally tugged his hand and whispered, "I think you need to take me back to the room."

"Are you sure?" he asked. "The stars—"

"Mistral, if you don't, I'm going to take care of things myself," I warned him. A glass of wine and dark chocolate had me hungry for bigger and darker things. "You can stare at the stars while I entertain myself."

He looped his arm around my waist and hurried for the elevators. When the doors closed behind him, he grabbed my hand and guided it to the bulge under his long tunic. "I've been losing my shit for an hour. I was waiting to see how long you would let me stall you. You cracked first."

"You're awful," I said.

When we emerged from the elevator, he hiked me over his shoulder. I squealed with laughter. He backed into the door and didn't put me down until he tossed me onto the huge bed. I watched with hunger as he shed his jacket, then yanked him closer so I could unbuckle him.

"Hungry girl," he teased.

"It's not my fault you're so hot," I replied, releasing his cock from his snug briefs. Without another word, I took him into my mouth, holding his hips lightly as he slid in further. One hand rested atop my head as he worked into me slowly, gently. I pulled off of him, breathless. "What's on the menu tonight?"

"You are," he growled.

He started to pull away, generous to a fault, but I grabbed his belt and kept him close. "Let me finish this first," I said. "Why don't you tell me what you're planning to do? You talk, I'll listen."

He chuckled. His voice was strained as I continued to suck him eagerly, his hips working slowly to meet my mouth. "Well, I'm definitely tying you up."

"Mm," I agreed around his shaft. His body jolted, and I laughed, making it even worse. I loved feeling him losing control. It was a lot of work to deal with him, considering he was built like a stone statue and thick enough that I could barely get him into my mouth. But I loved the way he responded, loved the way his eyes would glaze over, and the way he'd wake up in the morning and say *you remember that thing you did with your tongue? That was amazing.*

He was always worth the effort. And I'd figured out that I could just about knock him unconscious with a couple of fingers massaging right under that pulsing knot.

"Legs over your head," he said. I moaned around him. "And then I'm going to eat your pussy, so slow and sweet that you're going to beg me to speed it up." I made a questioning noise. "Torture, Helena."

I withdrew, stroking him as I caught my breath. "Oh, really?"

"Oh, yeah," he said.

"I don't think you can take your time. I think you'll lose your resolve," I said.

"Careful about challenging me," he warned. His eyes drifted down, and I resumed my work. "Then I'm going to fuck you deep and hard." I let out a moan that surprised me as my body ignited. "You won't be able to touch me. Just me touching you and fucking you until you lose your mind."

His hips jerked, and I could hear his breathing turning into a quick rasp as I brought him closer and closer to the edge.

"This whole place is going to hear you," he teased. "They're going to—" I employed my secret weapon, gathering some of the slickness from his shaft and finding that secret place on his *dzirian*. His voice rose and fell in a noisy, undignified groan as I finished him off, his cock jerking in my mouth. I swallowed him down, sucking him slowly until he cupped my face to pull away. Then he bent to kiss me.

He made quick work of my clothes, and I was practically vibrating with excitement as he threw one of his bags onto the bed. He still wore his pants as he approached and said, "Give me your hands."

There was a stern roughness in his voice that I loved. I knew that he saw me as his equal. I saw it play out every day that we were together. But I loved the silent assurance when he took charge of my pleasure and making sure that I was thoroughly sated at all times.

I held my hands together. "You have your pants on."

"Maybe you should take them off," he teased. He waited for me to reach out and slide them over his hips, revealing the powerful legs beneath. Gods, he was so beautiful. Before I could grab his underwear, he shook his head. "No," he said firmly. "Hands."

With a shiver rolling over me, I put out my hands, watching intently as he wrapped silky red rope around my wrists, carefully looping and tying to create pretty knots that looked like flowers. As he did, he occasionally leaned over to kiss me, the soft underside of my forearm, my chest, everything he could reach.

I was calm and quiet as he tied both wrists, then lifted me by the waist. He stretched my arms out, binding the loose ends of the ropes to the bed. Then he slid a finger under the rope cuffs, always concerned with my safety. "Everything okay?"

I nodded. "Yes," I said. "It feels nice."

He chuckled, then lowered himself to kiss me, lazy and sweet. Eventually, he worked his way down, caressing my breasts. He teased at my nipples, rolling and pinching until they were tight and sensitive. His warm mouth closed over one, and I gasped at the hard pressure. His deep voice rumbled against my chest as he chuckled, then switched sides.

I shivered in anticipation as he worked his way lower, but he bypassed my sex, already wet and pulsing with desire. When he reached my ankle, he wrapped it in rope like he had my wrists, bringing it down around my foot in a pretty little lattice before finishing it off. I flexed it. "That's pretty," I said.

"So are you," he replied. He wrapped the other, and I felt a twist of anticipation as he lifted both my ankles over my head and spread my legs wide. "Keep them up."

As he tied the loose leads to the bed frame near my wrists, I did my best to keep my legs up for him, realizing I was about to be utterly vulnerable and helpless. It was thrilling, though I couldn't have imagined ever letting myself be this way with someone other than Mistral. He finished his work, then sat back on his heels as he ran those big hands up the backs of my thighs.

"Now, that is a beautiful sight," he marveled. Before I could ask, he slid a pillow under my back. He took his time touching me, running those huge hands all over my body, awakening my nerves until they were all singing for him. I closed my eyes, sinking into the sweetness of it. I sighed happily when his mouth finally found that warm place where I needed him. I rolled my hips toward him as he licked and sucked, drawing me into his mouth and ravaging me with his tongue. His fingers joined the party, teasing at my clit when he broke away to nibble at my inner thighs, just barely grazing his teeth over the tender flesh.

He had learned my body, had learned what I liked, and he wound me tight until I was whimpering and keening with need, trying in vain to get closer to him. "Please, Mistral," I begged. "I'm so close."

"I know, sweet rose," he murmured. "I know. I told you I was going to make it last."

He wasn't kidding. I was nearly incoherent as he drew it out, teasing and bringing me just to the edge before breaking away to kiss my thighs. Finally, when I was shaking with need, he drew my clit between his lips and flicked his tongue over it. The rasp of his tongue sent me over the edge, and I squealed with delight as I came, and he devoured my pleasure, still licking and stroking as my body squeezed and strained for something to hold onto.

My head fell back as I tried to catch my breath. "I love you so much," I blurted.

"Mm," he agreed. "I love you." The bed shifted beneath me, and I raised my head to see him lining up his cock at my entrance. I had nowhere to go, but I still wiggled my hips as if I could somehow bring him in.

He teased into me, just a few inches at first, moving in tiny, slow strokes. My body fluttered around him, and I tried to clench down him, to bring him in. He gripped my thighs, spreading them wider for him. "Bossy," he said, his eyes closing as he slid deeper. He glanced up as he put more weight against my legs, bending me nearly in half. "Is this okay?"

I nodded. "I'm great," I said.

Then he thrust himself deep, all in one stroke, until he was buried to the hilt, and I let out a terrible, undignified sound as white-hot sensation rolled over me. And true to his word, he fucked me deep and hard. I had no leverage, no way to get any closer, no control whatsoever. I was all his, and he took care of me just as promised.

My whole body was quivering with need, ready to blow apart, and still, he somehow spread me wider, drove deeper into me until I was seeing stars. I couldn't speak, could only stare up at him in awestruck wonder as he imprinted himself onto me, reminding every cell in my body who I belonged to.

Bracing one hand above me, he brought his other hand to my pussy and strummed against my clit. His pale eyes were intent on mine as my hips bucked. I had been on the edge for a while now, and it took only a few seconds of him touching me to throw me into the abyss again. My throat closed, and I gasped in a silent cry as orgasm flooded me. No coherent thought, no shame, nothing but feeling.

And still he thrust into me, his eyes half-closed as he neared his climax. I could see the flex in his stomach, the way his shoulders hunched ever so slightly before he came. His cock jerked in me, and he groaned as he pitched forward, thrusting in tiny little strokes as he spilled into me. "Fuck," he groaned. "Fuck, Helena."

My body roared to life again, an echo of that beautiful haze, fluttering around him as he finished. He reached up, entwined his fingers into mine, and gazed down at me. He was breathless, just letting his feelings wash over me. Through our bond, I felt the fuzzy white sensation. It was soft and shapeless, the way he sometimes felt early in the morning, before he'd really woken up but he was stirring as I rubbed his back.

"Hi," he said quietly, head resting against my calf. The ridged curve of his horn tickled at my sweat-slick skin. His eyes were practically glowing. I no longer had to ask him to stay a while. We both loved the 'echo,' the way our bodies synced while we were still locked together.

"Hi there," I said, staring up at him through the frame of my own bound legs. "You better tell your girl she missed out on a good trip."

He laughed. "Her loss."

I wiggled my fingers. "Will you please let me out? I want to touch you."

He smiled, that sweet shy smile that was only mine, and complied. As he released me, he gently rubbed my wrists and hands, then kissed them delicately. He did the same with my feet, then bundled me up to his chest, where I could feel his heart pounding still. "When we did this the first time..."

"By this, do you mean when you fucked me on the Aedelia or when you tied me up the first time?" I said.

He laughed. "The Aedelia," he said. "I thought that I'd better enjoy myself while I could, because it couldn't last."

"And here we are," I said.

"Here we are," he agreed.

I lifted my head and kissed the line of his jaw. "What if you get tired of me?"

"Impossible," he said. "Do you think you'll get tired of me?"

"Never," I said. "Tired of feeling safe and happy? Never going to happen." I kissed his jaw again. "I love you, Vethylas Khel."

"And I love you, Helena Cage."

"Do I get to be a Khel, too?" I asked. "Is that how it works?"

He chuckled. "It's a family name, and technically none of us are related except for Viper and me. I say you can call yourself whatever you want." He nuzzled into my neck. "As long as you call yourself mine."

"Obviously, silly. Helena Khel has a nice ring to it, doesn't it?" I said.

"I like it," he said.

I raised my head. "Want to have some dessert in the bathtub?"

"Is that code?"

"You know it is."

The End

The Rogues of the Zathari continues with **Viper**.

Bored and restless after seeing his twin brother settle down with his human mate, Viper takes a job as the muscle for a massive heist on an intergalactic cruise ship. Along the way, he falls fast for spunky, sexy Kiersa Brynn, a human housekeeper.

But when he discovers that the heist has been pinned on Kiersa, he drops everything to cross the universe and get her out of trouble. With the Dominion hot on their heels, Viper will risk everything to earn Kiersa's forgiveness and give her back her life...even if it means sacrificing his own.

Keep reading for a sneak peek!

If you love Helena and Mistral, I've got a sweet little bonus scene just for you! (Warning...this scene is pure sugar and spice!)

You can scan here and sign up to access the scene on BookFunnel!

VIPER: A SNEAK PEEK

Kiersa

With the tension rumbling in my stomach, I was either going to pass gas or open an interstellar wormhole somewhere in my lower intestine. Who knew that raging anxiety was the key to intergalactic jump technology?

My afternoon meal consisted of limp vegetables and synthetic proteins molded into a pink, meat-like brick, so it wasn't exactly appetizing to begin with. And it was free, courtesy of my Malonumas employee badge, so at least I wasn't wasting money by leaving it untouched. I sighed and pushed the tray away.

The Malonumas Voyages employee cafeteria was halfway full, with most of its patrons in casual clothes for the last time before the next high-priced voyage launched. Some of my acquaintances had splurged on a meal at the Stargazer's Retreat, an outrageously expensive restaurant here on Azuras Station, but I'd passed.

Even if the restaurant had been closer to my budget, I didn't particularly like Ardolan's circle of friends. They had a way of making me feel stupid and unimportant without a single unkind word. It got old to be on the outside of the jokes, not to mention feeling so damned jealous all the time. I didn't need to break the bank for expensive appetizers and an all-you-can-eat buffet of inadequacy.

Instead, I'd joined several of my friends to eat in the employee cafeteria, where the *very* humble meals were free. One of my coworkers, a fellow Bronze Deck employee named Lomon, nudged me. His half-Zathari heritage gave him a tall, wiry frame with lovely, dove-gray skin and brilliant green eyes, though he lamented that he had only a bumpy skull and not majestic horns like his father. His voice was comically affected as he wrinkled his nose. "Is the grilled not-meat not to your liking, Miss Brynn? Shall I fetch the chef to cook you another protein brick?"

The others laughed at him. Mer, one of my frequent drinking partners and fellow housekeeper, leaned in. "I find the quality of this protein brick utterly appalling," she said in a snooty, high-pitched voice. "I wish to speak to your supervisor at once. At once, I say!"

I smirked despite the anxiety sitting in my belly like a lump of concrete. Lomon raised his eyebrows expectantly. Lightly mocking wealthy, out-of-touch guests was a downtime tradition. Knowing that we'd get to reenact their worst-behaved moments made it much easier to deal with ill-mannered snobs on our long voyages.

With a deep breath, I lifted my nose and imitated the breathy rasp of one of our celebrity guests from the last voyage, whose treatment of the lowly staff was as horrific as her singing talent was lovely. I placed one hand to my chest dramatically. "Just the smell of this foul substance has made me poorer. I fear it has even reversed my most recent face lift," I whined. "Fetch me your freshest fruits from Zaalbara, juice them directly into my mouth, and don't even think of bringing me anything picked more than thirty-eight minutes ago."

They laughed, and Lomon helped himself to a limp vegetable from my tray. "There you are. You looked far too serious."

"It's assignment day, Lolo," Mer said. He frowned, and Mer nudged him. "She tested for the Short Skirts again."

I winced at the word *again*. Not that I needed a reminder that this was my third test in a year. By now, I could practically recite every line of the handbook.

And every time, I got the same *thank you for your interest, not at this time* message in my inbox.

"Why?" Lomon said, going for another vegetable. "It's barely any more pay and way more hassle."

I shrugged and pushed my tray toward him. "I don't know. I just want to."

"But—" He hissed in pain and stared down at his feet.

Mer fixed a sweet smile on her face, her white teeth dazzling against her brilliant blue skin. I appreciated her attempt to act natural, even if it was utterly transparent. "Good luck, Kiersa," she said sweetly.

"Good luck," Lomon echoed, his voice pinched by pain.

We spent the rest of our lunch hour chatting about what

Lomon, Mer, and the others had done in their week-long leave. Azuras Station was a massive space station with hotels, restaurants, and all sorts of expensive amusements crammed into its rotating silver rings. It also functioned as the launch point for all Malonumas Voyages cruises. The narrow window between cruises was the only time we commoners could roam the station freely, though most of the amenities were far too expensive for us to enjoy.

During the break, Lomon and one of his buddies from maintenance had taken a shuttle down to visit New Terra, the colony where most of us planned to settle when our cruise contracts with Malonumas ended. Mer and one of our other housekeeper friends, Inekta, had indulged in a spa day and spent the rest of the time sleeping in and enjoying not waiting on anyone else for a few days.

I'd spent my time on the corporate side of the station, beneath the expensive boutiques and high-end restaurants. I'd spent from dawn to dusk poring over the employee manuals, roleplaying scenarios, and finally, taking the much-dreaded tests.

And today was the day when I would get yet another rejection.

After lunch, Lomon was the first to rise, saying he wanted to pick up a few things from the commissary before report time. Our ship assignments were abundantly clear as we cleaned our table. After thirty seconds, our table was spotless, the chairs arranged at perfect angles and spacing.

Before leaving, Lomon caught me in a hug and kissed my cheek. "Good luck," he whispered.

My heart thumped as I headed to the employee communications kiosks on level B2. The polite female AI—Sona, the silver-tongued voice of all Malonumas vessels—greeted me at the security door. "Good afternoon, Kiersa Brynn," she said.

"Good afternoon, Sona," I said.

I hurried down the hall and into a long, narrow room divided into dozens of private cubicles. Quiet conversations wove into a soft buzz as other employees chatted with distant family and friends. A green light beckoned me to the end of a row, where I found an empty cubicle. Inside, I swiped my badge over a scanner to activate the curved screen.

When my Malonumas employee portal appeared, a bright red indicator caught my eye, with a number 3 blinking inside. I tried to be optimistic, like Ardolan always advised. Even in the silence of my own mind, I felt like a phony, but I envisioned myself opening the message to see *Congratulations!*

Before I could lose my nerve, I touched the screen. My first message was a standard employee briefing, a compulsory document we got before every voyage. I swiped past it to see the next two messages. My head swam when I read their titles: *Examination Results. New Work Assignment Details.*

This was it. "New work assignment!" I blurted.

Maybe all of Ardolan's *positive thoughts attract positive outcomes* bullshit had worked after all.

One tap later, my hopes were dashed.

Dear Kiersa Brynn (Employee MV-XU-8912)

We appreciate your interest in the Concierge training program. Here at Malonumas Voyages, we value hard work, aspiration, and a commitment to excellence. We thank you for striving to learn more about the company and how you can make it better with your gifts.

At this time, you have not been selected for the Concierge program.

The rejection was followed by several paragraphs of conciliatory corporate jargon, which I couldn't see thanks to my blurry eyes. I knew what it said without reading it all. *Blah blah, high standards, low acceptance, and you never had a chance, Kiersa Brynn, you should have known your place.*

At the bottom of the message was a handy ranking, just in case I needed to know why I'd been passed over again.

Knowledge of Malonumas Voyages Company Culture: Excellent

Politeness and Attitude: Excellent

Appearance: Good

Adaptability: Insufficient

I was a little offended at my appearance being only *good*, but compared to some of the concierges, I was plain. Ardolan had suggested a boob job, but if I could afford to upgrade my cleavage on a whim, I wouldn't be scrubbing toilets on a luxury cruise liner.

Adaptability was where I always failed, because that came down to my personality. No amount of studying could calm the temper and hair trigger that had come with me from Earth like a case of bedbugs.

I'd watched a dozen trainees go through their exercises. When several of them crashed and burned, I'd quickly visualized how I would have done things differently. By the time they called my name, I was ready to be aggressively polite.

Two minutes into my test run, the trainer threw a cold drink in my face and told me I'd just insulted her culture by bringing her a cocktail with ice. As far as I knew there was no Raephon taboo on ice cubes, but I'd apologized and promised to make it right. Despite my calm demeanor, she'd picked up the ice cubes and lobbed them at me one by one. Even with sticky soda soaking into my expensive white shirt, I maintained my calm demeanor, right up until an ice cube hit me in the eye hard enough to hurt. When I wiped my eye, I came away with a handful of smeared mascara and one of the false eyelashes I'd carefully applied that morning.

Even then, I took Ardolan's advice, saying, "Let me make this right for you," in a slow, sweet voice while I reminded myself that this wouldn't matter ten minutes from now.

When the trainer snapped back, "I'll have your fucking job, you little twat," I practically heard the *twang* of my last frayed nerve snapping. I probably shouldn't have told her that I could bring her some more ice for her chapped ass. And I definitely shouldn't have told her that I could bring a pair of pliers and some grease to apply the ice internally. It had gotten a boisterous laugh from one of the other applicants, but the trainer just gaped at me before scribbling furiously on her tablet.

Stupid, stupid, stupid.

But God, I was so embarrassed and flustered I could barely think. My feet hurt from prancing around in the stupid high heels, my thong was crawling up my ass, and I had barely slept for two days because I'd been studying.

I knew they did it on purpose to knock out people like me who might lose their tempers and anger their wealthy customers. The last thing Malonumas wanted was a viral video of one of their employees melting down.

Whatever. Another voyage, another month of making beds and scrubbing toilets and being selectively blind to our guests' unusual toys and suspicious stains. At least I could wear flat shoes and drop the jaw-aching smile.

I swiped up to clear the rejection message, then opened the *New Work Assignment Opportunity.* My brow furrowed as I read the message.

Dear Kiersa Brynn (Employee MV-XU-8912)

Congratulations on your reassignment to the Platinum Deck. This reassignment comes with recommendations from your superiors as an acknowledgement of your excellent service aboard Malonumas Voyages. Pending a short probationary period to consist of two voyages, you will receive a generous stipend at the end of each subsequent voyage.

Upon boarding for voyage preparation, please report to your immediate superior, Zhenya sul Voras at Room P-21.

Regards-

Malonumas Voyages Staffing

This was technically a promotion, but not the one I'd hoped for. As I closed the screen, I caught a glimpse of my sour expression. The Concierge manual had a three-point checklist for an optimal smile. Head up, medium smile with no teeth, soft eyes with lifted brows. "Now that's the Malonumas way," I teased myself.

Smile when you're pissed, and never let them see you cry.

Or offer ice for their chapped asses.

※

Sixteen hours later, the Star Treader was ready to welcome her wealthy guests and begin a launch to the stars. As one of the cleaning staff, I was not expected, nor even permitted, to appear at the boarding zone. The VIP Concierges would be there in their tailored lavender uniforms, most of them extraordinarily attractive and young. While Housekeeping scrubbed and polished every inch of the Star Treader, the Short Skirts were plucking and polishing to perfection in the corporate spa.

That was the Malonumas way, too.

In another wonderful twist, my cabinmate, Ardolan, had been promoted to VIP Concierge. As she dabbed lipstick on her newly plumped lips, she nodded eagerly. Clearly, she'd spent her break getting a little extra cosmetic work done. "We're practically working together now, Kiki," she had said sweetly. "I'm so excited for us."

Mer called Ardolan a *plastic android bitch*, and I was inclined to agree when we first met. With her syrupy sweet voice and vacant stare, you could have mistaken her for an AI. Her Vaera heritage gave her the most beautiful rose-red skin, copper-streaked hair, and delicately pointed ears, which she adorned with pretty little jeweled caps. Company-approved, of course.

But after more than two years of sailing with Malonumas, eighteen months of that with Ardolan as my cabinmate, I'd realized she didn't have a mean cell in her perfectly proportioned body. She was just impossibly clueless in a way that came from living on a nice, temperate planet, where her biggest dilemma was whether to go to university or work for a few years before she married another wealthy denizen who would nod along eagerly to her tales of when she worked among the poor before whisking her off for another luxury vacation.

Three months into our tentative friendship, I'd realized she was far from stupid. Ardolan van Sherras could recite any menu from any restaurant on the ship, rattle off the ingredients for a hundred unique cocktails, and ask thoughtful questions about virtually every culture represented by our guests. And I could guarantee that Ardolan wouldn't have threatened to give the theoretical Raephon customer an ice cube enema.

"Me too," I lied. "But I was really hoping to be a Concierge."

"Oh, I know. And you're so pretty, I don't know why they haven't picked you," she said. She startled me with a big hug from behind, almost lifting me off my feet. "But honestly, it's all the same in the end, right? Finish the contract, and then we're done. Who cares?"

That was easy to say when she was rubbing elbows with our wealthy guests and getting roped into pictures with celebrities. Sometimes I felt like I'd never left Earth, where I was forever gazing through dust clouds at distant stars, wondering why I couldn't be chosen, just once.

But she wasn't wrong. And there were probably people back on Earth that would have killed to be scrubbing toilets on a Malonumas vessel, even the perpetually befouled public restrooms near the daiquiri bar. I had a room of my own, three decent meals a day, and my cabinmate didn't steal from me. So I was going to wear that company-approved smile even if I had to bite down so hard on my resentment that I cracked my own damn teeth.

On launch day, we ate breakfast together, and I mostly meant it when I wished her good luck at her new assignment. While she headed back into Azuras Station to prepare for pre-boarding, I headed to the Platinum deck to meet my new boss.

Before knocking on the door of P-21, I paused to reapply my company-approved smile. My new boss, Zhenya, was intense and stern, giving me an appraising look as I presented myself for our meeting. The tall Vaera woman was elegant, with close-cropped scarlet hair that flipped over to one side. She leaned over, put her hands around my waist, and lifted my knee-length skirt to examine the embossed label.

"Excuse me," I protested, fixing my skirt back over my snug shorts.

Ignoring my protests, she bustled into the supply closet and pulled out a neatly pressed maid's uniform. It was similar to my current uniform, but with embroidered details and a neat little blue scarf and star pin. There was even a dapper little blue hat hanging from a pin loop. "Change into this one before going on the floor," she said. Then she tapped her computer to activate a holographic display, where she swiped through several headshots of women's hairstyles. Each wore a sleek braid, bun, or twist. "One of these. No ponytail."

I absently touched my hair. "I'm sorry, ma'am. I didn't know."

"Now you do," she said. "Fix the hair after final checks."

Despite my trepidation about being the new girl, I found there were two other new housekeepers when I joined the pre-launch meeting in a small ballroom on the Platinum deck. Crystal decorations glittered in every corner, while a vidscreen of fish on the ceiling made me feel like I was inside an aquarium. A catering crew stocked a corner bar while a technician checked the display domes on each of the small tables.

Our briefing included details about our celebrity guests, including a tech baron from Firyanin, and the intergalactically-renowned pop star, Tempesta. I glanced around and saw the other staff as stone-faced as ever, which made sense, when

Zhenya sternly reminded us that there was to be no gawking, videograms, or other unseemly behavior.

I was surprised to learn that VIP housekeepers were assigned to only three cabins each. Not only were we responsible for cleaning them twice daily, but we could be called by a button inside the cabin or the app our guests received. If a client asked for champagne or towels or personal lubricants—not unusual—we were to deliver right away. When not doing a scheduled deep clean, we assisted cleaning common areas, breakdown after events, and resetting tables in the main dining room.

Just after Zhenya finished her announcements, there was a pleasant chime from the speaker system. "Platinum guests board in fifteen minutes," Sona said. "All Star Treader staff are advised to prepare for boarding protocols."

When I worked on the Bronze deck, I'd have been on break while passengers boarded. But on the Platinum deck, the fifteen-minute call was our cue to start delivering chilled wines and snack trays. I pushed a refrigerated cart down the hall and tried not to be bitter that each bottle probably cost more than I earned in a month.

Each cabin was quadruple the size of the crappy apartment I'd shared on Earth with my burnout family, to say nothing of the glorified closet Ardolan and I shared. Soft, gray-and-white decor brightened the rooms, while warm daylight bulbs glimmered off the delicate crystal chandeliers. Each VIP cabin had a large sitting area, where I had painstakingly arranged the pillows on the couches to precise schematics.

In the small dining area, a chilled basin was set into the table. After verifying the temperature, I placed two bottles of wine inside. A neatly printed card explained the provenance of the wines, which I placed, along with a perfectly folded origami flower centerpiece. In the refrigerator, I left a tray of fruits sliced into small flowers.

I hurried along to my other two rooms, then returned the refrigerated cart to the kitchen. While I was checking two extra bottles of wine back into the storage cellar, my wrist buzzed. I checked my watch and flipped up the matte tan cover. Cabin 9 was already calling.

Excitement bubbled inside me as I hurried down the hall. Back on Earth, my mother had laughed in my face when I told her I was going to be a housekeeper. "You're going to clean up after rich people?" she'd scoffed, all but spitting in my face. "What a waste!"

As if staying on Earth to run drugs for shark-eyed men who'd gut you for looking at them sideways was somehow better. She hadn't always been that way, but losing Dad had changed her. Grief had carved her open so her awful sister, Auntie Lora, could fill her up with poison and spite. And high-grade Blitz, a scarily addictive street drug, had poisoned what Lora hadn't touched. Mom had done everything she could to keep me on Earth, leaving me with no choice but to take a contract with Malonumas. Cleaning toilets for rich people was the only chance for me to break out of her orbit.

Regardless of what dear Fernanda Brynn thought, I liked my job. Even the rude customers gave me stories to tell, and I liked the satisfaction of checking boxes and doing things correctly. And so, even if I was nothing more than the human help, I was going to be the best damn housekeeper that the guests in Cabin 9 had ever seen.

Amidst a pleasant spill of music, guests filed down the halls like little ducklings behind the lavender-clad VIP concierges. While most guests would go through safety briefings in the halls or in the open atriums, VIP guests had their own lounge with a featured launch day cocktail. Every second of the voyage would remind our wealthiest guests of how special they were, lest they venture too close to the little people and their messy reality.

I ducked into a side hallway and waited for the crowd to pass. After all, *out of sight unless you're needed* was one of the top priorities of a Malonumas housekeeper. When they were gone, I headed to Cabin 9.

The door was ajar, so I knocked lightly. "Housekeeping. May I come in?"

There was no response, so I crept inside. A cluster of suitcases stood in the middle of the big suite, and a man's coat was tossed over the nearest couch. Water ran in the first bedroom. I froze, debating whether to bolt. It wouldn't be my first time walking in on a naked passenger, but it tended to make things weird.

"Housekeeping," I said again. "Did someone call?"

A heavy hand fell on my shoulder. I yelped in surprise and whipped around to see a big man looming over me. And he wasn't big like Lomon, who was tall and wiry. This man was *big*. Broad shoulders threatened to split through his snug white shirt. The dark gray skin and slender black horns meant he was probably Zathari.

"What are you doing here?" he said, rolling down his crisp white sleeves over muscular forearms.

I couldn't help staring at him. Not only was he outrageously attractive, but his left eye was...well, it was something. The right was a beautiful pale blue, framed by dark lashes. But his left was clearly a prosthesis, with an eerie blue glow inside a glass lens. There was a faint line outlining a fist-sized patch around his eye. The subtle seam rose over his brow and curved down to his cheekbone. It wasn't his skin, though it was a perfect match for his coloring, right down to the subtle flecks of darker pigment that gave it a lovely, stone-like dimension.

His right eyebrow lifted. Oh God. I was staring.

Say something, you colossal dumbass.

"Do you need towels?" I blurted.

His eyes drifted down to my empty hands, then back up to me. "What?"

"I apologize, sir," I said. Gods, I could not screw this up on my very first day. This was about to be the ice cubes all over again. I averted my eyes, then realized it was rude not to look at him when I spoke. But looking at him made my stomach tie in a knot and start whispering naughty suggestions to lower places. "I'm..."

His head tilted, one corner of his mouth tugging up in a coy smile.

What in the hell was my name?

I looked down at my nametag. "Kiersa! Kiersa Brynn," I said, as if I'd just cracked an impossible cipher. "I'll be taking care of your housekeeping services during your adventure with us."

"My adventure," he said, his tone almost mocking. "That's cute. Very picturesque. It's nice to meet you, Miss Brynn, but I didn't call you."

"You didn't push a button?" I glanced at my watch and

noticed a code next to the alert. "Maybe in the washroom? There's a button on the wall."

His lips curved into a smile that turned my legs to jelly. "Must be it. I was trying to turn on the lights, but I didn't realize there was a button that summoned a gorgeous woman straight to my door. Malonumas should really put that on their advertisements."

My cheeks heated with the compliment. There was a wonderful twinkle in his right eye. I spared a smile. "Well, now you know there is. I'll send one for you right away. I'm afraid we only have blondes today, but we'll restock a full selection in the morning."

"Beautiful *and* funny," he said, smiling even wider. The broad grin carved a dimple into his right cheek. God, I had to quit staring at him. He chuckled and extended his hand. "Ihrin Sabane."

"Mr. Sabane," I said politely. His big hand enclosed mine, giving it a firm shake. I bit my lip. "Mr. Sabane, of course it's your business, but you should probably attend the safety briefing. It's in the executive lounge just down the hall."

He smirked at me. "Should I? Perhaps you could give me the short version, here. I'll bet it's much more interesting if you do it."

Was he...was he flirting with me?

It wouldn't be the worst thing to happen. When I first got hired, I was shocked to learn that Malonumas Voyages did not forbid fraternization between employees and guests, so long as employees were not on duty nor on call. And I was certainly not shy. I had seen quite a few wonders of the universe, both in space and in bed. As it turned out, some of our guests were just as intrigued by a woman from Earth as I was by...literally everything.

"Ah, I'm afraid I'm not qualified to give you a safety briefing," I said.

He took a step closer, forcing me to look up at him. Shit, he even smelled good. "Then perhaps you can take me where I need to go. Are you qualified for that?"

"I think I am," I said. "Follow me, Mr. Sabane."

★⋆★

You can find VIPER on Amazon in paperback and electronic format!

ABOUT THE AUTHOR

Despite dreams of the stars, Stella Frost lives on Earth, where she writes steamy, action-packed science fiction romance. She loves aliens with horns, smart mouths, checkered pasts, and golden hearts.

You can visit Stella online at her website!

She also has a serious TikTok problem, and you can catch up with her latest silliness by following her there.

For fun with Stella and several other amazing alien romance authors, check out the Facebook reader group, Interstellar Ever After!

ALSO BY STELLA FROST

The Rogues of the Zathari

Prequel: Bishop

Book 1: Havoc

Book 2: Mistral

Book 3: Viper

Book 4: Wraith

Made in the USA
Columbia, SC
15 September 2024